Rest and Be Thankful

HELEN MacINNES

Rest and
Be Thankful

LITTLE, BROWN AND COMPANY
BOSTON

To Gilbert and Keith,
my favorite cowboys

Contents

Rest and Be Thankful

CHAPTER I

Road to Nowhere

THE ROAD climbed westwards, twisting through the green hills and high pastures. Ahead lay a towering wall of mountains buttressed by rock, covered by dark green fir trees. The paler grass from the meadows stretched round the mountains' base like a sea, forming inlets here and there as the forest receded, or an isolated lake where the trees marched down to encircle the invader.

Then the road stopped climbing, as if it had decided it had wasted quite enough breath, and turned abruptly to run in crazy twists along the high valley which suddenly opened out under the shadow of the mountains.

"How very unexpected," Mrs. Margaret Peel murmured, and sat forward with interest as if she were trying to catch a better glimpse of the stage in a crowded theater. Sarah Bly, who shared the back seat of the touring car and all the bumps and jolts, held on to her hat with one hand and on to the map with the other and wished Margaret were a little more conscience-stricken and less delightfully surprised. To run into an unexpected valley following an unexpected direction was slightly depressing at six o'clock in the evening. If this were Switzerland or the Austrian Tyrol, you could depend on reaching a little village every hour on the hour, and it would only be a matter of deciding which one had the best inn for a well-cooked meal and a comfortable bed. But this was Wyoming. And here was Margaret, who once insisted on taking her doses of Nature by well-diluted teaspoonfuls, now drinking it in by the gallon and becoming so intoxicated that she had quite forgotten this road was all her fault. It was a short cut, she had said, three hours ago.

3

Sarah Bly said, "We are now fifty miles from nowhere, heading for Canada. We might as well admit we took the wrong road and tell Jackson to turn around and drive us back to the State Highway." She glanced at the stolid neck of Jackson in front of her, and noted that he was still registering disapproval in his own persevering way. He hadn't once admired the view, and he was no doubt wondering if they would ever reach San Francisco in time to let him have his two weeks at Atlantic City before the snows set in. Jackson's idea of a journey across America was a smooth highway white-lined, and eighty miles an hour.

"It is quite incredible!" Margaret Peel said, as if she hadn't heard her friend's suggestion. She was watching the golden peaks, the blue-shadowed canyons, the continuous rise and fall of pasture land and forest. Then she added consolingly, "At least, we've left those miles of plains behind and all those herds of white-faced bulls. After a few days of that, I'd thought I'd scream. Nothing but eyes and eyes all watching me speculatively. Reminded me of a lecture I once gave, somehow."

"They were cows, darling. There just can't be so many bulls in the *whole* of America."

"Well, they didn't look like cows." Her voice became less doubtful as she abandoned that problem for their more immediate one. "We must be fifty miles from *somewhere,* Sarah. And we haven't reached Montana yet, far less Canada."

"I was only trying to drop the gentle hint that we may be lost. I just can't find anything recognizable on this map." Sarah's mood was one of rebellion. It had begun that morning when she awakened to find it was her birthday and she was actually thirty-seven. Margaret hadn't been sympathetic about it. "Why," she had said, "take a look in the mirror and you'll cheer up. Your hair is fair, your skin is excellent, your eyes are a clear blue, and you've a good figure. Thirty-seven means nothing. Now, if you were fifty-three, like me!" Which hadn't exactly been any consolation to Sarah, for Margaret Peel had reached the point of even beginning to take pride in telling the truth about her age.

Mrs. Peel caught the sound of rebellion in Sarah's usually quiet

4

voice. "Sarah," she said affectionately but firmly, "the man in New York said *everything* was clearly marked on that map. Perhaps you aren't looking in the right place. This is Wyoming, dear. Let me see." She studied the map between increasingly wild lurches of the car. "Why, there we are. Or almost." She pointed to the town where they had slept last night. "The pass over the mountains lies just west of there."

"West by the State Highway," Sarah Bly reminded her. Then she smiled in spite of herself at Margaret's usually neat hat, now cocked drunkenly over one eye by that last jolt. But Mrs. Peel was too busy frowning over the brown splotches and green patches on the map to notice. She was a handsome woman. The features in her face were finely molded, and the warmth of her quick smile matched the humor in her bright, brown eyes. Their vitality offset her white hair and her pale skin.

"I suppose we'll have to stop the car," she conceded suddenly. "Don't worry, Sarah: this road must lead someplace. That's the nice thing about a road. It's all my fault, I know. I suppose I just got carried away by a view. Still, you must admit that this *is* one way of seeing something of the country."

Sarah Bly admitted it, and stopped thinking about the fate of the Donner party as the car halted. Jackson, somewhat melted by Mrs. Peel's frank admission that she needed his help, began giving his laconic advice. Yes, Sarah Bly thought as she straightened her own hat, that was indeed the purpose of this tour — to see something of America. And originally it had been her idea: it was she who had persuaded Margaret, last winter in New York, that it was about time they gave their own country a chance.

For almost twenty years — and Margaret, in fact, could recall more than twenty — they had lived abroad. They had housekept in Paris, in Rapallo, in Dalmatia; they had collected people, paintings and recipes; they had given amusement with their American money and they had been amused, in turn, by the ideas and customs of foreign lands. It hadn't been pointless: at least two of the penniless writers who had dined with them so constantly in their Paris flat had become almost famous; and the little press, which Margaret had

5

subsidized, had printed some essays and poems which were now collectors' items. In Italy, there always had been a group of writers and painters staying with them. And in the charmingly straying castle which they had rented in 1939 in Dalmatia, their guests had overflowed its ramparts right down into the outskirts of Ragusa. But all that was over: those days were gone, now. And gone, too, were most of their friends.

So many had been killed, Sarah Bly thought unhappily as she stared at the wall of mountains across the valley. Or they had disappeared, or they were shut away behind political boundaries. And those that were left? Postwar politics had embittered or twisted them. . . . So we came home, back to a land we had neglected for twenty years, strangers in our own country except to the few people in New York who had known us abroad. And all that was left of those twenty years was Jackson; and this motor car; and our zest for travel.

She turned her eyes quickly away from the wall of mountains, back to the twisting, narrow road. At this moment, she could wish that Margaret's zest for travel had not become quite so uncontrolled. And the car, too, was as good as ever even if it was of a 1933 vintage. But where was Jackson? While she had been daydreaming he had disappeared.

"I've sent Jackson to spy out the land," Mrs. Peel explained. She was walking around the car slowly, breathing the fresh cool air with maddeningly obvious enjoyment. "You really did get lost among those mountains, didn't you? Now, do get out and stretch your legs, Sarah. You'll feel much better."

But Sarah Bly kept her eyes on the road and waited for Jackson.

"Yes, it was all my fault," Mrs. Peel admitted. "Still, Jackson has quite forgiven me." She looked reprovingly at Sarah. She held out two candy bars wrapped in metallic paper. "Look, he brought these along specially for us. What would we do without Jackson?"

Sarah Bly took the candy and unwrapped it. "Oh, no!" she cried. She held up the boldly printed name on the silver paper. "GOODIE TWO CHEWS. . . . Oh, Margaret!"

Mrs. Peel studied the legend in silence. Then she unwrapped her

6

portion and began to eat it. "I simply will not be depressed," she said to the nearest mountain. "Look, what on earth are those brown things bouncing over that piece of hillside? Antelopes? There you are, Sarah. We've got antelopes playing, skies that are not cloudy all day, and all we need is the seldom discouraging word."

Sarah Bly smiled in spite of herself. Besides, the candy was good. And Jackson would be back any moment, and the car would be turned round — for just at this point in the road it could be turned safely. Here, grass edges had taken place of steep banks and sharp cliffs; the hillside to the right of them was joined to the road by a sloping stretch of ground, and to the left of them the green slope continued into a broad meadow — as if the road, at this point, did not separate hill from valley but formed a natural bridge. It was impossible to deny that this view, with its mountains and teeth of rock, bore a certain resemblance to the Dolomite country in the South Tyrol. Perhaps the Dolomites, with a strange touch — in these neat, pointed, green hills and rich forests — of the Côte-d'Or. And surely, in these steeply-sloping fields, folding into each other, dipping, rising, a decided reminder of Scotland: here, there was sage instead of heather. And the boulder-studded grass had its thistles, too. "And blue lupines, and wild roses, and what's that flame-colored flower?" she said aloud.

"Thank you, Sarah," Mrs. Peel said. "That's much better. But what has happened to Jackson? I suppose it is all the fault of these turns in the road. They keep enticing you on."

"If he gets lost — " Sarah began in alarm.

"We'd have to camp out here until he gets unlost. It *has* been done before, you know. I expect this country, at one time, was dotted about with covered wagons waiting for scouts to turn up again. Cheer up, Sarah! The Indian wars are over, and the bears all spend the summer nowadays in Yellowstone to get their photographs taken. We've little to worry us. Imagine if we were sitting in a covered wagon, sixty years ago, and a band of Sioux were watching us from the top of that ridge over there! It must have been quite unpleasant to comb your hair out each night before you went to bed. So reminding. I think I'd have traveled with a shaven head, just

7

to annoy them." Mrs. Peel's eyes suddenly narrowed, and her voice sharpened. "Now, how did that get there?" She pointed to the ridge where she had placed her scalping-party, and stared angrily at the gray mist which was creeping over it, swirling lower, thickening, even as she watched. "Was that distant thunder?" she asked. She looked anxiously at the rest of the sky, still blue and brightly smiling.

"It's quite near," Sarah said. "And not thunder. Hoofs, I think."

"Oh, dear! More bulls," Mrs. Peel said, abandoning her pioneer-woman attitude and climbing back hastily into the car.

"Coming this way," Sarah Bly informed her with some satisfaction. Of course, they would only be cows; but still, she removed the red chiffon scarf which she wore tucked into the neckline of her gray flannel suit. "Poor Jackson. Do you think dodging a stampede is one of his secret accomplishments?"

"They aren't bulls, they're wild horses," Mrs. Peel called loudly above the mounting uproar, as a mass of flying manes and tails and pounding hoofs suddenly swept over a hillside and poured down towards the car. Half-circling them, urging them on, were five men on horseback.

"And this," Sarah said quickly, remembering the grass bridge at the edge of the road which made such a convenient turning-place for the car, "this is where they will cross!"

Mrs. Peel looked at her with horror.

"Cliffs, precipices, canyons," Sarah shouted in explanation, and waved her arms to the front and back of the car.

One of the riders raced towards them, while the others altered their half-circle to a flanking maneuver to turn the horses and slacken their speed.

"Get that car out of the way!" shouted the rider. Sarah Bly, ignoring her tight skirt, climbed desperately over into the front seat. She was rarely allowed to drive — Jackson had a well-developed sense of possession — but she knew roughly what to do. She did it, conscious of the man's furious look, of the angry voice, of his impatient horse, of the loud shouts and terrified neighs which were now alarmingly close.

8

"That's it!" the man directed. "Now turn the car across the road! Just there! There!"

Mrs. Peel wondered what Jackson would say if he heard the gears being stripped like that. But Sarah had managed it, bringing the car to rest before it fell over the bank on the left of the road. "But why?" Mrs. Peel said, "for heaven's sake why?"

"To form a road block," Sarah answered. "And stay in the car, Margaret!" She felt ridiculously pleased with herself, and with her guess, as the man now rode his horse over to the other side of the broad natural gateway and took his position there. In one hand, he held a ready loop; in the other, the rest of the long rope was neatly coiled. He had quite forgotten them, Sarah thought, as she watched his concentration. Then his eyes lifted towards the milling herd of horses, as its leaders were once more directed towards the road. The surging wave hesitated, gathered force, rushed suddenly with renewed speed, shook the car as it poured over the road, and thundered past to cover everything and everyone in a cloud of dust.

"My dear!" Mrs. Peel's voice rose chokingly, as a horseman appeared suddenly at the edge of the cloud on the high bank above them and, without altering speed, rode down its steep slope, swerved to avoid the car, and then disappeared down a steeper slope at a gallop to turn a couple of straying horses back into the mainstream.

It was over as quickly as it had begun. They were left staring after the moving mass of horses, listening to the fading calls of the circling riders.

"So that's a cowboy," Mrs. Peel said faintly, and sat down on the nice quiet safe seat of the car. "We really do choose our moments. . . . Imagine arriving in the middle of a rodeo!"

"A day's work for them, which we nearly ruined."

"They very nearly ruined us," Mrs. Peel said.

Sarah didn't reply; she was watching the man, who had guarded the road, now riding slowly towards them. He seemed to be paying more attention to recoiling the rope and fixing it onto his saddle than he was to the two strangers. He was a tall man, thin, muscular. His face, set in strong lines, was impassive. He reached the car and halted his horse. He touched the battered felt hat, wide and curved in the brim, which he wore pulled well down over his forehead. He sat easily on his horse, his body now relaxed, his right hand resting on his hip, his left arm leaning on the saddle horn. He said nothing. He sat there and he looked at them.

"We really are sorry," Sarah Bly said, and tried to smile. If we had been men, she thought, he probably would have sworn at us.

"It was very considerate of you to warn us," Mrs. Peel said, still flustered by her experience. "I suppose the horses would have scattered and divided and taken different directions and all that."

He nodded. He was less angry now. His eyes, a clear gray against the deeply tanned skin, had a smile in them. He shifted his hat farther back on his head, and then pulled it over his brow again. Then he looked at the car.

"Having a little trouble?" he asked. His voice, now that he had stopped shouting, was very pleasant: quiet, controlled, with a touch of humor in it.

"We are lost," Mrs. Peel said. "At least, we know where we are going eventually, but meanwhile —"

"Keep on for another six miles and you'll reach the ranch. It might be an idea to hurry a bit. Looks as if a storm's coming over these mountains." He lifted his hand to his hat, touched the flank of his horse as he wheeled it around, and was off. At the rate he was traveling, it would not be long before he overtook the horses.

Sarah said, "Did you notice the spurs, and the high-heeled boots?"

"Where's Jackson?" Mrs. Peel asked, trying to reassert herself. But she was in for another attack of bewilderment as Jackson's square-set figure came scrambling down from the hillside onto the bank above them. He stood there, looking down at the rough slope, shaking his head. Then he walked along to the more sedate path by the natural gateway to reach them. In his hand, he held a large bunch of wild lupines.

"Horses!" He was still shaking his head. "Horse come down here." He pointed to the bank. "In my country, many horses. Many horses, cowboys. But ground is flat." He waved the lupines in a horizontal line. "Flat. And grass. No this." He looked with wonder at the bank, and then at the boulder-strewn hillside down which the horses had raced.

"In your country? Cowboys? In Hungary?" In all her eighteen years of Jackson, Mrs. Peel had never heard him mention a horse.

"We'd better start moving," Sarah said to him. "Keep on for another six miles. Looks as if a storm's coming over these mountains." But both women stopped smiling when the first roar of thunder reached the valley. As the jagged lightning struck down at the pinnacles of rock, Jackson maneuvered the car around without one reproving look for the shameful way it had been treated, and drove with all the abandon of a Hungarian cowboy along the darkening road. They passed groups of trees, now, tracing the banks of a stream. At first, they could hear the angry rush of water, and then the rising wind silenced it as the tall trees groaned and bent. The lightning encircled them, cracking like a whip. The thunderclaps echoed across the valley, rebounding from peak to peak.

"Oh!" Mrs. Peel moaned, and put up her hands to her hat too late. Sarah laughed unfeelingly, for she had lost hers at the first blast of wind.

"Jackson!" Mrs. Peel shouted. But she couldn't compete with the thunder. And the rain had begun to fall, large heavy drops changing to a stream of wind-swept water. Jackson, driving as if the hounds of hell had been unleashed at his heels, was obviously not going to stop the car to put up the hood, far less search for hats on a hillside.

"Oh dear!" Mrs. Peel said, and hung on to the rocking car with both hands. The lights in the ranch house could now be seen, but at the moment they gave little comfort, for it would take another three minutes to reach their promised safety. And in this country, Mrs. Peel had learned, anything could happen in a matter of seconds.

CHAPTER II

Flying Tail

THE MEN came into the ranch-house kitchen, hooked their slickers on the wooden pegs at the door, shook their hats and threw them on the broad window sill, straddled the benches that stood on either side of the oilcloth-covered table, and reached unanimously for the bread. The full stewplates began to empty rapidly.

Mrs. Gunn waited until they had some mouthfuls of good hot meat and mashed potatoes inside them, before she started asking questions. She had been brought up on a ranch. Now, as she added another half-pound slab of butter to the table and refilled the bread plate, she looked around at the old-fashioned and cheerful kitchen with its large wood stove, then at the five wind-tanned faces enjoying her cooking, and felt content with her world. She was an elderly woman, big-boned and yet spare. Her movements were brisk and neat. Her red hair had whitened, her face seemed very pale in contrast to the men's tanned skin. There was warmth and kindness in her eyes, frankness in her look.

"Got the last horse into the south pasture just as the rain broke," Jim Brent said. "Very nearly didn't though. There was a car on the road, right where it shouldn't have been, and a couple of women with feathers in their hats, and a man, all dressed up in blue uniform, picking flowers. Darnedest thing I ever saw." He smiled, shaking his head.

"What were the women like?" Mrs. Gunn asked, her interest aroused by hats with feathers in them.

"One was kind of middle-aged . . . white hair, brown eyes and a quick smile. She was fussing a bit. The other — oh, she was all right, I guess."

"Climbed faster over that car than a colt trying to get to his mother," Ned put in. His handsome dark face had a ready grin. "That was after Jim got to hollering at her."

"Burst the seam of her skirt, too," Jim said, "but she had a nice way of not noticing. She had a nice way of smiling, too, quiet but steady."

"And where did this happen?" Mrs. Gunn wanted to know.

"Just below Snaggletooth. They couldn't have picked a better spot to scatter us if they tried. Seemed as if they were having a picnic."

"Didn't they know a storm was coming up?"

"Look, Ma," Ned said, "them Easterners wouldn't know a thunderhead even if they was swallowed up by it." Ned, who had spent an October calf-roping in Madison Square Garden two years ago, knew all about New York and its peculiar inhabitants.

"I told them to drop in, by the way," Jim said. "Better keep some of that stew."

"Them damn' Easterners, taking the meat out of a man's mouth," Bert grumbled, the furrows on his face deepening. He wasn't going to let young Ned, there, get away with all the information on the subject. He had met Easterners, too, for he had worked for some summers, before the war, over at a neighboring ranch that took in dudes. He poured his fourth mug of coffee, and stirred its thick layer of sugar vigorously. His long, pointed face had a comical twist to it.

Mrs. Gunn removed the stew dish from his reach, and brought over a bowl of peaches. No nasty cans on her table. Things were nicely served. She insisted on that, just as she insisted on everyone being washed and brushed up and boots scraped and no language in her kitchen. They were good rules, she had found. A new wrangler might think she was fussy, but he came to enjoy supper at her table as much as the others. It was a rough life they had, sometimes eating and sleeping in the hills for days on end. It didn't hurt to give them a little of the woman's touch when they got back to the ranch. She put a large plate of freshly made doughnuts at Bert's elbow to help him forget his disappointment.

"Well," she said, "whoever they are they're taking their time.

13

Ought to have been here by now. Wonder if that loose plank on the bridge gave them any trouble?"

"We'll have to dig them out of a hillside," young Robb predicted in his quiet, slow way. "That stoneface above the bridge was beginning to crack up again. I noticed it last week." His face was thoughtful, but the fresh color in his cheeks, and the light hair and blue eyes, made him look even younger than he was.

Ned said, "It's all that rain we get here." He came from Arizona, and anything more than a shower once every three months seemed flood proportions to him. His dark eyes had a laugh in them, ready to take on all arguments. But Robb, who came from Montana, wasn't taking up any challenges tonight. He was thinking about the storm.

So was Mrs. Gunn. "Hard to hear a smash on a night like this," she said and listened half-expectantly.

Bert helped himself to some more peaches. "They'll be taking pictures," he said. "Over at Fennimore's, there were a crowd of dudes, and all they did was take them pictures." He looked at Ned, defying him to contradict. "They come to the corral in the morning, all two hours late, with leather straps around their necks and leather boxes dangling on their chests. They was near as well harnessed as the horses."

"Dudes . . ." Chuck said reflectively. He was the oldest wrangler there — perhaps the oldest in the county. Age had made him still thinner, but his eyes had lost none of their alertness and the color on his lean cheeks was still fresh. He admitted he was near seventy-six, but the rest of the boys thought he was being kind of modest. He treated Bert, who was forty-five or thereabouts, as a brash young fellow from Idaho who had only spent twelve years of his life in this part of the world, so that the other thirty-three were negligible. Ned and Robb, twenty-six years apiece, and newcomers since they were demobilized, were practically in the kindergarten. Jim Brent had been born here and he had lived here most of his life, so even if he was only forty-one he made up for his youth by being not too ignorant about the country.

14

A hard ride nowadays took Chuck's breath away, as he put it. But now that the warmth of the food and the coffee were working on him, he was ready to join in the talk. "Dudes," he said reflectively. "First bunch of dudes I ever seen, back in 1898, was —"

Jim Brent, who knew all Chuck's stories and wasn't even expected to listen to them, rose to his feet. "Come on, Bert. You know all about Easterners. We'll take a couple of shovels in case that flower-picker has gone wandering into a ditch looking for watercress." He moved stiffly over to the door — he had been in the saddle since six o'clock that morning — and started to pull on his slicker. Bert followed him, saying nothing, listening to the increasing gusts of wind, the renewed thunderclaps. They both halted for a moment, before they opened the door, and listened to the wind and the rain outside.

Mrs. Gunn said, "Perhaps they drove right on to Sweetwater."

Jim shook his head. "Didn't know if they were coming or going, far less that Sweetwater ever existed. Ready, Bert?" They plunged into the night and it took both men to close the door.

"There was five of them, all straight from St. Louis," Chuck was saying.

"Sure rains here in Wyoming," Ned said. "Ought to have known it. At the Garden, the Wyoming ponies had webbed feet. Kind of puzzled me at the time."

"Sure, sure," Robb said. "And the Arizona ponies all had humps in place of withers. Crossed them with camels, they tell me."

"Now, boys!" Mrs. Gunn said. "Anyone else want a doughnut? If the ladies come here, they won't touch them. Bad for their figures, they say." She laughed, and patted her own gaunt hipbones. "It's not the eating, it's the sitting, if you ask me. Well, I'd better get a couple of beds ready. Robb, give me a hand with some logs. We'll need a fire in the guest room to cheer them up. Hasn't been used now for almost seven years." Her smile faded as she thought of the changes the war had made, and she left the kitchen quickly. Fortunately, she thought as she climbed the stairs to the linen closet, she had always kept the house aired and cleaned and polished as if all the Brents were still living here. It would be nice to have the guest room used again.

In the kitchen, Ned stretched his long thin legs towards the bright fire. Like Chuck, he was going to wait to see the arrival of this flower-picker. He rolled a cigarette and listened to Chuck, whose breath had fully recovered and now matched his memory.

CHAPTER III

Rest and Be Thankful

S ARAH BLY awoke first.

She lay quite still, enjoying the soft warmth of the bed, the deep silence, the pale sunlight filtering through green curtains, the comforting disorder of opened suitcases, the feeling of having slept so well that no more problems existed. If they did exist — for, after all, the car was still in the ditch, and their clothes were probably shrinking to nothing as they dried in the warm kitchen downstairs — they would be solved. That was the kind of morning it was. Cold, too, she decided as she stepped out of bed. But she had to see what lay outside of the green curtains.

Mrs. Peel stirred, yawned, and then looked around in a dazed way. It was the pleasantest hotel room she had seen in a long time. She stared at the fireplace with its evidence of a log fire, and gradually she remembered. She drew the four blankets and wool comforter more tightly around her. At least, here was safety. Last night — She shuddered. She closed her eyes, but she could still see the three miserable, drenched, mud-covered scarecrows being brought into a warm, cheerful kitchen. And that thin, white-haired woman, Mrs. — Mrs. Pistol — taking them in charge, helping them unpack their suitcases, finding them dry clothes, lending them an extra cardigan, heating up stew and coffee for them. All in the quietest way, as if this were nothing unusual. Yes, everyone had been like that, all the strange expressionless men who didn't say much but looked politely at the bunch of lupines which she had still clutched in her hand as she walked into the kitchen.

After all, she couldn't hurt Jackson's feelings by leaving them to drown in the car: she had told him so often that blue flowers were her favorite ones, and he had picked the lupines yesterday to cheer her up for having been so wrong in insisting on that road. Jackson never explained, because he still thought in Hungarian and that kept him silent except in moments of great excitement. Once, Mrs. Peel had suggested that she would learn Hungarian and then he would have someone to talk to. But the proposal had alarmed Jackson. That, Mrs. Peel had understood too. It was Jackson's consolation that he was able to do one thing that very few people in France or America could do. Whenever he felt perplexed by the Western world, he would smile, knowing that if he started talking Hungarian he could bewilder it too. She couldn't take that smile away from Jackson. He had admitted the logic that, if she wasn't to learn Hungarian, then he would have to be renamed. "Jackson" was something she could pronounce without having her tongue trip over a weird assortment of strange sounds. Too many sneezes, Sarah had agreed.

"Sarah!" she called. She lifted her head to look across the room. But the other bed was empty, and the bathroom was silent.

"How extraordinary," Mrs. Peel said, and began to worry. Sarah never behaved this way. What could have happened to her? Where was she?

This was a strange house in a strange — a very strange — place, and they were miles from civilization. The people had been very kind last night, but now that she came to think of it, hadn't they been also very quick? Yet there was a little town only twenty-five miles farther along this road — Mrs. Pistol had talked about it — and there must be a hotel there. Never, in Mrs. Peel's long and varied experience of getting lost, had she been welcomed as a guest overnight in a strange house and treated as a friend. Either she had been directed politely to the nearest inn, or if she stayed, she paid.

Mrs. Peel sat up in bed, shivered, searched for her watch under the pillow, and couldn't find it. Her purse — she couldn't remember where she had laid it last night, but she had put it somewhere in this room — wasn't visible, either. She stared wildly around. Twenty-five miles to the nearest house, she remembered. She set out bravely for the door.

A sound of chopping came upstairs from the kitchen. Then, as she hesitated on the landing, wondering if she should dare call Sarah once more, she heard Mrs. Pistol's voice and Sarah's laugh.

"Sarah!" she called sharply, angry with herself and with Sarah. As she heard Sarah's high heels leave the kitchen, she turned and ran back to bed. She was cold. She was hungry, too, and the tantalizing smell of eggs and bacon and coffee which had drifted up from the kitchen had sharpened this unaccustomed early appetite.

Sarah, looking most attractively healthy, carried a tray into the bedroom. She was alarmingly cheerful, too, for this time of day.

"Lazybones," she said. "It is practically midmorning, ranch time."

"My watch —" Mrs. Peel began fretfully.

"It had fallen on the floor. I put it on the dressing table. Now, have something to eat and you'll feel much better."

"You know I never eat in the morning," Mrs. Peel said.

Sarah only smiled. "You'll be surprised how good ham and eggs are, after all these years. I'll have a cup of coffee and give you the news of the day. No morning papers, here, you know." She laid the heavy tray on Mrs. Peel's lap, and then went over to the broad stretch of windows. She drew back the green curtains and let the bright sunshine spread into the room. The sky was blue. The clouds were white and innocent. A treetop stirred in the gentle breeze and fluttered its fresh green leaves.

"What time is it?"

"Half-past nine," Sarah said.

"You made me think it was noon," Mrs. Peel said accusingly, and sipped a cup of strong black coffee. "Did you have breakfast with the cowboys?"

"Good heavens, no. They had breakfast hours ago. I only got downstairs about half-past seven. And they seem to be called wranglers."

"If cowboy was good enough for the West for fifty years or so, it's good enough for me," Mrs. Peel said rebelliously. "And they are all out riding again. . . . What an incredibly romantic life!" She was becoming more human as the cup of coffee took effect. She looked at the inviting slice of ham and the two perfectly cooked eggs. "I'll just have a little taste," she said, and cut into the first yolk.

"Not entirely romantic," Sarah said. "It seems there is a lot of work around a ranch, and it's done by them without outside help. We've rather added to their chores, I'm afraid. Jim Brent — he's the tallest one, with graying hair and gray eyes, who spoke to us on the road yesterday evening, and he's the owner of the ranch, did you know that? Jackson was quite surprised, and rather pleased, when he heard that: it made him feel much better, somehow, about eating supper along with us last night. You know how feudal he insists on being, sometimes! Anyway, Jim Brent has gone with Jackson and Robb — comes from Montana I hear — to get the car back on the road. Once that is done, Jim and Robb have to clear the road to Sweetwater, where a tree fell last night. Ned — who has that very attractive Arizona drawl — is repairing a saddle. Later, he and Bert (he's middle-aged and quietly amused by things) have a job of mending fences to do. But meanwhile Bert has gone to clear the stream with Chuck (the very old man: he's worked on this ranch for years and years, even before Mrs. Gunn came here), so that the water-supply won't be blocked by the storm."

"And didn't Mrs. — Mrs. Gunn have time to tell you about herself?" Mrs. Peel was enjoying the second egg, now.

Sarah laughed. "She has been here for fifteen years. She used to be the Brent family cook. Now she is a kind of caretaker for the house. Do you know, Margaret, this house is practically empty now? Isn't it a shame? It is the most charming place you can imagine. No, don't look at me like that. . . . It is beautifully built, and it is in the most perfect setting."

"Setting for what? The Ride of the Valkyries?"

Really, Mrs. Peel reflected as Sarah talked about the house, about the scenery, Sarah was in the best of spirits this morning. Her blue eyes sparkled, her skin had been tanned to a warm glow by yesterday's sun on that misleading road, and her hair curled just sufficiently around her neat head to be attractive. Mrs. Peel wondered what her own hair would look like after that storm last night. And she never tanned nicely. If she couldn't find calamine lotion by this afternoon, she would have a face like a broiled lobster. Oh well, what did it matter at her age? But it was slightly depressing, at this moment, to see Sarah looking frankly not a day older than thirty. Even Sarah's excitement over this new place was a young excitement. And it was infectious.

"Sarah," she said reflectively, "an experience like yesterday's may be good for us after all. I mean, we are getting into a certain kind of groove. All we do, all we think, is the kind of thing we have done or thought ever since we were twenty-five."

"Oh, our arteries haven't hardened already!" Then Sarah Bly looked ruefully at her friend and smiled. "Or have they? Is that why we have been so — so baffled in this last year, ever since we came back from Europe?"

Mrs. Peel sighed. "It's horrid to think about . . ." She looked down at the tray, now emptied of food. "Well, that's one long-standing rule I did break." Then, as she poured the last quarter-cup of coffee, she said, "Remember Paris in 1930, when you had just arrived there? And then, two years later, when we set up house together? How very full of experiment we were then . . . we'd try anything, once. But nowadays when we want to feel happy, all we say is 'How this is like what we once loved!' It is all a kind of seeking-back — a sort of middle-aged retreat."

Sarah said nothing for a few moments. "All right, then. Come and try some more new things. Wash in ice-cold water, put on your warmest clothes, and come and see the house. It is built on a green island, where the stream divides round these trees. And all around are mountains, for the island lies in the center of a valley."

"I'm afraid mountains have lost something of their charm for me this morning. When do we leave for that little town? What's its name?"

"Sweetwater."

"Beg pardon?"

"Sweetwater. Mrs. Gunn thinks we ought to wait until the evening at least, to let the road have a chance to recover from the rain. It is said to be bad, and it is all downhill, twisting and turning. Besides, the car may be slightly rebellious after the treatment it got yesterday."

"But we *can't* force ourselves on strangers like this. And I need calamine lotion, anyway."

"Mrs. Gunn says baking soda is just as good."

Mrs. Peel stared at her in amazement. "What on earth have you not been discussing with Mrs. Gunn?"

"There seems to be quite a lot to talk about. Frankly, I'd be sorry to leave at once. I don't know why. I was prepared to hate every minute in this place when we staggered into the kitchen last night. But . . ." Sarah Bly shrugged her shoulders. "Do hurry, Margaret. We've wasted so much of the morning already. And bring your camera and plenty of color film."

Mrs. Peel's face brightened. As she got out of bed and headed for the bathroom, she asked, "What ranch is this, anyway?"

"Flying Tail Ranch. The large mountain overlooking us is Flashing Smile. The rushing stream at the front door is Crazy Creek. And the green island on which this house is built is known as Rest and Be Thankful."

Mrs. Peel looked round the bathroom door, toothbrush poised in mid-air. "Say that all again." She listened raptly. "It sounds like Stephen Vincent Benét," she said, and having established a literary flavor went back to scrubbing her teeth enthusiastically. Suddenly she was at the door again. "It's snowing! The sun is shining, the birds are singing, and it's snowing."

"That's the cottonwood trees along the creek. They are shedding little white fluffs of cotton, and it floats down in clouds."

Mrs. Peel stared. "Sarah, are you developing a Western sense of humor?"

"I can't keep my face quite straight enough for that."

"No one *ever* told me this. It really is all so — so different. Tell me, why do movies about the West always insist on bandits; and long, long, bars; and women having fights in spangled skirts?" She didn't wait for the answer, but disappeared once more into the bathroom.

"Because this is the day of the Classified Character," Sarah said to the open door. She began to tidy the bedroom as she waited. "All heroines are slender; heroes are never bald; rich men are ruthless

22

privateers or tolerable old fools; politicians are stupid or crooked; all children are cute; poor men are victims of other men; all Frenchwomen are chic; all Englishmen keep such stiff upper lips you can't hear what they're saying; all Italians are so human; all people in authority are petrified; all professors are dehydrated; all scientists are devoted to test tubes. Do you want me to go on? I've a long list."

"What was that, Sarah? The water was running and I couldn't hear you, I'm sorry." Mrs. Peel returned shivering from the bathroom, and began dressing with lightning speed. "I suppose they would have considered it a sign of weakness if I had lit a fire? Well, this is one morning when I won't take very long to get ready."

Her voice became somewhat muffled as she struggled with a sweater. "You know, Sarah, most of the books we read abroad about America weren't of much help to us. It wasn't our fault entirely that we knew so little about our own country as it is today." Then her voice became more normal again as she at last got her head through the sweater's neckline without disarranging her hair too badly. "I mean, we learned a lot about some aspects of America, especially when they were squalid or harrowing. The realistic school of writing is so deceptive, implying the part is the whole." She frowned thoughtfully as she fastened her skirt. "No wonder foreigners are baffled between one writer's enthusiasms and another's prejudices. You know, in these last few weeks as we traveled slowly across America, I've been amazed and excited. Now, where are my shoes?" As she rummaged in her suitcase, she went on, "And I've been learning all the time. There is so much to learn!" She was over at the dressing table now, combing her hair into place. "Why don't writers tell us about *all* kinds of things — the good and the bad and the middling? If they aren't all described, then you get an overweighted picture. It is the completeness of writers like Dickens and Tolstoy that makes them live, isn't it?"

"The lady will now descend from her soapbox and advance into the unknown countryside on a voyage of discovery," Sarah Bly suggested, opening the door.

Mrs. Peel, collecting all the rest of her necessary equipment, followed her at last. She was still frowning, though. "I wonder if there are any traveling scholarships for writers — traveling in America, I mean?"

"Give them a car, some money, and tell them to get lost, young man, get lost? But perhaps they are just like us when we were young," Sarah suggested. "When the word travel is mentioned, they think of Paris."

Mrs. Peel said nothing more. She was remembering the days when their little flat off the Rue de Seine had been the meeting place of ambitious writers with all their arguments, hopes, plans and manuscripts. The days when . . . Would she ever be able to stop referring to them? The days *now*, she told herself firmly. But she couldn't persuade herself to feel happy. Last winter, she had attempted a little *salon* in New York, inviting those she had known abroad, along with the few American critics and writers she had met, to her Friday Night. One of her most faithful guests and bitter friends (he was European import, vintage 1939, to give New York its due) had named it "Maggie's Saloon." That had been rather hard to take.

"Now what's holding them up?" Mrs. Gunn asked the alarm clock on the kitchen window sill, as she finished preparations for noon dinner and began mopping the floor. Outside, her morning's laundry was bleaching nicely on a rope strung between two linden trees.

Bert, riding back from the creek, with a spade over his shoulder, stopped for a cup of coffee at the kitchen door.

"You'll get plenty of water now," he said. "And the car is out of the ditch. That dark-faced fellow is tinkering with it and muttering to himself. Hasn't stopped to pick a flower, yet."

"Did any of you find the hats?"

"No. Guess them feathers took wing."

"Well now, I did want to see a Paris hat," Mrs. Gunn said disappointedly. "In fact, I haven't seen a new hat in five years since I visited my husband's folks in Omaha."

"You'll see plenty now," Bert said out of the side of his mouth, as the two visitors appeared at the hall entrance to the kitchen. Mrs. Peel, in beige tweed, was armed with sunglasses, a large-brimmed hat, an umbrella (to be used as a sunshade), a raincoat (rescued from the bottom of her suitcase so that she might sit on a specially nice piece of grass), her pocketbook, and a camera. Miss Bly thought she was equally suitably dressed for the West. To her neat wool suit she had added a heavy silver bracelet and a gay silk scarf over which red horses leaped appropriately.

"We are just going out," Mrs. Peel called gaily and startled Bert, who had scarcely thought they were dressed for going in. "When should we return for luncheon?"

Bert handed the coffee cup back to Mrs. Gunn, and they avoided catching each other's eye. For a moment his gaze flickered over the camera. Then he gravely touched his hat and left. This, he figured, was something for Ma Gunn to handle by herself. He'd take bull-dogging, any day.

CHAPTER IV

Inspection

THAT MORNING, Rest and Be Thankful set out to please. The miseries of last night had only served to make today's joys all the more enchanting. The two visitors returned from their leisurely walk not only filled with enthusiasm, but with their interest quickened. Mrs. Peel was conquered even as Sarah had been. The house itself was built of stone, which was unusual, and yet appropriate; for the stones had come from the road through the valley, where the Stoneyway Trail had once led towards the Oregon Trail. Mrs. Peel yesterday, in her little jokes about covered wagons, had not been very far wrong historically. And the house was built well, with charm and dignity and strength. Around it were stretches of green grass bordered by the tall cottonwood trees that followed the branching arms of Crazy Creek. And once the creek had encircled the house and its grounds, it joined again to go rushing through Stoneyway Valley down to Sweetwater in the plains.

After midday dinner was over, there was a short pause for irresistible sleep (to be blamed entirely on six thousand five hundred feet of altitude, Mrs. Peel hoped). And then there was more talk, more discussion; and they went out to walk under the shade of the cottonwood trees to talk and discuss still more. By this time, they had discarded coats and sweaters; and Sarah undid the top buttons of her silk shirt and rolled up its sleeves, while Mrs. Peel kept the umbrella-sunshade over her head. But it wasn't very long before all talking ceased. The peace of the valley and the deep silence of the hills enfolded them.

As Mrs. Gunn sprinkled the laundry and rolled it into neat packages to await ironing, she could see the two visitors every now and again from her kitchen window. They were strolling around the house, pausing to look at the vegetable garden, then the flower garden now overgrown with weeds, then the creek where the trout swam boldly. They looked up at the mountains; and they looked towards the hilly pastures, where the horses were grouped together and tossed their heads and whisked their long tails in protest against the midday flies. Then the trees hid the visitors from Mrs. Gunn's sharp eyes, for they walked towards the ranch which lay over the bridge and at a little distance from the house. So she couldn't see them pause at the corral with its massive five-barred fence, or look at the log buildings which lay around the corral — the saddle barn, the stable, the smithy; or quicken their pace slightly as they passed the Wranglers' Roost, where the boys were cat-napping in the heat of the day before they rode out to the north pasture to check on the mares and the colts.

But Mrs. Gunn had seen enough. "A regular tour of inspection, like they were prospecting the place," she said aloud, and spat on the hot iron to test it. Then she became too busy to pay much more attention, and she had almost forgotten her remark when the ladies appeared at the kitchen door, apologetic for this intrusion and their mud-coated shoes. They sat and talked to her as she ironed, and the questions they asked — all very polite and kindly meant — were enough to let them learn a good deal about the ranch.

Yes, Mr. Brent lived here by himself now. No, not in the ranch house, but in the cabin over near the Wranglers' Roost. The house was too big for one person, he said. Once, there had been eight of them here. Old Mr. Brent had died two years ago, and his wife had followed him within three months. The younger son, Martin, was killed in Normandy. Martin's wife had taken their two little girls back to Baltimore. Jill Brent, the only daughter, had married a New Zealander she met in India during the war. And of course there used to be a lot of friends visiting them here. In the summer, the house was full, and the younger people often had to sleep over in the guest cabin down near the creek.

Yes, you could say it had been a lot of work, even with extra help,

27

but it had been real nice too. Kind of lonely nowadays. It was still lonelier, though, when the boys were away at the war. Only old Chuck, and his friend Bridger from Sweetwater, to look after things, with the help of a couple of school kids. Of course, the horses had been taken over by the Government, and by the end of the war Chuck and old Cheesit Bridger were just caretaking the buildings and land. Now, things were getting back to normal. Not quite, though. No money in horses, today. Cattle was the thing. No, not cows or bulls. Steers. (This was one exchange of looks between the ladies that Mrs. Gunn couldn't fathom.)

Oh, yes, horses used to be a paying proposition. The Army buyers came out here regular — Cavalry and Artillery, you know. And the French used to buy a lot too, for overseas service. And old Mr. Brent just liked horses. That's why he kept running them, even after the First World War. Now that Jim was in charge, he was trying to change over to cattle. He had made a beginning, but cattle took a lot of acres to make any profit on them at all. If he wanted to increase the size of the herds, which cost money, he would have to sell some of his land. And then he wouldn't have enough acres for the steers. It was a problem, any way you looked at it.

Why didn't he sell the horses? Well, he had been trying to do that. But there were only a few dude ranches around this district (dudes were awfully sore on horses) and apart from that, there were just the local buyers who would only pay thirty dollars for a good horse. They'd only give about a hundred and fifty for a quarter-horse. Easterners might pay five hundred, but what they wanted nowadays was mostly thoroughbreds; and that took some raising and coddling, for a thoroughbred couldn't run wild or fend for itself in the winter, not even on the lower pastures. Almost as stupid as steers, who didn't even know enough to scrape away the snow with their feet to let them get at the grass.

How big was Flying Tail? Oh, just medium. About 20,000 acres. Some of it wasn't much good either: the part that lay south near the plains, for instance, Jim would like to sell, but no one would buy that piece of land and you couldn't blame them. And when you calculated that each steer needed about twenty acres grazing land

28

in this part of the country, well then — just figure that out for yourselves.

The two visitors exchanged glances again. They had got lost somewhere among the quarter-horses, but they managed to grasp that it was all a problem, any way you looked at it.

"This house must be rather a white elephant, then," the younger one said, getting muddled a bit in her geography. But her pretty blue eyes were full of sympathy.

"It is such a perfect setting," the older one said. "It is just the place for people to be happy, to have a holiday away from cities and machines and worries and frustrations. Mrs. Gunn, would you think it impertinent of us if we were to ask you to show us over the house? It is so enchanting from the outside, that we are sure the architect must have been just as inspired indoors."

Mrs. Gunn gathered, in spite of the strange accents, that they wanted to see the house. She had no objections. It wasn't that she was actually hoping for anything: she was only at the stage of thinking, "Wouldn't it be nice?"

There were seven bedrooms, four bathrooms, and four other rooms — a large living room, an ample dining room, a study (old Mr. Brent's refuge from his wife's innumerable guests), and a very small sitting room with a glass-enclosed porch and a view of the mountains that silenced Mrs. Peel completely. Miss Bly remarked that Mrs. Brent had put out not only a lot of money on the house, but taste and thought as well. "Those were the days," Mrs. Gunn said and startled her visitors into wondering if she were a mind reader. But Mrs. Gunn wasn't thinking about money so much, for she added, "And they could come back again, if only this house had the right mistress."

As they returned to the old-fashioned kitchen, Sarah Bly said, "It seems strange — " She stopped, realizing her tactlessness. She cleared her throat, ignored the smile in Margaret's quick brown eyes, and changed her course. "How attractive your kitchen is."

"I like it," Mrs. Gunn agreed heartily. "It's not like the new kitchen, thank goodness." She opened a door and showed them a narrow white room with streamlined equipment for cooking and washing.

"That looks very efficient," Miss Bly said with renewed interest. "It would be very easy to have guests, wouldn't it?"

"Yes," Mrs. Gunn said grudgingly, "but it still looks like a hospital to me." She led the way back to the cheerful wood stove and the comfortable rocking chair. As she made them a cup of tea, there were other questions to be answered: the little guest cabin by the creek, the quarters for the help, the electric plant that hadn't been used for some time, water running hot as well as very cold. "It all costs a mint of money," Mrs. Gunn said truthfully and sadly. However, the ladies accepted another doughnut and praised Mrs. Gunn's light hand; and when they went upstairs to rest for a little (altitude or old age? Mrs. Peel wondered again), Mrs. Gunn decided that really they were as nice as could be even if they did use an awful lot of extra words. No wonder they tired so easily.

"I can't quite believe it," Mrs. Peel said. But whether she was referring to the house, or to the two doughnuts which had tempted her so successfully, or to the invitation to supper (relayed by Mrs. Gunn) with the master of the house in the dining room tonight, Sarah Bly wasn't sure.

For a while they were silent. And although they felt exhausted, they were too excited to sleep.

Then, "I wonder if you are thinking what I am thinking?" Mrs. Peel asked.

Sarah stared at her, and then laughed. "We *are* idiots," she said. "We decided only a month ago that we had reached retiring age, remember?" She rose from her bed and went over to the windows and opened them wide. The steady murmur of the creek, the rustling of the cottonwood trees, the notes of a robin singing two lines of a song came drifting into the room.

"Nonsense," Mrs. Peel said brusquely. "That's what it was. This idea is just the sort of thing I need to keep me alive. If we are idiots, then we are idiots with a good idea, and just enough money — which is equally important."

"Unless the price of this house were too high."

"We could always lease it, of course."

"That wouldn't be the kind of money he needs. Besides, he might not like our plan at all." Sarah Bly remembered Jim Brent's determined jaw line and decidedly firm mouth. The eyes, too, were uncompromising. He might want to keep the house as his own, even if it was a white elephant. Men were like that.

"Well, we are having dinner with him aren't we? Let's be thankful the electricity isn't on, and that candlelight has a softening effect."

"He will think we are crazy," Sarah said. "And how on earth do we get anywhere near the subject?"

"Leave that to me," Mrs. Peel said. She was already in her most persuasive mood as she began to brush her hair. "After all, think of the benefactor he would be if he sold us this house — why, he might be responsible for a completely new phase in his country's literature."

The future benefactor was at that moment changing into a clean pair of well-faded, well-shrunk jeans. As he stamped his way into his best high-heeled boots, he was cursing Ma Gunn's idea of hospitality. What had made her suggest that the guests should have supper in the dining room tonight, and that he ought to be host? They had accepted before he had been given the chance to make a polite excuse. They were nice enough women, he supposed, but he had a hell of a lot of paper work to do in his office tonight. And where the devil was that clean shirt? He cursed everything within reach in turn, before he managed to leave his cabin.

The boys were lined up, outside the Roost, to encourage him with a cheer. Bert, caked with mud from the afternoon's work, volunteered to come and serve them cocktails. There were numerous other suggestions too, including Ned's guitar playing, Robb's recitations, and old Chuck as the Singing Cowboy. And Jackson, they thought, could pick flowers for the table.

But Jackson was sitting on his cot, upstairs in the Wranglers' Roost, thinking dolefully that everyone else sounded much too happy. His hands itched and burned with red blotches that had

31

spread up his arms and, since he had wiped the honest sweat off his brow several times in the course of this hot day's work, were now appearing on his face. He rose to look in the small, cracked mirror that hung beside Robb's cot. He closed his eyes to blot out the horrible sight. Before he came to Wyoming, he thought gloomily, he had been a handsome man—his taste ran to square-shaped jaw, heavy eyebrows above large brown eyes, and thick black hair. But now, his eyes were puffed into slits; his nose had swollen and spread. He was no longer the Hungarian *émigré* or the Paris *boulevardier,* or the smart New York chauffeur. He was a Tibetan pig. He sat down on his cot and wondered doubtfully if Atlantic City would ever look at him again.

CHAPTER V

Action ...

JIM BRENT found he was enjoying himself, after all. That was
something of a surprise, for he had entered the dining room in
a definitely bad-tempered mood. By way of apology, he set out to be
a good host; he listened sympathetically, and he even talked a good
deal more than he usually did with women. He was admitting to
himself that he had jumped to several wrong conclusions about
them. And so they found him a much easier companion than they
had expected. They couldn't guess from his face that his opinion
of them (and they had never guessed that, either) was undergoing
a complete revision. They weren't as silly as he had thought: perhaps it was only natural for women to be as upset as they had
been, last night, by the loss of their Paris hats. People, when they
were badly shaken, often made more of a fuss over a trifle than over
the real danger. And they weren't as useless as he had thought:
they might joke about their life abroad (often turning the joke
against themselves, which was the best kind of joke anyway), but
it took a lot of organization to get a printing press going; and it
took a bit of courage to carry it on hidden from the Germans, while
it printed Resistance leaflets instead of poetry.

"I had the most wonderful time," Mrs. Peel was saying. "I wrote
the editorials, you see. They were only ten lines, of course, for
we were strictly a one-page affair. But that was awfully good
discipline, I'm sure."

"For writing telegrams," Miss Bly suggested with a smile.

"But our useful days ended in December 1941."

"When we became, officially, enemies of the Reich."

33

"And so we were smuggled out of France by friends. By way of Marseille."

"But we ran into a storm — you know, it really *can* blow in the Mediterranean — and we found ourselves in Sicily of all places. Still, it was an interesting month in a way."

"Thirty-three days, Sarah. They are written on my heart. Then we got re-smuggled, fortunately. People can be very kind."

Brent managed to get three words in. "And where, then?" He didn't usually ask people questions about themselves, but this one seemed worth asking.

"To North Africa," Mrs. Peel said lightly. "Wasn't that lucky? We had never managed to get around to North Africa in any of our summer holidays."

And that was all they would say, apart from a bare little remark by Miss Bly that they had spent the last years of the war in London doing some work with the Free French. But as he hadn't mentioned his incursion into Europe by much their same route, only in reverse, with Italy as a digression between Sicily and Marseille, they all came out about even.

It was just in this most vulnerable of all masculine moments, when he was admitting to himself that he had been mistaken about them, that Mrs. Peel made a frontal assault.

"Mr. Brent, have you ever thought of renting or selling this house?"

He could only stare at her.

She went on, "It stands on its own little island, quite apart from the ranch and your own cabin, so really you wouldn't be troubled by people."

He was too amazed to reply. As a matter of fact, he had thought of trying to raise money by selling the house. But unless he liked the people who bought it, he would be better off leaving it unsold. Sometimes he wondered if it was a problem he kept postponing, just because he didn't really want to solve it. Yet it had to be solved soon.

"The fact is," Mrs. Peel went on, while Miss Bly kept her eyes fixed on her coffee cup, "we are enchanted by Rest and Be Thank-

34

ful. We would like to lease it, or to buy it just as it stands. We aren't speculators, Mr. Brent. We just like the house, the situation and the scenery."

Brent looked at both of them. His tanned face was quite expressionless, and only its mounting flush gave the ladies any clue to his feelings. And that was very little, for Mrs. Peel felt she had embarrassed him and her cheeks flushed too. Miss Bly flinched and thought, he is angry. They both looked so upset that he found he couldn't tell them that they were idiots: "I think you shouldn't make up your mind too quickly about that," he had been about to say.

Instead, "This house is too big for two people," he said.

"I agree," Mrs. Peel said. "I think it would also be very selfish for two women to keep Rest and Be Thankful all for themselves."

Sarah Bly said, "Our idea was that we would invite a small group of unknown writers to spend a few weeks here, where they could look at hills and mountains and sky, where they could relax and talk and work. The sense of peace is so wonderful. Out here, in this quiet valley, they could think and imagine. It is all so different, and yet so *real*."

Mrs. Peel agreed so vehemently that the white curls on top of her head slightly lost their symmetry. "You would be a real benefactor to writers if you let us have this house, Mr. Brent."

"Me?" He was dumfounded for a moment. "Now this is all your idea, Mrs. Peel. I've nothing to do with it." He looked at them gravely, feeling suddenly sorry for them. Just two women who had inherited a lot of money, who had too much time on their hands.

Mrs. Peel said, "Writers are really such *nice* people, and the unknown ones have *such* a difficult time."

"I always figured writers had a pretty soft life. Any of the boys here would think so."

"Oh no! Not today. Once — well, you wrote a terrific success and the money rolled in from every country and the taxes were very low. So a writer could invest his earnings and live very comfortably on them. Some, with good business sense — investments, you know — became really quite wealthy. Actually — " Mrs. Peel hesitated. She blushed. Then she went on, "I was one of those."

Sarah Bly stared at her friend in amazement: Margaret must be really determined to persuade Mr. Brent to let them have the house, or she would never have given away that secret. No one, except her publisher, her literary agent and Sarah Bly, knew about Margaret Peel. By Margaret Peel's own very definite request.

"Of course," Mrs. Peel was saying, "this is between us, Mr. Brent. Did you ever hear of Elizabeth Whiffleton?"

Mr. Brent hadn't.

Mrs. Peel seemed relieved. "Well, I was she."

"Was?" asked Jim Brent.

"Definitely," Mrs. Peel answered with considerable force. "Never, *never* again. Elizabeth Whiffleton spent two years of my life in writing a book. Just one book. And it made money. Well, that was very nice because I needed money. My husband had died, he was really a darling but the world's worst businessman. So Elizabeth Whiffleton sat down and wrote a story to keep me alive. It was published in 1925. And do you know what happened? It sold and sold, and I found I was quite well-off. Then, because my husband had never been able to manage our finances when he was alive, I was fascinated by the stock market. I began to buy when the market was low and sell when it was high. It is *so* simple, really. I doubled, and then trebled my capital, and by 1928 I was too rich to feel honest. So I stopped then. Fortunately, as it turned out. Now you see how I feel every sympathy for young writers, and try to help if I can."

"Try to teach them to play the stock market?"

Mrs. Peel laughed. "No. I mean — if they have to write for money, often they can't write what they want to write. I know. You see, I always wanted to write a book, but not the Elizabeth Whiffleton kind. I wanted to write a book, a very serious one, that the very best critics would acclaim."

"And which few people would read, probably," Sarah said with a smile. "And you certainly wouldn't have had the fun you've had out of life, Margaret."

"But at least I could have told my friends I was an author," Mrs. Peel said with unexpected spirit. "Now I have to sit quietly, as I've

36

done for twenty-three years, while they discuss *their* books. It would be very frustrating if it weren't so funny."

Brent said, "I would think you'd tell them about the book you wrote."

"About *The Lady in White Gloves?*" She was too shocked to answer.

"Was it banned?" he asked, looking curiously at the earnest, kindly brown eyes. He couldn't imagine this white-haired, serene-faced woman writing dirt. He didn't like the idea, either.

Sarah Bly sensed his thoughts. She said quickly, "No. It wasn't that kind of book. In fact, I'm afraid it wouldn't have enough sex interest for a smash hit today. What was daring in 1925 is school-room reading, now."

"The truth was," Mrs. Peel said sadly, "that all my particular friends considered the book to be tripe. They *are* very literary, you see."

"They disliked it simply because it sold," Sarah said in swift defense. "They never really gave it a chance." She won an admiring look from Jim Brent. He might not be able to understand why anyone should be ashamed of a book just because a lot of people bought it, but he did understand loyalty.

"Prender Atherton Jones must have read it," Mrs. Peel said, defending her friends in turn. "He reviewed it. Shatteringly. He was one of our group in Paris," she explained to Brent. "He had considerable reputation as the reviewer for *New Dimensions.*" Mrs. Peel spoke the name with such awe that Jim Brent raised his eyebrows.

"Four book reviews a year, and thought he was being slave-driven," Sarah Bly said, and won another look from her host.

"Now, Sarah, I have to admit it wasn't the kind of book I wanted to write. But I *was* desperate for money. I had exactly two dollars and thirty-seven cents in my pocket when I received the advance on signature. That is" (with a kindly look to a bewildered Brent) "the money advanced to me by my publisher as soon as I signed the contract on the completed manuscript."

"Well, that was all of twenty-three years ago," Jim Brent said. "Why didn't you write another book?"

37

Mrs. Peel looked embarrassed. She glanced at Sarah.

Sarah said quietly, "You've been much too busy all these years." But she knew, as Margaret knew, that being busy with people was one way of postponing the fearful day of having your pencils sharpened or your typewriter newly ribboned, of sitting down to stare at a white sheet of paper. She thought, too, of her own efforts at serious literature. Poetry. That was what she had been going to write when she arrived in Paris in 1930. She had been nineteen, the stuff that dreams are made on. And they had all gone sour. No one published her poems except Margaret. And to keep herself independent, so that later she might travel with Margaret with a free conscience, she had begun writing cook books. They sold, and were still selling. And even if she tried to tell Margaret that she was wrong to worry about what people, like Prender Atherton Jones, thought, she herself had published the cookery recipes under another name. And she had never mentioned them to Prender, or any of the rest of their little group.

Jim Brent looked at the two downcast faces. That was just like women, he thought, to have imaginary troubles if they couldn't find real ones. He said, quite frankly, "I don't understand it. Why hide what you've done, Mrs. Peel? If it is these literary friends you are afraid of, then what kind of friends are they?"

His question certainly had results, for they stopped looking so gloomy, and they stared at each other for a moment. Miss Bly even laughed.

Mrs. Peel said, "We told you all this, Mr. Brent, because you ought to know what we are and who we are. Of course you will want references. Would my publisher be sufficient? There's our lawyer, too."

"Just a minute," Jim Brent said, conscious that Mrs. Peel had passed mysteriously from the romantic mood to the realistic. "Just a minute, Mrs. Peel. . . . We're going ahead pretty fast."

"But we have to," Miss Bly told him earnestly and gave him one of her warmest smiles. "We shan't see you tomorrow morning, and when we leave — well, we've gone for good, haven't we? And this idea of ours would be lost forever. Which would be a pity, for it might benefit us all."

"All of us?" he asked, his eyes smiling. "I'm thinking of you two," he explained. "Do you know the writers personally?"

"No," Sarah Bly admitted. "All we are interested in, frankly, is the fact that they are unknown writers. They haven't been published yet."

"Mr. Atherton Jones knows them," Mrs. Peel said. "He had planned a summer group for August of very promising, but quite unknown, writers. He rented a delightful old farm built in pre-Revolutionary days in New England. We heard from him, only a week or so ago, that he is in a fearful quandary because all the group is arranged but the house has begun to fall down. It has just been condemned as unsuitable for human habitation. He doesn't know what to do. Here's the group of writers all ready for August, and there's the house — "

"Falling down," Brent said. "Seems to me he has a better eye for historical architecture than he has for simple foundations. It also seems to me that he must have made some money out of literature, too. That kind of idea costs money. So if I were you, Mrs. Peel, I wouldn't worry too much about that book of yours."

"No, he hasn't made money," Mrs. Peel said quickly.

"He hasn't exactly starved, either," Sarah Bly said.

"That's because he has been lecturing ever since he came back to America, Sarah. And you know how he hates it. Actually, Mr. Brent, he was arranging his summer group on a very businesslike basis, but without any profits at all. The writers were to pay fees, and that would cover living expenses as well as the cost of the lectures that Mr. Atherton Jones's friends were going to give about the art of writing. But *no* profits. He made that quite clear to us all."

"Will you charge fees?" Brent asked.

"No. Fares out to Wyoming will be a big enough item."

"We don't want fees and we don't want lecturers," Sarah Bly said. "We don't see it that way."

"The writers will merely be our guests, and I assure you that

39

writers make very quiet, delightful guests. Have no fear of that, Mr. Brent."

"If they aren't," Sarah Bly said, "we'll put phenobarbital in their coffee."

"They will," Mrs. Peel continued, silencing Sarah with a shake of her head, "not trouble you at all, Mr. Brent. Or the ranch."

"Mrs. Peel," Jim Brent said, "I don't think I've made up my mind just yet."

"Of course you must have time to think about it," Mrs. Peel murmured. "But if you did think about it, what kind of price would you ask?"

"About fifty thousand dollars, I guess." They'd never meet that. It was as polite a way of refusing as any.

"For everything?" Mrs. Peel was amazed. "Furniture, guest house and everything?"

"It's worth much more," Sarah Bly said. "I'm sure it is."

"It's isolated," he replied. "And it is expensive to operate. You'll need extra help, unless you're willing to do a lot of work yourselves. And there's Mrs. Gunn — she may not like this idea. She's made her home here for years."

"We couldn't do without Mrs. Gunn, either," Mrs. Peel said quickly. "I do hope she approved of us."

A sudden thought struck him. "Did you ask her to arrange this dinner here, tonight?"

"Good gracious, no!" Mrs. Peel said with such vehemence that there was no disbelieving her.

"Then she probably approves," he said. He began to understand why Ma Gunn hadn't disturbed them to clear the coffee cups away.

"You will let us have the house?" Miss Bly was asking.

"At that price? Isn't that a lot?" He was amazed in turn. The house and grounds were well worth fifty thousand dollars. But he had expected some Eastern haggling. Whenever you had to sell anything, you were always told that the market was poor and you would be lucky to get half the value. When you had to buy, it was peculiar how high the market value had suddenly become.

Mrs. Peel and Miss Bly looked at each other.

40

"I'll take it," Mrs. Peel said, as if she had been born and raised in the West.

"I'll think it over," he said.

Sarah Bly ended the discussion by saying, "You know, during the last ten minutes I began to wonder whether *you* were buying the house and we were trying to sell it!" He smiled, then.

They said good night in the hall, and he waited at the foot of the stairs until they reached the landing. Then he turned away, picked up his wide-brimmed felt hat from the hall chest, pulled it well down over his forehead, and left the house without another glance around it. But as he entered the strip of cottonwood trees to reach the bridge and the road to his cabin, he halted. He looked back at the house. It lay in darkness, except for the dim candlelight in the guest room.

It was a house where he had been happy, but that was a long time ago. It was too large, built for a family and their friends. A man, living alone there, would feel he was a relic as much as the house.

He turned away, walking confidently in the dark along the twisting path and over the bridge, knowing each rut in the road, every jutting branch. He might as well be as frank as these two women had been. He needed the money. If the choice had to be between selling valuable acres and selling the house, it would have to be the house. A house didn't provide grazing land for cattle, and without cattle the ranch would close down. Then why hadn't he agreed at once to sell the house? Perhaps because it was a problem he had postponed for many months. He resented it being solved so quickly. Then he entered his cabin, kicked aside the clothes he had thrown on the floor earlier that evening, lit the oil lamp, and, as he threw his hat up onto the antlers above the door, wondered irritably how the devil he had ever got into this evening's predicament.

In the guest-room, Mrs. Peel stood near the blazing fire and watched it thoughtfully. All the talk downstairs about Paris had recalled memories she wanted to forget.

"What's wrong, Margaret?" Sarah asked. "Regretting your buying impulse?"

Mrs. Peel shook her head.

Sarah went on creaming her skin in front of the mirror. She took more trouble tonight than usual. "How old do you think Jim Brent is?" she asked, keeping her voice casual. She studied her face in the glass. No wrinkles yet, she noted thankfully.

"About forty, I suppose." Mrs. Peel forced her thoughts back to the present. "I like his eyes. A nice warm gray. But sad and watchful. Of course, he has his worries. Doesn't he ever laugh, though? And how thin all these men are!" Her voice grew more cheerful as she talked, if only to please Sarah. And somehow, thinking of the house and the ranch and people like Jim Brent, she became more cheerful.

"I'm going to visit a hairdresser in New York," Sarah announced suddenly. "You won't recognize me when I return here!"

Mrs. Peel stared at her friend. "You'll be too busy in New York explaining to the lawyers that we haven't lost our minds. Mr. Quick would really like me to die and leave all my money intact to cat and dog homes. Much pleasure that would give me under six feet of earth! I'll telegraph Prender Atherton Jones tomorrow and get him to send you a list of his stranded writers. Do you think he will be annoyed with us for not consulting him first? He does like to manage things."

"My dear, why do you think he wrote you about his tumbling-down house? He wanted your help. And he has got it."

"Oh no!" Mrs. Peel said in disappointment. Really, Prender could be quite feline at times.

"I'll get a plane from the airport at Sweetwater," Sarah was saying as she climbed into bed. "I'll be back here in five days with everything organized. Margaret, do you think you can manage things here? There is so much to be planned. We have only six weeks until August."

"Go to sleep!" Mrs. Peel said, much in the same voice as she had said "I'll take it." She had no doubts at all about the future. It must be this air, she thought, as she obeyed her own command.

... and Reactions

I N A PLACE where newspapers arrived late and radio reception was temperamental, the news about Rest and Be Thankful spread as fast as a forest fire. The town of Sweetwater (population 853, except on Saturdays when it reached 1200 or more) felt itself to be implicated in the change. There the reaction was swift and varied.

"Better lay in a big stock of fancy shirts," Mrs. Dan Givings warned her husband, who owned the Western General Emporium. "And some beaded moccasins and Navaho rugs and silk rodeo ties and postcards and frontier pants." Dan thought they'd better wait a bit: women always seized on any excuse to spend money. "That's just it," his wife said. "There'll be women among these visitors. And if we don't sell the stuff this year we can sell it next year. These dudes never know what they want to buy unless they see it. Give 'em plenty to see." So the Western General increased its stock, and Mrs. Givings changed the windows from Christmas gifts to something real fancy.

The B Q Bar put up a new neon sign, added three new slot machines with the jack pots tantalizingly full of silver, and ordered an extra shipment of Sheridan Export beer. The Teton Bar, not to be outshone, put up two neon signs. It also added six slot machines to supplement its crap table and black jack. The Foot Rail and the Purple Rim, having their own steady Saturday trade, contented themselves with repainting their names.

The Reverend Teesdale of the Methodist United suggested a Welcome-to-Sweetwater Social. The Reverend Buell of the Evangelical Lutheran wondered if he should call, as Father O'Healey, over at Three Springs, certainly would.

Bill's Drugstore rewrote its menus, and ordered film, Kleenex and sun-tan lotion. Upstairs, its Zenith Beauty Shop put up new curtains across its two booths, and added oil shampoos to its repertoire. But Mrs. Bill drew the line — even for Easterners who spent money so wildly — at facials. "If they're as crazy as that, let 'em go to Yellowstone and jump in the mud volcano," she said.

There were other rebels in Sweetwater, too, particularly among the old-timers who liked their cow towns straight. They didn't care whether that new movie, which startled them ten years ago, ever opened its doors in the evening. They took a very poor view of Milt Jerks (who ran the log-cabin gas station on the outskirts of town) when he rented a front room on Main Street next his movie house, filled it with fishing tackle and leather goods, and brought an old plug — fully saddled and bridled — to stand patiently by the hitching-rail at the edge of the board sidewalk. And when Jerks (he was a newcomer from St. Louis who had settled in Sweetwater just over fifteen years ago) suggested everyone should dress Western this summer, and bought himself a shiny blue tie and an embroidered shirt, feeling ran high in the Purple Rim Bar.

"Hell," old Cheesit Bridger said, "we was here before he were and all them damned dudes either. An' what kind of way does he think we dress now? It sure ain't Eastern." His friends around the Purple Rim spat their agreement. Their father had fought off Indians, had killed bears and snakes and badmen, had built a little thin line of wooden houses and a schoolroom and the first church, with no help or encouragement from anyone except their wives who could shoot and saw and nail as good as any man. Then after the Indian troubles, there had been the war between the big ranchers and the settlers which had spread from Johnson County into this part of the country. And there was a time when the outlaws from Jackson Hole had tried to run Sweetwater as well. But ever since 1914, when the fighting was taken over by Europe, there had been peace in these parts. The railroad had been kept a good ten miles to the east of Sweetwater, and the State Highway was only reached by a second-class road from Main Street South. As only a few rough roads branched out from Main Street North to the ranches and farms hidden in the surrounding hills and valleys, Sweetwater had been spared invasion by busloads of "towrists." The old-timers considered the building of the airport (a wooden hut on a grass field) as only the Thin End of the Wedge. For dude ranches were increasing each year since the airport had been organized.

Although Cheesit and his friends had to grant Milt Jerks that dudes had money in their pockets to match the jingle of their new spurs, all *they* got out of it was that they'd be wrangling dudes instead of horses. Horses were easier on the nerves. And here was the news that Jim Brent had sold his house to more dudes. Not that they blamed Jim. Everyone knew he had been having a bad time. They blamed the Easterners.

"They ain't regular dudes," old Chuck said, suddenly overcome by loyalty to Rest and Be Thankful. He had ridden over to Sweetwater to discuss the news with Cheesit Bridger at the Purple Rim. "Seems they're kind of writer fellers."

"Dudes with brains," snorted Cheesit in disgust. "Maybe long hair too." He shook his head slowly. "That's worst of all."

And the Purple Rim fell into deep gloom, with only the slap of a bottle of Sheridan Export on the long, dark counter to break the silence.

Back on Flying Tail Ranch, there was also gloom; but here, it was tempered with stoicism. The boys did not like the idea of a lot of strangers wandering around the corral. (Jim might say that the ranch was now separate in every way from the house, but seeing was believing.) Yet they liked the idea of finding themselves without a job even less. Flying Tail was all right. So was Jim Brent.

Bert said he only hoped them writing fellows didn't come into his saddle barn with notebooks in their hands and pencils all sharp as their noses.

Chuck, remembering Cheesit Bridger's predictions, sustained himself with an anecdote about the Texas Invasion. (That had been repulsed eventually, leaving Wyoming triumphant.)

Ned thought that Ma Gunn would be needing extra help. He knew a nice girl in Las Vegas who would like to summer in Wyoming.

Robb, suddenly brightening, said there was a nice girl in Butte, too. Ma Gunn said she would also get her niece, Norah, from Three Springs. Norah thought a lot of writers. And if the ladies seemed in a bit of a hurry, well, that was the way Easterners were. And why not? The house was there, and the summer was before them. She was to keep her kitchen as her own place, and the boys would always find a cup of coffee and a slice of pie to help out Chuck's cooking. By September, the Easterners would all be back home again. The summer wasn't so long.

Bert remembered there was always next summer, and the summer after that, and after that. Besides it worried him, when he was over to Sweetwater, to hear Mrs. Dan Givings and Milt Jerks saying this was all a trend: wouldn't be long before Upshot County was as full of dude ranches and tourists as its neighbors were.

"Well, you get used to anything," Ma Gunn said. "And we may as well look on the bright side: we'll get one good laugh a day." There would be plenty to talk about in the long winter evenings when she was visiting her son and daughter-in-law over at Three Springs.

Jim Brent said very little after announcing his decision. He only interrupted his routine for one day, in which he hired a Piper Cub from the Sweetwater airfield to fly to Warrior, the county town, to see his lawyer.

Mrs. Peel talked at great length. Mrs. Gunn listened as she counted sheets and towels and cups and silverware, and observed that it was just like reading a dictionary, which was always something she had meant to do. One of her cousins, over at Greybull, had spent many a pleasant winter with a dictionary by a man called Sam Johnson, and had reached the letter T before he was knocked down by a bus traveling to Yellowstone. "Never knew what hit him," Mrs. Gunn ended, in a shocked voice. "They were wearing these shorts and brazeers, too."

Mrs. Peel puzzled over this for a little, so that her flow of eloquence ceased, much to Mrs. Gunn's disappointment. But as Mrs. Peel was preparing to visit Jackson, with more poison ivy lotion and apple pie and a good book, she suddenly turned at the door and said, delightedly, "Tourists!" Mrs. Gunn nodded, and went on counting blankets. For someone as educated as Mrs. Peel must be, she had a very peculiar way of pronouncing words. "Toorists," Mrs. Gunn repeated to herself, and had her good laugh for that day.

Mrs. Peel was able to talk at great length to Jackson, too, for the Wranglers' Roost had miraculously emptied as she was seen timidly approaching the corral. It was fortunate that Jackson never did say very much, for she had so much to reassure him about. He was much better, today, in every way. He was dressed in his neat blue chauffeur's uniform, and his black hair was expertly combed into place. He was pleased by the haircut which Chuck had given him, and he was delighted by the tattered copies of *Western Stories,* with plenty of pictures, which Ned had heaped on his cot. Yes, he was definitely much better today; yesterday, there had been a gleam of mutiny in his eyes. Perhaps the thought of spending the summer at Rest and Be Thankful was beginning to seem less strange. To make quite sure, Mrs. Peel talked about his eventual trip to Atlantic City as a definite promise, and offered three weeks instead of two. As for California — well, that would be a pleasant exploration for the winter months, when Rest and Be Thankful would be closed. (Mrs. Peel believed in the pioneer spirit up to a point: beyond twelve inches of snow, no.) She left him, feeling slightly happier, and hoping he was more reassured.

He was, much more than she had guessed. The men, who shared the large room with him, were friendlier than he had first thought. Whenever they paid you an insult, it was a compliment. Whenever they kept their faces solemn, it was a joke. So all he had to do, when they mentioned flowers, was to smile as if he were enjoying himself. That had had amazing results. Bert had even searched for a bottle of Dr. White's Poison Ivy Lotion in the bottom of the small wooden chest, where he kept special things like mateless socks and buttons and letters and broken knives and bits of wood to carve into ornaments. He also found some Sure Cure Snakebite and Sore Tail Ointment, and he presented these to Jackson too. Just in case, as he confided in Ned, the Hungarian Cowboy was going to show them all how to ride. Ned agreed that this was the kind of guy that always caught trouble; kind of helpless; made you think of a

47

roped calf just at the moment it stopped kicking and turned its big brown eyes up at you. Robb suggested that — when you got right down to it — they might act just as helpless in a place as peculiar as that Hungary. This remark was followed by a period of silence. Chuck nodded his head: he never had any objections to this foreign fellow — best listener he had found in years.

So Mrs. Peel returned to Mrs. Gunn's kitchen, where she was given a nice cup of coffee to reassure her still more. "We couldn't do without Jackson," she explained, rocking herself gently in Mrs. Gunn's chair. "Which is funny. . . . At first, you know, he was so dependent on us. He couldn't even speak much French when we met him. He was earning a pittance in a Paris garage doing odd jobs. He had been a refugee, you see, from Bela Kun."

Mrs. Gunn didn't see, but she waited hopefully.

"The Communist," Mrs. Peel went on. "Jackson's father was a farmer. Although I don't quite understand how Communists will go around shooting farmers who disagree with them, and then blame their famines on countries that don't shoot their farmers."

Mrs. Gunn said it seemed kind of unreasonable to her, at that.

"He was so lost in Paris, poor Jackson. His name was Tisza Szénchenyi in those days, which complicated life considerably I'm sure. And he was so proud, he wouldn't admit he was lost. We engaged him one summer to drive us through Provence — we wanted someone who *didn't* know the way, so annoying to be *taken* on a tour — and he has been with us ever since. Now, it is we who would be lost without Jackson. That's why I'm so relieved to feel he will probably stay at Rest and Be Thankful. I noticed, for instance, just as I was leaving him, that Robb came in before going to Sweetwater to measure him with string for some suitable ranch clothes. So clever the way Robb put knots in it. I was fascinated. But *how* does he remember which knot is which? Or has he a system? Which reminds me, what should I wear out here, Mrs. Gunn? I don't feel quite right in these clothes, somehow." Besides it was silly to wear good clothes, even of prewar Paris vintage, where they were never noticed.

"The ladies over at the dude ranches dress just like cowboys,"

Mrs. Gunn said, and smoothed her flowered apron over her neat blue dress.

"Oh dear!" Mrs. Peel said, thinking of her hipline. "But I am *not* a cowboy. Wouldn't it look rather silly to pretend I was? Perhaps I'll send Miss Bly another telegram, though. Abercrombie and Fitch must know what we ought to wear out West."

Mrs. Gunn looked puzzled, recovered, and said, "If it's clothes you need, the stores in Sweetwater have some nice things. This dress cost me only seven forty-nine."

Mrs. Peel smiled vaguely. "We must drive in, sometime, and have a look at the shops." And then she went away to battle with the telephone, so that the telegram could be sent off at once to New York.

The news about Rest and Be Thankful spread very quickly in New York too, even if there were plenty of worrying headlines to read in the newspapers. It only took one morning for all last winter's visitors to Maggie's Saloon to get onto the phone to each other, as soon as Prender Atherton Jones had called them and read the telegram he had received from Rest and Be Thankful, Wyoming.

". . . Can you imagine?"

"So very rugged, my dear."

"Sounds fun. Do you know, I've never seen the West. Did they say how many bedrooms?"

"Are they setting up a printing press, too, along with free beer and pretzels?"

"They are crazy."

"I'm *almost* an unknown author. Do you think I'd qualify?"

"She must be weighted down with money. Did you say old man Peel was a millionaire? And she never told us."

"Do they need any lecturers?" . . .

Some might laugh, some might sneer, but the idea caught many people's fancy — especially those who hadn't yet arranged how to spend the summer. Even Dewey Schmetterling, who had been unable to resist coining "Maggie's Saloon," felt the urge to re-establish friendly relations with Margaret Peel. After a minor triumph in securing her full address from Prender, he telegraphed his congratulations, beginning O PIONEERS! He would have been furious if he had known Sarah Bly was, even at that moment, arriving in town. A luncheon at the Ritz or, as a last resort, a dinner at Twenty-One would have ensured an invitation to spend a week or two on the ranch. He would have mentioned, casually, that he was about to leave to visit friends on the West Coast (what an amazing coincidence!); and Sarah would have smiled with pleasure and said, "Well, *do* come and see us on your way." Sarah and Maggie were goodhearted girls, if a trifle odd. Take this Rest and Be Thankful. Probably bought the place to have that address on their notepaper, with Telephone Sweetwater Seven Seven on the side. Maggie would be quaint even if it killed her. He had to see her in cowboy clothes . . . Maggie Oakley . . . That would be a gem for his collection.

But Prender Atherton Jones hadn't been too explicit about the telegram. He was planning to give Sarah dinner at Twenty-One, himself.

So Sarah's arrival in New York went unannounced, and she could spend an explanatory morning with Mr. Quick, their lawyer; and another equally wearing morning with Mr. Jobson, their pet banker; and an afternoon with her hairdresser; and, in between, she scored items off long lists in bookshops, music shops, garden shops and gadget shops. Thanks to Prender Atherton Jones's discretion, there were no friendly interruptions.

Her days were complicated enough, anyway, by the quick succession of telegrams from Wyoming:

GET BLUE JEANS BLEACHED AND PRE-SHRUNK AS ADVERTISED *New Yorker*. PLENTY OF SHIRTS LAUNDRY DIFFICULT. NO SATIN DEFINITELY NO SATIN.

MEDICINES WE KNOW AND TRUST. DON'T FORGET POISON IVY RATTLESNAKES FLIES MOTHS CALAMINE LOTION SUNSHADE FLANNEL NIGHTGOWNS HOT-WATER BOTTLES.

BOOTS HALF-SIZE LARGER AND START BREAKING THEM IN. SOCKS TOO.

The last telegram did full justice to Margaret's ten-line editorializing: SKIING UNDERWEAR. This put Sarah in a better humor, even while shopping in New York's most blistering mood, when the sight of wool was enough to cause a third-degree burn. Some telemark under-vests and Schneider crouch panties, please. Her private joke was abandoned, however, before the eighth store had lifted its eyebrows at such an unseasonable request but managed to retrieve some wool objects for her from its bargain basement. They looked tentlike, but they would shrink: you could depend on wool. She scored off the last memorandum on her crumpled shopping lists, and prayed that she would be safely in the plane for Wyoming before the next telegram arrived.

On the last evening, Sarah was to have dinner with Prender Atherton Jones. She had her third cold shower, changed her clothes again, and put on her hat and lipstick most carefully for Twenty-One. Just as she was almost ready to leave, Prender phoned to say that they might have dinner instead in a little French restaurant around the corner: it was so much easier to talk there. Poor Prender, his intentions for dinner were always good but they invariably flinched two hours before the check was presented. Now, if she hadn't answered that telephone call! But she stopped feeling amused as she entered the hot street, and felt the warm waves of air surge up from the sidewalk. The little French restaurant "just around the corner" was too near to justify a taxi, too far for pleasant walking in this weather. It would probably be having difficulties with its air-conditioning.

It was, for it relied on a fan. Prender's face, she was glad to see, was already having its difficulties too. This would be a dripping, oozing, brow-mopping evening.

"How well you look!" he said truthfully, and then he added a trifle too truthfully: "Years younger! What have you been doing to your hair? Most attractive that way." He guided her to the tight little seat behind a small table with a checked cloth. "Isn't this very Left Bank? Reminds me of the days when I used to visit you in Paris." His voice became suddenly practical. "And what's this new adventure you have engineered? We are all dying of curiosity. My phone has been ringing for the last three days."

There was no need to answer his question, for Margaret Peel's telegram to Prender had been remarkably explanatory. So Sarah smiled and said, "Thank you for sending me the list of writers who might be interested in coming to Wyoming. I've spent today telephoning the names you marked specially."

"I made that list as soon as I got the telegram," he assured her. "I knew how desperately urgent it was for you."

Sarah Bly felt her eyes widen. Somehow she had thought the predicament of the unhoused writers would have been a desperately urgent problem for Prender. He might even have said thank you to Margaret Peel. But at this moment, as he ordered red caviar and *madrilène,* to be followed by *sole amandine* (flounder with nuts on), it was obvious that he was Margaret's benefactor. He finished his assault on the French language with a little domestic wine suitable for a lady, and then remembered that Sarah Bly had an excellent palate. He covered his confusion by firing off questions, amusingly phrased, in his crisp way. He had great charm and used it as expertly as he managed his excellent hands. They pulled information out of you, Sarah thought: she was amazed at her own power of describing Rest and Be Thankful.

"It sounds delightful," he said. "I think we shall have a most enjoyable holiday. What other lecturers have you decided to ask? I'll give 'The Subconscious in the Novel.' Or perhaps 'The Approach to Kafka'?"

Sarah's smile faded. "We hadn't planned any lectures."

He was incredulously amused. "But you must have lecturers, Sarah!"

"Frankly, we cannot afford their fees. This is an expensive undertaking — much more so than we had imagined, I'm afraid. Wages and prices in America are so much higher than in Europe, you know."

Ridiculous nonsense, he thought. Margaret Peel could easily have afforded to finance his Literary Festival; and she could certainly

52

now offer her Rest and Be Thankful to him for the summer. Instead, she had financed her own idea and stolen his writers. He was deeply wounded. He passed his hand over his thick white hair, lightly enough not to disarrange its carefully encouraged wave. This was a sign of distress. His light gray eyes, rather too closely set together in an otherwise handsome face, looked at Sarah reproachfully. "My own summer was all built around the writers," he said.

Sarah tried to murmur something about accommodations being limited, but he waved that aside.

"If you aren't having lecturers — " He looked at her unbelievingly. "What *are* you providing for my writers?"

"Wyoming," Sarah said. She was angry, now.

He noticed the expression on her face. He counterattacked. "You know, Sarah," he said with a smile, "it isn't exactly fair to ask writers to be your guests, so that you can have intelligent companions to brighten your evenings. Is it?"

She was silenced. He made it sound so painfully true. He had certainly succeeded in killing her enthusiasm. She wished she had never heard of these writers, never seen Wyoming. She wondered, suddenly, how someone like Jim Brent would handle this situation. And surprisingly, she regained courage.

She said quietly, but decidedly, "We aren't trying to take away your writers, Prender. If you feel we are, then let's call the whole thing off."

He hadn't quite expected that. He passed his hand over his hair once more, straightened his dark blue tie, and took a sip of wine. He had never seen Sarah in such a difficult mood. She was usually very amenable. It had been a grave mistake to cancel the table at Twenty-One. "Now, Sarah," he said, even managing a smile, "that would be very disappointing for the writers, wouldn't it?"

And after that, he set out to charm. Dinner ended on a friendly note with a dissection of their acquaintances in New York, Paris and London. Everyone knew Prender, if they were celebrated enough; and he knew them — if they were especially celebrated — by their pet names. Twiddles, Dickie, Booboo and Bibi came slipping into the conversation as easily as allusions to Tom Wolfe, Lorenzo, Gertrude and Alice. Sarah's alarm subsided. She even began to feel a little ashamed of herself for her suspicions.

But when they parted, "I'll write and let you know when to expect me," he said. "I'll draw up a programme for you. I know Merrick Maclehose would lecture without a fee if I asked him. He's due for a Pulitzer Prize any year now. And Aubrey Brimstone — he's starting a new magazine, didn't you know? — he would be another good man to have. We ought to have a publisher, and perhaps a literary agent, to visit us too. Good for morale. Of course, we need only have *them* for a few days."

But Prender Atherton Jones would stay all of August and more, Sarah Bly thought dejectedly as she walked back to her hotel. And he would plan everything, unless she saw that he didn't. And that would be unpleasant, too.

She looked at the rows of lighted windows, shining high above her in the warm dark sky. The tall narrow silhouettes of the mid-town skyscrapers were outlined clearly by the glow from the bright canyons at their feet. But even the view of New York by night couldn't comfort her. By next winter, Rest and Be Thankful would be another of Prender's discoveries. Next summer, it would even be his Literary Festival. Forever and ever.

"We'll see about that," she told herself grimly, by the time she reached her room. Then her words startled her. Few rebelled against Prender, and they were cast into the wilderness of the un-mentioned. She could hear Prender pronounce her own obituary: "Poor Sarah, of course, always did have reactionary tendencies." "Reactionary," the damning word. The word that implied that new ideas must always be better than old, that progressive thinking — good in itself — couldn't have bad results. How easily we can be blackmailed by a word, she thought.

She undressed quickly, had her fourth shower, dropped into bed, drew a sheet over her, threw it off again, and settled patiently to endure a sleepless night. She began to compose a letter to Prender which would make everything quite definite. No fees. No lecturers.

No guests except the writers. And Prender? She could hardly refuse him, after all.

She stared up at the shadowed ceiling, circled by dim bands of light as the procession of taxis and cars came from the closing theaters. She listened to the street noises, to the hum of engines, the roar of an accelerator, the protesting scream of brakes, the ebb and flow of rushing wheels as the traffic lights changed. Her irritation increased. She became angry with her own weakness.

She found herself wishing she had Jim Brent's independence: he didn't give a damn for anyone. Then she found herself smiling as she thought of his probable comment on some of the prize exhibits in Prender's circle. That cheered her up considerably. In a way, it would be amusing to see Prender Atherton Jones trying to dominate Wyoming.

CHAPTER VII

One to Get Ready, Two to Get Steady...

EVERYTHING, Mrs. Peel decided, was most satisfactory: she hadn't had so many arrangements to make since her summer on the Dalmatian coast in 1939. The house was almost ready for the invasion. The invitations had been sent out, and six writers had definitely accepted them. Additional help had been engaged. Friendly relations had been established with the storekeepers in Sweetwater, who were relieved to hear that the new owners of Rest and Be Thankful weren't going to order staples from Omaha or Chicago. A Mr. Milton Jerks had announced he could provide gasoline, a car, souvenirs of Sweetwater, a laundry, a Piper Cub, and movies changed once a week without fail. And all Sarah's purchases in New York had turned out well, except the skiing underwear which preferred to stretch. The new books were added to the shelves in the study, which now could be called the library. The radio-phonograph and records were installed in the large living room for the use of their guests. The small sitting room with the glass-enclosed porch would be their own retreat. (Even in her exuberance, Mrs. Peel felt that retreat might sometimes be the better part of valor.)

Prender Atherton Jones had not yet announced his arrival. In fact, he had not even answered Sarah's letter, sent by special delivery just before she left New York.

"I wonder when he *is* coming," Sarah said, as she helped Margaret put up some pictures in their sitting room. With magazines and books, flowers from the garden where delphiniums and hollyhocks grew wild, and little personal knickknacks (with which Margaret always traveled as insurance against bleak hotel bedrooms), the

56

small room was becoming definitely their own. Now the pictures (reproductions from the Museum of Modern Art) were being inspected, judged for size and color to suit the shapes and lighting of the three available walls.

Neither of them had mentioned Prender for almost an hour, but Mrs. Peel, as she stood back to frown at a picture, could answer, "We'll have a telegram, any day now."

"Perhaps we ought to have told him how to reach here." Sarah felt that the responsibility, somehow, would be hers.

"He never asked us. Besides it is all quite simple. First, you take the big plane to Denver, and then the little plane to Sweetwater. Then that very efficient Milton Jerks sends you here by car."

"He may not fly."

"Then that, darling, is his problem. There are such things as information booths in New York's stations. Now, don't worry about Prender. Why, anyone would think you really wanted to see him arrive."

"I've been hoping for a telegram that said he couldn't come."

"You do jump from one extreme to the other, Sarah. After all, if he wants to come here, then that is that. We cannot offend him, you know."

"Why not?"

"Sarah! You know we've never antagonized anyone! Except those Nazis in Paris. And then it did annoy me that we had to do it so secretly. Besides, Prender isn't a Nazi: he's so much the opposite politically. You know how advanced he always is."

"Yes, that makes him sure he is intelligent."

"Sarah, what has come over you? When you met Prender in New York you must have been so exhausted by all that shopping that you became a little bit fretful. Now, you know you do, Sarah, whenever you are tired. You do get cross."

"Only if people make me cross," Sarah said determinedly, and reached for the hammer and nails. "Now, if anything, you are much too kind. I cannot understand how you always make such an effort to be nice to Prender. He did hurt you once, you know."

Poor Elizabeth Whiffleton, Mrs. Peel thought. Ah well! . . . She

57

said nobly, "If someone hurts one, then one must try all the harder to be nice to that someone."

Sarah, hammer in hand, looked down from the chair on which she now stood in stocking feet. "Translate that, will you? And hold the rest of the nails meanwhile."

Mrs. Peel said patiently, "You have to try all the harder to be nice to anyone who has hurt you."

"Why?"

"Because it's so tempting not to be nice."

"It would seem easier to give into temptation, just once, and even the score. Then you could all start over again."

"But Prender knew nothing whatever about Elizabeth Whiffleton; at least, I hope not. If I had ever been rude to him, he would have immediately wondered why. And he is very clever at finding out, you know."

"In other words, we are afraid of him. Just as most others are. But why? I've kept asking myself that for the last few weeks. He has never done a thing for us, Margaret, except tolerate us or use us. In fact, that is what he does with everyone."

"Sarah, you mustn't talk like that." Mrs. Peel was scandalized. "Besides, I *do* want a pleasant summer for a change. You know how upsetting last year was."

Because we knew too many people like Prender Atherton Jones, Sarah thought, and banged the nail home. The plaster cracked, splintered and fell.

"That's a decided improvement," Mrs. Peel said acidly.

Sarah said nothing. I am *not* fretful, she told herself.

At that moment, footsteps left Mrs. Gunn's kitchen and came towards the sitting room. Jim Brent halted in the doorway. "Hello!" he said. "May I pay you a visit?" He looked at the two flushed faces turned towards him, and then at the fallen plaster. Excitable creatures, women.

"How nice of you to come in," said Mrs. Peel, recovering herself first. "Do have a seat, Mr. Brent. You see, we are making ourselves comfortable." She waved her arm around the room.

He dropped his hat on a chair and looked at Sarah. "Need a little help? Plaster on that wall never did dry right." He took the hammer from Sarah's hand and helped her down from the chair. "Now where would you like the nails hammered in?"

Mrs. Peel showed him, while Sarah struggled into her boots. "I'm breaking them in," she explained as she stamped and tugged. Probably she looked ridiculous to him in her checked shirt, blue jeans and bright new boots. Somehow, she wanted to justify her appearance. "These clothes are so sensible," she said, which was true enough. She had been amazed how practical and comfortable they were.

"That's maybe why we wear them," Brent said, with a hint of a smile.

Mrs. Peel, who had taken one look at her back view in blue jeans and given a piercing scream, glanced down at her tweed suit. It was beginning to show signs of wear, and the nearest cleaner's was at Three Springs, the town with the railway station, ten miles beyond Sweetwater. It took such a long time to lose five pounds, she thought dejectedly. Sarah, whose appetite had been quite as large as hers, showed not one extra ounce. In fact, she looked extremely neat in these blue jeans. Life could be very unfair.

"I'm afraid they are too gay for my age," Mrs. Peel said diffidently.

"You'll get used to them," he said. "They sort of bleach out with weather." He finished hammering in the nails, which this time did not even crack the plaster. Mrs. Peel watched him gratefully: he hadn't tried to minimize her age, and yet he hadn't made her feel she might look odd in a checked shirt and trousers. She could hardly see herself doing anything in "weather," which probably meant wind and rain, except retiring to her room with a new book. However, it was flattering to be taken for a pioneer woman, just as it was relaxing to have her age accepted as something natural. Age happened to everyone, if they lived.

"That's splendid," Mrs. Peel said. "Now, Mr. Brent, if you'd help us lift the pictures into place, we can all sit down and admire them."

He looked at the pictures, and then at Mrs. Peel before he lifted them, one by one, to set them squarely in place.

"That's such a help," Mrs. Peel went on. She glanced at Sarah.

Why was she so quiet? Surely she hadn't taken the remark about being fretful too seriously. "Isn't it, Sarah? We really should have asked Jackson to do this, but he has got so involved in the plumbing over at the guest cabin."

As Jim Brent stepped back to look at the effect on the walls, he thought that Jackson might be well out of this.

Sarah Bly spoke then. "You don't like them, do you?" She said it softly, half-shyly.

He looked embarrassed. "Do you?"

"Of course!" Mrs. Peel cried. "Look at the composition, the feeling of unity, and yet the sense of separate individualities. The colors are odd, but they are balanced in a very unexpected way, so — " She looked at Sarah for help.

"That one is called 'The Three Dancers,'" Sarah said.

"I'm certainly glad you told me." He smiled back to her.

"Of course, not three modern dancers," Mrs. Peel explained. "See, the details of their costume — it's seventeenth-century, Italian comedy — are marvelously correct once your eye penetrates the composition."

"Supposing," he said, "you were to see that picture for the first time in your life. Supposing no one could tell you its title. Would you know that it was three dancers?"

The question was so honestly put that Mrs. Peel hesitated.

"Would you?" he asked Sarah. She was equally taken aback. After all, she had to admit she had heard about the picture by its title even before she went to see it in an exhibition, where it had been labeled and catalogued. The picture and its name had never been apart in her mind.

"Well," he said, "that makes me feel better. But I still think you've been cheated. All you've got is two-and-a-half dancers."

Sarah laughed, much to Mrs. Peel's amazement.

"And what pictures do *you* like, Mr. Brent?" Mrs. Peel asked, as they all sat down at last. She suddenly thought that he seemed perfectly at home, but then why shouldn't he be? She looked embarrassed.

"The kind I used to want to imitate when I was in Art School," he admitted with a grin.

60

"In Art School?" Mrs. Peel was caught off balance completely; but she was smiling, as Sarah was, for the grin was infectious.

"It only lasted three years. Nothing serious."

"Why —" Sarah began, and then stopped. She would be disappointed if he did start talking about himself, for that was what all men did when they wanted to impress you. Little allusions here, little side lights there, all adding up to prove to you that they were someone who mattered.

He said, "I came over to see you about the horses you'll need for your guests."

"Seven, I think," Sarah said quickly, halting the questions she saw rising in Margaret's eye about art school, and did you go to college, and what made you return to the ranch?

"But not wild horses," Mrs. Peel added. "I'm sure few of us have ever ridden very much."

"We'll pick quiet ones," he assured her. "They'll be in the west pasture — that's nearest the corral. It will make it easier for Jackson when he brings them in to be saddled."

"Do you think he will manage?" Mrs. Peel asked anxiously. What she had seen of these horses had convinced her that they were quite capable of lassoing Jackson and bringing him into the corral. "Of course, I have every faith in him, and he was a farmer's son and did know about horses — I suppose — but after all, this isn't Hungary and that was years ago."

"Horses are horses, anywhere," Jim Brent reassured her. "Jackson is quick to learn. Uses his eyes. Follows advice. He'll do, all right. I'll send him out with the boys during the next few days to learn the trails around here. Then he can guide your guests, and we won't have to worry about sending out searching parties."

"You mean people can get lost?" Mrs. Peel asked in horror.

"It has happened."

"Oh dear!" Here was another hazard. . . . "Perhaps," she said hopefully, "our guests will be too busy to go riding."

"Perhaps. I've looked over the saddles we once used, just in case they aren't too busy. I set Jackson to cleaning them off."

"Thank you," Mrs. Peel said, and felt extremely helpless for having foreseen neither saddles, nor corral, nor pasture, nor Jackson as a cowboy. What *would* Jackson, the New York chauffeur, have to say to that? He had already accepted the position of gardener with a frown; but perhaps he had only been thinking of poison ivy.

"Well, that's about all." Jim Brent rose. "Would you care to walk over to the west pasture now? Your horses are already there."

"I'd love to," Sarah said delightedly. He must be six feet three, she thought as she looked up at him.

"I'd love to, too, but — " Mrs. Peel looked at her neat shoes, remembered the six inches of mud all over the ranch this morning, " — it did rain rather hard, last night."

"Laid the dust," Jim Brent agreed. "By the way, I was over to Three Springs railroad station, this afternoon. I heard there was a trunk waiting for Rest and Be Thankful. Seemed to belong to someone called Jones."

"Oh!" the two women said together and looked at each other.

"I suppose we'll have to send for it," Mrs. Peel said, wondering if Sarah could possibly manage the car on the twisting canyon road which led down to Sweetwater from Rest and Be Thankful. Jackson was too busy with saddles and vegetables and trails and horses to be lassoed. Thank goodness he had fixed the car, after days of work on it. Oh dear, she must get him to see to that awful bridge: someone might choose that road into the ranch when the light was failing. Signposts, she must remember them too: small, discreet ones to cheer people on, if they were coming by car. Maps had been sent to the guests, of course, but you couldn't mark all the hazards into them.

Jim Brent watched the worries chasing over Mrs. Peel's pleasant, kindly face. She reminded him constantly of his mother's sister, who used to take so much trouble to give him a good time at Christmas when he was at school, two thousand miles from home.

He said, "I brought the trunk along with me, Mrs. Peel. That always saves a journey. I'll give Jackson a hand with it tomorrow."

He left with a nod and a smile, without waiting for thanks, and Sarah followed him.

"Really," Mrs. Peel said aloud, remembering Mrs. Gunn and the boys and Mr. Brent during these last weeks, "they are all remarkably patient." She looked at her pictures, straightened one of them, rearranged the flowers, tidied some magazines, and then sat down with the Sunday *New York Times* to catch up on the troubles of the world.

The evening sunlight streamed over the rim of the mountains to the west and glanced through a corner of the porch. Robins sang in the chokecherry bushes, an aspen tree quivered with each breath of wind, blue delphiniums pointed to a blue sky, and the scattered white clouds changed softly to pink and gold.

Mrs. Peel put aside the newspaper thoughtfully.

Then she rose and walked through the porch into the garden, across the grass towards the edge of the creek. She turned to look at the house. Her house, she suddenly thought.

It gave the effect of being low, spread out, nestling naturally into the grass and the trees between the arms of the stream. It was part of its setting; just as the meadows and hills, folding into each other, and the mountain peaks, towering massively behind the rounded hills, were all part of the house. In the slanting rays of the sun, each fold and hollow was emphasized with highlights and shadows, each spine of rock stood boldly in relief. The pine forests were bands of rich velvet. The valleys and canyons grew deeper and darker, reaching further into the heart of the mountains. The peaks were more jagged, third-dimensional, elaborately carved by wind and torrents into giant cathedrals with ridged buttresses of primeval rock.

As she watched, the sun disappeared and the valley was suspended in golden light. For a deep moment, she no longer existed. Then the shiver in her spine, the hot tears stinging her eyes, reminded her she was alive, a human being humbled into worship. She was glad she was alone.

She walked on. She became more composed. This place did

make you thankful, she reflected. But how odd that she had had to live so far away, for so many years, before she found it. Was she really growing old? Was the thought of living here for four months every year necessary to help her through the other eight months back in civilization? "Civilization! Pew to you!" she said scornfully. She then had the guilty thought that, by October, she would be opening her eyes wide as she saw the tall buildings of New York rising one behind the other, and she would be saying "Civilization!" in quite a different way as she read *Cue*'s enchanting lists of where to go and what to see. "Pew to you!" she repeated determinedly, but she laughed as she wondered if she weren't speaking to herself this time. Sarah would say that we were all the — But where on earth was Sarah? By Mrs. Peel's watch, it was an hour and a half since she had left with Mr. Brent.

The light was failing now, and the clear lines of the hills were fading. All the colors — the greens of grass and trees, the blue shades of mountains, the golden yellows of cliffs and canyon walls — were losing their sharp vitality, gradually merging into the anonymous gray of dusk. The landscape was already half-asleep.

Mrs. Peel walked towards her house, noticing the sudden dampness in the grass, promising herself the comfort of a log fire. Sarah returned then, moving somewhat stiffly, trying to appear very nonchalant. But her voice was excited, and as she came into the hall Mrs. Peel noticed that her eyes were shining, her cheeks were pink, her even teeth were very white against the honey-colored tan of her smooth skin, and her hair was just wind-blown enough to make it very attractive. Mrs. Peel thought that she had seldom seen Sarah look so — so healthy. Which is a woman's way of saying that another woman is astonishingly pretty.

"Guess what?" Sarah said. "I've been out riding!"

"On a horse?" Mrs. Peel was horrified.

"It wasn't a dolphin, darling. Margaret, it's perfectly superb! When you get up there" — she waved her arm roughly in the direction of the mountains, which she obviously expected Mrs. Peel to see as clearly as she had, in spite of the walls that surrounded them—

64

"the whole valley ripples out like a cloth of gold underneath you."

"But how did you get up there?"

"Jim Brent guided me. We were trying out my horse. And you've nothing to worry about . . . the horses can pick their way over any mountain trail. I just relaxed and held on; Whitesock — that's its name — did all the work."

"It?"

"Well," Sarah said doubtfully, "perhaps he. Or it. They are geldings. That's the horse equivalent of a steer."

"What color is he?" Mrs. Peel was interested, even if she still felt somewhat deserted.

"Henna-brown, with a white ankle. Your horse is a deep cream, with a platinum-blonde mane and tail. He's called Golden Boy."

"Well, hadn't you better go upstairs and take a bath? With Epsom salts?" Mrs. Peel asked, slightly cheered by the description of her horse. It might bewilder Mr. Brent, but it gave her a very clear picture.

"I'll go upstairs and inspect the damage," Sarah agreed. "These blue jeans are very rigid, you know, especially the seams. If I were you, Margaret, I'd start jumping on yours to soften them up. For once, laundries are too gentle."

"But these Western saddles look so comfortable," Mrs. Peel said in amazement as another unnecessary problem faced her.

"I suppose so, once you get used to them." Sarah mounted the stairs with difficulty. "The best thing for us is to get broken in as quickly as possible. Then we can welcome our guests without hobbling around like a couple of Civil War veterans."

"You don't make this new experiment look too attractive," Mrs. Peel remarked as she watched Sarah's progress.

"Well, I'm sure it has taken pounds off," Sarah called back.

Mrs. Peel went into their sitting room, lit the log fire, and brooded about that.

When Sarah came downstairs at last, wrapped in her long wool dressing gown, Mrs. Peel said, "I believe I'll try Golden Boy, tomorrow. He *does* look quiet?"

"As Chuck says, he's broke gentle. And he is beautiful." Jim Brent couldn't have chosen a better horse to entice Margaret into riding. Had he known that? I bet he did, Sarah thought with a smile. "I've a surprise for you," she added. "Golden Boy is all your own. Mr. Brent has given these two horses to us."

"My dear . . . !"

"Yes, I was just as taken aback as you are. It's so long since anyone gave us anything, except a box of chocolates or a jar of bath salts as a thank-you-for-having-me note. I was so amazed, *I* almost forgot to say thank you adequately. Mr. Brent only said it would be a pity to live here and not have your own horse. Which means, when translated, that you just can't cover enough ground on your own two feet in this country, and an automobile is useless if you really want to enjoy yourself. You know, when he says anything, it is very much to the point. We sometimes use ten words when two would do."

"Why not one? And keep it monosyllabic?" Mrs. Peel suggested. "Actually, I am inquisitive enough to wonder about your conversation on horseback. Or does that make him more talkative?"

But Sarah refused to be drawn out, either by Margaret's affectionate amusement or by the friendly, relaxing fire. She stretched out her feet in their comfortable leopard-skin slippers, and eased her bruised thigh against a soft cushion.

"Oh, you just ask questions," she said noncommittally.

"Isn't that being too much the inquiring reporter?"

"Oh, *not* questions about himself! About the country — the early settlers, Indians, battles, massacres, trails, all that kind of thing. His grandfather came here as one of the first ranchers. His father was born while the Cheyennes were circling round these mountains on an impromptu war party."

"And what did you talk about? Paris, Rapallo, Venice, Ragusa? How I wish I had been there to listen! A study in contrast."

"I'm sure he found it just as amusing as you do," Sarah said, flushing brightly. Had she really appeared so ridiculous?

"Sarah, my dear!" Mrs. Peel was alarmed.

"Well, I don't know why you laugh at him just because his taste prefers Rembrandt to a modern distortionist."

"I'm not laughing at him," Mrs. Peel said. "I'm quite aware what is one man's Shostakovitch is another man's Haydn. That's the nice thing about good art — there are plenty of differences to suit anyone who has taste at all. Besides, if I *did* smile a little, I am quite sure he evened that up by having a little smile over us. After all, 'The Three Dancers' and the West are rather odd together, I suppose."

"Some attempts at modern painting would look odd, anywhere. Too many imitations, perhaps. You can imitate technique; that's all right, for you can learn that way. But you can't imitate feelings and emotions and experiences: that's something an artist has got to supply out of his own life. I *am* getting tired of gasworks and linoleum patterns and jig-sawed anatomy."

"Sarah, my dear — "

"Did you see the clouds, tonight? Weren't they worth painting? They were lying all on the same level of the sky, as evenly based as if the wind snipped them off in a straight line. And they rose to different heights, large round puffs of white smoke. It was as if a giant had taken handfuls of foam and laid them on a glass-topped table, and we were underneath looking up. Or did you see the ripples of hills and fields when the sun slanted sideways on them, and the grass turned gold?"

Mrs. Peel looked at her friend, half-puzzled, half-alarmed. "Please don't talk to Prender this way, Sarah," she said earnestly. "Just imagine next winter, and all the gay remarks you'd have to listen to. They'd be calling you Nature Girl."

"Margaret, sometimes I wonder if we've spent most of our lives making the wrong friends. Oh, I know they are intelligent, and bright, and highly interested in everything that is new and remote and difficult to understand. But darling, I am sure there must be intelligent people who *are* kind too. Only, why don't we meet them? Is something wrong with us?"

Margaret Peel didn't answer. They sat in silence, watching the last flickering log. At last — "Time for bed," she said, suddenly brisk in voice and movement. "Tomorrow is a busy day."

Sarah rose too, slowly and carefully. "I've two bruises," she an-

67

nounced. "I wonder if Jackson could give me some tips on how to mount a horse without flinching. You know, he *is* very good. I watched him tonight, riding his horse round the west pasture. He was talking away to it, teaching it Hungarian I think. He wears a large hat, Indian-style, with the crown quite undented. And he has wrapped a broad sash around his waist. An imposing figure."

"Jackson, too!" Mrs. Peel was now resigned to her own first appearance on horseback. "Well, I suppose this was all inevitable if we did choose to live in the West. Did he look depressed, or just resigned? I'm afraid we'll lose a good chauffeur. After this summer, he'll use his savings to buy a little repair shop near his beloved Atlantic City, and we'll never see him again."

"And then we can drive the car ourselves, with no one to shake a gloomy head." Sarah set the fireguard safely in position, switched off the lights, and followed Margaret slowly upstairs.

"Really, Sarah, that does sound ungrateful. After all these years."

"It sounds more ungrateful keeping him, after all these years, if he wants to leave. Besides, a lot of women do drive cars nowadays: think of all the traffic accidents."

When they reached their bedrooms, Sarah Bly halted. "Margaret, why on earth do I keep calling myself Sarah?"

Mrs. Peel, halfway into her room, for their goodnights were sensibly brief, looking round in surprise. "Because it's your name, my dear." Oh, she thought, we've forgotten to lock the front door again.

"But it sounds so — well, so sedate and old, somehow. Why not Sally? I used to be called that."

"Why not? It's *your* name," Mrs. Peel said sleepily. She smiled as she added, "Good night, Sally." She watched Sarah enter her room. Not Sarah. Sally.

CHAPTER VIII

First Arrivals

I T WAS Saturday, the last day in July.

"No one is going to come," Mrs. Peel said gloomily. She had reached the stage of all hostesses who have prepared too well and now only have to wait. "Except Esther Park. And that's almost no one."

"Nonsense," Sally Bly said cheerfully. "The others were just too busy to let you know how they are arriving. Writers are always so preoccupied."

Mrs. Peel agreed. Then she looked down at the list of names in her hand. She knew it, and yet she felt she didn't know it. It would be awful if she were to start talking to a novelist about his short stories.

"Yet, somehow," Sally said, looking out of the sitting-room window and admiring the perfect evening, "somehow I wish they weren't coming."

"Sarah!" Mrs. Peel was shocked into forgetting her friend's new name. "That would be very selfish of us."

"It might be nice to be selfish for one summer," Sally said, quite unrepentant. "Whenever you discover anything you like, Margaret, you always rush to share it with others. Really, I thought Europe had cured you of that."

"You never used to object." Then she handed the list with a smile to Sally. "Would you mind? I just want to be sure I know them all as soon as they arrive. New faces and new names are so nerve-racking when they come together." She looked apologetic. "I know it's silly of me," she said.

Sally took the list without any enthusiasm. "All right," she said, "we'll do our homework. And then we'll go up to the corral. Ned is practising calf roping tonight. There's a rodeo in August in Sweetwater, you know. Bert has entered for bulldogging, I hear."

"That will be interesting for our guests."

"And for us," Sally said wryly. "We come into the picture, too, sometimes. Now, let's see this list. The women first. We've met Carla Brightjoy. She attended those meetings of the New Trends in Literature Group, last winter in New York."

"Brown hair, draped long. Glasses. Fantastic hats all filled with bits and pieces. She writes short stories."

"All the women do. They mentioned it when they accepted our invitations."

"Such a good idea of yours, Sally, to ask them to give us any details they'd pass on to their publishers. It makes them less strange to us."

"Now, what about Mimi Bassinbrook?" Sally asked, glancing out of the window. If she could hurry Margaret, there would be still time for a ride this evening. Jim Brent would be waiting at the corral.

"I've heard about her, I seem to remember. A Southerner?"

"From South Brooklyn, I'd imagine. Don't you remember her at Prender's parties? She has red hair and green eyes. Young. Excellent figure. Dresses with what is called a *flair*. Short stories, she says, but I'm sure she'll write a historical novel. She could project herself into it."

"Mimi Bassinbrook . . ." Mrs. Peel said thoughtfully. "Now, how did I never notice her?"

"She was always surrounded by a phalanx of men, darling."

"She must have talent. I mean, Prender said all these writers had talent."

"Plenty of talent," Sally agreed with a smile. "Now, who's the third woman?"

"Esther Park. She wrote us ten pages and told us nothing really. She mentioned short stories, novels and plays. Just like that! Prolific . . . Frankly, I've never even heard of her."

"Nor I. I only know that she kept on talking when I telephoned her in New York. She accepted right away, I remember."

"Oh . . ."

"Now, the men," Sally went on quickly. "We have met two of them, thank goodness, so who is the third one?"

But Margaret Peel refused to be hurried. She counted them one by one on her fingers as she recited, "First, Karl Koffing. He said he was working on a novel about New York. Born in Red Gulch, Iowa. Age twenty-four. Thin and dark and intensely critical of everything. Unfit for military service, wasn't he? That's why he couldn't go overseas. Poor Karl. . . ."

"I've never heard him be critical about that," Sally said, interrupting Mrs. Peel's sad thoughts about young men who suffered from bad health and the tragedy of it.

"Then next, there's Earl Grubbock," Mrs. Peel went on, ignoring Sally's smile. "He's twenty-seven. Ex-Army. Sergeant, wasn't he? Fair-haired, but losing some of it. And he has put on a lot of weight, hasn't he? I suppose all that muscle which sergeants have just turned to — "

"Writes about Southern hardship," Sally prompted her.

"Yes. Wanted to know if we were being 'restricted,' because if so he wasn't coming. Whatever did you answer to that, Sally?"

"I wrote we were definitely restricted to writers who hadn't been published yet. No reply, so far. Perhaps he isn't coming, but I hope he does. He can write, if only he wouldn't discard every manuscript halfway. He seems to get discouraged, but he *will* chose discouraging subjects."

"I'm sure that kind of attitude is all a matter of metabolism," Mrs. Peel said. "Have you talked over the menus you've planned with Mrs. Gunn? Of course, she is a very plain cook." She paused, and then added wistfully, "Do you remember Rapallo and the food we served there?"

"Don't worry, our guests won't starve."

"Simple food at regular hours. Plenty of sleep," Mrs. Peel murmured, as if persuading herself. "That's what we all need after a winter in New York. And I am sure we were right not to worry about wines. As for other drinks — well, cocktails can be disastrous at an altitude of six thousand feet. Or do you think they'll expect such things?"

"We can offer them beer or a mild Scotch in the evenings. And if they want real Western life, they can save up for Saturday night in Sweetwater as the cowboys do. But how did we get there? Ah yes, Earl Grubbock . . ."

"Yes," Mrs. Peel said, equally thoughtful. "Well now, the third man is Robert O'Farlan. Working on a war novel. He's rather old for that, isn't he? Fifty, he said. But perhaps he was in O. S. S. I've always wanted to talk to someone important in O. S. S. You know, I'm quite sure that the nice Sicilian who smuggled us so cleverly to North Africa must have been an American. No one else in the wide world could speak *Siciliano* with such a delightful Chicago inflection."

"Important O. S. S. men don't talk. Any who do weren't important. But why should Mr. O'Farlan be O. S. S.?"

"Well, he could hardly be a parachutist, not at fifty. And he was very uncommunicative about himself. All we know is his age, his address, and that he is writing a war novel. Of course, he might have been Navy."

"We'll know, soon enough. Well, that's all." Sally returned the list to the folder marked "Urgent" which lay on the writing desk. "But they sound so much more than six, somehow. Come along, Margaret, we've worried too much about all this."

"I may as well admit I'm nervous: this is our first house party in America. Oh, I do hope it goes well! I suppose writers are much the same all the world over. They will work in the mornings, read in the afternoons, and talk together after dinner. It will be pleasant to hear some intelligent conversation again."

Sally laughed. "Thank you, darling. And what about the great outdoors? Or is it just to be a background for intelligent conversation?"

"Oh, it will be there," Mrs. Peel said vaguely, as she led the way to the kitchen to get two carrots for Golden Boy. "It always is. But you mustn't judge others by yourself, Sally. We don't all throw ourselves with such abandon into the Wild West." She glanced at Sally's tight blue jeans and then at her own tweed skirt. Three more pounds, she thought, and I can risk it.

"Golden Boy needs exercise. Why don't you try him out, tonight?"

"I'm getting to know him first." And she also had to finish the article in the *Encyclopædia Britannica* on Horsemanship and Riding.

They crossed the yard, passed the garage, and entered the road that would take them to the corral and the west pasture. "I've an idea," Mrs. Peel announced. "I'll let Jackson exercise Golden Boy meanwhile. That will cheer him up: he really is so gloomy, these days. What can be wrong?"

"Ask him," Sally suggested. Then she stopped short. "Good heavens! What's this?"

"This" was a young girl with gleaming gold hair, narrow hips snug in tight pearl-gray trousers, green satin sleeves swinging loose from her white buckskin waistcoat, who stood near the entrance to the saddle barn. Beside her was a black horse with an elaborate leather saddle. An enormous dog of undistinguishable breed lay at her feet, but its long coat had been as carefully brushed as the horse had been curried and polished.

The cowboys had gathered around, of course. Jackson was there, too, sitting on the five-barred fence as if he had always been accustomed to perch eight feet from the ground. Ned looked as if he had found something other than calves to rope. Jim Brent was there, with his horse saddled and bridled for an evening ride, but now it was tethered to the hitching-rail and quite forgotten. Mrs. Gunn and her pretty niece Norah (who had arrived from Three Springs only that morning) had come up for an evening stroll to see Ned's calf roping. They were trying to stand somewhat aside, and yet they too were caught into the group, fascinated by what they saw. The girl's long gold hair, braided into two plaits reaching just below her shoulders, was tied with bright green ribbon bows. Her hat of fine white straw, broad-brimmed, with its edges curving like peregrine wings, sat as demurely as the Empress Eugénie's over the center of her brow. Her feet were small in the narrow pointed boots of fine green leather.

For a moment Mrs. Peel, remembering the carrots (which she knew were not the correct Western approach to a horse), hesitated. Then, holding them openly in her hand, she walked bravely on with Sally. Mrs. Gunn came to meet them.

"It's the girl from Las Vegas," she explained quickly, in a hushed voice. She shot a glance at Ned, and shook her head. "She's just arrived." This time she looked hard at the bright green car and the gleaming aluminum horse-trailer which had been parked at one side of the saddle barn. "If she can clean as well as she can ride, she'll be good."

"You mean she's the nice girl from Las Vegas Ned told us about? Our new upstairs maid?" Sally asked, keeping her voice equally hushed. Mrs. Peel was still fitting Mrs. Gunn's glances into a pattern.

"That's her." Mrs. Gunn looked at Ned again. "I kind of think we're lucky that Robb's nice girl from Butte went and got married last week."

By this time, the three women had approached the group round the corral. Ned stopped his conversation, to turn to them with a proud smile. "Mrs. Peel, Miss Bly, I want you to meet Miss Drene Travers."

Miss Drene Travers put out a neat little hand and gave a firm grip. She had very large dark blue eyes, with black eyelashes and skilfully marked brows. Her skin, incredibly untanned, had the same smooth finish that the slender straight-haired girls, forever hurrying along Lexington Avenue in New York with mysterious patent-leather hatboxes, always displayed as they turned a photogenic chin line to their passing public. She smiled slowly, showing even white teeth between the deep red lips. "Hello, how are *you*?" That was all. But Sally had to admit it was devastating.

Mrs. Peel, unaccustomed as she was to public welcoming, had the feeling that a few phrases would not be out of place. The silent men around her, who had been such good hosts themselves, obviously expected her to rise to the occasion. They were presenting the new-comer to her as Ned's friend, a stranger to be made at home, an interesting piece of decoration which would bring the bright color and humor of Madison Square Garden to the workaday world of

Flying Tail Ranch. Mrs. Peel, if puzzled by the respect with which they looked at the girl (for she had arrived too late to see Drene's exhibition of riding which had won even Mrs. Gunn's admiration), put it all down to Western gallantry. She had been impressed by it, from the very beginning: men, here, believed that you were all right until you proved you weren't. So, as she admired Drene's long flickering eyelashes, she made a neat little speech hoping Drene would like Rest and Be Thankful. She was conscious of the smile in Sally's eyes, and she took the last hurdle with a crash. "Mrs. Gunn will show you where to sleep," she ended. Now what on earth had made her bring *that* up? She added quickly, "I was just going to tempt Golden Boy." And she smiled gaily and waved the carrots to distract all attention. She succeeded.

Drene's black horse stretched his neck towards them. The green satin sleeve billowed as the neat little hand came smartly up and clipped him sharply over his face with the reins. Only Mrs. Peel and Sally Bly were startled. And they flinched again as the horse was pulled sharply around and struck once more. Drene's narrow, pointed toe seemed to spring into the stirrup as she swung herself lightly on to the saddle. Her shoulders were neatly held, her hips moved in understated rhythm, and her body fell into a compact, well-timed jig as the horse broke into its dancing trot. The enormous dog rose, and loped along at the heels of the horse.

Sally had only to look at the eyes of the silent audience to know this was very good, very good indeed. Ned and Robb had mounted too, and were urging their horses into a canter. The others looked as if they were ready to follow, too.

"She's very good," Sally said, watching the horse and rider as they cantered around the west pasture.

"A well-trained horse," Bert said, and shifted his hat more over his eyes. Jackson, shifting his hat too, nodded. Chuck agreed.

Mrs. Peel held the carrots less conspicuously. But I couldn't hit Golden Boy, she thought despairingly, even if that *is* the right way and this (she looked at the carrots) is not.

Jim Brent came over to Sally. "Like to go for a ride?" he asked.

"Not tonight, thank you," she said, keeping her voice as casual

75

as his. Not after that, she thought: I'd feel like a sack of flour bouncing around on the saddle. She looked at the hillsides, now veined with shadows, and persuaded herself it was much too late anyway. Margaret might have the wit not to stand there looking so damned amazed either.

At that moment, fortunately, the next distraction arrived in the long black shape of a Lincoln. It prowled up the road from the bridge with a rich, satisfying hum that drew all heads around, as if they were paper clips turning towards a magnet. The car slowed down, became undecided, stopped. A man put an excellent brown suède shoe carefully onto the roadway as if testing the dusty surface. Then he stepped out. He was tall. He wore his light camel's-hair coat draped round his shoulders as if it were a cape. His hair was white and carefully waved. He shielded his eyes against the sloping rays of the sun.

"It's Prender," Mrs. Peel said.

"Is this Rest and Be Thankful?" he called, and turned for a moment to say something to his two companions in the car. A girl's voice laughed gaily and a man answered jokingly.

"And I think that sounds like Dewey Schmetterling with him," Sally said in amazement mixed with horror.

"But what is *he* doing here?" Mrs. Peel said, and handed the carrots quickly to Jackson.

The riders had noticed the car's arrival too. They had also decided their evening ride was over, for they came — the green sleeves first, the men rather unwillingly after — at a gallop towards the corral in a fine flurry of flying manes and tails. Yet Miss Drene Travers, as she pulled up so spectacularly beside Jim Brent in full view of the astonished newcomers, was not looking at the car. She didn't dismount; she sat superbly in golden silence and turned her quiet eyes to the hills. Sally could only spare one admiring look for such an exquisite still-life, before she had to hurry towards the car. Margaret Peel stopped to murmur to Mrs. Gunn, "*Please* take charge." She glanced at Drene as she spoke, but the expression on her face told Mrs. Gunn that the car had brought its own set of problems too.

Jim Brent, also, had noted Mrs. Peel's expression. Just as he had noted Sally was walking with a very firm heel-to-toe stride towards the car. She walked that way only when she was angry about something and was making up her mind to take action.

Bert said to him, "Hey! Some of them writer fellows must make money."

"It would seem that way," Robb said, watching another camel's-hair coat step into view.

Jim nodded. He hadn't expected this kind of arrival. Nor had Sally Bly, he was damned sure. He unsaddled his horse, turned him loose into the west pasture, and carried the saddle with its blanket and bridle into the barn. He didn't give a second look at the car or at the girl on the black horse. It had amused him to see the reaction she caused, but he wasn't the kind of man to prolong a joke. If she did her work to please Ma Gunn, and didn't cause any trouble among the boys, then he didn't object. Besides, she was a bit of brightness for the evenings when the boys gathered around with little to do. She was probably a decent kid, just another rodeo-struck girl who worked in the summers and performed in the winters. Having decided he was only taking a thoroughly practical attitude to the whole business, he walked out of the saddle barn, gave a general good night to all of them, and started towards his cabin.

He glanced briefly at the car as he passed it. The second man was young-looking, small, thin, dark-haired. He was looking towards the corral, studying the group there with obvious delight. A girl, with smooth red hair and redder lips, was standing with considerable elegance, her slender feet posed ballet-fashion in flat-heeled slippers. She wore a very wide, very long skirt, flaring from a small, belted waistline. She looked at Jim and smiled. Well, he thought, the boys are hardly going to miss the movies at all, this summer. Mrs. Peel was too busy talking to notice him go by. The men were too busy looking at Drene on horseback. But it seemed to him that Sally's smile was too small and somehow pathetic.

"We'll leave the car here," Mrs. Peel was saying, "and Jackson will put it away, we'll take the luggage, the house is just beyond the trees, how ever did you pass its entrance, didn't you see my little signpost at the bridge?" She ran out of breath, but if she didn't keep talking, she was going to be rude. So she talked on, angrily aware of Dewey Schmetterling, the uninvited guest. Not only uninvited, but totally unimagined. And there he was, as coolly under control as if he had been expected. He hadn't even bothered to explain his arrival. But then, Dewey never explained. Surely we have entertained him quite enough, Mrs. Peel thought bitterly; in Paris, in Rapallo, in New York. Why has he come here? I'm positive our charms aren't so marked as all that.

"And is all this included with the sunset?" Dewey Schmetterling asked, watching Miss Drene Travers dismount by swinging her leg forward, across and over the flowing black mane. "*And* a perfect three-point landing. Mimi, you will have some new postures to learn, thank God. If I spend another winter at parties, tripping over girls' splayed feet and pointed toes, I'll abandon New York."

"Yes, darling," Mimi Bassinbrook said so amiably that Sally buried her very feminine thought that ballet slippers had been out of vogue by last winter, too.

Prender, who had been remarkably silent, now became businesslike as his eye counted the numerous suitcases. "What about one of these men doing this job?" He looked, as he spoke, at Jim Brent's retreating back.

"No!" Sally said sharply, and stopped Prender's ready command just in time. "This isn't our territory," she explained more quietly. "This is Flying Tail Ranch. We only pass through it on our way to ride."

"The natives seem friendly," Dewey said, and Mimi Bassinbrook laughed. She had a pleasant laugh to match her pretty face. Prender Atherton Jones seemed less amused. Perhaps, Sally thought, he had travelled two thousand miles with that laugh. Or perhaps (as she noted how he left the heavier suitcases for Dewey to carry) there were other reasons. Prender had a slightly ruffled air, as if he were in one of his deeply wounded moods.

"What a marvelous sunset!" Mimi said, and pointed with charming delight. Sally looked at the red hair gleaming brightly in the

78

sun's yellow rays. All this, she thought, and Drene too: what a summer we are going to have.

"A very grade-A sunset in the very best technicolor," Dewey said.

Prender spoke — rather sourly, Mrs. Peel thought. "We'll be in a much more admiring mood after dinner."

"After dinner?" Mrs. Peel looked in alarm at Sally. "Didn't you have dinner at Three Springs or Sweetwater?"

"No. It was much too early. It is absolutely impossible to digest anything calling itself dinner at six." He glanced at his watch, and nodded approvingly. "It is not quite eight o'clock now. We'll wash and have a quick cocktail, first. Is this the house?" He stood for a moment, looking at it. "Delightfully rustic, my dear." He opened the large double screen door and passed into the hall. He nodded approvingly once more and put the suitcases down where the servants might find them and carry them upstairs to unpack.

"Isn't this *darling*?" Miss Bassinbrook said, glancing from the white hall into the green living room.

"It will be, after I've had a couple of drinks from a tall frosted glass," Dewey Schmetterling said, and let his suitcases fall. He leaned against the bannisters, a slender elegant young man, and was conscious in a most unconscious way of Mimi's admiration. Prender frowned heavily.

Mrs. Peel stood quite silenced. She was wondering if a cheese *fondue*, or an omelette and a salad, and some canned soup would be enough. She was worrying about a room for Dewey Schmetterling, the totally unexpected. She was thinking that their solitary bottle of Scotch was going to be insufficient. She was remembering that Prender always insisted on Daiquiris in summer. Remarkable how she had forgotten about that.

But Sally took charge. She smiled charmingly. "Come upstairs. While you are washing, I'll make some sandwiches. I'm afraid dinner is over. We eat at half-past six, you see, so that we can go out riding in the evening. And our help is quite free, once the dishes are all washed up, so — " she lifted Miss Bassinbrook's hatbox, "let's move these, shall we? Housekeeping is a little different out here, you know. Delightfully rustic, as Prender would say. Margaret, will you attend to the fire in the living room?"

Mrs. Peel, as she lit the kindling under the logs, was lost in amazement and admiration. Living room, Sally had reminded her; *she* would have led them into the little sitting room and established a bridgehead for future invasions.

Then she went into the kitchen and started slicing Mrs. Gunn's excellent home-baked bread for sandwiches.

Sally came downstairs smiling. "Well, this *isn't* Paris or New York," she said in reply to Margaret Peel's raised eyebrows. "They may as well get into the picture, right away. They have hot and cold, electric light, clean towels, and good beds. They have someone to prepare their meals and wash their dishes, and someone to pay for it all. If they don't think that's enough, they can go back where they came from." They both laughed, then.

"I begin to understand that, for the first time in my life," Margaret Peel said, referring to Sally's last sentence, and went into another fit of laughter.

"Coffee," Sally said, becoming practical again, "gallons of it. That will help our Scotch situation, I hope. I wish I had the courage to offer Prender some beer! And here's plenty of fruit for dessert. I'll serve it on ice, Spanish-fashion, and add an exotic touch."

Sally has become so practical, Mrs. Peel thought, as she carried dishes into the living room, where they had set up a card-table complete with supper cloth and a candlestick for the impromptu meal. Of course, Prender might have written to say he was coming, or he could have telephoned from Three Springs: that would have saved all this trouble. She sank into an armchair wearily, for she had been on her feet practically all day. There had been so many little last touches to give each room. All involved so many journeys, up and down stairs: books, flowers, candlesticks, writing paper, matches, soap, ash trays and all the rest of it. In Rapallo, now, they could have nine maids for the cost of one in America. Europeans, or almost-Europeans like Prender, kept forgetting that. In Rapallo, too, no one — not even Prender — had expected everything to be run like the Ritz: everyone had laughed when things like plumbing went wrong and said, "The Italians, they are so charming, aren't they?" But here, two thousand miles from New York, with the nearest store some twenty-five miles away and not a lime to be seen, Prender had wanted his Daiquiri.

"Cheer up," Sally said, carrying a large pot of coffee into the room, "August has only thirty-one days. Besides, the rest of our guests won't be like this, I'm sure. It is only Prender being very Atherton Jones. I like Miss Bassinbrook. She was appreciative, at least. Just *loved* your darling flowers on her *divine* writing table. And such a *sweet* bed lamp which really *worked*. . . . I wonder what's keeping them?"

She placed the coffeepot near the glowing logs. "Between you and I, as they say in polite circles, I am furious about D. Schmetterling. He isn't invited. He isn't an unknown author. He had a smashing success with his book of satires on his unfortunate family. He has enough money of his own, thanks to his family, to rent a whole dude ranch for himself. So it's *damnable* that he should be taking up a room here. We need the space."

Mrs. Peel didn't even flinch at Sally's vehemence tonight. "I know he doesn't like us, yet he keeps *haunting* us," she said miserably.

"I shouldn't be surprised if we are part of his studies for his next smashing success. I'm sure he sees us a mixture of Lucia and Tish. And I rather dislike being spread-eagled on a slide under a microscope."

"Oh no! He couldn't! He wouldn't!"

"He could. Besides, he has no imagination. So he *has* to write from life: one of those specimens who've got to borrow because they can't invent. Margaret, I'll really get fighting mad if he picks our guests for copy."

"I'm sure he isn't staying. . . . It just happened that he was driving across the country to California, and so Prender and Miss Bassinbrook came with him. I'm sure it was all as simple as that."

"It just happened," Sally said. "But how I wish Prender wasn't always tempted to save money. A train ticket would have been much cheaper in the long run, for all of us."

"Sarah," Mrs. Peel said sharply, "I don't think your trip to Europe last year did you any good at all."

"On the contrary," Sally said equally sharply. "If it hadn't been for that, I might never have grown up at the ripe age of thirty-seven. Pippa's passing is definitely from the kindergarten to the first grade. And it's Sally, Margaret. Sally. . . . I am no longer anyone's kindly great-aunt. I've discovered a very good rule: from now on, anyone I spend time on has got to justify *his* existence in my life."

Mrs. Peel said nothing. She stared at the little dancing flames stitching the logs together.

Sally reached out a hand and touched her arm gently. "You certainly justified your existence in my life. Remember 1932? That hideous day in October when I was — well, I wasn't very happy, was I? You didn't know how unhappy, when you came to see me that night because you were worried about me. And you stayed to talk until dawn came. You didn't know; but you — you saved my life." She spoke the last words with difficulty and embarrassment. How often the truth sounded trite; and the untruth, witty.

Margaret Peel's gentle face turned towards her friend. The brown eyes, which could look so young, were now old with deep wisdom.

Yes, she had known. She had talked that night to a girl clearly marked for self-destruction. She had talked against time, and waited for the first sign that the dreadful determination had weakened. Then it had been safe to stop talking, but not to leave alone. She had brought Sarah to her flat. It was then that this easy partnership had begun. But from Paris to Wyoming had been a long journey in years. It had taken all that time for Sarah to speak of that night.

She touched Sally's hand in reply.

Then, "The coffee is going to boil," she said, pulling out her handkerchief to move the pot further away from the blazing logs.

Sally rose. "They are coming downstairs. Thank goodness." She went to welcome the guests, invited and uninvited.

CHAPTER IX

Sally

M IMI BASSINBROOK had changed her dress and her face. Mrs. Peel, taking one look at the off-shoulder blouse, gave up her chair next to the fire. After all, that was less of a sacrifice than having to nurse a guest with pneumonia.

Prender Atherton Jones was more cheerful, having tested the mattress, the plumbing, and the view from his window.

Dewey Schmetterling was imperturbable. His dark hair was smoothly controlled. His face — which once had a tendency to be full-fleshed and volubly expressive — was fixed in its carefully disciplined mask. As a boy, he had become conscious of the fact that his nose was more prominent than his chin; so he carried his head high, with an almost imperceptible backward tilt. He had decided his eyes were too large, too emotional, and so his eyelids were trained to narrow them to a coldly appraising stare. His eyebrows looked best in a slightly quizzical frown, so they stayed that way. He held his lips tightly to give his mouth a firm line. All this had been so constantly remembered — just as a determined woman can improve her waistline by pulling in her diaphragm even during the most intellectual conversations — that it had become seemingly natural. His appearance, made to match the character he had adopted, was that of a handsome bird of prey, waiting for the moment to strike. Among men, he found, this more than made up for his height; he could do little, though he had tried hard enough, to extend his five feet four inches. For men were wary of him. Women, because he seemed incalculable and indifferent, found him interesting. When he did turn on the charm, at moments of his own choosing, the effect was overwhelming. For the charmed one, a little nervous, a little apprehensive, a little doubtful that she was quite up to Dewey's standard, suddenly felt she was not only the most enchanting and beautiful but certainly the wittiest woman in the room. Five minutes of that made a whole evening memorable. Other men were puzzled that Schmetterling, as in all branches of his career, could achieve so much by working so little. They explained it in terms of women's natural instinct for wealth. Dewey, dressed with superb understatement, was surrounded by an aura of good living, clinging as unobtrusively, but tantalizingly, as the scent of the costliest French perfume round a pretty woman's throat. No expense, provided it was in good taste, was spared: the best was not too good for Dewey.

"My dear Sarah!" he said now, looking at the plate of sandwiches and conveying the right amount of amazement and amusement. "And coffee, too. How delicious! We'll stay awake all night and tell each other stories. A Western *Decameron*." He looked appraisingly at Sally's checked shirt and tight levis, as he lifted a sandwich. Then he turned unerringly on Mrs. Peel and stared at her tweed suit.

"Maggie, you disappoint me. Where's your fancy dress? I expected a pair of pearl-handled revolvers at least. You must let me send you them." He looked at the sandwich in his hand reflectively. "As a bread-and-butter letter." He kept the phrases, as well as the accent, of the school in southeastern England where he had been educated.

"I'm the spangled-skirt type, I'm afraid. Not Annie Oakley," Mrs. Peel said, trying to smile. But a pink spot of annoyance spread over each cheek as she turned to Mimi Bassinbrook.

"I adore the West, don't you, Mrs. Peel?" Mimi said. "Wasn't it clever of Prender to have thought this up? He has the most original ideas. I know we are going to have the most wonderful time." She smiled up at Prender Atherton Jones, and patted the chair next to hers.

Prender was half-gratified by Mimi's renewed allegiance (it had been a hideous journey, with Dewey winning most of the laughs and almost all the attention), half-embarrassed at the look in Sally Bly's

84

eye. As Mimi went on chattering gaily to Mrs. Peel, he spoke quietly to Sally. "Mimi has a genius for getting things slightly mixed. That's one of her attractions, frankly."

"I think she has many," Sally said, and was very efficient with the coffee cups. "Two lumps, cream; here you are, Prender. Dewey? Black and strictly unsweetened? Tea for Miss Bassinbrook? Why, of course. Shan't be a minute."

When she returned from the kitchen with the teapot, the group had settled cozily around the fire.

"To think," Mimi was saying as she watched the blazing logs, "that it was over ninety degrees in New York on the day we left. And the humidity! My fingers slipped all over the typewriter keys, and the sheets came out all permanently curved as if they had lock-jaw or something."

Mrs. Peel, interested, said, "And what are you writing, Miss Bassinbrook?"

"Oh . . . just a few odd things at the moment. New York is so distracting, you know. I hope to really get down to work here, of course."

Better start by giving up split infinitives, Sally thought. But then, she was slightly soured at the moment by the lemon she had forgotten to bring from the kitchen, and which Miss Bassinbrook now requested most charmingly and naturally. Sally left them talking about humidity, New York, Singapore, the Amazon jungles, and returned with the sliced lemon to hear them arguing about politics. At least, Prender was making gloomy predictions and passing dire judgments.

"We are, in fact," he was saying, "approaching the police state."

Sally looked at him sharply. "If you had lived in Nazi-occupied France," she suggested, "you wouldn't throw around that charge so lightly."

"Intellectual freedom is dying," he said, ignoring the interruption.

"How?" Sally asked. Prender was always so evasive with direct questions: he preferred to make broad general replies, decked out with noble phrases, which proved that anyone disagreeing with him must be narrow-minded and mentally limited.

85

He descended to Sally's practical level with obvious distaste. He said coldly, "I am talking of political investigations. Witch hunts. Opinions are being persecuted. Is that clear enough, Sarah?"

"You'd tolerate all opinions? Even destructive ones?"

"The air in Wyoming must be full of fire and brimstone," Dewey said. "And are you going to run for Congress, Sarah?" The prospect amused him highly.

Mrs. Peel said, "It isn't a laughing matter, Dewey. I've seen how Communists can use tolerance to get into power. And once they are in power, they aren't tolerant. Last year, in Paris — "

"Freedom cannot be qualified," Prender said.

Mrs. Peel sighed. If only he'd let her finish her story. A practical example, too. She tried once more. "You know, Prender, last year — "

"I may disagree with a Communist," Prender went on, "but I shall fight for his right to disagree with me."

"Naturally," Mimi said, looking thoughtful and sympathetic.

"And for his right, eventually, to send you to a concentration camp just because you continue to disagree with him?" Sally asked.

Prender shook his head over Sally's rabble-rousing. "If we ever were to reach that stage of — of concentration camps, we'd resist. We'd fight violence with violence. Then our conscience would be clear. That's my whole argument: we must keep our conscience clear."

"Even at the expense of our country's future?" Sarah asked. "Wouldn't our consciences be clearer if we were to fight ideas with ideas now?"

Mrs. Peel said, "Let me lend you my little edition of Demosthenes to reread, Prender."

He looked at them in turn. "I never knew you were both so politically minded," he said and dismissed them with a smile. "It's hardly your line, is it?"

"Last year, in Paris," Mrs. Peel said indignantly, "we — "

"Wyoming must do something to women," Dewey said. "That's why they got the vote here in 1869. In London and New York they were still chaining themselves to policemen as late as 1919, but all

86

they had to do in Wyoming was to argue. My dear Sarah, your flights of fancy have given me a hell of a thirst. Or did the women in Wyoming use their vote to make it a dry state, too?"

Sally rose to find the Scotch and open it. Mrs. Peel added two logs to the fire, and went to find soda and ice. Mimi removed the fruit plate from the rug at her feet, and handed it to Prender to discard on the mantelpiece. Dewey stretched his legs comfortably, watched them all, and found much to amuse him.

When Mrs. Peel returned with the news that Sally had used all the available ice for her Spanish fruit bowl, the conversation had definitely lost its social significance. She calmed her feelings, which had gone on ruffling themselves in the kitchen, but she still felt despondent. Political subtleties were painful enough in Europe, but to find them rearing their ugly heads in New York and coming to invade the peace of Wyoming was unbearable. (If the Atlantic was of any use at all, it was to give people here a breathing-space to learn. Some nations in Europe had never been given the chance of that breathing-space: they were plunged into disaster before they even started arguing.) She had found Wyoming an escape into a place of reason, where politics meant discussions on the merits and failings of either Republicans or Democrats, where such hideous things as concentration camps for political opponents weren't even imagined.

Prender was now launching into his experiences on the journey westwards. He seemed to have forgotten the bitterness that had been stirred up. So Mrs. Peel sat down with relief beside Mimi Bassinbrook, listened, and tried to stop being despondent.

"Thank you, Sarah," Dewey said, and took the tall glass which she brought over to him. "Or is it F. Nightingale mixed with Joan of Arc? You do surprise your friends, Sarah."

"Not Sarah. Sally," she said gently.

"In heaven's name, why?" He noted she kept a special kind of smile for him.

"Because I like it."

"And if I call you Sarah?"

"I won't hear what you say."

87

"Efficient," he admitted. Yes, there was always California and Liz Beaton, who was the nice awed type that Sally used to be. Still, a day or two here might be rewarding. Mimi, for one thing. And for another, the arrival of The Great Unpublished. And Prender, for a third. For instance, poor Maggie had been trying to tell them, too, about some of her experiences on her journey here; but, at the moment, she was only able to add less than half a sentence at a time while Prender's saga unfolded. Prender was swinging into full stride now, with all the makings of a most successful addition to his lecture season. In spite of his protests about calories, he had eaten enormously of the sandwiches, and as he stood in front of the fireplace, looking down at the half-circle of faces turned towards him, his eloquence was as limitless as the country over which he had traveled. An impressive if somewhat boring performance, Dewey thought; like St. Paul's Cathedral, fog-capped.

"I am delighted," Sally said at last, when Prender paused for a drink. "Because it proves we were right, and that happens so rarely."

"Proves?" Prender asked, a trifle shaken.

"Yes. Remember Margaret and I suggested last winter — I think it was at one of your parties, actually — that it was odd how so many of us knew New York and Connecticut, but how few ever traveled west of Chicago or Cincinnati? Apart from reaching California in an air-conditioned train, of course. Well, if we hadn't decided to travel leisurely across the continent, we wouldn't have found Rest and Be Thankful. And if we hadn't found Rest and Be Thankful, you wouldn't have traveled across the continent, either. So I am delighted, for you are obviously impressed by your own country for the first time in your life. Perhaps the rest of our guests will share your enthusiasm. That was what we hoped for. It makes all the trouble we've had well worth while."

"Trouble?" Prender was more perplexed.

"My dear, you don't imagine that you can set up housekeeping for nine people" — she glanced at Dewey — "for ten people, twenty-five miles from the nearest store, thirty-five from the railway and a decent road, without a lot of planning? Things just don't create themselves, you know. Everything is made so easy for us in the cities that we forget how much energy and time it takes to arrange the minimum necessities in life."

Prender nodded, memorizing that idea. He had to admit he was amazed that he had traveled as far as from Paris to Istanbul to reach Sweetwater from New York.

Dewey said, "Do we trap or shoot our meat? Or do we use a nice old-fashioned hatchet?"

Sally smiled. "And what did Dewey think of the journey? How many neon-lighted hamburger stands lie between here and the Atlantic? I'm sure you counted them all. And how many fat women wearing shorts? How many Miss Tomato-of-the-Year contests? How many funeral parlors designed as Corinthian temples? Dewey, you must have treasured them . . ."

Dewey rose to pour himself another drink.

Mimi Bassinbrook laughed. "Miss Bly, *how* did you guess? He just loved all of them."

"There are so many different things to see, so many ways of life in America," Mrs. Peel said in her most understanding manner. She shot a warning look at Sally, who ignored it with a still brighter smile.

"Yes," Sally said innocently, "and what you see depends on what you are determined to see."

"Dewey *insisted* we spend last night at one of these drive-in places where you rent cabins," Mimi went on.

"Was it called a motel, Dewey?" Sally asked.

Prender Atherton Jones, now in excellent humor, said indeed it had been. Dewey had insisted on driving for an extra thirty minutes to reach a motel advertised as the Pop Inn.

Dewey, watching Sally with a new wariness, joined in the laughter if only to turn it away from himself. "We slept," he said in the quiet, precise voice which he had carefully cultivated, "on beds that were described in Basic American as Kumfy Kots; and the lamps had the trade name of Brite Lite. It was a very pleasant evening."

"I'm so glad, Dewey," Sally said. "How horrible for you if you had had to sleep at an ordinary hotel with ordinary beds. Absolutely uninspiring. Which reminds me — where are *we* going to put you? In a tent?" She spoke lightly, gaily, as if it were a pleasant problem.

Mrs. Peel shook her head and restrained a smile.

Prender said quickly, "Dewey is only staying here for a night on his way to California. He's going to visit Elizabeth Beaton."

"How nice for Elizabeth," Sally said. "Does she still keep her tame seal in the swimming pool? Dewey, you can teach it tricks — tray balancing, so that it will serve cocktails while you are floating peacefully among the wax water lilies."

Dewey smiled, poured himself a third drink, and tried to think of something to say. Usually, he held the floor whenever Prender yielded it. But tonight, Sally had kept him silent merely by talking about the kind of things he had been about to mention. She even was adopting his kind of phrases. He hadn't been so angered or bored for many a month. Tomorrow, he thought, adding another jigger of Scotch to his glass, it will be California. But as he drank to that, Mimi — who, for the last hour, had been giving Prender extra attention to calm his disturbed memories of today's journey — rose and went over to the radio-phonograph.

"Music!" she said so enchantingly that only a monster among men would have thought about her sure grasp of the obvious. She gave Dewey a small signal as she pulled out the record albums, and sat down on the floor to arrange them around her. Sally admired the entire arrangement as she wandered over to Mimi, too.

Sally was being damned annoying tonight, Dewey thought. In a way, he had to admit, she was also being useful; for Prender, after a quick frown towards the corner of the room where the phonograph stood, seemed reassured, and he sat down beside Mrs. Peel to start talking about Aubrey Brimstone's new magazine, which Prender might possibly edit, if he had time.

"Bach, Haydn, Beethoven," Mimi said delightedly.

"Long hair," said Dewey, although he fought for tickets to the Boston Symphony Orchestra just as determinedly as Mrs. Peel. He looked at Sally challengingly.

She accepted. "Sweet corn, too, for those who like to hum a tune. And here's bebop for the initiated." She picked up a record and studied the printed center. "Tiberius Tantivy and his Fourtet. Now, Dewey, that's another for your collection."

Dewey seemed shocked by such sacrilege, for Basic American in advanced art must be taken seriously, unlike Basic American in advertising. He rejected Sally's offering, to pick a record of his own. "Stravinsky," he said.

"The Bebops' bible," Sally murmured. "What a pity we all read *The New Yorker,* isn't it?"

Dewey stared at her, a man whose words have been stolen most blatantly right out of his mouth. Unforgivable.

"What is wrong with Sarah?" Dewey asked, as he and Prender went upstairs to bed. Mimi, from her bedroom door at the far end of the corridor, waved a plaintive good night.

Prender shrugged his shoulders. All that worried him was that Dewey, as soon as the writers arrived and if he stayed, would be moved into his room. That was completely unsatisfactory, not only from the point of view of sleep but of pleasure. Sarah had been quite obdurate: the writers must each have a room to themselves, and neither pointed suggestion nor gentle sarcasm had been able to shift her from that most decided stand. There were two things on which he had determined: Dewey must leave for the ample charms of Liz Beaton and her psychopathic circle; and Sarah would be sorry, next winter in New York.

"Pity about Aubrey Brimstone and Merrick Maclehose," Dewey Schmetterling said, suddenly more cheerful.

"Yes."

"Too late to write them. When did you expect them to arrive?"

"On Monday."

"Ah well, there's always Western Union. Good night."

Dewey may have sounded almost gay, but he had his own particular problems. What did an author do when one of the ineffective, funny characters in his new satire had suddenly become charged with electricity? It wasn't fair. He would have to kill her off, somehow, and that could always be made clever-cruel and amusing. But a pity, nevertheless, for she had been good for several more laughs before the end of the book was reached. Thank God, Maggie had stayed in character. Almost. She talked less, but perhaps that was only a mood tonight.

It was a dispirited satirist who fell asleep. His room was cold. His bed had not been turned down. His suitcase had not been unpacked. And they had known how he hated sandwiches.

As they waited for the fire to burn low enough before they would leave it, Mrs. Peel was much amused and a little shocked.

"Sally, I've never known you to be so inhospitable."

"After making all those sandwiches? And dashing around with slices of lemon? And our precious bottle of Scotch all gone and not another one to be found this side of Three Springs? Besides, do you want Dewey to stay?"

"I wouldn't expire with grief if he left. But Prender — "

"Well, he should have remembered he didn't own this place. I wrote him, you know, about lack of bedrooms for lecturers."

"He suggested the writers could share rooms." Mrs. Peel was almost half-persuaded. It was hard to refuse Prender.

"They mustn't! Not here. Prender imagines everyone who lives in New York is as comfortable as he is in his borrowed penthouse."

"But Aubrey Brimstone — "

"Can afford several kinds of holidays."

"But — "

"Margaret, let's have our own way for once. Everything we start gets twisted out of shape by other people to suit themselves. Whose life are we living, anyway? Theirs, or ours?"

They watched the fire die slowly.

"People *will* put one into such difficult positions," Mrs. Peel said sadly. "They make it so hard for one *not* to look in the wrong, even when one is more or less right."

"A matter of technique. It's about time we recognized it."

The last charred log broke in two.

"It's about time we went to sleep," Mrs. Peel said. She rose and began collecting coffee cups and plates in a vague way.

"Go up to bed. I'll cope with this litter." Sally looked with distaste at the cigarette stubs in the saucers.

"Mrs. Gunn —"

"I know. She has only one pair of hands and tomorrow is baking day. I'll leave the kitchen as we found it. Go to bed, Margaret."

Mrs. Peel was too tired to refuse. When you were as tired as this, it was pleasant to be persuaded into laziness.

Sally, as she dried the last glass in the kitchen, was reflecting that — thanks to the inventiveness of Lord Sandwich — she wasn't scouring pots and pans at midnight.

Jim Brent, taking a restless walk after a dull evening of accounts and business matters, noticed the lighted kitchen. As he drew near, he could see Sally. He stood in the shadow of a cottonwood tree and watched her for a moment. On impulse, he went over to the kitchen door and knocked. He smiled as he heard a glass fall and Sally's description of herself.

The door was opened a bare three inches. "Need any help?" he asked.

Sally, still startled, could only shake her head. She opened the door fully, laughing at her own caution. "Give me time and I'll get accustomed to this part of the country," she said. "Do come in. I've just finished — by breaking a glass." She held up the remains for him to admire.

"Too late for a walk?"

She shook her head. "I'll get a coat." She got rid of the broken glass, hung the drying cloth on its rod, and then ran to the hall for her coat. He noticed the quick decisive movements, and thought how typical of her they were. He wondered if the broken glass in her hand had been her idea of an improvised weapon. It would take some time, he thought, before she forgot France under the Nazi occupation. She had told him, when he had teased her about locking the front door to the house, that when she got back from Europe even as late as last year, she had found herself clutching her purse and her shopping packages as if they were about to be lifted out of her arms. She hadn't been the only one to have formed that habit, either: everyone coming back from Europe would hardly trust a porter to take charge of a suitcase. It was one small result of the war: people, hungry and desperate, were quick to pilfer. "You don't blame them, really," she had said. "You just learn to be careful."

Now, as she came back with her coat round her shoulders, he said, "Sorry to trespass, but the light kind of welcomed me."

"I'm glad it did. I'm afraid I gave you a poor welcome."

He smiled. "My grandmother used to hold a gun when she opened the door in the dark. There were some wild customers roaming around, then. Trainloads of ex-convicts and gamblers poured into Laramie: the railroad stopped there, you see. It was sort of tough on Laramie."

"I take it that Laramie attended to its uninvited guests?"

"It had to. And once the citizens started shooting, you'd be surprised how the lawbreakers faded out." He steadied her by the arm as she stumbled. "Better wait a moment and let your eyes get accustomed to the night."

"You keep a very beautiful sky in Wyoming."

"You miss it when you go away," he admitted. "I guess cities shut out the sky."

Then they walked down towards the bridge, and across the creek, to reach the road by which she had first come to Rest and Be Thankful.

"How are the guests?" he asked unexpectedly.

"Oh, all right."

"I see." He didn't sound convinced.

They halted by the noisy creek which ran by the roadside. It was none of his business. He couldn't even suggest that if she needed a man with a few forceful phrases to keep her from being bullied, then he'd oblige. Why they hadn't chosen to spend a quiet summer here by themselves was still a puzzle to him. But women were puzzling. Men simplified life. Women always seemed to want to complicate it.

"I sold the last batches of horses today," he said.

"Oh, I'm sorry," she said truthfully, impulsively.

He was grateful for the emotion in her voice, emotion he couldn't

94

afford. "I've kept a few," he went on in the same controlled voice. "A ranch isn't a ranch without horses, somehow."

"And how are the steers you bought?"

"Oh, all right." His voice was noncommittal. He had his worries, too. Ranchers, whose grazing land was high in the mountains, bought their steers in the late spring, fattened them through the short summer, and sold them in the fall. This year, he had taken a chance, bringing up his steers to his land about two weeks late. Still, the grazing was good; and they'd fatten up enough before the end of September if there was no drought. He'd ship them east as late as possible. That, too, depended on the weather. It was a gamble; but stock men always took a gamble. Drought or disease could wipe them out in a few weeks. A grass fire could wipe them out in a couple of days. He had safeguarded himself in one way: he had kept his herd small, this summer. Next year, if everything went well, he would invest in a bigger herd, and hire more hands to take care of it. If all went well . . . "I suppose," he said, "I'll get more enthusiastic about them in time."

She began to laugh.

"I like a good joke as well as the next man," he said.

"I was thinking your new steers and our first guests seem to have a lot in common."

He laughed then. It was the first time she had heard him laugh, and she felt happy. They stayed, watching the night sky, conscious of each other, and all the more consciously avoiding the personal as they talked.

A night wind from the mountains came rustling through the trees. It had a bitter touch, and she shivered.

"Better go home now," he said. He was quick to notice. He took her arm and led her back along the dark road with its strange shadows, guiding her carefully over the rough surface. Something between them had altered. She couldn't guess what. But even if her body shivered, she was warm. Warm and happy.

When they came to the house, she stood for a few moments at its door, reluctant to enter.

"Good night," she said at last. "And thank you for trespassing."

He said nothing. He was watching her face. Then he spoke, still holding the hand she had given him. "Why didn't you go out riding this evening?"

"Oh. . . ." She took her hand away, suddenly embarrassed. "All these guests arriving . . . it was difficult."

"I guess so," he said. But the guests had arrived after she had refused. "Tomorrow night?"

"Tomorrow night."

"Fine."

"Good night, Jim."

"Good night, Sally." He still hesitated, but she went indoors.

He waited under the cottonwood tree until he saw the light go on in her room. Then he turned, walking into the deep shadows, past the silent corral, towards his silent cabin.

CHAPTER X

East Meets West

JACKSON had scythed and then mown the grass in front of the house. It now stretched, as smooth as a bright green carpet, down to the edge of Crazy Creek's bank where the tall cottonwood trees grew. In the warm afternoons, the guests liked to gather there, near enough the shade of the trees to give them the feeling of coolness, while they listened to the chattering creek and perfected their sun tan. Only Prender Atherton Jones sat on one of the garden chairs. The others preferred to stretch out on the soft cool grass. Today, like the three days that had already vanished, found Mimi Bassinbrook the center of the group. She might not seem to notice that; but she had dressed in the minimum of midriff blouse and brief tight shorts, which were as becoming to her figure as the reclining pose she had adopted.

Carla Brightjoy had compromised with Breton sailor's red trousers, rolled almost to the knees but not quite, for her knees were knobbly and her thighs were too thin. Her Hawaiian shirt was loose and full, and looked elegant, she believed, with its tail hanging out. Her small face was made still smaller, thinner, by the large round glasses she liked to wear. She gave little nervous darting glances around her as she sat hugging her knees and moving her neat feet restlessly in their Mexican sandals. She tried not to look too often at Mimi's figure, stretched with effortless grace on the grass beside her. And she tried to persuade herself that her own clothes were much more suitable for the West. Yesterday, Mimi had worn a jade green *maillot* and never even entered the water. Yet, in spite of her objections she had to admit that Mimi looked attractive. The men obviously thought so, too. Not that clothes, or looks, really mattered. Still . . . But even as the wish sprang into her mind that she might look like Mimi Bassinbrook, she comforted herself with the knowledge that Mimi would never be a writer. You could feel that, just looking at her. (She'd marry someone rich like Dewey Schmetterling, and have a house like this, only in California where she could wear patio dresses and be photographed at a new angle for *Vogue*.) It really was difficult to understand why she had been included in this house party. Surely Mr. Atherton Jones didn't think she *could* write? Yet, his judgment was said to be so good. Last winter, when he had praised two of Carla's own short stories, she had walked around for days in a secret exultation of hope and joy. That excitement had made even the dreary hours of standing all day in the Cosy Corner Book Shop seem less tedious. For whenever she felt exhausted and depressed now, she reminded herself that these hours brought her food and clothes and the little room in Greenwich Village — where she was free (after she cooked her evening meal, and washed out her underwear, and ironed a blouse or sewed a clean collar onto her dress) to write. Free? She looked around her slowly, studying the house placed so peacefully against its background of mountains and blue skies.

Carla sighed, and then frowned in embarrassment as the others lifted their heads from the grass to look at her. She felt she had to say something now. "It must — it must be wonderful to have a house like this. I mean, one could write so well here." She smiled, thinking how pleasant it was to discover such places in the world.

"Sure," Karl Koffing said, and his bitterness startled her. "All you have to do is marry a rich man, get him to die young, and then choose the house you want where you want it." He dropped back onto the grass again, threw his arms out as he yawned, and lay crucified. His brown eyes stared up at the blue sky angrily. He forced his mind away from the bucolic scene around him. This world of trees and flowers and rushing streams was the unreal world, the temptress to lull you to sleep and make you forget. He closed his eyes as he returned once more to the world of his novel — that was real enough. He could smell the stink of First Avenue and

98

hear its snarling city noises, he could feel the bitter chill of the small sordid room where Mike Krinling lived. Then why the hell couldn't he get on with writing about Mike Krinling? For three days now, he had done nothing except try to recapture the mood of the last chapter. Winter — freezing temperature inside the room — Mike's unfinished manuscript on rickety wooden table — best friend Bill lying on ramshackle, unmade bed — Mike astride wooden chair — a little food, very little, on window sill — half-finished bottle on floor between the two men. Bill about to accept a job that will take him over to the enemy — trading independence of mind for security of flesh. Bill's methodology weak. Argument savage. Outside — pulse of the giant city — Mrs. Quacelli next door shouting at her drunken son (victim of environment) — phonograph, playing its only record, from Marianna's room upstairs together with man's coarse laughter (Marianna another v. of e.) — children, dirty and ragged, yelling on side street, dirty and squalid. Mike's dialectic wins argument. Bottle finished. What next?

That was where he had stopped writing and packed for the journey West.

Marianna? Or Hoolihan's Bar round the corner?

Hoolihan's Bar. Marianna would be coming there, anyway. And that punk of a huckster from Beekman Place would be there, too, trying to make her; throwing his money around like his opinions, the phony liberal, afraid of the change in the future, trying to play safe, afraid of the Mike Krinlings, apologizing for his earning power, always aiming to be on the winning side, fine example for Bill to see. Argument clinched. All right. Next chapter at Hoolihan's.

But when to begin it? This evening, P. A. Jones, Esq., was holding forth on Existentialism. Tomorrow morning there was riding. Tomorrow evening, then? But that was what he had said yesterday. And the day before. Those damned birds, he thought, suddenly sitting up and glaring at the linden trees where the robins liked to sing, didn't they ever shut up? "Hell of a row," he said angrily.

"Relax, Karl," Earl Grubbock said. "I'm trying to think." Earl rubbed his chest, stretched his leg muscles and tightened his diaphragm. Still too much weight there. He turned over on his stomach, partly to hide the extra inches, partly to let his back get equally roasted. He had been getting out of shape ever since he had gotten his discharge. A protest against Army discipline, probably. He had been as lean and tough as any of these wranglers only three years ago. Well, he'd start toughening up again: it wasn't too late. And he'd start a program of work, too. Keep to it, this time. He'd settled down to work tonight. His new idea for a short story wasn't bad, not at all bad. A house like this one, only in the South — two elderly women living in dreams of their own faded world — a lynching at their door. . . . What then? He must talk more to Mrs. Peel and get an idea how she would face violence and injustice. Suicide? Insanity? Or deeper retirement into her dream world? Yes, he'd start on that story tonight, when the idea was still hot, when he felt full of energy and strength. He closed his eyes and pillowed his cheek on the grass. The warm sun, the firm earth: energy and strength. Then he remembered Prender Atherton Jones and the lecture on Existentialism. Hell's bells, he had forgotten the flaming good-will hour.

Carla Brightjoy, still watching Karl Koffing, still looking at the house, summoned her courage to say, "But couldn't you *earn* the money — I mean, *not* marry it — to buy a place like this? After all, there are lots of writers with farms in Connecticut and Pennsylvania." She smiled, but the smile froze as Koffing turned his eyes away from the linden tree and gave her a look. Then he settled back on the grass again.

He could be so handsome, she thought — a strong face, with its high cheekbones and well-set chin and large eyes; brown eyes, the sort of eyes you might expect to be kind. But at the moment, they were contemptuous and the face was hard. He was so — so difficult. She looked nervously around at the others. Fortunately, Mimi hadn't seen anything: she was pretending to be asleep. Earl Grubbock had his face buried in the grass. Mr. Atherton Jones, over in the cushioned armchair, was too busy talking to that awful Esther Park. And *she* was practically kneeling at his feet, her head turned to him as she listened. That left only Mr. O'Farlan, sitting in the shade with his back against a tree, reading a newspaper. Had he noticed? Yes, he was looking at her, and then at Karl Koffing, and then at her again. But of course, he didn't get on with Karl. That might explain why he smiled to her now. She looked down at her clasped hands.

Robert O'Farlan had seen Carla being put most thoroughly into her place again. He smiled, partly to cheer her up, partly because she looked like a timid little marmoset, crouching nervously, frowning to keep herself from crying. He saw her hesitate, look down at her hands clasped tightly around her knees; and then she looked up and smiled so wholeheartedly that he was still more sorry for her. He lowered the newspaper. To his alarm, she rose suddenly and came across to the tree.

"Have you really done much work, here?" she asked, trying hard to please. "I do admire the way you plan your day." He was the only one of them who had seemed to do any writing at all since he arrived. She smiled, and then she sat down beside him, slipping into an imitation of Mimi Bassinbrook's reclining odalisque.

He had asked for this, O'Farlan realized. He gathered the newspaper together and folded it up philosophically.

"Does anyone want the *New York Times*?" he asked.

"Four days old," Karl Koffing said contemptuously to a small white cloud sailing through the sky. "And the radio is almost as bad — nothing but firecrackers being let off whenever you want to hear anything. God, no wonder these people out here were isolationists. How can they live?"

"They do," O'Farlan said crisply, "and very nicely without our help, too. And what makes you think they were isolationists? As far as I can learn from Mrs. Gunn, there were no punctured eardrums out in this district when the war started." He eyed Koffing's Army-surplus pants contemptuously. O'Farlan was wearing them too — as all the men were, except Jones, who preferred well-cut riding breeches — but he had, at least, been in the First World War. He would have been in the second one, too, if he hadn't been rejected when he volunteered. He would have been in it, not because he liked war (as Koffing tried to make out), but because he hated the whole damned thing so much. And to volunteer, to hope that you'd be taken, was one way of atoning for all the damned politics you had preached before the war, for misleading yourself and misleading others.

Carla Brightjoy, feeling herself being pushed out into the cold shadows again, said hastily, "Mr. O'Farlan, how long have you been working on your novel?" She meant to be sympathetic, but he tightened up once more, back into the gray-haired, white-faced, worried man who rarely smiled. She forgot her adopted grace and hunched her body in nervousness. She couldn't think of another thing to say.

Mimi's voice said softly, "I like newspapers four days old. It is just no use worrying about their headlines, because, by the time you see them, someone *must* have done something about them somewhere."

"In the wrong way, too," Earl Grubbock said gloomily, rolling over on his back to watch the pattern of the leaves against the sky. "Next time, I'll sit the war out. I'll get me a good safe job and make some money for a change."

"You wouldn't," Mimi said. "You aren't *that* kind."

Grubbock looked pleased in spite of himself. "Well," he said, sitting up and wiping the loose strands of grass from his shoulders, "if war starts, we are all for it, all of us."

"And what did war ever decide, anyway?" Koffing said, still watching the sailing cloud.

"Plenty, if you've learned your history," O'Farlan said, "or if you haven't purposely forgotten it. If we had lost the last war, who would have been in Washington, now, as occupation troops? And if that doesn't move you, who would have been in Moscow?"

"I'm against beginning a war," Grubbock said angrily.

"Who isn't? You haven't a patent on that, I can assure you."

Grubbock glanced at Koffing, but Koffing kept silent now. "Look at the preparations we are making," Grubbock said. Why didn't Koffing talk up? He knew all the facts and figures about that.

"Sure," O'Farlan said sarcastically, "don't think of fire insurance until your house burns down!" His voice changed to bitterness.

102

"Did pacifism ever stop anything unless you were dealing with pacifists?"

Grubbock flushed. Koffing looked at the vanishing cloud with narrowed eyes. Prender Atherton Jones stopped Esther Park's adulation of Sartre with a half-raised hand. Carla Brightjoy murmured "Oh!" and watched everyone anxiously.

Mimi sat up and said, "*Will* you all please stop this? If I hear any more politics, I'll *scream*." She looked around. Dewey Schmetterling wasn't going to appear after all. Where could he have been all afternoon? Did that little blonde cowgirl, who dusted the bedrooms so abstractedly, have *every* afternoon free? It was maddening how clever Dewey could be about such things. Of course, he was only being amused by the braids and the bows. Drene Travers . . . what a name! Some people, Mimi Bassinbrook thought as she looked at her long slender legs and wondered if they'd really tan properly here what with wearing blue jeans most of the day, some people have the most awful names.

She swung herself gracefully onto her feet, to the admiration of all the men and the envy of Carla, who sighed and took off her glasses and rubbed the itching bridge of her nose.

"Do you have to wear these things?" Robert O'Farlan asked.

Carla frowned at the glasses in her hand. "I work in a bookshop, you know." She stared at the round lenses, glinting owl-like back at her, and then looked up at Mimi. She could see her almost as clearly, almost. In fact, quite enough. She pulled down the legs of her pink denim trousers, pressing out the wrinkles with her free hand. It was no good. She looked worse than ever. She stuck the glasses back in place defiantly.

"I think I'll take a walk to the corral," Mimi announced. She looked at Grubbock, smiled at Prender Atherton Jones, and started off towards the path through the cottonwood trees.

No one moved.

Prender Atherton Jones had decided to discipline Mimi. He smiled, but made no effort to join her. Mimi, spurned by Dewey for the sake of a little cowgirl in tight frontier pants, was something to see. Tomorrow, when she had learned this little lesson he was now teaching her, he would take her riding with him.

The others were silent, too, as they watched Mimi leave. Earl Grubbock looked as if he might be about to follow, and then he saw that Atherton Jones was watching him with a suddenly alert eye. It was too much like stealing the apple off the teacher's desk, Grubbock decided: fun, but hardly worth it. Besides, Mrs. Gunn's niece Norah was a pretty little piece. She hadn't been spoiled like Mimi. When you shared a bar of candy with her, she said thank you as if it were orchids. He contented himself, now, by enjoying the pleasure of watching Mimi in motion in her tight brief shorts.

"What about a swim?" Grubbock said suddenly. He prodded Koffing's ribs with his elbow.

"If our legs don't freeze and drop off . . . all right. In and out?" The idea repelled Koffing, but he was willing to show Grubbock that it took more than ice-cold water to freeze his guts. He was, although he tried to make little of it, always conscious that Grubbock had fought in the war and he had not.

But Grubbock didn't move. He wondered, why the hell bother? He had jumped into plenty of water, waded through plenty of surf, with full equipment pulling him down. Here, he didn't need to do one damned thing unless he wanted to, when he wanted to. Here, the sun was warm, the grass invited you to stretch out and look up at the sky, time was nothing. "Too damned lazy," he said, and he lay back with his hands clasped behind his head. He hadn't had so much a sense of peace in years.

"Make up your mind, for Christ's sake," Koffing said irritably. That was like Grubbock — ideas never fully worked out, plans never quite finished, plenty of energy but it needed direction, plenty of the right emotions but they needed to be channeled. Koffing could see himself as the missionary with his first convert, and it was a picture that both pleased and excited him. By the end of the month, he would have Earl Grubbock arguing better against O'Farlan, unmasking that diversionist's ideology and seeing it clearly for what it was. Given a few more months in New York, and Grubbock would be a sound and loyal sympathizer.

"Relax, relax," Grubbock murmured sleepily. "This is the first real holiday I've had since the damned war."

Koffing looked sharply at Grubbock.

But Grubbock had closed his eyes.

Carla Brightjoy seemed asleep, too. But she was wishing she had the courage to walk up to the corral as Mimi had done. How wonderful it must be never to feel that you might be intruding, never to entertain the terrifying thought that you were superfluous.

Robert O'Farlan thought of his work, waiting for him in his room. Time to start it, again. But the dappled shade around him was cool, and he was unwilling to leave it, to step out into the brilliant, blazing sunshine. He felt lazy, comfortable, and pleasantly tired. He could blame that on the altitude. Unlike the others, he hadn't started riding — too damned busy in the mornings for that. The others could afford to waste time: they hadn't been writing a book for — well, counting the years he had thought about it, worried about it, partly written it, scrapped it, chopped it, changed it — for almost twenty years. He had completed four drafts. He had torn them up and begun again. And the longer he waited, the more varied the angles, the wider and deeper the conception had become. Now, he was almost at the end of the fifth version of his novel. This one might be all right. It excited him. Was that a good or a bad sign? Two chapters to go . . . two that had baffled him and benumbed him for the last few months. But here, he might get enough confidence, enough energy and peace, to finish them. As Carla Brightjoy had said, this was a good place to work. *If* you were determined to work.

He thought of his four-roomed apartment in Queens: three small rooms and a kitchenette, to be more accurate. He thought of Jenny, who complained and criticized and, yet, still insisted on living with him. For the children's sake? Or did she enjoy martyrdom? Or what? As a novelist, he ought to have the answers to the problem of his own wife, but he hadn't. . . . He admitted he had never been much of a bargain — he had spent a good deal of the ten years that followed the First World War in veterans' hospitals; and, once he was fit enough, he had begun to teach school. But she knew all that when she married him. So why criticize, now, the three thousand dollars a year he could earn as a teacher? Why talk about his novel to people in just the way she did? "Robert's writing a war novel, didn't you know? A novel about the *First* World War!" Pause, while everyone laughed and the usual fool said that was original anyway. "And he can't find a title for it! I suggested *Forever All Quiet* but Robert doesn't seem to think that's funny." More laughter to prove everyone else did.

Stop it, O'Farlan warned himself. The purpose of coming to Wyoming was to get away from all that. Jenny and the children were having the usual summer with her people in New Jersey. His summers were spent in New York, with a visit at the week ends to Jenny's people as a polite gesture. This year, he was being impolite, but the novel would be finished. He looked at his watch, and rose.

Carla, suddenly very wide awake, glanced up at him. "Work?" she asked, with her timid little smile.

He felt he had to make himself seem less of a machine. "I thought I'd visit Mrs. Gunn for a cup of coffee, first," he said. Why explain, why apologize? Human beings were strange creatures: even the way they all gathered here, when each could have had a private corner in this island of trees. . . .

Esther Park's voice cut across the peace of the garden. "Mr. O'Farlan, I think you are wonderful. How you work! You *are* wonderful. Isn't he?" She gave an encircling smile, meant, they felt as they tried to wriggle free, for each of them alone. "You must tell me how you plan your day. We all need lessons in that. Don't we?"

Robert O'Farlan, as the eager face turned back to him, felt as if he were watching a movie with a quick succession of close-ups, while the sound track boomed every time the face on the screen lunged towards him.

"I — " he began, and stopped. She was talking again.

She was an ostrich, he thought: all nose, no chin, too much neck. Eyes that protruded in her enthusiasms. Thick body, thin legs, large feet. Even her black hair, overcurled and thick, reminded him of waving plumes. She was an ostrich, gobbling everything, everyone.

greedily up. But what terrified him most was her manner — the hand laid on his arm, the breathless question, the painted line of eyebrow that formed a question mark as he answered, the beady black eyes noticing everything, the notebook which she always carried under her arm ("My best ideas are so unexpected. Aren't yours?"). She talked about Her Work.

She had tried this on all the others, turning on the full blast of her charm. After the first half-hour, there was a firm movement away from her, an equally firm determination never to be caught again. Dewey Schmetterling was the only one who had spent part of an evening with her, but that had seemingly been enough even for his peculiar tastes.

All right, all right, O'Farlan thought as he stooped to pick up the newspaper he had almost forgotten; you're the guy who took twenty years to get the characters in your novel straightened out, but you've got everyone here classified and dissected after a few days. Standing up, he looked at Esther Park. There was a limit to all honest politeness. He turned away, leaving her still talking.

Carla scrambled to her feet. "May I come to Mrs. Gunn's? If you don't mind, that is?"

O'Farlan, who did mind, said, "Come along." He suddenly knew by the look on her face that she would never have had the courage to visit Mrs. Gunn's kitchen alone, and he was glad he hadn't refused.

Esther Park wasn't going to let them escape so easily. "Why don't you come to my room, instead? And have a drink?" She smiled round the group again. "Why don't you *all* come?"

"Too early," O'Farlan said, and he could hear Carla's little intake of breath in her relief.

"Going out riding," Grubbock mumbled. Koffing nodded. They both rose as if they had to catch a horse at four-thirty leaving on Platform Five.

"I've some notes to look over," Prender Atherton Jones said as he glanced at his watch with a frown. His was quite the most finished performance, but he had had much longer practice in the gentle art of disentangling. They all avoided looking at each other as they got ready to take wing and fly.

Esther Park was less embarrassed than they were. "Ah well," she said brightly, "I'm going to see Mrs. Peel. She *must* have known Sartre or Camus." And tucking her notebook under her arm, she pranced off with her spring-heeled step.

"Don't believe she cares a bit," Grubbock said, surprised and relieved.

Or she's learned to hide it through years of practice, O'Farlan thought as he waited. Carla was gathering up her sun tan lotion, and a book, and a bag, and a handkerchief. Now don't go being blackmailed through pity, he warned himself, or else you'll have Esther Park around your neck for the rest of the month. He looked at Carla, and wondered why women had to hang on . . . and on. . . . But suddenly, she looked up, gave her nervous smile; and he felt ashamed of himself.

Carla was saying, "And I want to see Jackson too. I need his advice about riding. I just can't seem to get on a horse without pulling the saddle all sideways." She stopped in embarrassment: why admit it so openly? All the others seemed to take to riding so easily, so naturally. At least, they didn't *look* the way she felt. Jackson was quiet and unworried; he gave lessons without making you feel you were wasting his time. She could learn from Jackson.

Koffing laughed. "*That* dumb bastard," he said in an undertone to Grubbock. "Doesn't know his knee from his elbow, if you ask me."

But Carla's hearing was quick. "I wasn't asking you," she said so sharply that the four men stared at her. If Jackson had been an exiled Communist, no doubt Karl would have approved of him. Then she blinked quickly, bit her lip, and looked at Robert O'Farlan for help.

"Let's get that cup of coffee," O'Farlan said.

"Come on Karl," Grubbock said. "We'll visit Chuck and see if he has any beer left. Pity we killed that bottle last night. That's one thing you learn out here: ration yourself."

"We can go into Sweetwater tomorrow and stock up again,"

Koffing suggested as they walked up to the ranch. "I want to collect my mail, too. I'm expecting some newspapers and magazines. Take a damned long time to arrive. Wonder what's delaying them?"

"Tomorrow, we are having our first long ride. Deep Canyon, remember? That's the scene of Chuck's story about the Indian massacre. I can drink myself to death in New York, but I can't go riding into Deep Canyon. I'll ask Bly to get us some liquor in Sweetwater. She's always shopping there, anyway."

"And if you ask her to bring more than a couple of bottles, she'll open wide her big blue eyes." Koffing laughed, and then imitated Sally as she offered them a drink in the evenings: "Another Scotch, Mr. Grubbock?" He looked with amusement at Grubbock's face. "Why don't you take that third drink in the evenings, anyway? Scared of her?"

"Well, she thinks she's being generous," Grubbock said uncomfortably. If Sally Bly hadn't offered him another drink, he would have resented it. But she offered it. And by taking it, he would have proved he couldn't refuse. In New York, he used to say that he could take a drink or leave it. But he must have taken it oftener than he had left it, for the one thing that annoyed him about Rest and Be Thankful was the fact that the nearest bar was twenty-five miles away. And he hadn't enjoyed finding out that it could annoy him. I can take it or leave it, he told himself angrily.

"You'll be drinking Coca-Cola before she finishes with you," Koffing warned him.

"The hell I will," Grubbock said. Then he halted, looking at the blue sky over Flashing Smile Mountain, and changed the subject willingly. "Hey!" he said, pointing. "There's an eagle!"

CHAPTER XI

Peace, It's Wonderful

HIGH in the blue sky, the eagle soared over Flashing Smile Mountain. It circled slowly, turning in a wide curve, traveling surely with pinions seemingly motionless. Yet it had left Flashing Smile and was over Deep Canyon even as you watched; then past Deep Canyon, past the forests, to the cloud-shadowed hillsides. Its brooding circles brought it lower, its giant wings outstretched as if to cover its kingdom. It seemed to halt. For a moment, its large hard shadow hovered over the trail. You halted too, waiting, watching. It circled once more, alert, majestic, dominating. The black shadow swept over the hillside, betraying the speed and power of the eagle's flight. Then suddenly, as if its body had lightened and had lifted triumphantly in some unseen current of air, it rose high into the sky once more. Your heart lifted, too. But you still watched it, traveling now across the first ridge of mountains, planing over the sea of rocky pinnacles to soar away into the vast stretch of blue.

On the green hillside, there were only the harmless shadows left — the moving clouds; the steers bunching together as they moved down the trail; the three riders urging them on watchfully, bringing them slowly and carefully to new pasture land.

A group of three steers, then two more, then three again, broke from the herd. One of the horsemen spurred his horse into a gallop, as smooth and as effortless as the way the eagle had traveled, flanking the strays, drawing them together, edging them back into the herd with swinging rope and repeated short sharp-pitched yell. Then he waited, his body now relaxed, the horse still eager but obediently motionless, until the herd had passed and he could follow it.

* * *

Mrs. Peel watched the distant eagle until she could see it no more. Then she turned away from the window of the living room and continued with her afternoon rest which, today, took the shape of putting away all the phonograph records in their proper albums. She discovered five beer bottles behind the couch along with the missing third record of Shostakovitch's Seventh. Thank goodness, Karl Koffing still considered it "artistically great." There were so many composers whom he now spurned, and writers, such as Huxley or Eliot, who might never have written for all he ever mentioned them. Mrs. Peel frowned. . . .

Of course, Karl wasn't a Communist. That was what he had said yesterday in that bitter argument. "Sure," Karl had said then, "smear everyone with liberal views as a Communist, so that no one will listen to him."

But now, as she thought about it, it was rather a clever remark. It implied that Communists had liberal views. And yet they hadn't: they followed a philosophy which, when put into practice, killed liberalism.

"What we all need is a thorough training in simple logic," Mrs. Peel said to the album of Shostakovitch records as she patted it into order next Sibelius. "And a thorough training in semantics, too." Take this newly fashionable word "smear," for instance. A "smear" was another way of saying a "lie," nowadays. Yet if anyone had been lying last night, it was Karl; he had been quoting the Communist explanation for everything all evening, and then, when challenged by O'Farlan, had denied he was following the Party line, by saying he was being smeared. If Karl believed he *was* being smeared, then he implied he despised pro-Communist views. If he despised them, why did he express them so constantly?

"If a man refuses meat at every meal, and talks about the virtues of vegetables, why should he say he is being smeared when he is called a vegetarian?" Mrs. Peel demanded of the neat row of record albums. If only she could think of these things, in time to say them at the correct moments! She placed the beer bottles on the table so that she would remember to take them to the kitchen, and looked around the room to see if she had missed anything. Today was

III

Norah's day off, and Drene Travers had been responsible for cleaning the living room. Ah yes, these ash trays. . . .

"I thought someone was with you," Esther Park said behind her. She had come in so silently that Mrs. Peel jumped, and lifted her hand to her heart.

"No. Not at all. I was only arguing aloud. Don't you ever talk to yourself?"

Esther Park had already reached the couch. "No, *never!*" she said quickly. She looked at the empty beer bottles and then at Mrs. Peel. She had her notebook under her arm, the case for her eyeglasses in one hand, and a large straight-brimmed felt hat swinging from the other.

Well there's no need to be so emphatic about it, Mrs. Peel thought.

"How do you like me?" Esther Park asked suddenly, gaily, and pirouetted around. She was in full Western costume, with every possible detail and expense. And, of course, she wore her frontier pants tucked inside her elaborate boots.

"Oh!" Mrs. Peel said. "Why, it's — it's — "

"You never noticed! And I went upstairs especially to put them on for you. They only arrived today. I ordered them in Sweetwater when I came, but of course they all had to be taken in for me." She tugged at the tight satin blouse and the bulging frontier pants. Then she fingered the broad, silver concho belt nervously. "I think the effect is worth waiting for, don't you? I could have got everything in New York, of course, but I *did* want to capture the real Western flavor." Then she smiled as she glanced down at herself, pleased with what she could see, and threw her hat with its striped chin-strap onto a far chair from which it slipped and rolled to the floor.

"Let's have a *long* talk, shall we?" she asked with her most brilliant smile and sat down on the couch. "Tell me about your life in Paris. I love Paris. It's so — *so* — you know! Rome, of course, is beautiful in its own way, and I adored, simply adored Athens. Didn't you? The Aegean . . ."

"Yes, yes," Mrs. Peel said at the end of a wild Baedeker ride which had lasted almost ten minutes, "you love Paris." For they were back there again.

"Of course, the people — " Esther Park said darkly.

"The people?"

"Well, the men . . . Mrs. Peel, what *makes* men like that?"

"Like what?"

"*You* know." Esther Park looked at Mrs. Peel critically. "Or perhaps you don't. Some women aren't so — well — "

"So young? So attractive?" Mrs. Peel's sense of humor reasserted itself. She was smiling.

"Well, it does depend on the woman, doesn't it, after all? But honestly, men are so, so predatory. Do you ever walk in New York?"

Mrs. Peel's amazement returned. "I've lived there since last September," she suggested mildly.

"Have you ever walked in Central Park?"

"Frequently."

"At night?"

"But why at night? I've all afternoon to go walking."

"Then you don't know."

"Don't know what?" Mrs. Peel asked irritably.

"The dangers."

Mrs. Peel looked partly in distaste, partly in pity at the middle-aged woman who faced her so expectantly. "Well," she said, her voice more brusque than usual, "you can stop worrying about all those dangers here. You'll find Wyoming perfectly safe." And probably dull, she thought.

Esther Park smiled. "Is it?"

Mrs. Peel stared.

"Do you know what happened last night? Someone tried to get into my room. I always lock the door, fortunately. But I heard the handle being turned; I heard it. Again and again. Quietly. I thought I would die."

"Why didn't you scream?"

"You don't believe me. You are laughing at me." Esther Park was mortified.

"Miss Park, there are so many noises at night in the country.

113

The wind rises and a window rattles, the temperature falls and a beam contracts, a mouse runs down a wall, a packrat scurries in the attic, a squirrel drops from a tree onto the roof, a coyote calls on a hillside. I used to worry about them, at first, but now — why, we don't even lock the front door any more."

"And I think that's terribly dangerous. I do, Mrs. Peel. There *were* people moving around last night. There were. Dewey Schmetterling left the house and didn't come back for two hours. And I heard Mimi Bassinbrook, too."

"That's really none of our business, is it?" Mrs. Peel rose, and hoped that her guest would take the hint. But she didn't.

"Mimi went to a party at the guest cabin. That's where she went."

"Well, what if she did? Why shouldn't Mr. Grubbock and Mr. Koffing give parties?"

"And the girl who cleans the bedrooms, Drene Travers, she was there too. After she left Dewey Schmetterling."

"How remarkable," Mrs. Peel said coldly, "that you could see so much from your bedroom window."

Strangely enough, Esther Park was silent.

"You really shouldn't worry, Miss Park. I'm sure you — and everyone else — will be as safe here as you want to be. Just go on writing your book. And stop worrying."

"But that worries me too. . . . I did want to discuss My Work with you," Esther Park said, watching Mrs. Peel gather up the beer bottles. "I need your advice. I've so much material, *so* much. It is so difficult, isn't it, when you have too much richness? I mean, to decide just what to use?" She fumbled with her notebook. "Of course, I have the title." She held out a page, and Mrs. Peel saw *The Mirrored Darkness: a Mezzotint in Four Shadows.* "I think 'Mezzotint' is good, don't you? It's so much more sensitive than just saying 'a novel,' isn't it?"

Mrs. Peel laid down the beer bottles. She had waited hopefully for her guests to mention their work to her. Now, one of them had — and if Mrs. Peel was sure of anything at this moment, it was that Esther Park had never written, couldn't and wouldn't. She tried to shake herself free from this idea, but it persisted.

"What is the trouble?" she asked encouragingly, trying to forget all about the title. But the outpouring of words that answered her added to her depressing discovery. She said, if only to dam the torrent, "Well, show me the last chapter you've written so that I can see what you mean by difficulties. I've had quite a lot of practice in reading manuscripts, you know. In the old days, I used to — "

"Oh, I can't, I'm afraid. Mr. Atherton Jones is reading it. He is such a good critic, isn't he?"

In Esther's excited contortions over an excuse, her notebook fell onto the carpet. She bent quickly to pick it up, and the leather case for her glasses fell in its turn. The case hit the ground with a solid thud, the clasp unsnapped, and Mrs. Peel saw the neat handle of a small revolver, just as she was thinking how odd it was that Esther never seemed to wear the eyeglasses she carried around so constantly.

Esther Park looked up and saw Mrs. Peel's startled face. "I had the case made for me, specially," she said casually, and smiled.

"For Central Park?" Mrs. Peel asked, recovering herself.

"I take it everywhere. It is such a comfort."

"But hardly necessary here."

"Oh, you never know," Esther Park said hopefully. She rose. "I think I'll go up to the corral. I suppose you are too busy to walk up? Poor Mrs. Peel, always so busy. We must have another talk soon. Perhaps in your little sitting room tomorrow afternoon? That would be so cozy. I'll *try* to slip away from the others. Mr. Atherton Jones tells me you know all about Sartre." She picked up her hat, and settled it firmly on the back of her head. "Well, see you tomorrow. About two o'clock?" She waved the spectacle case playfully, and clumped on her high-heeled boots into the hall.

Mr. Atherton Jones, Mrs. Peel thought angrily, Mr. Atherton Jones had a number of questions to answer. Mr. Atherton Jones had better have a few replies that were not only quick but plausible. She picked up the beer bottles and the overfull wastebasket, and carried them along with her bad temper into the kitchen.

Mrs. Gunn had just put something into the oven. The kitchen smelled of spices and baking pastry and hot coffee. Robert O'Farlan and Carla Brightjoy were seated comfortably at the long table under the opened windows, talking to old Chuck and Ned. Mrs. Gunn added her comments to the conversation, very much in the way she sprinkled the correct touch of seasoning into a cooking pot.

"I'll get you a nice cup of coffee," she said to Mrs. Peel, with a quick eye for the worried face. She took the empty bottles and the wastebasket, shaking her head over that Drene. She glanced at Ned, wearing his best black shirt too. He might have known he wouldn't find Drene here in the kitchen. Gallivanting around the countryside with that Mr. Schmetterling in his big car.

"Hello, Mrs. Peel," Ned was saying, "how are you?"

"Fine," Mrs. Peel said, giving the correct answer to the correct greeting. "Hello, Chuck, how are you?"

The two men had risen as they welcomed her to the table. O'Farlan remembered in time, only to manage halfway to his feet. He grinned. "I'm getting lazy. Shouldn't have stayed here so long. Mrs. Gunn's kitchen is much too comfortable."

"We might call it the Five O'clock Club," Carla said gaily. The warmth in the kitchen had set her eyes and lips smiling; her face was flushed, and she looked a full ten years younger.

"She's nice without glasses, isn't she?" asked Mrs. Gunn. "Now, if she'll just eat a bit more, she's going to be winning one of these beauty competitions when she goes back to the city."

That, Mrs. Peel decided as she looked at the delighted Carla, was a slight exaggeration, but it obviously did no harm.

"Miss T-bone 1948," Carla said, and then bit her lip, wondering if she had insulted anyone.

But Chuck was grinning. To his mind, the description was apt. Ned half-smiled. Then, by contrast, he thought of Drene. He stopped smiling, stared at the table, and threw Carla into a panic of remorse. She looked nervously at the dark young man with the unhappy dark eyes, quiet, unsmiling now. She couldn't tell whether it had been her silly joke that had hurt him. Then he looked up, saw her watching him, and gave her a reassuring grin. But it was still unhappy. Mrs. Peel had noticed it too, for she began quickly to talk about the eagle she had seen this afternoon.

Ned had his own thoughts, as he sat gravely listening. Where was Drene, now? She was free every afternoon from two until five, and even if he tried to get all the jobs around the ranch, little did he see of her. Out with that store dummy again, showing him the trails from his automobile. Sure, it couldn't last . . . she'd be back, riding in the evenings, listening with a smile, walking around, she'd be back. Sure. But it was hell while it lasted. Don't know if I care for her to be back, Ned thought with hurt pride, not a girl who ditches me so damned quick. Less than a day here, and she ditches me. Don't know if I care. He rose suddenly. "Time to get back to the corral," he said. He didn't want to see her coming in with the patent-leather-hair guy driving up the road as if he owned it.

"See you at the party!" Carla called after Ned.

"Thanks for the coffee," Chuck said to Ma Gunn, and lifted another piece of cake as he followed Ned out of the door. "Sure get tired of my own cooking."

Carla said to Mrs. Peel, "You're invited too; everyone is."

"Just singing and dancing," Mrs. Gunn explained. "The boys thought they'd like a bit of fun, tonight. Miss Bassinbrook has been coaxing them to have a party in the barn. She found out that Ned plays the guitar. And Robb gives a good recitation, too. Writes some of the poetry, himself."

"Songs about sleeping on the wide prairie?" Carla asked, too delightedly.

"You'll all have to perform," Mrs. Gunn said as an answer. "It's only fair if you get a laugh at them that they get a laugh at you."

Carla looked guilty. "But *what* could we do? I can't do anything, really."

"Nor I," O'Farlan said hastily.

"Oh, you'll manage something," Mrs. Peel said. "After all, there are talents in the East, too."

Carla looked as if the idea of the party wasn't quite so amusing now.

"It will be fun, I'm sure," Mrs. Peel reassured her. "Oh dear — " She choked on a mouthful of coffee.

"Burned your mouth?" Mrs. Gunn asked sympathetically.

"The lecture. Mr. Atherton Jones's lecture. It's tonight."

There was a short silence. Mrs. Gunn opened the oven to inspect a large roast, and baste it.

"Too bad," O'Farlan said with a sudden smile. He rose. "I'd better get some work done before dinner, if I'm going to a party tonight. Thanks for the coffee."

Carla laughed. "I bet we aren't the only truants," she said delightedly. "I think I'll go up to the corral now and see Jackson."

"Jackson drove Miss Bly into Sweetwater this afternoon," Mrs. Peel said. The car was being troublesome again, and Sally had had a worrying journey by herself yesterday. The road was a difficult one, all curves and twists as it descended to the plains. Jackson had insisted on driving today, much to Mrs. Peel's relief.

"Oh . . ." Carla said. "Well, I'll go up to the corral, anyway."

"All roads lead to the corral, I'm afraid," Mrs. Peel said as she watched Carla's wrinkled red trousers follow the path to the ranch. "I hope my guests aren't being a nuisance to Mr. Brent."

"No," Mrs. Gunn said thoughtfully, "but — "

"But what?"

"Oh, it all evens out," Mrs. Gunn said, and began peeling potatoes to roast in the gravy of the meat. "Jim feels the corral has given you some trouble, too. Ned telling me that Drene was a good worker!"

"Poor Ned." Mrs. Peel looked as if she were to blame somehow.

"Have a nice piece of cake. It was baked today."

"No, thank you," Mrs. Peel said virtuously. She looked down at her blue jeans to encourage her to resist. I just made it, she thought, just. Now all she had to worry about was to get Jackson for half an hour to herself, to show her the easy way to climb on a horse. There must be an easy way. Everyone wanted to find it: that was the reason so many visits were being made to the corral.

"Don't people out West ever use mounting blocks?" she asked Mrs. Gunn.

"Never heard of them."

"But the horses are so big . . . My stirrup is practically at chin level."

"Pick a hillside," Mrs. Gunn suggested practically. "Plenty of *them* around here."

"I've tried that. Then I find, somehow, that I've got Golden Boy on the upside and I'm downhill, and he looks round at me as if I've lost my mind. Perhaps I should learn to mount from the right-hand side, too, and solve all problems."

"Don't try that, *ever*," Mrs. Gunn warned. "When he's the wrong way round, just move him. Put your shoulder against his forequarters, and shove."

"He weighs eleven hundred pounds, and I'm down to one hundred and thirty-two," Mrs. Peel said gloomily. "What I need is spring-heeled boots. Or a rope ladder — one tied to the saddle horn, to be let down when necessary."

"Maybe you'll pick up a tip or two at the rodeo," Mrs. Gunn said, and counted the potatoes. Not many of the guests would eat them, and that made her work easier, but she shook her head over their lack of appreciation of good food. What use was gravy without potatoes? Well, by September she would be cooking for the boys again and she'd have plenty of potatoes to peel. Poor Chuck, getting tired of his own cooking. And the boys? They'd be glad when September came around. These guests had complicated a lot of lives, and they didn't even know it. Poor Ned, for instance. And poor Miss Bly, running in and out of Sweetwater with lists of this and that to get for them — couldn't they remember all they needed, once a week, and give her some time to enjoy herself? And Mrs. Peel — all she got was just to be plain worn out.

"If I was you," she said to Mrs. Peel (who was at that moment reflecting on Golden Boy and his little ways — except when he decided it was high time to go home, he really was a most amiable horse), "if I was you, I'd stop worrying about them. Let them drop things all over the place, and let them do the picking up or live in a pigsty, whichever they prefer. I'd let Drene go, and save *that* much money — goodness knows it's all costing you plenty, and who's going to pay for the laundry? The first lot went out today, shirts and everything, special two days' service that Milt Jerks offers at double rates, and I bet they'll come back charged to you. And all that liquor they drink at night. They *don't* think, that's all. They give Miss Bly lists of things they find they need, and never calculate the trouble or gasoline or wear and tear on the car with each trip down that road to Sweetwater. They don't *think!*"

Mrs. Peel was still with Golden Boy. She wakened up to the last sentence. "They do," she protested. "Really, it is amazing how much they can think. Whenever we come to a patch of flowers, I can see Golden Boy weighing up the situation. What kind, this time? How long will I get away with it? Two minutes? And if I urge him on, he breaks into a canter just to discipline me. You know what I've discovered? Horses don't only think, they've got a sense of humor. Why, the way he looks round at me if I choose a very steep path, as much as to say, 'Are you sure you mean this? You'll be sorry!'"

Mrs. Gunn said nothing. It did her heart good to hear Mrs. Peel laughing, even at herself partly. You couldn't blame her for paying so much attention to the horse: he was nicer to her than most of the human beings around here. Miss Bly was kept so busy with the shopping in Sweetwater through the day, and riding with Jim in the evenings. And the others were busy too, pestering the boys when they weren't arguing among themselves.

"He's a fine horse," Mrs. Gunn said at last. "And you look fine riding him."

"Do I?" Mrs. Peel was so pleased that Mrs. Gunn refrained from finishing her remarks, which were about to be "if you don't look so nervous."

Mrs. Peel pushed aside her coffee cup. "That was just what I needed, Mrs. Gunn. Now I must go and change the flowers in the living room. They are wilting, and Mr. Atherton Jones would hate to look at faded flowers in between his paragraphs. Oh, but of course, there won't be a lecture this evening. . . . Or will there?" She looked in dismay at the dough now being rolled out on the marble-topped table where Mrs. Gunn's perfections were made.

"Blueberry pie, tonight. That will put him in a good humor."

"Oh dear . . ." Mrs. Peel's worries flooded back, and she remembered all the things she had meant to ask when she had first come into the kitchen. "Mrs. Gunn, what shall we do about Drene?"

"I'd tell her to go. She's little use to us. Just a waste of money."

"But Ned?"

"He'd understand. Besides, he's got his troubles with her, too."

"If only Mr. Schmetterling would leave!"

"That wouldn't improve her work. Carries a duster around as if it would bite her."

Mrs. Peel considered that. She said slowly, "You know, I don't like to discharge her. A month is not a very long time, anyway, to have her around. And she really *is* so decorative. Silent, of course. Does she ever speak?"

"I don't mind that. Norah talks too much." Mrs. Gunn had been hurt.

"Norah's a bright girl, Mrs. Gunn. She's in her third year at college, isn't she?"

"Yes," Mrs. Gunn said with justifiable pride. "And even if I say so, she's a pretty girl. Not Drene's style, of course. Thank heaven for that."

"But Drene isn't a bad girl. . . . I mean, she attracts men; but you can't blame her for that, Mrs. Gunn. Now, can you?"

Mrs. Gunn pursed her lips. "She doesn't try to hinder the attraction. She's going to do some riding at the rodeo." Mrs. Gunn sniffed openly.

"Then I couldn't discharge her, not now," said Mrs. Peel in relief.

"Why not?"

"Well, the rodeo probably means a lot to her. It would be a blow if she were to miss it because we had sent her home."

"You sort of like her?" Mrs. Gunn was scandalized. "Why, she's only good for posing her eyelashes against a sunset."

Mrs. Peel began to laugh. "True," she said. "But consider the lilies of the field . . ."

Mrs. Gunn folded the dough, refolded it, and then rolled it out for the fifth time into a smooth thin circle. "Just like Mary choosing the better part. . . . Sometimes I wonder why any of the rest of us went and chose the other." Mrs. Gunn slapped the dough angrily into a large pie-dish.

"It isn't so easy," Mrs. Peel agreed hastily. "Oh, if only Mr. Schmetterling would leave, that would solve everything, I'm sure. I'll speak to Drene about the cleaning. She always listens so charmingly, as if she wanted to understand. And if she doesn't improve, Mrs. Gunn, then we'll ask her to leave."

"If that isn't too late. For Ned, I mean. His mind isn't on his work, these last few days. Hasn't practised any calf roping, either. Fine showing he'll make at the Sweetwater rodeo. And he's missing other rodeos. He should have entered for two, this week. He will never get enough points to qualify for Madison Square Garden." She shook her head gloomily.

Mrs. Peel had never imagined anything like this. "I shall talk to Drene," she said. "And please believe me that we really do appreciate the work you do, Mrs. Gunn."

"Ah, well," Mrs. Gunn said, mollified, "the back is made for the burden." And she shrugged her strong shoulders, and smiled.

"Ned . . ." Mrs. Peel said reflectively. "Is he the only one who has found our guests, well — troublesome?"

Mrs. Gunn was intent on placing the pie in the oven. Then, as Mrs. Peel waited for an answer, she turned round. "No," she said frankly. "There has been a bit of bother with Mr. Koffing."

"Oh?"

"The boys thought he was kind of funny at first, but he's just getting to be a plain nuisance. Keeps telling them they ought to have a forty-hour week."

"Oh!"

"And he wants to see the land divided fairly among the workers, so that everyone can have their right share. He thinks a lot of a new system being tried in some countries in Europe, where the farmers get twelve acres each. 'But this is America,' Bert says, meaning the grazing is probably different here. Mr. Koffing picks him up wrong. 'All right, then. This is America. Everything bigger

122

and better. Double that twelve-acre estimate. Does that suit you?'
Chuck says, 'Twenty-four acres for me?' Mr. Koffing nods his
head, serious as could be. 'There's plenty of land and too few people
on it,' he says."

Mrs. Peel was speechless.

"He says all ranchers are making fortunes, while people in the
cities can't get meat unless they pay a dollar and twenty cents a
pound."

"He means well," Mrs. Peel said gently.

"Maybe. But he don't *know* much. That's what the boys say. He's
plain ignorant, or he wouldn't talk that way. Chuck says, imagine
us working a forty-hour week when the stock don't know anything
about union rules. When they need you, they need you. And Bert
tried to explain that the steers cost us twenty-six cents a pound, and
that after a summer's work of moving them from pasture to pasture
and giving them feed when the grass isn't good enough, we'll be
lucky to get twenty-eight or -nine cents a pound for them. If it was
a drought year, half of them'd be dying off, and the other half
would be skin and bone and no weight on them at all. But it was
the twenty-four acres that raised the biggest laugh. As Chuck said,
they'd be able to have one steer and a fifth, apiece."

"But didn't they tell him all this?"

"He's not the kind of man who listens to what *you* say. Mr.
Grubbock did, and he asked a lot more questions. But Mr. Koffing
just began talking about the way the ranchers were going to steal
the National Parks."

"But Mr. Brent wants to leave the National Parks as they are!"

"And so do most of us. Our fathers had to fight the big ranchers,
once, when this country was being opened up. We don't forget
that battle. Why, the big ranchers even got Texas to invade Johnson
County, and that's right near us. It was only fifty-six years ago."

Mrs. Peel was at a loss for words. "I'm so sorry about all this," she
said at last. "Oh, the idiot!"

"That's what the boys say."

"What can I do?"

"I'd leave it to Jim and the boys."

Mrs. Peel was alarmed. "Oh no!"

"Don't worry, now. It will all be settled in a nice way. *You* don't think we are savages, do you?"

It was a justified rebuke. Mrs. Peel flushed. "No," she said, and put all thoughts of a fight out of her mind. "I suppose that people who talk too much underestimate those who don't."

The sound of a car returning from Sweetwater drew nearer. It was approaching the bridge.

"Now we can relax, Mrs. Peel." Mrs. Gunn listened to the car. "Running better, too."

Mrs. Peel nodded.

"Don't worry so much," Mrs. Gunn went on in her quiet kindly voice. "The ranch is doing well and your guests are having a fine time. Some of them may not know it until they get back to New York, but they are having a fine time. We've been lucky, too. No accidents, so far. Bert tells me that Fennimore's Dude Ranch has had two broken arms, one broken leg, one smashed jaw, a collarbone, and three broken toes this summer."

Mrs. Peel could only say, "And that could happen here, *too?*"

The moving cloud of dust traveled slowly down the trail towards the south pasture. The herd of a hundred and fifty steers was coming safely in. Flanking it, Bert and Robb were riding confidently. Jim was following up the bunch, keeping a watchful eye on the stragglers. The noise of the slowly moving herd, the never-ending lowing and bellowing, the heavy plodding hoofs, was broken with the shouts and oaths of the men, the cracking of Bert's bull whip, the changing gaits of the quick horses. The body of sound moved along the peaceful valley, splitting the silence of the mountains as sharply as lightning struck at their peaks. Then the babel of noise receded into a diminishing chord, and the quiet of the hills returned.

The new wire fence was ready around the south pasture. Chuck and Ned had ridden up to open the gate, and then had taken a wide sweep over a rough hillside to meet the herd without turning it. Robb gave them a whoop of welcome: all hands were needed now for the last stage of the long journey. The riders, in careful formation, headed the leading steers towards the gate. The strays at the edge of the mass of brown-coated, white-faced steers crowded back towards the others. The leaders had sensed water ahead of them. The herd's lumbering pace increased. There were few stragglers now. Those that had stopped to graze, all along the way, pushed forward as greedily as the others. There were no set fights now, either, except for a bad-tempered lunge at a competitor who was forging too heavily ahead.

"Steady!" Jim yelled at them, "you dumb bastards, steady!" They would be ripping themselves up on the barbed wire, pushed into it by those that followed, blinded by their mass excitement. First, they wouldn't go, and then they'd go with a rush, shoving madly, pushing headlong because they were scared, not knowing what they were scared of, not needing to be scared. It was only with the mens' cursing and yelling and a cracking bull whip that they'd calm down. The damned silliest bullheaded bastards. Jim Brent yelled again and spurred his horse on. So did the other cowpunchers, as they tried to brake the pace of the herd and yet keep it bunched together.

The cow ponies moved quickly, carefully, obeying the least command. They were as alert as the men, as quick to feel sudden trouble. They were good cow ponies, well trained, and they enjoyed knowing that. They patrolled the flanks of the moving column watchfully, proudly. And at last the steers, persuaded into a reasonable pace by swinging ropes and shouts, began to move into their new pasture. The horses stood still now, surveying a job well done.

Down at the corral, Mimi and Carla stood with Grubbock and Koffing, and they watched the horsemen on the sloping hillside. They said nothing, just watched.

The last steer was through the gate. The riders waited until Ned closed it securely. Then, grouped together, talking a little, laughing, they rode at an easy pace down to the ranch. If they saw the watchers by the corral, they gave no sign.

Koffing moved away, back to the house. Grubbock, with a last look at the hillside, followed him. Mimi and Carla were still watching.

*   *   *

The hum of the car filled the yard. "Yes," Mrs. Peel agreed, as she listened, "it sounds *much* better." She went to the door to welcome Sally and Jackson with their armfuls of parcels and bundles.

"How was it in Sweetwater?" she asked.

"Hot as hell," Sally answered. And Mrs. Peel asked no more questions.

Jackson counted the parcels, nodded, went back to the car for one they had overlooked.

"If it hadn't been for Jackson," Sally said, accepting some tactfully iced coffee, "I'd have had a nervous breakdown right in the middle of Main Street. It was all these first- and second-choice colors in shirts, and six-buttoned cuffs, and blue jeans guaranteed to shrink just two inches, that nearly set me off." She glanced at the long shopping list and shook her head. "Zero hour was three o'clock, with the sun at its hottest. I was tempted to buy an egg and fry it on the sidewalk in front of the Bank. Only, we hadn't our camera along to take the picture of the year. Camera . . . Oh, Jackson, we forgot Mr. Atherton Jones's films. *Oh* blast!"

"Well I'm glad to see your language has been cooled by the iced coffee," Mrs. Peel said. She eyed all the packages on the table. "Didn't Mr. Grubbock order some liquor, though?"

"Not today. Perhaps his waistline has something to do with it."

"One does become conscious of one's waistline on a horse," Mrs. Peel agreed and looked virtuously at the cake which Jackson wasn't refusing.

"You'd wonder why they don't get all the things they needed once a week," Mrs. Gunn suggested, as she set aside the batch of rolls to rise and began splitting the pea pods into an enormous bowl. She looked at Sally pointedly.

"They still have the New York corner-drugstore complex . . . open twenty-four hours a day just around the corner. But that's an idea, Mrs. Gunn. Worth trying, perhaps. Now, I'll clear all these packages into the library, and set up shop there. And I'll give you a hand with the dining-room table. I bet Drene has forgotten it is Norah's day off. Margaret, there's a party tonight. Jackson is going to teach us the czardas."

126

Jackson grinned, and interrupted his conversation with Mrs. Gunn about the merits of their horses to say he had forgotten most of the steps.

"Then you invent them. No one will be any the wiser."

"Bert dances a nice Varsoviana," Mrs. Gunn said.

"It will be fun," Sally said, and wondered if Jim Brent would be there. "I suppose *everyone* is coming?"

Mrs. Gunn nodded, and watched Miss Bly's happy face with interested speculation.

"I'll be late," Mrs. Peel said gloomily. "After all, one of us must turn up for the lecture."

Sally said, "I had forgotten all about it!" She looked at Mrs. Peel in dismay.

"I'll handle the situation," Mrs. Peel said. "It's my turn to struggle through a temperature of ninety in the shade."

"Ninety-six," Jackson said proudly, and helped Sally to gather the parcels together.

"The nicest thing about going to Sweetwater is coming back here, high up into the mountains and the fir trees and the rushing streams. You know, Margaret, the name of Rest and Be Thankful really means something."

Jackson was no longer smiling. He stared at the parcels in his arms thoughtfully, and a dark gloom settled over his face.

Mrs. Peel watched him anxiously. "Jackson," she began timidly, and then she decided that her question would be better asked when she and Jackson had no audience. Did he really dislike being here so much? Every time anyone praised Rest and Be Thankful, he looked sad and thoughtful. Were Atlantic City's attractions so powerful, even at the distance of two thousand miles?

Jackson had looked up at her as she spoke, but fortunately Earl Grubbock and Karl Koffing appeared at the kitchen door.

"We've been waiting for you," Grubbock said. "We had an idea we'd go riding before dinner, but our horses weren't so easy to catch. What about a lesson in lasso work, Jackson?"

"Roping takes a few lessons," Mrs. Gunn suggested.

"Then the sooner we start the better. What about now?"

"Go ahead," Sally said. "And I got that thirty feet of rope you wanted. There it is on the table, under the straw hat for Mimi. Tell her that it's waiting here to be dipped in the trough and shaped into a bullrider's crush."

Jackson picked up the rope. "It will have to be stretched," he said with a most professional air. And the three men left.

The women watched them go. Perhaps they *are* enjoying themselves, Mrs. Peel thought hopefully of her two guests. But Jackson? The truth is I'm afraid to ask him if he wants to leave: what isn't asked, isn't answered.

"I noticed some of them were looking at the fishing rods in the hall," Mrs. Gunn said. "That was real smart of you, Miss Bly."

"What was?"

"To leave the fishing rods in the rack in the hall and never suggest fishing. I kept wondering at the waste of all that tackle, until I saw the men having a look at it this morning. They'll be taking pack trips into the mountains, and they'll all quieten down and stop arguing except about the fish they didn't catch. Real smart of you."

Sally laughed. "I begin to think you see right through me, Mrs. Gunn." Then she flushed, wondering just how much Mrs. Gunn did see.

Mrs. Gunn smiled. It might have been with pleasure as she looked round her kitchen at the well-ordered preparations for dinner. She opened the door of the oven and basted the roast methodically. "Everything is going to be all right," she said as Mrs. Peel and Miss Bly left her.

Prender Atherton Jones, having gargled his throat, changed his tie, and gathered his manuscript together, came downstairs. This, he decided, even if he wasn't being paid his minimum two hundred dollar fee, would at least be useful practice. For it was a new lecture, still to be timed for length, tried for effect, and groomed for next season's stardom.

There was unusual silence in the house, and only Mrs. Peel in the library. Through a half-opened window, came drifting the far-off sound of a four-part chorus. "The natives sound festive," he said to Margaret Peel with a smile. Then he looked once more at the empty chairs, and somehow they became emptier as the distant singing surged to a crescendo.

Mrs. Peel said quickly, "Prender, the most awful thing has happened. We all thought today was tomorrow!" She crossed over to the window and shut out the close harmony. It sounded most inviting, she thought regretfully.

"Today was tomorrow?"

"Yes, they thought the lecture was tomorrow." She turned to face him, and tried to smile. "You know how dates get all muddled, out here."

"I don't know," he said stiffly, still too shocked to be angry.

"Everyone is crushed."

"So I hear," he said bitterly.

"And they *are* looking forward to hearing your lecture tomorrow."

"Then they'll be disappointed." His hand smoothed his hair. "And of all the excuses — today is tomorrow, yesterday is next week, Friday was Sunday. . . ."

"Prender," she asked gently, "what *is* today's date?"

"It's the — " He hesitated. Perhaps Margaret was right. It was inconceivable that anyone would have willingly forgotten his lecture. He gave a wry smile and looked down at his notes. "It would be useless to give the lecture. I haven't written it down to the level to which their minds have obviously sunk." But he still fingered, almost regretfully, the pages of his manuscript.

Mrs. Peel, knowing suddenly what she had to do, said bravely, "I would be sorry to miss the lecture. It's new, isn't it? Would it be too much trouble to read it to me?"

"Not at all," Prender said, his eyes no longer tight and hard. He added, with an attempt at diffidence, "That is, if it isn't a bore for you." He watched her face. Then he said, "Would you time it, Margaret? And let me know if the peroration is too sudden, won't you?"

"Why, of course!" she said, as delightedly as she could. She chose a chair to face him and composed herself into the eager listener. She tried to forget the insistent lilt of a folk dance, beating out its gay rhythm, faint, far-off, and yet tempting.

Prender stood beside the table, adjusted the lamp, poured himself a glass of water, clutched his lapels, cleared his throat, and began. "An obvious manifestation of the intellectual turmoil . . ."

It's "Turkey in the Straw," Mrs. Peel thought. She restrained her tapping foot and set her eyes upon the clock.

CHAPTER XII

Problem and Paradox

Prender Atherton Jones brushed his hair, admired its effect against the deep tan of his skin, looked approvingly at a diminishing waistline, and walked away from the mirror in a sudden attack of good temper. It didn't last long. From his bedroom window, he looked down upon the garden. Esther Park was sitting there, and none of the others. She looked up suddenly as if she had felt his glance, and he drew back behind the green curtain.

They had been here over a week now, he thought bitterly; and she still haunted him. If he slipped out through the kitchen, he might reach the corral unseen. But what then? In his depression, he had to admit that riding on Sunday mornings in Central Park might be enjoyable, but riding on a Western saddle, up and down mountains, edging along canyon trails, was quite another thing. It wasn't riding. He had shown both Grubbock and Koffing, neither of whom had ever ridden before, the correct way to sit a horse and to post. They hadn't listened. Instead, they were out-cowboying the cowboys — slouching on the saddle, sitting the trot, breaking into a canter to pass him on the trail, urging their horses into a gallop (which they insisted on calling a lope) to leave him far behind. The women were just as bad: they watched him tolerantly as he mounted, and they didn't seem to object to the barbarous lack of either mounting block or hand-up. And yesterday, when they had been approaching one of those interminable gates, Mimi had said in front of O'Farlan (who had only begun to ride and admitted he just hung on and hoped for the best)—"Let me open this one, Prender. I can do it easily." That was enough.

He looked cautiously around the curtain. Esther Park was still there, sitting beside his comfortable chair. He frowned and picked up the latest copies of *Vista* and *New Dimensions*, which had just arrived across the Atlantic. He was cheered by noticing a promising article on Kafka in *Vista*, and a most interesting analysis of the new and almost unknown poet-philosopher Wehmut Schaudichan in *New Dimensions*. (Schaudichan's doctrine of Atomism was definitely on the way up.)

He might find peace to read in the library. No one used it nowadays. They were always out riding, or fishing, or picnicking, or talking to the cook in the kitchen, or watching the cowboys around the ranch. Of course, if he had been given the guest cottage, with its bedroom and sitting room, all would have been well. Instead, Grubbock and Koffing shared it. They seemed to use it mostly for parties, which were invariably over before he ever heard of them. It also seemed that no one over thirty was asked to these parties. He compressed his lips and gave a parting look in the mirror.

In the library, Mrs. Peel was talking to one of the cow hands, the tall thin fair-haired one.

Mrs. Peel looked up to say, "Don't leave, Prender. I was giving Robb a book he might like. *Martín Fierro* . . ."

Robb looked at the book in his hand. "Thanks a lot, Mrs. Peel. Now, I'll be getting back. We had a bit of trouble with two of the colts."

"Where?" Mrs. Peel asked anxiously.

"Down the road a piece. The little fellows got on to the wrong side of the fence from their mothers."

"And they tried to get through?" Mrs. Peel was horrified. "Oh, that dreadful barbed wire! Why do you have it, Robb?"

"A steer don't understand anything else." He looked at the book again. "Well, I'll get going. I'll take right good care of this, Mrs. Peel."

"What will happen to the colts?"

"Jim and Bert are taking them to the vet. They'll mend. They're young enough." He was wishing now that he hadn't mentioned the colts. Mrs. Peel had a soft heart. That was what the boys liked about her. Didn't think of herself all the time. He looked at Atherton Jones, and his quiet blue eyes were no longer warm and friendly. He pulled his hat down over his brow and left.

"I do hope it wasn't any of the palominos," Mrs. Peel murmured anxiously. "I wonder if they'll be scarred? Robb said they would mend, though. You know, Prender, there is always some tragedy going on here. To look at these mountains, you'd think there was nothing but peace and safety. And then you see the bleached bones of a horse on some lonely hillside — 'one that didn't get through the winter,' as Bert said to me when I asked him. Or you come across a canyon where every tree is splintered and charcoaled. . . . Only last week, one of the young steers fell down a precipice and broke its legs. The eagle got at it. You've seen him, haven't you, soaring over Flashing Smile? And last spring — "

"Yes, yes," Atherton Jones said with a touch of amused impatience.

Mrs. Peel was suddenly nettled. "How can you stay here without being interested in everything that goes to make this place? A ranch isn't just a Madison Square Garden show put on to amuse Easterners. It is something that lives, and has its own life and its own problems."

"Well, the despised Easterner has *his* own problems," Prender Atherton Jones said. "I've quite enough, without starting to imagine a young colt entangled in barbed wire. You and Sally were always inclined to dip deeply into local color. In Paris or Rapallo, that could make sense. But here — my dear Margaret, where does it lead you except to start thinking like a farmer, acting like a yokel?"

"Yokel!"

"Certainly! They call us 'doods.' When they tack such names onto us, then they are merely asking for an equivalent response. Besides, what else is in their minds except horses and weather and cows?"

"Steers," Mrs. Peel corrected firmly. "Let's have the *mot juste*, Prender. You were always a stickler for that. And what's in their minds? What is in anyone's mind? You've got to delve deep down for that, wherever you are. You shouldn't underestimate people, Prender."

"I? My dear Margaret . . . only yesterday Sally said I over-estimated people!"

133

"So you do, Prender." Then as he watched her with a puzzled, tolerant, almost pitying smile, she said a little angrily, "You overestimate people who have a reputation, and you underestimate those who haven't. Take Robb, for instance."

"Who on earth is Robb?"

"The young fair-haired cowboy from Montana, the one who writes poetry. Why, you just saw him!"

Atherton Jones smiled. "And does he sing over the radio, too?"

Mrs. Peel ignored that. "Why do you think I was giving him Hernández's *Martín Fierro* to read?"

"Why not Whittier and Longfellow?" Prender Atherton Jones asked with a continuing smile.

Mrs. Peel looked at him. "Robb had a schoolteacher who liked poetry, and got him interested. Robb can also write poetry." But Prender had picked the most comfortable chair and was examining the contents list of *Vista* with a thoughtful frown. She moved over to the window and glanced out to see whether the early clouds had blown away or would she need her raincoat this morning. "Old Chuck said we were in for a change," she said in a puzzled way. The sky looked much brighter to her eyes. "Why, there's Esther Park. Waiting for you, Prender?"

"I beg your pardon, Margaret?"

"All right, I'll leave you in peace. If you get any with Esther Park around, that is."

"Is she still out there?"

"She's coming this way, actually."

He rose quickly. "Margaret, let's go to your sitting room. We can go on discussing your cowboy poet there. What kind of stuff does he write? Four-line stanzas?"

In order to answer him, Mrs. Peel had to leave the library, too. He had crossed the hall at an amazed speed, for he was already in her private sitting room, and once she entered he closed the door swiftly and locked it.

"Ssh!" he silenced her. "It's the only way. Don't answer if she calls."

Esther Park didn't; she knocked, and she tried the door handle, but she didn't call. They listened to her footsteps leave the hall.

"Poor Esther . . ." Mrs. Peel said. She frowned at Atherton Jones. "We shouldn't have done that!"

"I'm being driven crazy, Margaret. I simply can't stand it." He sank wearily into the deepest armchair and looked around the room with approval. "Do you use this place much?" he asked suddenly.

"I'm afraid we don't use it as much as we had hoped," Mrs. Peel said with gentle irony.

"A pity to let it go unused."

Mrs. Peel suddenly realized where the current was setting. She looked embarrassed, wondering where Sally was, offered Prender a cigarette, and sat down. "Oh, it isn't altogether uninhabited," she said. "Now, about Robb. He has real talent, a lot of instinctive taste, and a surprising amount of reading behind him. I was wondering, Prender, if you could advise — "

Prender said, "You know, Margaret, I think the cottage would have been more suitable for me. I do need a room to work in, and my bedroom — charming, of course, and most comfortable — is distractingly bedroomish. The cottage has a pleasant sitting room."

"If Dewey Schmetterling had not arrived with you, Prender, you could have had the cottage. He really complicated all our plans. Or didn't you guess? I sometimes wish that Karl Koffing hadn't been so quick to suggest he would share the cottage with Earl Grubbock. Then Dewey wouldn't have got a bedroom to himself. In fact, he would have had to share yours, and he wouldn't have stayed on." That would have solved several problems. Mrs. Peel thought of the beautiful Drene, whose dusting and mopping were more absent-minded than ever. Dewey Schmetterling had been with her constantly for a full week; and then, in these last three days, he hadn't been with her at all — as if he were avoiding her. Yet he still stayed. And Drene looked still as serene and aloof. And poor Ned was still ignored, still waiting, still hoping.

But Prender's indignant voice interrupted Mrs. Peel's thoughts about Dewey and his unfathomable behavior. "And I was to suffer Dewey in *my* bedroom so that he would leave quickly?" Prender was asking. "Margaret, really . . ." He was hurt and horrified.

"Well, *we* aren't exactly responsible for having him here."

"Now, you know that was a mistake. I've admitted it." It was so like women to keep reminding you of small errors in judgment. "I don't see why I have to be the only one who suffers for it."

"The *only* one?" Mrs. Peel thought of Ned.

"Or why I have to bear the brunt of Esther Park."

"I've borne a little of that brunt, myself, in this last week," Mrs. Peel reminded him. "I don't even get my siesta, any more. . . . Prender, frankly, why is she here?"

Atherton Jones smoothed his hair, lost the look of martyrdom, and said with his most engaging simplicity, "Frankly, Margaret? It was a mistake."

"What? Another one?"

"My secretary's mistake, this time," he said quickly. "Esther Park had enrolled for my Literary Festival, and my secretary included her name on the list that was sent to Sally in New York. Sally was so hasty about phoning all the writers on it, that the damage was done before I could stop it."

"But —" Mrs. Peel began. Then she halted, completely bewildered.

"I *am* sorry. I apologize for my secretary's stupidity." He looked so miserable, at having unloaded all this unpleasantness on his friends in Wyoming, that Mrs. Peel didn't have the heart to question him any further.

"There's no need to look so hurt, Margaret. Mistakes do happen," Prender went on. His voice was too assured, again.

Mrs. Peel looked at him quickly. "I'm more than hurt. I'm inclined to be really angry. Doesn't she realize she is taking up the place of someone who could have benefited from this holiday? She can easily afford to pay for her own holidays, judging from what she spends on clothes and liquor and all these extras she is forever ordering from Sweetwater. That's the only thing she *has* got — money."

"Well, that is scarcely her fault: her people are frightfully rich. But they spend their money wisely. They bought Shenquetucket Island, and restored the manor house and village. It is now one of the early colonial showplaces, you know."

"And Miss Park is part of it, no doubt. All she needs is a village pond and a ducking stool to complete the illusion."

"There's no need to be so upset, Margaret. After all, *I* am the one who suffers. She haunts me. You must have noticed it. That's why I'd like the cottage, where I can have my own sitting room and a door to lock."

"You knew her before we did," Mrs. Peel said sharply. Then she stared at him as she realized he had known, too, that Esther Park had only the desire, but no talent at all, to be literary.

The doorknob turned and then rattled. "Are you all right, Margaret?" It was Sally's voice.

"What's the idea?" she asked as Mrs. Peel unlocked the door and she entered. Then she saw Prender Atherton Jones, who seemed as ruffled as if she had interrupted an assignation. Sally looked at both of them with some surprise.

"We were hiding from Esther Park," Mrs. Peel explained quickly.

"The coast is clear now," Sally said, looking pointedly at Atherton Jones. "Miss Park waylaid me in the yard and talked to me for full fifteen minutes. When last seen, she was heading for the corral. And there, she'll pester Jackson until he hands in his resignation and escapes from the lunatic fringe to the comparative sanity of Atlantic City. Why don't you go and rescue him, Prender? After all, he is the totally innocent bystander."

"I'll be in my room if anyone wants me," Atherton Jones said without looking at Sally. His parting glance at Mrs. Peel was reproachful.

"Sally — you were almost rude," Mrs. Peel said worriedly as the door closed behind Prender Atherton Jones. But so was I, she thought; I should have offered him the use of this sitting room when he wanted it.

"You might have been really rude if you had talked to Miss Park for fifteen minutes. She is going highly literary, this winter: she's helping to back a 'little' magazine in New York. And didn't I hear Prender mention an editorship of a little magazine this winter? There's your problem solved: now we know why Miss Park is here.

He daren't say no to any of her whims, not at this stage of his plans. She's the money behind his magazine."

"Oh, no!" Mrs. Peel was shocked. "I can't understand it. He isn't — well, I mean, he can be so likable, so charming. But he really hasn't behaved too well since he has come here. What's gone wrong with him?"

"Nothing. He is as he was and always will be. We are just seeing him more clearly. It is so easy to be charming and likable *if* you don't foot the bill. It is so easy to be liberal *if* someone else pays. And I don't mean money, either, although he is quite adept at that too. Prender is the supreme paradox, Margaret: the egotist who believes in his own unselfishness, the materialist who condemns materialism."

"Then have *we* changed that we can see him more clearly?"

Sally shrugged her shoulders. "Perhaps. Or perhaps it is the background that puts him into proper proportion." She pointed to the window, and Mrs. Peel looked and saw the soaring peak of Flashing Smile. Below it, lay the deep gash of canyon which led to more mountains, more forests, more mountains.

"Perhaps," Mrs. Peel agreed. "These mountains shrink us all to little men with little problems. Very little problems." For several moments, nothing more was said.

"He isn't happy here," Mrs. Peel said suddenly. "Why doesn't he leave?"

"Egotists have pride. They don't like to admit that mountains can make them or their problems as little as they are." Then Sally looked at her watch and said, "Heavens, what happens to time out here? I ought to have been halfway to Sweetwater. What about the little problems on this blasted shopping list? Nothing to add?"

"Nothing," Mrs. Peel said with a smile. "Well, you've solved the riddle about Esther Park as well as Prender for me. I wish you could do something about Dewey, though."

"Why not convince Esther Park that Dewey has succumbed to her fatal charms, and let her chase him away?"

"Her charms might be more fatal than you think. Remember her gun." Mrs. Peel spoke lightly, but she was beginning to worry again. How did you get someone as determined as Esther to hand over that ridiculous gun? Prender had laughed when he heard about it, frankly disbelieving. Earl Grubbock had thought it was a joke. Even Sally didn't take it seriously. And Mrs. Peel hadn't had the courage to speak to Jim Brent about it: why convince him that Easterners were neurotic? Or he might possibly think it was only Esther's idea of Western dress. Heaven only knew that was peculiar enough.

Sally was talking about Dewey. "I've a theory," she announced.

"I've given up all my theories about him," Mrs. Peel said, discarding Esther's gun and thinking now of Drene and Ned. "He took Drene from Ned. He spent a week with her. Then suddenly, overnight, he began avoiding her. Yes, avoiding her. Yet, he stays here and he makes no move to leave. I give up."

"He's in love."

"*What*?"

"With Drene. For the first time in his life he is really and truly in love. And he doesn't want to be in love with Drene. He wants to leave. And he can't."

"But why avoid her, why sit around by himself, why?"

"Because he can't bear to find himself in love with her. Imagine what his elegant friends in London and New York would say if they knew! Can you imagine what *he* would have said if someone like Prender had fallen in love with a cute little girl with cute little bows in her hair? With someone who did tricks on horseback? It would have been a field day for Dewey, and he knows it."

"But what makes you think — oh, it's nonsense. Not Dewey. Complete nonsense."

"He was attracted to Drene from the first."

"Good material for his next satire. You *know* Dewey."

"It may have begun that way. In that case, there is justice in this world; for he is suffering plenty, now. Have you noticed him in these last few days? Silent, nervous, unobservant. He doesn't even enjoy coining a phrase about people's mistakes any more. He doesn't even notice their mistakes."

"He's probably bored."

"When he is bored, he leaves."

"But she scarcely utters a word!"

"That might have its attractions."

"Whatever gave you this fantastic idea?"

"Dewey likes to ride, but he doesn't risk it here. Drene is so good that he doesn't want her contempt. Instead, he took her out in his car, where he could do the impressing."

"And he hates to use his car on these roads. He lends it to no one." Mrs. Peel looked at Sally, half-convinced. "No," she said suddenly. "It won't do. Not Dewey. Think of all the women he's had, and never been in love. Besides, they only met less than two weeks ago."

"Time doesn't matter when you fall in love," Sally said, and her cheeks colored slightly.

"What about Drene?"

"I can't guess about her."

"No one can," Mrs. Peel agreed. "Would that be one of her attractions for Dewey?"

"Could be. And she's a study in contrasts. She looks the most helpless piece of decoration, and yet she arrived here, complete with horse and dog, all the way from Las Vegas. That takes sense and courage."

"I've always admired her secretly for that," Mrs. Peel admitted. "Not one of us women here could have done it." She shook her head in defeat. "I've tried to imagine myself traveling from New Mexico to Wyoming with Golden Boy in a trailer."

"With sacks full of carrots?"

Mrs. Peel laughed. "Well, they do get results. He comes now when I call his name. He doesn't need to be lassoed."

"Roped, darling. Don't use lasso in Wyoming any more than you'd tuck your trousers inside the legs of your boots or wear a diamond clip on your bathing suit. Well, I'll have to rush. . . . Dewey and Drene have made me later than ever."

"Couldn't you telephone to Sweetwater and get the obliging Milton Jerks to deliver?"

"I would. Except there are colors to be matched, and stripes just so broad and no broader. Not to mention rodeo ties — those little sawed-off things that look like rabbit's ears when they are knotted."

"What gave our guests that idea?"

"I assure you I didn't. Good-by, darling. See you at dinner. In a bad temper, no doubt."

"I wish Jackson could go with you."

"He's too busy nowadays. Don't worry. I'll manage."

Sally left. Mrs. Peel, watching the neat figure in its trim jeans and shirt, remembering the clear eyes and the bright skin and the lithe movements, shook her head in amazement. Three months ago, Sally couldn't have driven down that appalling road to Sweetwater. And now . . . Well, we all changed. But as for Dewey Schmetterling — that was something Mrs. Peel couldn't believe. Yet Drene . . . *my gracious silence.*

Mrs. Peel rose suddenly, and went into the living room.

Drene was there, as Mrs. Peel had hoped.

She was dressed, now, in a plain shirt and blue jeans. She wore red bows on her braids, and sneakers on her neat little feet. She was holding a duster as if, to quote Mrs. Gunn, it would bite her. She gave each piece of furniture a gentle flick and a nonseeing look. There was grace in every movement.

She half-turned as Mrs. Peel entered the room and she smiled, tilting her head slightly to the side, holding it there as her large blue eyes (violet-blue, gentian-blue, deep deep blue) widened for a moment and the long eyelashes flickered in recognition.

"I left a magazine here by mistake," Mrs. Peel said quite unnecessarily.

Drene nodded graciously. Mrs. Peel bent her head over the table.

When Mrs. Peel looked up again, Drene was standing by the window. She seemed quite unaware that, as she turned her profile to the garden, Mrs. Peel was watching her in admiration. It was the way she held her head that fascinated Mrs. Peel — the perfect line of cheek and jaw and throat. Does she do this often, Mrs. Peel wondered?

"It's pretty," Drene said, turning round unexpectedly. "You've made it real pretty, Mrs. Peel."

"Jackson did that. He is very good with flowers."

Drene smiled and nodded. So I've heard, her glorious eyes said. Mrs. Peel could almost hear the word "Lupines."

"He's very good with horses, too, isn't he?" Mrs. Peel said quickly.

Drene's perfect eyebrows contracted. "Well . . ." she said at last, and gave a warm smile which took the edge off her unspoken criticism.

"At least, Jackson likes horses and understands them, doesn't he? Of course, few people can ride as well as Ned, for instance. He is superb."

Drene's face was once more in repose and gave no answer.

"Ned's appearance helps, I think," Mrs. Peel went on. "He is just the type we all like to see on horseback, isn't he? Tall and dark and so very handsome. He is very good at calf-roping, isn't he? He is going to enter for the Sweetwater rodeo." Mrs. Peel cut short another *isn't he?* just in time. But it seemed the only way of forcing an answer. "And I heard you were going to do some — some riding at the rodeo, too. We shall all come and see you. I hope you both win."

Drene lowered the long eyelashes. "Maybe," she said. Then she lifted her eyes to the green garden once more. She was a thousand miles away. Perhaps she was thinking of New Mexico, where the mountains rose in sunset colors to steal the glory of the evening sky.

"One thing worries me," Mrs. Peel said gently. "You haven't been riding enough, Drene. You can't win unless you practise, can you?"

There was the suspicion of a frown, the slightest shrug of the neat small shoulders. She was still watching the garden.

Mrs. Peel said, "I hear Ned is going to practise tonight, just after supper. In the south field. We are all going to cheer him on." That had been Sally's idea. Ned needed encouragement. He'd practise hard if people were watching him. Just like any other art, Sally had said: your public kept you encouraged. And so, at breakfast this morning, everyone had agreed to be Ned's public, everyone except Prender and Dewey of course. Dewey never came down to breakfast anyway.

Mrs. Peel hurried on, "You'll be there, too? You'll have a very appreciative audience. But of course you mustn't take *all* the limelight away from Ned." She laughed at her little joke, and Drene smiled. The eyelashes flickered, the head turned towards the garden, and the perfect line was once more achieved.

When Mrs. Peel left the room, an unwanted magazine tucked under her arm, Drene had gone back to dusting. She was once more a thousand miles away. Mrs. Peel was tempted for a moment to stop, to say something, to bring her back. But she went through the kitchen on her way to the corral. She was beginning to see what could have led Dewey further and further into the quicksands.

"I've paid a little visit to the living room," she said to Mrs. Gunn. "And we had a little talk."

"Hope it helps her dusting," Mrs. Gunn said, and went on kneading an enormous bowl of dough.

"It *is* very preoccupied," Mrs. Peel admitted. "Bread-making day? Well, I shan't spoil it. I'll go up to the corral to rescue Jackson from Miss Park."

Mrs. Gunn, left to herself, memorized a new phrase. Preoccupied dusting. Didn't make too much sense, but it had a fine sound to it. A lick and a promise would have been a better way to describe Drene's work. And all these things right under her nose that she never even noticed — the full trash basket, the cluttered ash tray. Why, if they had been a snake they would have bit her! Perhaps all this Mr. Schmetterling business was a mixed blessing for Ned, after all. He was better off without Drene, if only he knew it. If Ned married her, he'd be eating store bread and canned vegetables for the rest of his life. But you couldn't tell a man that when he was in love. When he was in love, his brains weren't in his head.

143

CHAPTER XIII

Snapshots

M IMI BASSINBROOK waited until Sally had left for Sweetwater. Then, with her straw hat in its well-shaped bullrider's crush (Robb and Bert had shaped it for her with the help of the horse trough), she stepped lightly towards the corral. Her red hair was brushed smoothly with only a casual curl allowed to fall over her brow, and she wore one large bow at the nape of her neck. Carla Brightjoy, Esther Park, and Mrs. Gunn's niece Norah had all imitated Drene's two braids, two bows. But Mimi preferred to adapt rather than adopt. She did it most effectively: if there was one thing on which the cowpunchers and the writers, masculine, could agree it was on Mimi. She was, as old Chuck said, a right neat little number. At this moment, with her green bow to match the stripes on her shirt and the color of her eyes, she was a very neat little number indeed.

In front of the large red barn — which was strictly Flying Tail territory, unlike the smaller saddle barn where Jackson was in charge — there were two trucks. Into each, a mare and her colt were being led.

Mimi paused and seemed to consider. Then she crossed over towards them. Bert was there. And her luck was in at last, for there was Jim Brent too. For once, she had guessed right.

"Hello, how are you?" he asked.

She suddenly felt as nervous as a girl of sixteen. She smiled. "Fine," she said. "How are you?" She looked towards the trucks and the colts. "Not so good?" She looked worriedly into his eyes. They were gray. Suited him.

"We've had a little bit of trouble," he admitted.

"So I heard. Are you taking them in to Sweetwater?" This, she decided, was the way a man should look. Not fat, folded, rubber-skinned, sallow. He was carved down to the essentials, physically and mentally. I'm tired of boohaha boys and middle-aged men with a paunch and two ideas to support, she told herself.

"That's right," Jim Brent said. "All set, Bert? Let's get going."

"Mr. Brent . . . would you give me a lift in to Sweetwater? I've some shopping to do, and Sally has already left."

"I don't think you'll find it too easy, riding in the truck."

She smiled, her teeth white against the well-shaped red lips and tanned skin. She tucked a straying curl behind her ear. "I don't mind that. Besides, I'd like to talk to you."

Her frankness brought a smile to his eyes.

"You haven't talked very much to me, you know," she said. "Not even when I ask you to go out riding with me in the evenings. You aren't angry, are you, when I join you then? You know so many interesting trails."

"I'm not angry," he said. He was more angry with Sally, who never seemed to have much time for riding nowadays.

Mimi said, laughingly, "I'm beginning to think you dislike red hair."

He held the door of the truck open for her. "If you're set on coming, climb in."

"Are you sure I am not being a nuisance?" She was already inside the truck.

Jim Brent looked at Bert, and they exchanged a grin.

"We'll bear up," Bert said. He walked over to the truck he was going to drive. He gave old Chuck, who was standing at the barn door, a broad wink as he hoisted himself up. Then he started the engine, and the truck moved evenly and carefully down towards the road.

"It will be a slow ride," Jim said, watching Bert's truck intently. "We have to take it fairly easy."

"Mr. Brent, I do believe you don't want to give me a lift." She had a very charming laugh.

145

"Sure, I'll be glad to give you a lift," he said hastily, and he climbed up into the driver's seat beside her. He looked at her for a moment. She was watching him with a mischievous smile; he found he was smiling, too.

"Was that Miss Bassinbrook in the truck?" Esther Park asked, arriving too late.

"Think so . . ." Chuck answered, and turned to go into the barn. Yep, he was saying to himself, and that's how it's done. He shook his head admiringly.

"Chuck —"

"Sorry, Miss Park, I've got a sick horse on my hands. Got to go and take his temperature."

"May I come too? I've never seen a sick horse."

All open-eyed and pretending to be a little girl, and not even with red hair or a good figure to excuse it. That's how it's done, he thought again, but not to me. He rolled a cigarette.

"He's got distemper," Chuck explained. "You don't want to go catching distemper, do you now?" He concentrated on licking the cigarette paper.

"Well, what about you?"

"Had it three times. Can't catch it no more." He struck a match with his thumbnail and lit the cigarette. He broke the match in two and threw it into the shallow puddle of water beside the trough.

"Well . . ." she hesitated, and then as he turned to go into the barn she started back to the corral. "See you later," she called.

Chuck nodded. No doubt. No doubt about that at all. Then he thought of the pretty redhead who had gone driving into Sweetwater with Jim. Had she picked up any wrong ideas about Jim? When she asked so many goddamned questions about him, it came only natural to tell her he was the biggest and best rancher in three States. It didn't hurt no one, Chuck reflected. Or did it? Girls had funny ideas, no sense of humor at all. And their funniest ideas were about ranchers. Got them from books, must be.

Chuck waited for a few moments, just inside the barn doorway, to make sure the black-haired woman had gone. Estes Park. Queer

146

name to give a woman. A queer woman. He went over to the horse box. "I feel kind of sorry for her," he told his patient, who looked at him dolefully. "She's like a stray hound dog. Pat her on the head just once, and you've got her on your doorstep each morning for the rest of your life. Yes, I sure feel kind of sorry for her. But not so sorry as I am for you, you sonofabitchn old pony. What did you want to go and get distemper for?"

"Jackson."

Jackson's brows lowered. She was back again.

"Jackson, did you ever have distemper?" Esther Park asked.

Jackson stared at her. He turned away abruptly, and went to open the gate into the corral for the returning riders. I may be dumb, he thought, but not as dumb as that.

"Mrs. Peel," Esther Park said, "Jackson has just been inexcusably rude."

Mrs. Peel glanced across the corral. Jackson looked as if he had decided to leave tomorrow. "Oh, dear!" Mrs. Peel said. She wondered if anyone had ever told Esther Park she was the last straw. "Have you seen Dewey Schmetterling?" she asked.

"No. Why?"

"He worries me, that's all. He always seems to be so very much alone, these days." Heaven help me, Mrs. Peel thought. Or is this really me speaking?

"Oh . . ." Esther Park thought over that one. She lowered her eyes to study the ground. She suddenly smiled and looked up at Mrs. Peel. But Mrs. Peel had fled.

"Tomorrow is Wednesday," Earl Grubbock said as he and Koffing, unsaddling their horses, were carefully watched by Jackson. They didn't need his help, now, except for that business of roping their horses in the corral before they could be saddled. But that would come, too, with practice. If Jackson had learned, they could. They were quite sure about that.

"Tomorrow is Thursday," said Esther Park. She was standing,

they suddenly discovered, at their elbow. Grubbock looked startled, then annoyed. She was always slipping up like that, trying to edge in. Why the hell didn't she go out riding in the mornings as all the others did? Instead she hung round the corral, waiting for them to return, setting a kind of ambush for them.

"Today is Tuesday," Grubbock said without another glance in her direction. "Tomorrow is Wednesday and Sally's day in Sweetwater. I've a list of things for her to get."

"Today is Wednesday and Miss Bly left for Sweetwater an hour ago," Esther Park insisted.

"Today's—" Grubbock's angry voice halted. He looked at Koffing. "What's today?"

"Damned if I know." Koffing thought for a moment. "Saturday, we went into Sweetwater with Robb and Bert. Sunday, we recovered. Monday, we went that all-day ride over Snaggletooth. Tuesday. . . . Hell, today *is* Wednesday."

"Well, what the hell happened to Tuesday?"

"Search me." Koffing unfastened the cinch, and lifted off the saddle and blanket. He unbuckled the bridle and slipped it free. He carried the harness into the saddle barn. Then he stood at its door, looked at the dusty corral encircled by its high fence and the hills beyond. The grass was turning yellow, now, so that the fields had a golden color to them. The fir trees were darker by contrast, and at the edge of the highest mountains there was a band of deep purple as if someone had taken a colored pencil and emphasized the outline of each peak.

Koffing looked with pride at a forest-covered canyon, biting deep into a mountain slope. I was there, he thought. Just an hour ago, I was there. He felt good about that. A difficult ride, and he had made it in quick time. He still felt the pleasure of the speed with which he and Grubbock had ridden down the mountainside, over the hills, across the rocky creeks back to Rest and Be Thankful. It had been a good ride.

Grubbock was still trying to coax his horse to let the bit drop out of his mouth. "Come on, Brighteyes. Spit it out. *That's* the way. Good boy."

"Got a cigarette?" Koffing asked.

"Lost mine too. These damned pockets . . . we'll have to get some of those buttoned jobs that the boys wear — one to each pocket and six to the cuff."

"Have one of mine," Esther Park said eagerly. She produced a gold cigarette case with a flourish.

"Not right now, thanks," Grubbock said, and elbowed Koffing aside to get into the saddle barn with his pile of harness. "There you are, Jackson. Didn't need any help today. We'll soon be graduating. Magna cum laude."

Jackson nodded, but he had his own thoughts about that as he looked at the sweating horses. He had better let them cool off a bit before he opened the corral gate to let them get at the trough.

"If you didn't ride so hard, you wouldn't lose your cigarettes," Esther Park said, offering Karl Koffing a lighter to match the cigarette case. "You shouldn't gallop so much."

"No? Look, Miss Park, you just ride your way and I'll ride my way. How's that?" Koffing was smiling, but his voice had tightened as it did when he was angered.

Grubbock, coming out of the saddle barn, wondered how she would take that. She didn't go riding very much these days; and when she did it was at a slow walk with both hands clutching the saddle horn. She blamed a sacroiliac, but the truth was that the other guests had all developed a sixth sense: whenever she showed up at the corral, they formed their groups and rode off quickly. Well, Grubbock thought, she is Mrs. Peel's headache: we didn't invite Esther Park here. He picked up his coiled rope from a bench, and said, "How about some roping practice?"

"I'm going down to the house to see if that wandering mailman has got round to delivering our letters and papers. What the hell keeps them so late, anyway?"

"Still think they are being tampered with?" Grubbock asked with a grin.

Koffing flushed. What was getting into Grubbock nowadays?

"What is tampered with?" Esther Park asked with sudden interest.

"Oh, shove off." Koffing began walking towards the house.

"Did you hear that, did you?" Esther Park asked the corral. But Grubbock was intent on making a loop in his rope, and Jackson was rubbing down the horses.

She looked round the corral and the silent barns and found them desolate. Dewey . . . why, she had almost forgotten about him! She wondered if he'd like a drink. She had been too cruel to Dewey, perhaps. She had seen quite a lot of him for the first evening. And then she had dropped him. Of course, she had Her Work to do. He must understand that. It was the only reason, really, why she hadn't had time to see him. It was shameful the way everyone had been avoiding him. She'd find him, wherever he was, and cheer him up. She set off determinedly towards the house.

Robert O'Farlan straightened his back, stretched his arms, and looked down with satisfaction at the completed paragraph. He re-read it. Yes, it was all right. The second-last chapter finished. Only one to go.

He pushed aside the small table on which his typewriter stood, rubbed his shoulders to ease them, and walked across his bedroom to the window. Go on, he told himself, let out a war whoop, yell your head off, shout out the news. You've got it licked. The last chapter would be easy — it was almost written, even if there wasn't a word on paper. You've got it licked.

But he only leaned against the window sill and smiled quietly. Funny, you never reacted the way you had imagined.

This second-last chapter had been the difficult one. Sally Bly had been right. If you are stuck, leave it; don't force it; go fishing and catch a few ideas. Perhaps. Perhaps not. It won't matter, for they'll come sometime. If they aren't forced.

So he had gone fishing.

He thought with pleasure of the afternoon before him. High trees arched overhead, the sun filtering between leaves and branches, the cool clear water swirling over the rounded stones, a bird's unfinished song and the flutter of bright wings. There, time passed so easily that you lost count, and losing count you felt that there was all the time in the world. No hurry. No worry. Just time. You lost the nagging ache of doubt at your heart, the tight strangle hold of worry round your brain. The chattering waters never raised, never lowered their voice, and kept you company, buried in the peace of a green glade.

Down at the creek's edge, Dewey was sitting with a book on his knees. It had stayed open at page three for the last half-hour. He was wearing gray flannels and a faded blue blazer — a relic of fifteen years ago — with the worn emblem of a minor Oxford college on its pocket. His hair was carefully brushed, his shirt and tie were exquisite, his elegant socks were tightly drawn over his neat ankles. His shoes — he frowned at them. They were the only blemish, beginning to crack where the dust had worn into the grain. It was really too much to have to drive to Sweetwater in order to get them polished. He inspected them with distaste. And yet, in a way, they were a badge of honor: he hadn't let his standards be changed by this place. Not altogether. He glanced towards the living-room windows, carelessly, hardly noticeably. The man who didn't give a damn, he thought. And he didn't. He moved restlessly, the book fell, and as he bent to pick it up he could glance, without fear of being detected, towards the living room. Yes, Drene was still there.

He was delighted to see she had been watching him. Delighted? Nonsense. But he felt suddenly happier than he had been all morning, or since yesterday morning when she had been looking out of the living room window.

I'll leave tomorrow, he decided.

What had come over him? How had all this come about, anyway? I'm stark staring mad, he thought. What had ever prompted him to notice her? Or failing that, for she was scarcely the unnoticeable type, notice her any further? He stared at the creek as if he were mesmerized by the leaps of water flowing brokenly over the stones' uneven surface: the same stones, never changing; the same strands of water, gleaming as they unfolded in the sunlight. Like silk. Like hair, silver-golden hair. He turned his eyes sharply away, and forced them to look down at the page of cold prosaic print.

He would leave tonight.

He should have left here after the third night.

But oh no, she had said, oh no, not yet.

He should have left after the fourth night. But oh no, not yet . . . If she had paid any further attention to that cowboy from Arizona, if she had fallen for Grubbock's passes, if she had flickered her eyes to Koffing's come-hither look, he would have been cured long ago. But she hadn't. She only had eyes for him. Here, she promised him silently, here is something for you alone, yours for the waiting, but oh no, not yet. And he had stayed.

He'd leave now, at this moment. Why not? His bag had been packed for days. And he had stayed. Like a fool.

A fool? He thought of her hair falling loose over her white shoulders, the firm curve of her breasts, the slender, the incredibly slender hips. Diana. Diana of Versailles. . . . In the Louvre, he had stood silently before her. "What, no criticisms?" his companion had asked. (Who was she that day, anyway? The English girl with the ghastly father, the red-faced Marquis — what the hell was her name? Rosalie, Rosamund, Rosalyn?) And he hadn't even had an answer for that, only the wish that Rose by whatever name would drop dead.

He must get her to stop calling herself Drene. Diana was the right name. A year in seclusion, or in a well-chosen background, and he could produce her anywhere. Playing Pygmalion? Well, that might be an experience, too. And with her, he'd bring to life a satire on all women, on all the beauties who had bored or snubbed him, the duchesses, the actresses, the daughters of millionaires. Look at her . . . see what one year and my love can produce. More correct, more elegant, and more beautiful than you, who think you are ordained by divine right to be admired.

He closed the book angrily. I'm leaving now, he repeated, and strode towards the house. He almost halted at the living-room door. But it was silent. He passed it by. He might as well put the book on a shelf, and so he entered the library. But she wasn't there, either.

Instead, Mrs. Peel was arranging flowers.

He slipped the book onto a shelf.

"Did you like it?" Mrs. Peel asked pleasantly.

152

"Amusing." He almost smiled. Then he stood hesitating, looking at the flowers. "You do have a knack, don't you?" he said of the arrangement in the vase.

"Thank you." She looked at him with some surprise. "That's the first real compliment you've ever paid me, you know."

"First? Oh Margaret, come!"

"In fourteen years, to be exact," she said with a smile.

He lifted a cigarette and lit it thoughtfully. If he said it now, there could be no retreat. "I think I'll leave this afternoon, Margaret. I haven't been feeling too well recently — altitude, perhaps. Or it may be Wyoming water. A stupid but rather painful reason for leaving, I admit." Give them a reason over which they could laugh, and they would not look for any other.

"You haven't been looking quite yourself, Dewey. Perhaps you didn't get enough fresh air and exercise. I'm sorry you didn't ride. Once you get up into the mountains, you see the most superb scenery. In fact, it has quite silenced Sally about the Dolomites, as you've probably noticed."

He smiled agreeably. If I see another mountain in my entire life, he thought, I'll vomit. I've had enough scenery watching me make a prize ass of myself. "I'm sure it is superb," he said.

Mrs. Peel finished arranging the roses against a background of delphiniums. "You are supposed to throw away half the flowers when you think the vase is perfect, and begin again," she remarked. "But, really, I couldn't throw any flowers away. I'm not the tortured-chrysanthemum-against-bending-bulrush kind of arranger, I'm afraid. So, in spite of your compliment, I'll never win a prize."

Dewey Schmetterling had no answer. The girl has addled his brains, Mrs. Peel thought. She felt almost sorry for him. Then, remembering his long and happy career among women in Europe and America, she concentrated on feeling thankful for Drene's escape. She'd make a nice gay wife for Ned, who probably knew how to fall in love honestly. There was, she reflected as she looked at the dark handsome face, a limit to what one could get without giving in return. Dewey would have to learn to give. She was suddenly aware that he was embarrassed. This amazed her so much that she stared quite frankly at him.

153

He replaced a paperweight, fumbled with a table-lighter, switched on the lamp and then switched it off again. "Margaret," he began and then stopped. For a moment his face had looked vulnerable, and then it was once more in control.

"Are you going to California?" she asked in the uncertain silence that followed.

"I don't know. I think so. Anyway" — he took a deep breath — "I'll slip away after lunch. Don't mention it to anyone. I hate conscious conversations when everyone feels he has to be polite at the last minute. So I'll say good-by to you now. It has been a very — a very pleasant stay. So kind of you to ask me and all that. Give my love to Sally when you break the news to her. And do it gently. I'd hate to cause her any heart failure. Don't let her be too upset about my departure." He smiled, and left.

Outside in the hall, Esther Park's voice said, "Oh, Dewey! I've been looking everywhere!"

It was all so simple after all, Mrs. Peel thought. We've been worrying how to ask him to leave, and he simply came in here of his own free will and said (with an honest compliment included) that he was going to leave. She shook her head incredulously and then laughed. She crossed over to the bookcase to find the right place for the book Dewey had returned: he had just jammed it in, anywhere. But before she reached it, Carla Brightjoy came running into the room.

Carla's eyes were gay and excited, and her smile was happy. Would Mrs. Peel think her rude if she were to miss lunch? She was invited to a picnic down in the hayfield where Ned and Robb were working today. Mrs. Gunn had put sandwiches so quickly together, and added a blueberry pie to cheer Ned up, and really wouldn't it be fun, she hadn't ever seen haymaking except in movies, of course. Jackson had saddled her horse, and she was going to ride to the field. Alone? Why, of course; it wasn't so far.

By the time Carla's breath ran out, Mrs. Peel had forgotten the misplaced book. She was too delighted with Carla's shining eyes. No glasses, now, either. And the shirttail was tucked into the blue jeans. Her hat, with its brim rolled in the very best bullrider's crush, was set on her head exactly as Drene wore hers. And, as she turned to run out of the library, Mrs. Peel noticed that her straight loose hair was now neatly braided into two short pigtails, with bright blue bows to match the plaid in her new shirt. The stores in Sweetwater must be pleased with all the shopping that was being done. Mrs. Peel wished that Sally, too, could watch the confident little figure, hurrying to take the blueberry pie which Mrs. Gunn had baked for all the boys to see. It would make Sally's trips down to Sweetwater seem well worth while.

Robert O'Farlan came downstairs. He was whistling. Here's another who likes Rest and Be Thankful, Mrs. Peel thought happily.

"Any mail for me?" he asked someone in the hall.

"A postcard," Koffing's voice answered.

They said nothing more. Mrs. Peel moved, as a possible peacemaker, to the library door.

O'Farlan was reading the postcard with a frown. He could see it coming already: next winter it would be "Robert went off by himself to Wyoming and had the most wonderful time. Wives? Oh, they weren't wanted. Were they Robert?" Gay, brave laughter. Everyone else looking at him, laughing as Jenny was, but still looking. He might protest that she had been invited, as soon as Mrs. Peel had found out he was married. But their friends would then be told, "*How* could I leave the children?" Yes, it was coming. Now that she wouldn't be able to make remarks about his unfinished book, there would have to be others to take their place. That was Jenny's idea of marriage: a husband was the natural vent for all your frustrations. Once you unloaded your bad temper over the housework or the children onto him, you could face the rest of the world with a kind word and a sweet smile. Jenny's such a brave darling, her friends always said. When the children reached the age of eighteen and he packed his bag and left, they all would shake their heads and talk of the best years of Jenny's life and men, that's men for you. That a man might resent the best years of *his* life being turned into a desert, like fertile soil soured and eroded through careless misuse, would not be included among Jenny's unhappy thoughts.

155

She might even resent that he hadn't left sooner, when the children were younger, so she could have had *that* to complain about too. He jammed the postcard into his pocket, and walked into the garden.

"Had a good ride?" Mrs. Peel asked Karl Koffing.

"Fine." He sorted through the pile of envelopes and magazines which lay on the hall table. "Came back from Flashing Smile in an hour flat."

"Oh!" Mrs. Peel wondered what the cowboys were going to say about that. Of course, neither Karl nor Earl knew very much about horses. They weren't trying to be cruel; they just didn't know. They'd be worried if they had heard Bert's comments on them. "What's their idea? Gallop their horses off their feet right into the canning factory?" It made Mrs. Peel feel sick even to think of that word. Yet how could she tell the young men that horses could be ruined, could end up in that terrible place as dog food, because they wouldn't be able to get through a winter on the hills? They were both quite convinced they had mastered the job of knowing about horses, and they might even think that Bert, who had been handling horses since he was five, just resented the idea that it only took them a couple of weeks to learn his trade.

"Not bad," Koffing was saying, "considering our horses."

"Oh?"

"They're old, of course. Brent didn't give us any of the five-year-olds, I notice. Do you know how old my horse is? Sixteen, if it's a day."

"That isn't too old, Karl. Why, Mimi's horse is nearly twenty and he looks about ten. Horses last well, out here. That is, if they aren't run to death."

"If Brent had given us decent horses, they wouldn't be run to death."

"But they *are* good horses, Karl." Even Prender Atherton Jones had nothing to say against them.

"You don't catch the cowpunchers riding them. Their ponies are only four or five years old."

"And their ponies are still being trained. Horses aren't even

156

broken until they are about three years old, Karl! And don't blame Jim Brent: I asked him for reliable horses that were calmed down enough so that we wouldn't have accidents."

"They're certainly calmed down." Karl smiled. "Each time I ride into the corral, I can see Chuck standing at his cookhouse door, counting back to 1886 when he first taught my horse to carry a saddle."

There was a short silence. Karl looked down at the table. No mail, he thought. And no sense of humor, either: she wasn't even smiling. She didn't like him because of his politics, so whatever he said would be wrong.

"Karl," she said suddenly, "would it prove anything to you if I asked Jim Brent to let you pick out your own horse for a day or so?"

"I'd like that," he admitted. He had a very pleasant smile when things were going his way.

"Risks and all?" she asked.

"Sure. The more risks the better."

"I'll speak to Jim Brent," she said.

"And he'll refuse," Karl said moving towards the door.

"If he does, it will be for a good reason, Karl."

Yes, a political one, Karl thought grimly. You should learn to keep your mouth shut, he told himself, and just listen to all these hidebound Republicans and moralizing Democrats. Reactionary bastards.

Mrs. Peel watched him leave. The more risks the better . . . Was that how he felt about everything? He was so aggressive, always proving something. But to whom?

Mrs. Peel was still puzzling over that as she went into the dining room to tell Norah that there would be no Carla for lunch.

"Then that will be two places less, today," Norah said. "Miss Bassinbrook went into Sweetwater with Jim."

"Did she?" Mrs. Peel was a little amazed, for Mimi could have gone with Sally if she had wanted to. If . . .

Norah's pleasant voice went on talking about the weather, about the storm that seemed to be gathering; but perhaps it would wait until everyone got safely home from Sweetwater.

"Where's Drene?" Mrs. Peel asked suddenly, noticing that Norah was working by herself in the dining room.

"She likes to change before she helps serve lunch," Norah said, tossing one of her neat braids back over her shoulder. And she seemed different in other ways, too. She was prettier, somehow; thinner perhaps.

"Norah, are you getting too much work to do? I mean, you are supposed to be having a summer holiday as well, you know." Really, I must speak seriously to Drene after all, Mrs. Peel thought angrily.

"I'm having a fine time," Norah said with her quick smile. The pink cheeks deepened in color and the brown eyes widened. Then she hesitated, looking down now at the bowl of petunias on the table. "The only trouble is my aunt," she said slowly. "Mrs. Peel, would you ask her to stop worrying about me?"

"Worrying about what?"

"About the way I do my hair, and the way I wear my hat, and" — Norah raised her eyes — "about going into the dance in Sweetwater on Saturday."

"Well, I suppose we all worry about people we feel responsible for," Mrs. Peel answered. "And if we didn't, we wouldn't care. That would be a heartless kind of world to live in, wouldn't it?"

"And she worries about Earl Grubbock," Norah went on, making her main point at last. "Why, he is only a friend! He teases me about the West and about college and the things I learn there. It makes me feel so — so ridiculous when Aunt Gunn worries about it. There's no harm in it." The pink cheeks were now bright carmine. She was, Mrs. Peel reflected, a very pretty girl, all the prettier for being natural.

"Perhaps your aunt is only worried about Drene and that makes her cross with — "

"No," Norah said quickly. "At least, not altogether. It's all the fault of those war novels. She likes to read in the evenings, you know."

158

"Yes," Mrs. Peel said, "I know." She pulled out a dining-room chair and sat down. "I told her to borrow any book from our library whenever she wanted one. And she's been reading war novels?"

Norah nodded gloomily.

"And Earl Grubbock was a soldier? But so were all the cowboys except old Chuck, weren't they?"

"But my aunt *knows* them. She doesn't know anything about Earl except that he was a sergeant. And there is nothing good written about them in any war novel, is there? It's a wonder to me how we ever did win the war, if all the sergeants were so awful and all the officers were such fools."

Mrs. Peel could find nothing to say. She would like to have smiled but Norah was too serious. And so would I be, if I were Norah, she thought.

Norah said, "I wonder why writers want to make things more difficult for men? Why, in a few years, there won't be a woman left who'll trust a man when he is away from her. And to think it is the men who do that to each other! If it were a woman writer being bitter, you might say, 'Well, she's taking it out on the men, whatever they did to her.' But this isn't a war between the sexes. Often it stops being a war between nations. It's a war of men on men. They really hate each other, subconsciously, don't they? I said all this to Earl when we were arguing, and he couldn't find any answer. I was hoping he could, too."

Mrs. Peel rested her folded arms on the table. She looked at the girl with new interest. Never underestimate people, she told herself once more. Had that been Earl's thought, too?

"Tell me, Norah, you're at college, majoring in what?"

"Modern history."

"Are you going to teach?"

"I'm thinking of journalism."

"Ah, the big city? Chicago? New York?"

"No." The girl smiled faintly. "Three Springs."

"Why didn't you work on a paper this summer? Experience, you know."

"I worked on a paper last summer. But this year, my aunt told me that a lot of writers were coming here. That's quite an experience, too, seeing them when they aren't up on a platform making a speech or signing their novels at a bookstore."

"Oh," Mrs. Peel said in dismay. Then she looked at Norah's laughing, sympathetic eyes. "I expect you've found them very much like any other human beings."

"Yes," Norah agreed. "They're as muddled up as the rest of us. Only some of them *think* they aren't. . . . Like Mr. Koffing, for instance."

Mrs. Peel let herself smile this time. "Did you tell that to Earl Grubbock, too?"

"Well," Norah said politely, "he *did* ask me."

"Did he listen?"

"Why, of course!" Norah was startled. "He — he's very, well — "

"Not at all like the sergeants your aunt reads about?"

"Not one bit," Norah said, laughing now. "But you will tell my aunt not to worry about me?"

Mrs. Peel nodded. She watched Norah leave the dining room. Then she rose, putting the chair back neatly in place so that Norah's capable job of arranging the table would not be spoiled. A movement from outside the window caught her eye. It was Earl Grubbock, pretending to be studying the scenery. And probably cursing me, Mrs. Peel thought. She went out to join him. He couldn't see Norah just now, anyway.

"I was watching the creek," Earl Grubbock said. "Come over here and see this. Look, from this point, you'd think the water was running uphill. A neat delusion, isn't it?"

"Like most delusions." Mrs. Peel followed him and looked. "Why, so it is! A most original creek . . ."

He wondered if this would be a good moment to try to find out how Mrs. Peel would react to fear. (That story of the decaying gentlewoman with a lynched corpse on her doorstep hadn't worked out, so far.) But Mrs. Peel turned to him with such a delighted smile, a smile that made her young and very much alive, that he couldn't find the right question to ask her. Instead, he blurted out,

160

"It's an original place in every way." He looked around at the placid hills. "But I just don't seem to be able to write, here. O'Farlan is scribbling away; Carla's full of new ideas; even Mimi has reached the stage of deciding she isn't a short-story writer and is talking about a novel." Talk, of course, didn't mean you'd get a book written; he'd found that out.

Mrs. Peel had a way of expressing sympathy and interest even without saying a word.

He said suddenly, "I may as well admit it. I'm stuck. Perhaps I'm not a writer after all. Perhaps I'd better find me a permanent job and try to make something out of that." He stared moodily at the creek. But he felt better, somehow, for having put his thoughts into words at last.

"Whether you take a permanent job, or go on taking part-time jobs, I think you ought to keep on writing. In fact, you're the last person here among all our guests who should give up writing."

He looked at her. Her eyes were as quiet and sincere as her voice.

"You've a good style and a sensitive touch," she went on. "All that has been bothering you — " She stopped talking, and began to pace slowly around the garden. He matched his step to hers.

After a minute or two, he said suddenly, "Well, what's bothering me?"

"Advice is wrong unless it is really asked for."

"I've reached the asking stage."

"I said you had a good style and a sensitive touch. That's form. What bothers you is the content, the subject round which you'll wrap your style and tie it up with your touch."

"I write what I know about. I was born and brought up in the South. I know what I'm talking about."

"But do you want to write about it, or do you feel you *ought* to write about it?"

"Both."

"You want to reform."

"What's wrong with that?"

"Nothing. It is needed. Always. Everywhere. But I am never sure whether you can achieve reforms by denunciation as fully as you can by other methods. If people have pride, then denunciation is apt to drive them into a more determined stand. The only people who agree with denunciation and see all its truths are those who are already converted. The others only feel more alienated and bitter."

"You're jumping ahead of me. I haven't got anything published yet." His voice was bitter. "I can't even finish the short story I thought was all sewed up. I can't even manage a short story. I'm one helluva writer."

"Why short stories, anyway? They are much more difficult than a novel. . . . Look, Earl, why not a novel, something where you can show five points of view, ten, twenty if you like? But not just one? For you can't treat the South honestly from one point of view alone. And you know it; deep inside you, you know it. Perhaps that is one of the reasons you don't finish your story. You see, you could only hate the South for her faults as much as you do, if you loved her a great deal for her virtues. But you won't admit them openly, because they'd spoil your argument against her."

He stared down at the grass at his feet.

Mrs. Peel said, "Earl, you may be too gloomy about your work. Perhaps the short story is good, perhaps it only needs more time. I may be very far wrong in what I said."

He didn't reply. He started walking back to the house. Then his anger passed, and he stopped to wait for her. His face was worried, unhappy, but the anger had passed. "This grass needs cutting," he said. "Where do you keep the lawn mower? I'll try my hand at it this afternoon."

Mrs. Peel said, "It's in the garage. Jackson and I will bless you."

"Why didn't you tell us you needed help? We could have pitched in."

"We did ask you here for a holiday, you know. I could hardly start telling you about chores, could I?"

Earl Grubbock looked at her in amusement. "Where have you been living all your life? Look, after I've given this piece of grass a shave and a haircut, I'm coming to see you this afternoon. You can tell me frankly just where Koffing and I can lend a hand around the place. And another thing, I'd like to hash out all this problem about my work. You're the person to help me, if I can be helped. That's all."

Mrs. Peel felt her cheeks flush with pleasure. "I don't pretend to give good advice, Earl. But one thing I *do* know: you mustn't stop writing."

Through the trees, rising over their fringed tops to lose itself in the silent hills, came the sound of the bell in the kitchen yard.

"Lunch," Mrs. Peel said. "And you'll have to eat more, Earl. You've lost so much weight, we must be starving you."

He looked down at his waistline, automatically drawing his stomach in to meet his spine, throwing his chest out and his shoulders back. His skin was tanned, and there was a glow of health on his cheeks. The circles under his eyes had gone, along with the white, pasty, surplus-flesh look of his face.

"You know, when I saw you from the dining-room window," Mrs. Peel said almost truthfully, "I thought Robb had come visiting us."

He grinned. "Robb's got more hair on top."

"It isn't the hair that matters so much, it's this." Mrs. Peel thumped him hard on the ribs. "Well, see you after the lawn-mowing! It's a thirsty job."

"That's a date — but make it something innocuous. . . . What between altitude and isolation, I'm practically on the wagon. It's too much trouble keeping yourself supplied, up here. No bars on the way home, no handy little liquor store round the corner, no one asking you to parties and stuffing a glass in your hand."

"Yes," Mrs. Peel agreed, but she glanced at his waistline and thought it was also pleasant to feel as fit as you looked.

The bell rang again, with an extra clang to warn them that Mrs. Gunn's eyebrows were rising.

"It's a cheese soufflé!" Mrs. Peel said in sudden alarm. She broke into a run. Earl Grubbock followed her, laughing. Helluva lot I've got to laugh about, he thought. But a wide smile was still on his face as Mrs. Peel's pace became dignified again when they reached the hall, and they walked into the waiting dining room.

CHAPTER XIV

Stoneyway Trail Cutoff

S ALLY BLY was late in leaving Sweetwater. She stopped at Milton Jerk's log-cabin filling station. The boy who worked there looked at the Bugatti with professional interest. It was a good car, he said, a bit old-fashioned and queer-looking, but a good car all right.

"I think it needs some more overhauling," Sally said.

"Like to leave it here? Milt will be back from Three Springs in about an hour. He'll give you a lift to Rest and Be Thankful."

"I don't think I'll wait," Sally said, looking worriedly at the sky. The clouds were heavier, the air was hot and still.

The boy looked disappointed. He wouldn't have minded taking that car to pieces and putting it together again. "Guess you're right," he said, looking at the sky too. "Pity you didn't leave sooner. You'd have got a lift from Jim Brent. The trucks were in here, today."

"Were they?" She had seen them. She had seen Mimi, too. And for no logical reason at all, she had avoided them. That was one of the reasons why she had wasted time in Mrs. Bill's Zenith Beauty Shop for the last two hours. One of the reasons. She glanced at her hair in the mirror. Not altogether wasted, she thought. She gave the boy a smile and a wave, and drove off.

The car seemed all right, again. The boy at Milt Jerk's garage was efficient, and she could have left it there during the day for a checkup. Only, a Bugatti was a new experience for him. And Jackson, who had driven this car since they bought it in 1933 in Rome, would like to do the job of overhauling by himself. He'd resent anyone else touching "his" car.

164

The road from Sweetwater wound slowly, tortuously, up towards Stoneyway Valley. Once she reached the valley, the grade would be less steep, and there would only be a steady pull over the old Stoneyway Trail towards Rest and Be Thankful. She drove as quickly as she could, but carefully; for the twists and turns in the road, up through the forests and past the precipices of rock, were difficult. She was too busy concentrating on the road, on listening to the deep hum of the engine as it made the climb, to glance at the view of the plains as it lowered away beneath her. And the sky had darkened enough so that she didn't halt the car above the last turn on the road, as she usually did, to sit for a few minutes and wonder at the shapes and curves and colors of the land. A strong wind rose suddenly, catching the dust up into swirling clouds, bending the tops of the aspens and birches in sudden gusts. It was this threatening storm that decided her to take the short cut as soon as she reached Stoneyway Valley. It was more of a climb, but it shortened the fifteen miles which still lay ahead of her by at least seven. In wet weather, it was impassable. But the recent dry weeks had made it firm. It was narrow, but it was quick.

She swung the car into the cutoff. She was driving confidently now, even enjoying it. The back seat of the car was piled with parcels, but a quick glance behind told her that they were safe, although they jolted around with each bump in the dirt road. And then, it seemed to her that the car, still humming smoothly and powerfully, was traveling more slowly. Halfway up the first hill in the cutoff, it slowed down as the engine strained. She could smell burning rubber.

She thought anxiously, it must be the brakes. But how? Who ever had trouble with brakes going uphill? If she could reach the top of the hill, she'd stop there. But what then? The smell of burning rubber increased, and with it steam started pouring out of the radiator cap. She edged round the last curve on the hill, but the car stopped before it reached the top. It stopped dead, with the engine still humming. She cut off the engine, and sat there for a few moments, trying to make up her mind what to do. The brakes were fast: it was they that had stopped the car. The nauseating smell of burning rubber surrounded her. She looked for water. On one side of her was a pine forest, on the other a bank with a ditch at its foot; but the little stream there had almost dried up. She would have to try it. The radiator cap was smoking now.

She picked up her hat and scrambled down the bank for water, scaring the curious chipmunks that had come out onto a rock to watch her. I'm as scared as you are, she thought, and tried to fill her hat with water. The time she had to wait seemed enormous and frightened her still more. But at last, she had scrambled back onto the road with a hat almost full of water. Then with one hand, she had to pull off the cardigan, which she had worn tied loosely round her shoulders, to help her unscrew the radiator cap; even with its protection, she scalded her hand. And of course, she spilled some of the precious water. It wasn't enough, anyway. She slid down the bank once more.

This time, as she poured the water, and then stood back to look at the smoking dragon, it seemed to her as if the car moved. The brakes must have relaxed their grip, just enough. Instinctively, she dropped her hat and cardigan and sprang towards the front seat to get at the wheel. As she jumped in, she knew she was too late. She even, for a hideously blank moment, forgot what she must do. She got the engine started, tried to get it into first, and failed. Then she tried the brake, but it wouldn't work at all now. The car was moving downhill, preparing to gather speed, veering over towards the bank. She rose, trying to jump out. And the car, as if it were glad to get rid of her, suddenly lurched on the shoulder of the narrow road and threw her out. The swinging door struck her across her back. The jutting fender scraped savagely at her arm, but the wheel missed her. Lying in the road, she was only dimly aware of the car's crashing plunge down the bank.

She rose unsteadily, feeling the intense heat that swept around her. She backed slowly away, watching the mass of leaping flame. She wondered in a dazed way how long the car had been burning.

CHAPTER XV

Cowpoke's Corner

OLD CHUCK thought the stew smelled mighty good tonight, even if he did say so himself. It was nothing fancy, he thought of the supper, but he cooked it clean. And he always had it ready when the boys got in. The potatoes would take another ten minutes, so he went to the door of his kitchen and sat down on the step while he rolled a cigarette.

You're getting old, he told himself. Ten years ago — five, even — he would have gone to Jim and said to hell with all this cooking, and Jim would have given him a real job. He had thought of asking for one. But he knew that if there had to be a man to cook and do odd jobs around Flying Tail, then he was it. A twinge in his left knee, as he stretched out his leg, emphasized the truth of his words. He swore quietly, steadily, imaginatively, for a full minute. Then he rose, a thin slow-moving figure with the thin slow-burning cigarette held in one corner of his mouth, and went across to the barn to see if the sick pony was doing any better.

He looked over at the hillside where the horses roamed at night. They had already been turned out. He halted for a moment, hand on hip, his keen gray eyes narrowed. He recognized and named the horses, even from this distance. He could still see as good as anyone, he thought with some satisfaction. And he could ride better than most. It was the long trips that did for him, nowadays, them and the sleeping in rain and cold. Well, he had it good while it lasted. And there was worse ways to end your days, still working, still being useful. He'd be able to go on working here if he wanted to — Jim was a good boss. Didn't throw you out when you got a bit stiff in the joints. Yes, he'd work here, summers at least, until one day — Well, he thought, as he watched the horses scattered over the hillside, it'll be for me like it is for you. Some spring, when we ride up to get you, there'll be one of you that won't have got through the winter.

When he came out of the stable barn, Jackson was washing his face and hands at the pump. "Weather coming up," Jackson said, drying himself vigorously.

"Been coming all day."

"Stew tonight?" Jackson hung the rough scrap of towel to dry for the next man.

"And no cracks from you," Chuck said with a grin. "This ain't the Ritz."

"Wasn't thinking of none."

Chuck nodded approvingly over his pupil's progress. Jack had a real command of English now. Never used to talk at all. Now, he'd understand most anything, and when he spoke he used the words right. "And don't be going adding any of that red pepper stuff," Chuck said.

"Paprika. Makes stew well."

"Hey! Forgetting your English lessons? 'It makes a real good stew.' Got that? It don't, though. Stew's stew, without any of them fancy tastes added."

Jackson grinned. "And ketchup?"

"That ain't a taste. That's a necessity."

They walked back to the bunkhouse together. It was a neat, compact building of logs. Downstairs, there was a room for cooking and eating. Upstairs, a room for sleeping with a row of cots. Over the door, the sign WRANGLERS' ROOST had been taken down, for now there were few horses to be wrangled. In its place, Bert had nailed up the new name COWPOKE'S CORNER. Ned had said a comma had got out of hand there, and Robb, with all his poetry reading, had called it something that rhymed with pot of coffee. Bert said it was a plugging good sign and had taken the best part of a Sunday afternoon to do, and everyone knew them damned commas was as skittish as a colt to handle.

Well, whether it was WRANGLERS' ROOST or COWPOKE'S CORNER, it was home. Chuck spat the limp stub of cigarette from his lips, and ground it out automatically with his heel. "Best time of day," he said, watching the two trucks in the distance heading this way, as they wound along the narrow road in the valley. Then they disappeared among the trees as they neared Rest and Be Thankful. Their engines quietened for a minute or two when they reached the house. That would be Mimi Bassinbrook being unloaded, Chuck thought. He wondered how the little redhead had enjoyed her trip in a truck down to Sweetwater and back. Then he heard the trucks go into first and start up the hill. He moved through the door into the kitchen, and rescued the potatoes just in time from burning. He threw the can opener to Jackson, who had followed him. "Get busy on them vegetables," he said, pointing to the six cans of beans. He looked at the potatoes. "Goddamnit, you can't take your shriveling eyes off them perishing murphies without the bastards acting up."

"Let me get supper one night?" Jackson suggested, watching Chuck's heavy scowl over the potato pot.

"Hell, man, you're crazy."

"No! Like food fine."

Chuck looked at him now. "You kind of get your words mixed," he said sorrowfully. *Fine* was all right. *Like* was all right. You could say, "I like it fine." But somehow, you couldn't say "I like food fine." Hell, he's getting me mixed up. "Chow, man, chow. Not food." He was sure of that at least. "You trying to tell me you *like* to cook?"

"Sure."

"You got enough on your hands right now."

"Them damned doods," Jackson agreed. "If not here, I — " He closed his lips tightly, lowered his brows, and opened the sixth can of beans with a bang.

"You'd be doing some riding with the boys," Chuck finished his sentence for him. "Or helping me with this old chuck wagon. You sure aim to be a cow hand, don't you? What about that right pretty automobile you drove from New York?"

"Good to ride to Sweetwater, Saturdays."

169

"If you was a cow hand, you'd be riding in your old Chevvy or the pickup, on Saturdays."

"Okay, too."

"Spoken with the Boss, yet?"

"No," Jackson said gloomily. For what would Mrs. Peel say?

"Sooner the quicker. She's a real nice woman. Won't bite your nose off."

"Not that," Jackson said quickly. "Just — " He didn't finish the sentence, but Chuck was used to that by this time. Jackson thought unhappily of how helpless Mrs. Peel and Miss Bly were without him. That was his whole problem. He felt like a traitor, and that saddened him.

Chuck shook his head. Jack wanted to be a cow hand, but it would take a few years before he would know enough. It was pretty tough to start in when you were over forty. It was a hard trade that took a lot of learning. Still if you didn't mind rising before the sun was up, working in all weathers, long days of riding and watching, or days of ordinary plugging work on fences and gates and sluices and fallen timber, it was a good life.

"It's a good life," Chuck said. "I wouldn't have none other." He thought with nostalgia of the lonely nights on a cold mountainside that had given him rheumatism.

"Life for a man," Jackson, the ex-*boulevardier* from Paris, said so forcibly that Chuck felt somewhat embarrassed. He looked down at his thin legs and grinned.

"That too," he admitted. "Back in the fall of '88, I lost my roll — all of a season's wages — in three nights. That were in Jackson Hole, over by the Tetons, wildest place in Wyoming Territory. There weren't no State of Wyoming, then. I were a young fellow, full of mash and vinegar. Me and another fellow, Bill O'Brien it was from Buffalo, came riding over Toggarty Pass, all of ten thousand feet high if it's an inch, dodging the Shoshones, aiming to reach — "

But Jackson would have to wait for the story, for Bert and Jim Brent came into the kitchen and Chuck had something to say to

170

them. "Began to think you was roped and tied down in Sweetwater."

"Near enough," Bert said. "Sure as nearly didn't make it back up here. She *loved,* just *loved,* the Foot Rail Bar. Full of atmosphere, she said. What the hell did she mean, Jim?"

"Cigarette smoke and stale ale," Jim suggested with a grin. "Hello, Jack. Had a quiet day? No broken necks?"

"No trouble," Jackson said.

"Too bad," Bert said. "A nice little accident, nothing serious you know, makes it easier on the horses."

"How was the colts?" Jackson asked.

"All sewed up. They'll stay in Sweetwater for a week."

"Mimi thought it was 'so sweet' that we brought their mothers along for company." Bert's grin broadened. "Hey, Jim, how do you like being sweet?"

"Try and get a sick colt into a truck without its mother," Chuck said. "Grab your plates. Line up."

"Now, don't tell me," Bert said. "It couldn't be! As Mimi says 'It *just* couldn't be!' Well, well . . . it could." He looked at the stewpot, shaking his head.

"No cracks!" Chuck warned stonily. He looked round at the doorway. "About time," he said, as Robb entered. "Where's Ned?"

Robb threw his hat onto the nearest free peg on the timbered wall. He said nothing. He nodded to the others. When he didn't even make one small joke about stew, Chuck looked up at him sharply.

"Where's Ned?" he asked, meaning it this time. "Where's he at?"

"He's outside. He's coming." There was something in Robb's voice that caught all attention. They looked at each other. But Robb was concentrating on crumbling the hunk of bread beside his plate.

Chuck said, "Drene was up here about four o'clock. Asking for him. I told her he was down in the hayfield."

"Yes, we saw Drene," Robb said. "She came driving past the field with that Schmetterling guy. She made him stop the car, and she came running over to us." His tone kept the others silent. They had all stopped eating.

Robb went on, "She said good-by. She left Ned the horse to look after. She had the dog with her."

"She's left?" Jim asked. "You mean, Drene has gone for good?"

"Eloped. Drene's going to marry Schmetterling, she says."

"She says," Bert burst out with a roar. "And she left the horse to Ned. And she stopped to say good-by! That's mighty nice of her, mighty nice. Considering Ned bought the horse for her, and — "

Jim nodded warningly towards the door. Bert's voice quietened. He said, "You're just kind of lucky if you don't lose your roll when you meet up with that sort." Then he fell silent, brooding on the times he had lost his.

Chuck looked round at the worried, angry faces. He walked over to the door. "Come and get it, damn you, before I throw it out!" he yelled.

Then, at last, Ned came in. The others started joking about the food, and, for once, Chuck didn't stop them.

Ned helped himself to stew, and stepped over the bench to take his place at the wooden table. He said, "I was having a look at that little old pony of yours, Chuck. He's feeling mighty sorry for himself now, but right soon he's going to get frisky and start acting up again. Damned if he don't."

"By October, Bert will have broke him for a good cow pony," Chuck predicted.

Jim said Ned's own horse would need some more breaking in, if Ned didn't exercise him more.

Ned said that was right. Ragtime was getting as fat and lazy as one of them white-faced steers. He'd start tonight, and do some practising on the calves in the south field.

Robb said they'd have to hurry. It looked like bad weather. And heavy rain would spoil the ground for tomorrow, make it too slick.

Jim Brent, watching Ned now eating as quickly as the others, was satisfied. Ned was taking the news well. He wasn't going to leave the ranch and start wandering. When a cow hand started wandering, he'd lose his money more quickly than he had earned it, and certainly more easily. At the time, he might not care one red hell whether he lost everything. Later, he'd wake up and find he would have to start over again. That was all right when you were young. You could do it. And a good cow hand could get a job anywhere. But it wasn't a habit to learn, for, when you were older, it was hard to start over. When you were older, the broken bones and bruises and chills you had collected along the years began to trouble you. If you were a steady man, like old Chuck, that was all right: you'd always have a job. But if you weren't, then either you became one of the old vultures at the poker table in a bar, waiting for the young men to come in and work off their disappointments, or you were just someone with a good enough story to get another free meal and a free drink. "Atmosphere," Mimi Bassinbrook had said delightedly, when they left the Foot Rail this afternoon. She had talked about Gary Cooper and six-shooters and Marlene Dietrich in black-spangled skirts. Atmosphere . . . Jim Brent laughed suddenly.

"Something funny?" Bert said.

Jim, conscious that Ned was watching him carefully, began a story he had heard today when he was over to Sweetwater. It was about Milt Jerks and his proposal to brighten the Sweetwater rodeo with a couple of girls, dressed in tight short pants and twirling a stick above their heads, to march ahead of the school band.

Ned relaxed, and laughed with the rest. Jim relaxed, too.

The others finished their meal, and followed Ned out towards their horses and the south field. Jim said, "I'll be over to try my hand, too. Clearing up a little business first."

Chuck waited until the last man had left. Then he said to Jim, "Going down to the house?"

"Yes, I've got some explaining to do."

"Maybe they've heard already about this elopement."

"Maybe, but I'll have to go and see them."

"Well, have another cup of coffee while you make up your mind what you're going to say to Mrs. Peel." Chuck helped himself to the last of the canned peaches. "You know, I'm kinda sorry for that guy Smatterling. Doesn't know what he has let himself in for, with that Drene. Ned's well out of it."

Jim agreed. "Better now than later."

"Ned will get a good price for the horse, but not as much as he had to pay for it, I bet. And Milt Jerks will buy the fancy saddle and sell it to one of them doods. And what about the horse-trailer and her car? Ned bought them things, too."

"Schmetterling probably drew the line at a horse-trailer behind his Lincoln." Jim smiled. "That would have been a pretty sight."

"Cost Ned six hundred dollars, that trailer did. Well, he could use a new one, himself. He'll be arriving at the rodeos in style, for a change."

"He'll be arriving at the rodeos." Jim thought of the rodeos Ned had missed since Mr. Schmetterling had started complicating everyone's life.

"And when he starts hauling in prize money again, wonder what little blonde's hard-luck story he's going to listen to, this time?" Chuck asked. "Or maybe it'll be an old buddy from the Army, or from some ranch away the hell and gone in Idaho."

Jim nodded. There were two things which used up a cow hand's money: his horse and equipment; and other people. Ned was no exception to the rule.

"Well," Chuck said; poured himself a fifth cup of coffee, and began to roll a cigarette. "Give when you've got it. And when you haven't, you'll get it. That's the way it works out, here. Young Robb was telling me he might be traveling East to do some of that poetry-writing this winter. Miss Sally's been talking to him, it seems. But as I said, as far as I can make out, the cities don't live the way we live. He'll be real miserable. If he hits bad luck, there won't be no one to share it with him."

"Robb will have to find out for himself. He might like the East. Some do." Jim didn't sound too enthusiastic. He had had his own taste of the East. Although — as he admitted now to himself — it was hardly fair to blame the East.

Chuck licked the cigarette thoughtfully, and sealed the moist

174

edges of the yellow paper with a broken thumbnail. He spat a shred of tobacco out of his mouth with an expressive sound. "Do they?" he asked with a wry smile. "There were young Strausser from Double Emm, he were going to paint pictures. And there were Pete Devoe of Diamond Ess Dee, he were going to be a carver — "

"Sculptor."

" — because he was right clever at whittling things out of wood. And Jim Dalzell of Doubleyou Gee, he was to write stories. And Tommy Rosen, and Bob Tisdale, and Ralph Cusick, and all the others."

"Including me," Jim said, with a grin.

"I were only forgetting you out of politeness," Chuck reminded him. "What happened to them? Right back among the mountains, singing don't bury me on the lone prairie, and rubbing their tails off on a saddle. Didn't even wait to finish their training, some of them. Hitched the first ride West they could get. Now you stayed away four years and more. But I always figured that out as plain ordinary stubbornness."

"Maybe you were right," Jim said and laughed. He rose, pushed Chuck's hat further down over his eyes (Chuck only took off his hat in church or in bed), and left him.

As he walked towards the house, Jim was still wondering what he'd say to Mrs. Peel. He felt, as all the boys did, responsible for this new worry. And she worried so damned much. All Easterners did. They lived on worry, almost resented it being taken away from them when they couldn't get clear radio news bulletins or the papers on time. But after they had been here for a spell, they'd throw away their vitamin pills and sleeping tablets, and they'd even stop worrying about their worries.

CHAPTER XVI

Elopement

AFTER DINNER that night, the guests sat around the dining table with their last cup of coffee as if they were unwilling to leave. And for the first time this summer, Mrs. Peel thought, they were a united group. She sat at the head of the table trying not to worry about Sally's empty chair. She watched the steady glow of the candles, held above the twisted arms of silver, and listened to all the theories about Drene's disappearance. Everyone was exceedingly gloomy about her future, but they were gloomy in an excited way. Mrs. Peel, once the first shock was over, had become really depressed.

"I am sorry for Drene, I really am," Carla Brightjoy was saying. "And to think I saw her eloping, although I didn't know it at the time! When Drene called to Ned in the hayfield, he went over to meet her halfway. I stayed with Robb. And when Ned came back, he said nothing. But his face was really like death." That wasn't exactly the way it had seemed, but now it was all very clear to Carla. "He kept so silent. I couldn't help wondering. . . . And then I left to come home, and Mrs. Gunn told me all about it."

"Mrs. Gunn may have been wrong," Mimi Bassinbrook said. "Perhaps Drene only went for a long ride with Dewey. He never *said* he was leaving."

Mrs. Peel said, "He was, though. And Mrs. Gunn, along with Norah, saw Drene get into the car with her small suitcase. Dewey Schmetterling drove off before they could run outside to speak to her. She turned round, laughed and waved. She looked very happy, Mrs. Gunn said."

"Poor kid," Earl Grubbock said.

"Her dog was with her," Mrs. Peel went on.

"Thank goodness for that," O'Farlan remarked. "He was a nasty-looking brute. Perhaps he'll keep Schmetterling in order."

"It's incredible!" Prender Atherton Jones said. "I can't quite believe it." But he obviously wanted to.

"It is absolutely shocking," Esther Park said, her eyes indignant yet excited. "Is she going to live with Dewey, do you think?"

"That's their business," Earl Grubbock said curtly.

Karl Koffing said, "I'm damned sorry for her. I give her three weeks with Dewey, perhaps two. Then what?"

Everyone agreed with that. There was a short silence.

Mrs. Peel looked at the clock. "I wonder what can be keeping Sally down in Sweetwater?"

"She's met some friends probably," Robert O'Farlan said gently. "You know what it is like in a small town: everyone gets to know you."

"Yes," Mimi broke in quickly, glad of the chance to talk about her own visit to Sweetwater. "It was simply incredible, today. After we left the little colts beside their mothers in the vet's nice clean barn, we drove into Main Street and parked the trucks. We thought we might get a late lunch — just a sandwich, you know — at the Foot Rail. But before we got there, we were stopped twenty times if we were stopped once. And in the Foot Rail, itself — why, it is the most incredible place, right out of a Hollywood movie."

"Perhaps the Hollywood movie came straight out of the Foot Rail," Earl Grubbock suggested.

"I expected Gary Cooper to come in at any moment through the swinging doors, a six-shooter in each hand. And Marlene Dietrich ought to have been leaning against the blackjack table, with a spangled skirt and a welcoming smile. Earl, Karl, why didn't you *tell* me all about this? I do believe, Mrs. Peel, they wanted to keep the Foot Rail a secret for themselves."

"You should get Brent to take you to the Purple Rim, next time," Koffing said, and silenced Mimi. "The Foot Rail is pretty tame."

"Did you see any sign of Sally?" Mrs. Peel asked quickly.

"In the distance, only," Mimi answered, and made a charming little face at Karl Koffing. "He-man!" she jibed.

"Where?" Mrs. Peel wanted to know.

"Just along Main Street. Jim and Bert were talking to a ranger, one of those National Park men — now, Karl, there's a real he-man for you, you should have seen him!"

"And?" Mrs. Peel asked patiently.

"And by the time they had stopped talking, I didn't see Sally any more. She must have gone into a store."

"So Jim didn't see her?"

"I don't think so," Mimi answered casually, but with a touch of embarrassment as Mrs. Peel's brown eyes watched her keenly.

"Perhaps Sally met Drene and Dewey in Sweetwater," Carla suggested. "And she's been trying to persuade Drene to come back here."

"Hope it works out that way," Grubbock said. "The kid doesn't know what she has let herself in for."

"Well, I won't miss Schmetterling, for one," Karl Koffing remarked. He looked pointedly at Mrs. Peel, and congratulated himself on his powers of understatement.

"Nor I," Carla said cheerfully. "*Wasn't* he dull? He had nothing to say. It was really disappointing, because I expected someone very witty and amusing. I did enjoy his book, you know."

Prender Atherton Jones smiled. "Authors are often dull and disappointing to meet." And Dewey won't dare put me in a book, now, he thought with satisfaction: not after this little exhibition. It wasn't running away with a girl that amused Prender so much; it was running away with Drene, with pearl-gray pants and ribbon-bowed braids. Dewey and Drene . . . good God!

"That's discouraging," Earl Grubbock said with a grin. "Perhaps we shouldn't be so anxious to get published."

"Dewey called us 'The Great Unpublished.' I heard him one day when Sally was arguing with him about something," Esther Park volunteered. "And he also said we were Six Authors in Search of a Character."

"He would," Mrs. Peel said with so much bitterness that they all stopped thinking to stare at her.

"Don't worry," Earl Grubbock said. "You can score him off your guest list, from now on."

"But he wasn't *on* my guest list," Mrs. Peel protested. She looked at Atherton Jones with kindling revolt. Had he given the others the impression that Dewey Schmetterling had come here by *her* choice? "He arrived here uninvited. He stayed. And stayed. And now he's gone."

"With a bang," Karl Koffing said.

Robert O'Farlan looked sharply at Koffing. Had he forgotten his own interpretations of Schmetterling's visit here — some of them not too charitable to Mrs. Peel? Or was this just Koffing being very much Koffing: when you are wrong, never admit it, never apologize, and keep on talking so that others won't remember how wrong you were? It seemed that way. For Koffing was now talking hard about Drene.

"It would be damned funny, you know, if we hadn't all liked Drene," Koffing said.

"Reminds me of a Somerset Maugham story," Prender Atherton Jones said. "Remember? About the man in the British Foreign Office who became infatuated with a female clown in a third-rate traveling circus, and followed her all over France."

Mimi laughed. "Oh, Prender! I can't see Dewey following Drene all around the little country rodeos, adjusting her saddle for her, hanging around the chutes. In any case, he isn't like the man in the story. He isn't in love." She was quite certain about that.

"Sally thought he was," Mrs. Peel said mildly, and looked around the amazed faces. "Perhaps he is. But that's no excuse for ruining Drene's life."

Jim Brent entered the dining room as Mrs. Peel was speaking. He drew a chair up to the table beside her. "I see I don't have to do much explaining," he said. "Thanks, I'll have a cup of coffee." He looked around the group of faces. Mrs. Peel was as worried as he had guessed. Atherton Jones still looked a bit astounded, but satisfied; he always reminded Jim of a large prize Persian cat. Koffing was amused, and so was Earl Grubbock. Mimi was looking pretty. O'Farlan was thinking things out, perhaps wondering if he would have the courage to elope someday. Carla was upset. And the woman with the peculiar face — "The Chinless Wonder" Bert had called her — was more goggle-eyed than ever. "Where's Sally?" he asked.

"She hasn't come back from Sweetwater yet," Mrs. Peel said.

"Did she phone?"

"No."

Jim Brent frowned. He pushed away the cup of coffee, and rose. "I'll take a look. There's a storm coming up, and she may be stuck on the road."

"I'd be awfully glad if you did. She doesn't know much about cars, and the road is steep in parts."

"She'll be all right. I'll just hurry her along," Jim said.

"And what about Drene?" Karl Koffing asked. He was no longer amused. He was thinking that it was typical of Brent to come in here, brush Drene off with a phrase, and play the gallant rescuer for Miss Bly.

"What about her?" Jim asked.

"It seems to me she needs some help. She's got no friends in Wyoming outside of your ranch; no money; no family. We could start phoning the hotels in Three Springs. Then we'll know where to pick her up. She won't travel very far with the railroad fare that he'll leave her."

Jim said, "Look, Koffing, the guy is going to marry her. It's none of our business."

"Marry?" Koffing exchanged a half-angry, half-amused look with Grubbock. Simple-minded idiot. "Schmetterling *marry?*"

"Sure. She told Ned she was going to marry him. That's the same thing, in the end."

"Jim," Mrs. Peel said, "we feel rather badly about this. I assure you all Easterners don't behave this way. That's why Karl is so indignant."

Karl exchanged another glance with Earl.

"Well, you can lose that worry, Mrs. Peel," Jim said. "As a matter of fact, up at the bunkhouse we were feeling pretty badly about it, too. I assure you all Western girls don't behave that way, either."

Koffing cut in. "What's wrong with the way she behaved? She was a nice kid, out for some fun; and she got more than she asked for."

"Did she?" Jim said. Then he listened. "Here comes the rain." He left the room hurriedly.

"I'll go along, too," Earl Grubbock said unexpectedly, and ran after him.

"It seems," Atherton Jones was saying as Mrs. Gunn and Norah came in to clear the table, "as if Rest and Be Thankful blames Dewey, and Flying Tail blames Drene. That's rather odd. I should have thought it quite the other way round. Men usually blame the man, you know."

"Except the cow hands are siding with Ned. Naturally." Koffing shrugged his shoulders, disposing of the whole problem.

"And so you might, Mr. Koffing," Mrs. Gunn said. "If you ask me, they are a well-matched pair."

Women hate a pretty girl, Koffing thought. He wasn't the only man thinking that, either.

Atherton Jones said, "Now, Mrs. Gunn, we must be charitable. Think of the girl's people. They are going to blame Rest and Be Thankful." He looked, as he spoke, at Mrs. Peel. "They sent their daughter here, and — well, there was a certain responsibility attached to looking after her properly."

"Just a moment, Mr. Jones." Mrs. Gunn finished filling the tray and handed it to Norah. "You can start washing up," she told her niece.

It seemed to Mrs. Peel that Norah looked disappointed. She noted, too, that the braids and the ribbon bows had disappeared.

Mrs. Gunn cleared her throat, stood very erect, with her hands clasped in front of her, and began. "Mr. Jones, it might be easier if you'd all stop jumping to conclusions and get something straight, just for once." She shot a glance at Karl Koffing. Carla giggled nervously, and then looked apologetic.

Mrs. Gunn went on, her voice now less nervous, "Drene left her home when she was just newly fourteen. She has been on her own ever since. Doesn't even know where her people are. She was working in a drugstore outside of Las Vegas when Ned met her. She wanted to be a rodeo star. So he helped her. He bought her the horse, and the equipment. And he hadn't a spare dime when he started work here. The boys had to stake him — they've been paying his rodeo entrance fees and helping out with new equipment. If he wins, they get a cut of the prize money. That's how it's done when you haven't much to go on. Well — there's the real story for you."

She took a deep breath, and her voice became completely natural again, now that the strain of setting the facts right was over. "Ned has had a bit of experience which may help him save more of his money in the future. Drene is getting something bigger than working in a drugstore; that's what she thinks. And Mr. Schmetterling is getting a mighty pretty girl, who's shy and retiring; at least, that's what he thinks. I'm not pitying any of them. Jim could have told you all this, only he's too decent. He thinks no one goes making up false reasons when people keep silent." She looked pointedly at Koffing. Then she blew her nose, looked suddenly embarrassed, and seized the two nearest coffee cups to carry into the kitchen.

"And that," Atherton Jones said, "would make a splendid curtain for Act II." He rose from the table. "Well, as Mrs. Gunn says, we've got things straight for once." He mused over that with a smile. "Delicious. Servants in Wyoming are extremely refreshing."

"We have no servants in Wyoming. We have help." Mrs. Peel looked at him as coldly as she could. Sally was right: Prender was the complete egotist. At this moment, he was beginning to gloat over the predicament of Dewey Schmetterling. "For my part," she said, "I hope they *are* in love. In that case, any further discussion on our part is impertinence. Now, we shall all go to the south field, and watch Ned rope calves as we promised to do."

"It's raining," Esther Park said.

"It isn't heavy, yet. We are going. As if nothing had happened." She looked at Esther Park as she added, "No talk. No sympathetic words. If we can't learn anything else from the West, we can at least learn its dignity."

For a moment, she was amazed by the words and the calm, determined voice that had come out of her mouth. But everyone was agreeing with her. "Okay, General," Koffing said with a smile, and

182

walked out of the room beside her. The others followed. Even Prender made no protest as he went into the hall and pulled on his raincoat and well-worn tweed hat.

Ned was roping badly, but doggedly. He was getting his calf, but his timing was poor for his pony wasn't working with him. He cussed it steadily and cussed the calves and began to feel more normal. He made a little better time — twenty-two, then twenty-point-eight seconds. Still not good enough. But the audience thought it was wonderful. They had even forgotten about the drizzling rain.

"*Git* after him!" yelled Bert, releasing another calf through the gate. Ned streaked after it, standing in his stirrups, the noose swinging in a wide and then gradually quickening circle over his head. The calf twisted and turned, but the horse twisted and turned to follow. Again the pace of the swinging noose was increased. It flew straight as an arrow to rope the racing calf. As the noose tightened round its neck, Ned leaped off his horse and sprinted towards the calf. He threw it, kept it on the ground by the weight of his knee, and tried to tie-rope three of its ankles together. But the horse wasn't working properly. The rope, attached to its saddle horn, was slack. The noose around the calf's neck wasn't held taut enough: it thrashed wildly on the ground, kicking madly, struggling to rise. Ned, avoiding a broken jaw or a mouthful of smashed teeth, got an armful of three legs at last. He tied them quickly, surely. Then he rose, signaling with upraised arm, and walked back to his horse. Still too damned slow. He pulled sharply at the slack rope which stretched between the calf and the horse. "See that, you goddamned lazy sonofabitchn old pony you!" he said to Ragtime. He jerked the rope again, smacked Ragtime across the face to make him pay attention, mind his business, and back up. Ragtime backed, holding the rope taut, almost strangling the calf now that there was no need for it. "You do that next time," Ned warned him, "or I'll skin the goddamned hide off your back."

Robb untied the calf and let it run away. He brought back the tie-rope to Ned. "Better," he said. "Twenty-point-two seconds, that time."

The audience, perched along the fence, hadn't liked seeing Ragtime being disciplined. ("Ned's upset about Drene," Mrs. Peel explained.) But with his next calf, Ned made it in eighteen seconds flat. This time, his pony worked. No one in the damp audience, however, drew any inference from method to result. They just thought it was wonderful.

They stayed through the drizzling rain for almost half an hour. And then, the gusts of wind increased enough to make umbrellas useless, and the skies darkened still more, and the first roll of distant thunder came over the mountains. There was a general retreat towards shelter and a warm fire and something hot to drink.

Sally hadn't returned. There was no sign of Jim and Earl. And somehow, as the guests waited, they gathered in Mrs. Gunn's kitchen. Prender Atherton Jones did most of the talking. The others listened partly to his words, partly to the rising storm, partly for the hum of the returning cars.

It was almost nine o'clock before they heard a car. One car, not two. They looked at each other. Then they were on their feet, the women crowding round the door, the men out in the rain-driven yard. The bright straight shafts of lightning turned them into black shadows with white faces.

Jim Brent's car came slowly into the yard. Then he and Earl helped Sally out, and carried her towards the bright kitchen. Sally was saying, "I'm all right. I am, I tell you." But she closed her eyes and lay quite still.

"She took the cutoff to save time," Earl explained hurriedly to Mrs. Peel. "That's why we were so long in finding her. The car went over the bank. She got out before it burned."

Sally opened her eyes and tried to smile. "All that shopping," she said. "I didn't save a thing."

CHAPTER XVII

The Storm

BY THE TIME Mrs. Peel came downstairs to report that Sally was almost asleep and that Mrs. Gunn was going to stay with her, the others had lit an enormous fire in the living room and were gathered there. Earl Grubbock and Jim Brent were drying off in front of the blazing logs. Earl was answering the questions which Carla kept asking — not that he could give her much information about the accident itself. But he did describe the narrow dirt road, and the twisted mass of the burned car, and Sally some fifty yards away from it. She had traveled that distance before she found she didn't feel like traveling at all. She was unconscious when they found her, but at first they hadn't seen her — only the blackened burned-out car. That was a bad couple of minutes for both men. Then Jim's quick eyes saw the cardigan and hat on the road, and the search was started. They found her lying at the side of the road, near a blasted pine tree. Afterwards in the car, she said that she kept hoping lightning *didn't* strike twice in the same place, and that the chipmunks were very sympathetic.

Jim Brent said nothing. But he noted that Mrs. Peel's face was less worried, so Sally wasn't in danger. He relaxed, and he even smiled when Mrs. Peel admitted that Mrs. Gunn was a much better nurse than she was. Now all they had to do was to wait for the doctor to arrive from Sweetwater. "The road may delay him," Mrs. Peel said. "It is extraordinary how quickly a deluge of rain can turn a country road into a river of mud."

Earl Grubbock nodded his agreement and looked down at his boots. "Fine quality of liquid earth you keep here," he teased Norah, who was helping Mimi to pour out coffee and pass round the sandwiches. "You'd have thought a full armored division had been over that dirt road before we reached it."

Norah laughed. "There's more of the storm to come. You'll see plenty of fireworks in the next half-hour from these windows." She offered Jim a sandwich. "Lucky you weren't up in the mountains tonight, Jim. When are you going? Next week?"

Jim nodded. "I'd rather have this than snow. It's kind of depressing to wake up and find six inches covering you and the stores, and the horses broken loose as likely as not."

"Snow in August?" Mimi said, looking up from the coffee table.

"You can expect it any time after the middle of August, once you get into the mountains."

Earl said, "I don't think I'd enjoy my breakfast if I had to dig for it first. Why are you going into the mountains anyway?"

"There's a herd of steers in a pasture up there. We'll be moving them down to a lower one," Jim answered.

"All the boys going?"

"Except Chuck. He can't take the altitude so well, now." Jim looked at Grubbock. "Like to come along?"

"Sure." Grubbock was pleased. He looked across the room at Koffing, now deep in a bitter argument with O'Farlan about the November elections.

"Bring him too," Jim Brent suggested. "If he wants to come."

"Fine," Grubbock said, but a shadow of doubt crossed his face. He would have just as soon gone alone with the boys. However, Koffing had been asked in the Western way, and Earl would pass on the invitation. He changed the subject to the storm, which was now breaking with full violence among the mountains. "Fireworks," he remarked, watching the flashes through the window. "Lightning all shapes and sizes, sheet or forked. Have your choice."

"Fireworks in here too," Mimi said quietly, glancing over at Koffing and O'Farlan who had been joined by Prender Atherton Jones. He was now in the middle of an eloquent peroration. It seemed to Earl Grubbock that Atherton Jones always talked in paragraphs, never in sentences. And when they dealt with politics, they all could

186

be boiled down to one thing — an intellectual embroidery of the obvious. He should stick to literature, Grubbock thought, he knows something about that at least. Then he looked around, a little guiltily, for he had felt his remark so strongly that it might have been spoken. Perhaps Atherton Jones is a lesson to all of us, Grubbock went on thinking, perhaps we should all stick to our subjects. That's our trouble: if we are good at one thing, we think we must also be keen political minds. As if politics, in theory and practice, wasn't a science as difficult to master as any other. He looked at Atherton Jones with sudden distaste, and sipped the coffee.

"Too bitter?" Mimi asked. "Here's the sugar to disguise my efforts at cooking." She was smiling, and this time Earl knew she had guessed his feelings. Perhaps she shared them. And only three months ago, they had listened to Prender in New York as if he were the Oracle of Delphi.

"You need a drink, Earl," Mrs. Peel said suddenly. "We all do, tonight. Prender, will you attend to that?"

Perhaps she had asked Atherton Jones quite naturally — she had done it with her usual helpless flutter and charming smile — but it seemed to O'Farlan that it was as good a way as any to break up an argument which gave out more heat than light. And why hadn't Grubbock joined in to help Koffing? Well, well, he thought and moved over to the fireplace beside Grubbock and Brent.

"I hope you don't get colds," Mrs. Peel said.

Jim Brent exchanged a grin with Earl Grubbock.

"Haven't felt better in months," Grubbock said. It was true. He looked at the drink which Carla brought him. I can take it or leave it, he thought. He put it down on the mantelpiece, and drank the coffee.

"I wish the doctor would come," Carla said. She was still suffering from a sense of guilt: to think they had all worried over Drene running off with Dewey this evening, and had never given one thought to Sally, who had been lying on a lonely hillside.

"Mrs. Gunn says she doesn't think it's very much," Mrs. Peel said. "Perhaps a rib or two, bruises and cuts. Otherwise, apart from some scrapes and scratches, Sally seems all right."

"Not very much!" Carla said in horror. She looked at the others, who had now formed a wide half-circle in front of the fire. At that moment the lights went out.

The men swore and the women exclaimed — all except Mrs. Peel, who said quietly, "Well, we have plenty of candles in every room." And as she began to light those in the living room, she went on talking about Sally. "I do think a leg broken in two places is much worse, and Sally had that in 1941, when we were in Paris. And you'd never know, would you?"

You'd never know a lot of things, Grubbock thought suddenly as he watched Mrs. Peel's calm face. If he had wanted to know how she behaved in an emergency, he was learning now; and it wasn't as he expected. Thank God he hadn't asked her any foolish questions this morning.

Koffing leaned forward in his chair. "Were you in Paris in 1941?"

"Yes. And *not* as collaborators, Karl." Everyone laughed. Even Karl had to smile for she had said it kindly, humorously.

Jim Brent said quietly, "You were running a counter-propaganda paper, weren't you?" This time, everyone else stared.

"Yes. That's how Sally broke her leg in two places. You see, we had hidden our little printing press in a cellar. We had the help of four very good workmen — good in every sense — " She paused, and then went on, "They helped us to get it into the cellar, piece by piece. They set it up, and helped us run it. That was in June 1940. A friend of ours also helped us — he is the novelist André Mercier."

"Ah, of course. Charming man. Good writer," Prender Atherton Jones said. "At least, he used to be. He's fallen off badly. That last book of his — "

"Did you read it?" Mrs. Peel asked, suddenly very alert.

Atherton Jones looked annoyed. "Frankly, the reviews I saw didn't encourage me to waste any time on it."

"What reviews did you read?" Mrs. Peel asked, almost bitterly.

He stared at her. They had been in the literary magazines, published in Paris, which he had always admired so much: the French did these things so much better than we could, somehow. "I rely on my own judgment for — "

"And I'm still left in that cellar," Grubbock said to Mrs. Peel. If Prender A. Jones got started on his judgment, her story would be stillborn.

"Yes," Mimi said quickly, and won a smile from Grubbock, "I want to hear about the leg broken in two places."

"In that case, we are back in the cellar," Mrs. Peel said. "It was a small one, lying behind a much larger cellar filled with crates of aspirin. So we were fairly safe."

Carla laughed, and then looked apologetic. "Do go on. I'm sorry."

Mimi smiled, too. "It's so exactly like a Hitchcock movie," she explained.

"Except," Mrs. Peel said gently, "there was no background music, and the hero didn't always win, and the heroine was often old and ugly. And the cast would disappear, often unexplainedly. Forever."

No one spoke now.

"We were fairly safe," Mrs. Peel went on, "because aspirin was one thing that didn't attract the Germans. In fact, they were unloading it all over Europe as payment for value received. We never went near that large cellar, of course, once we got the printing press into the smaller one. We blocked up all traces of the connecting door with crates of aspirin. To reach our cellar, we had to come down a ladder from a trap door in the floor of a small room overhead. The caretaker and his wife lived there, and they covered the trap door with a scrap of rug and a heavy table. We worked out a very practical routine. The owner of the building was a friend of ours; he had been a dealer in antique furniture, but he hadn't much left after two months of Occupation except some worthless marks and many crates of aspirin. Everything was going better than we had expected; and then, one night, Sally missed her step on the ladder. That put her out of circulation for some weeks. But the leg mended nicely; and by the time we had to escape from France, she was perfectly all right. "Fortunately."

There was a short but deep silence. A look of surprise passed from one face to another. Jim Brent was watching Mrs. Peel thoughtfully.

"What then?" Earl Grubbock asked hopefully.

"Oh, *that* was just the usual story—alarms and fears and good friends and risks and much kindness. By that time, the underground movements were beginning to be well organized. We really had a very safe journey considering how extremely unsafe everything was." She had made her voice light, casual. And that, it told them, was the end of the story.

"Were many of your friends left in Paris, once you got back again after the war?" Robert O'Farlan asked.

"Not so many, actually." Her voice was now cold, almost hard. The bitter memories came flooding back. "Do you remember Marie and Charles Venault?" she asked Prender.

"They are running your magazine now, aren't they?" Prender had wondered about that. But perhaps, he thought, Margaret had tired of her one-time pride and joy.

"When we left France in 1942, we handed over our printing press to them. When peace came, they revived our magazine under its old name. It still pretends to be literary, but now even its book reviews are written with a political slant. If you are pro-Communist, your books get good notices. If you aren't, then either you are damned out of hand, or you get no mention at all. That's the treatment they gave André Mercier."

"But he was one of their friends."

"Until he was misguided enough to write a book praising the early resistance movements against the Nazis. He was damned, then. For, according to Marie and Charles, no resistance movements existed before the 22nd of June 1941. And after that date, they were good undergrounds only if they were run by Communists. Everything else was run by reactionaries in the pay of exiled fascists, or didn't you know?"

Then, as her sarcasm deepened, she noticed the faces around her: they were looking either uncomfortable or incredulous. Karl was the only one whose expression she couldn't judge. She fell silent.

"It simply doesn't sound possible," Prender Atherton Jones said. "Why, I knew them all well. Marie is a very charming and intelligent woman." He looked at Mrs. Peel disbelievingly.

"What I say is true," she said sadly. "And this is not an isolated case. Since the Liberation, many magazines and papers in France have fallen into Communist control. In fact, France has the biggest Communist press in western Europe. So you see, André Mercier and all the other writers like him haven't much chance, have they? Anything that he writes, from now on, is secretly blacklisted. And unless people like us realize what is happening, he is going to be abandoned to people like Marie and Charles."

"But, really, Margaret," Atherton Jones said, "literary magazines don't carry much weight in the political world. Aren't the Communists wasting their energies?" He smiled, shaking his head. "We mustn't exaggerate their danger, you know. That only leads to witch hunts."

"Communists aren't stupid. They don't underestimate the power that they can get from controlling words and ideas and opinions. And they've succeeded very well with you, Prender: you didn't even read André's last book, and yet you were ready to damn it. Don't tell me you've started to believe the lies about his private life that they are spreading?"

He looked a little uncomfortable. "Really, Margaret," he protested again, "this is all very hard to swallow."

"And impossible to digest, we found," Mrs. Peel said sharply.

Grubbock asked, "But why doesn't André Mercier complain out loud?"

"Probably he isn't as good as he thinks," Koffing said with a smile. "Even if his friends don't like it, he may have got the book reviews that he deserved."

Mrs. Peel looked at Karl. "I think," she said slowly, "you gave Earl his answer. If André were to complain, few would believe him — until it happened to them. The Communists would just say he was suffering from wounded pride, and the pro-Communists would help to damn him by repeating all kinds of false gossip about him. They are very clever at rumors, you know."

There was another silence. Jim Brent watched the disbelieving faces. Only Robert O'Farlan was thoughtful, as if he, at least, was weighing Mrs. Peel's words. Jim listened to the wind, trying to hear the approach of the doctor's car. The thunder had died away, but the rain still lashed the windows mercilessly. He waited for someone to speak, but no one did.

"Well, I believe you," Jim Brent said. "For the simple reason that I don't believe you'd make up a story like this, Mrs. Peel. I don't know much about book reviews or writers or any of that world. But I've known you this summer, and you've never said an unjust thing about anyone." He looked angrily now at the others.

"I believe you too," Mimi said unexpectedly, and gave Jim Brent a smile. "And I'm just thankful that I live in a country where the Communists aren't in any positions of power. Thank heavens, that couldn't happen here!"

There was a dead silence.

"Not a particularly happy phrase," Prender Atherton Jones said with a grimace, and raised a small laugh. "Ah, there are the lights again!" They all blinked at each other, smiling determinedly if a little uneasily, as the room was flooded with bright lamps once more.

"Thanks to Jackson," Mrs. Peel murmured, rising to blow out the candles.

O'Farlan said, "It seems to me that if we'd all face the fact that there are hidden Communists in this country, then we'd make quite sure it can't happen here. The trouble is, whenever I say that aloud, there's always some clever guy ready to yell 'reactionary' or 'witch hunt.'"

Grubbock looked over at Koffing. Nothing that had been said had moved him, either to worry or pity or anger. It was almost as if Koffing had closed his ears for the last ten minutes. Grubbock stared at his friend. Was he, or wasn't he? Well, if he was a secret Communist, what did it matter? Grubbock frowned and looked at the others. They were all a little upset by the story, even if they didn't quite believe it. Didn't *want* to believe it? Hell . . . was he seeing his own reflection? Only Jim Brent and O'Farlan seemed to accept it as possible. Mimi? She was just out to win a smile from Brent. She was watching Brent now, trying not to let any of the others see she was watching him.

Grubbock smiled wryly. This is one party, he thought, where you didn't make much of an impression on the pretty girls; you're losing your grip, Grubbock. But the Drenes and the Mimis would always somehow choose — however much they'd protest money wasn't everything and love was — someone with money. Brent must be rich, even if he dressed like a cowboy and worked as hard as any of them. For a moment, Grubbock felt the old bitterness returning: it was a hell of a life if you had neither money nor prestige.

Norah said suddenly, "There's the doctor's car." She was right. It was pulling up in the yard. She gave Grubbock a smile as she ran out of the room. No, Grubbock decided, it didn't have to be such a bad life, either. There were girls unlike Drene or Mimi. And you could try for money or prestige, and if you didn't go desperately grasping after them, you might have a good time trying for them. And if you didn't get them, you'd have found other things, perhaps richer and fuller than money or prestige ever were. You might have a good time finding that out, too.

Mrs. Peel had followed Norah to welcome Dr. Clark. Jim Brent had gone as far as the door. Then he paused, and came back into the room. "Glad he got here," he said. "I was beginning to think we'd have to send for Ned. He made a good job of Bert's foot when a horse stepped on it. The only time I've known Ned to fail was when he set Chuck's arm last summer. When it mended, it wouldn't bend. So they had to break it again and reset it. At least, that's Chuck's version of the story. I was down in Montana buying horses at the time."

"Good heavens!" Carla said. "Does that sort of thing happen often?"

"Not if you're careful. There's always a time when you begin to take a horse for granted. That's when the accidents happen."

Prender Atherton Jones said, "I wondered what you did here when you had an accident. After all the doctor is twenty-five miles away, and the hospital at Three Springs is another ten." Personally, he thought, I just concentrate hard on not having appendicitis.

"Oh, if it isn't too bad, we can patch it up. Ned's good. He got some medic work in the Army before he was picked out for officer's training."

"Was Ned in the Army?" Carla asked. All the women became interested.

"Sure. That's where I met him. He became my lieutenant. I offered him a job here as soon as he got his discharge. He's a good wrangler and cow hand, one of the best I've had." When his mind isn't set on a woman, Jim thought.

"What were you?" Mimi asked. "Captain or major?" Or it might have been a colonel: he would look wonderful as a colonel.

Jim Brent began to laugh. "I was a Pfc." He gave Grubbock a mock salute. "Sergeant! Thank you, sir!" he said.

"Same to you!" Then Grubbock was laughing too, and the women looked bewildered. O'Farlan smiled. Atherton Jones poured himself another drink. Koffing became interested in a magazine.

"Were all the boys in the war?" Carla asked.

"All except Chuck. He went down to the recruiting station in Sweetwater, said he could always be a cook. But he had to come back here. He took charge of this outfit, he and his old buddy Cheesit Bridger who came out of retirement to help us. Of course, the Government requisitioned the horses, so there wasn't too much to do — just a matter of holding the place together until the rest of us got back."

"Did you get wounded?" Esther Park asked. She had been silent for so long that everyone was surprised she was still there.

"You can't be lucky all the time. But I must say, you can get just as much cracked up if a horse starts really working on you."

"Once, a horse trampled my foot," Esther Park said. "And I had an arm broken when I was in Switzerland." The others looked at her politely.

Mimi said, "When I was a child, I remember — " and that began a whole chapter of amusing little accidents from Carla and Atherton Jones, too.

Esther Park looked angrily around. All that fuss over Sally, over Drene. All that fuss over Ned, and Chuck's arm, and Bert's foot. And no one even worried about her. I *had* a broken arm, she thought bitterly and looked at Mimi and Carla now discussing vaccination marks. I *had*. She went out of the room.

She hesitated at the stairs, looking up towards Sally's room. Its door was opening. She ran up the stairs, quietly, surprisingly lightly. She reached the landing as Mrs. Gunn came out.

"How is Sally? Is she bad? Does it hurt?" Esther Park asked. "Can I nurse her? I'd love to nurse her. I'm a very good nurse."

"That's nice of you to offer, but I think we'll manage, Miss Park. The doctor says she'll be up in no time." Mrs. Gunn bustled downstairs to make a sandwich for Dr. Clark and some fresh coffee: he had to get back to Sweetwater tonight.

Esther waited. Then the doctor came out of Sally's room, with Mrs. Peel saying good-by to him at the door. Again, Esther was full of anxious inquiries. They were embarrassed — as Mrs. Gunn had been — by her overemphatic anxiety. But Mrs. Peel was going to sleep in Sally's room and it was all arranged and Esther wasn't to worry. Mrs. Peel said good night, and closed the bedroom door firmly.

The doctor, as he went downstairs, glanced back at the lonely figure on the landing. Wonder if she could nurse? Looked like a neurotic to him, eyes, gestures, tone of voice. Probably just trying to get into the act. Give her a floor to scrub each morning and she'd be a happier woman. Occupational therapy, they called it nowadays.

Downstairs, Dr. Clark found it good to rest for half an hour by the fire, enjoying a sandwich and coffee before he started the bleak drive down to Sweetwater. Jim Brent was looking well, he was glad to see, and the rest of the writers were more normal than he had expected from that screwball on the landing. They were a nice crowd, talkative and friendly enough. There was an important-looking man, with a noble head and a good pair of hands, who seemed to be the host. He was making a fancy little speech about the fine life of a country doctor on his errands of mercy.

But as Dr. Clark stretched his sodden boots towards the fire, and remembered the child who had died of tetanus that afternoon, he was inclined to be less moved than his host was by the spiritual rewards. They must be very great, he was assured earnestly.

Before he finished the second sandwich, the telephone rang. The doctor was on his feet at once, his bag in his hand. "Tell them I'm coming straight over," he called to Mrs. Gunn in the hall, who had hurried to answer the phone. "Good night all."

Spiritual rewards, he thought as he plowed through the muddy yard with Jim towards his car. That kid with tetanus . . .

"Good night, Jim. Keep well!" he said, and drove carefully down the black, slick road.

CHAPTER XVIII

Good News and Bad

After a week, Sally was downstairs, suffering mostly from tight bandages. By that time, everyone had got accustomed to the idea that accidents do happen, and the household had stepped back into its ordinary routine again.

"An invalid's only interesting when he's about to die," Mrs. Gunn said shrewdly. She had brought Miss Bly a morning cup of broth, and found her alone in the little sun porch off the sitting room, reading through a pile of paper sheets, tattered and dog-eared. "But I'm glad to see you sitting still for a change. I've brought you the weekly bad news, too." She laid a collection of bills beside the manuscript on the table at Sally's elbow.

"Mr. O'Farlan's book," Sally explained.

"My, and isn't there a lot of it? And now it will be published!"

"We hope so," Sally said with a smile. "It's good, it's very good." She was as delighted as Mrs. Gunn, and a little surprised. Just wait, she thought, until Prender reads this! "But Mr. O'Farlan has a lot of work before him, yet."

Mrs. Gunn looked puzzled, so Sally told her about editing and polishing, about proof correcting twice over until you got to know every misplaced comma by sight.

"Why, there's more work to it than I thought," Mrs. Gunn admitted. "It's not all just a matter of sitting down and letting your ideas run away with you! Many's the time I thought I'd like to write a book, but — " She glanced at the pile of manuscript doubtfully. "If I were Mr. O'Farlan, I'd have made it a small book. Not so much trouble, I'm thinking. Now drink up the broth before it gets cold, Miss Bly."

"You're a strange one to be talking about avoiding trouble." Sally sipped the cup of broth dutifully, looked at the bills on the table beside her, and frowned. One of the envelopes, long and business-like, was from Lawyer Quick in New York. What words of warning was he giving them, this time?

Mrs. Gunn gathered up some petals, fallen from the mariposa lilies in the vase on the table. "Now don't let these bills go worrying you. And I do try to keep them down. But it is a multitude to feed and provide for, and they do like their food and all their etceteras."

"I wasn't thinking of the bills so much. I was thinking of Mr. Quick, our lawyer." Sally laid down the cup, and picked up his letter. She looked at it with distaste. "He takes such a gloomy view of everything. If only he would write, once, to say the world wasn't going to pieces and us along with it!" She looked down at the letter, then at the other envelopes: yes, all bills. She tried not to seem worried.

"It's the etceteras," Mrs. Gunn said. "I was the youngest in a family of ten, and all of us alive if it hadn't been for the war — the first one, that is. We had one dinner a day, plenty of gravy to make the meat spin out, plenty of potatoes to fill up the gaps. But it's not that way with city folks. Gravy is fattening, potatoes is fattening. So they've got to be filled up on other things. And Mr. Atherton Jones leaves all the piecrust on his plate — just eats the filling — and then thinks he'd like a bit of that Camembert to end with. Never seems to think that if he ate the piecrust, he wouldn't have room for the Camembert. And isn't cheese as fattening, too?"

"But he's very fond of it, so he forgets that. I'm glad that they at least enjoy their food here."

"They certainly do," Mrs. Gunn said with some pride. Then she added quickly, "Don't get me wrong, Miss Bly. If I'm cooking, I'm cooking. It takes just as long to make a good dishful of white fluffy potatoes as it takes to cook asparagus or mushrooms. But there's a heap of difference in the cost. That's what worries me."

"We'll manage. Guests are guests, after all. We can start economizing in September." She smiled up at Mrs. Gunn.

"Well — " Mrs. Gunn said slowly. "A giving hand is always getting. They say." But she shook her head as she scattered the petals into the cup's saucer, and gathered it up to take into the kitchen. "They don't last long, do they? Mrs. Peel put these lilies in that vase, only yesterday. That's what I always say when I get worried: nothing lasts forever. Not even troubles."

She glanced over her shoulder as she closed the door. Miss Bly was looking at the letter again. She wanted to tell her, "Open it. It may be good news, this time." But she had said more than enough already. It was strange, when she spoke about city folks, that she kept forgetting Miss Bly and Mrs. Peel were Easterners too. Not that she disliked city folks. When you got to know them, they were just like any other folks in most things. But they did take a lot for granted. Perhaps if they had to grow their own food, and kill their meat and dress it and keep it, they might eat anything that was nicely cooked for them.

She went into the kitchen and began to prepare the lamb chops for lunch. Two for each person. Chops weren't fattening it seemed, not even at a dollar and fifteen cents a pound. But Irish stew, which used only one half this amount of meat, was. And Mr. Atherton Jones said that any kind of stew was an apology of a meal. He had a way of saying things, she had to admit. She'd be nervous about serving stew for a long time to come.

Sally opened the letter and read it. She reread it. It was detailed, explicit and exact. She could hear Mr. Quick's voice dictating it to his efficient secretary; she could see him marking each point, as he spoke, with his thin paper knife tapping on the immaculate blotter in front of him. Sally, whose blotters got blotted and torn off at the edges for penwipers, was always amazed by the perfection of Mr. Quick's desk. But Mr. Quick never made any mistakes. . . .

She heard laughter in the hall, and then voices.

"Margaret!" she called impulsively. She wished she hadn't when Prender Atherton Jones came in with Mrs. Peel. He looked at himself in the mirror, and whatever he saw pleased him. He was in fine spirits.

Prender was thinking how tanned skin and white hair went well together. He pulled back his shoulders and admired his chest expansion under his yellow polo shirt. He was wearing riding breeches and English boots. He adjusted the navy and white spotted silk scarf at his neck, and smiled amiably. "How's the invalid?"

Then he noticed the manuscript. "What's this?" he asked sharply.

"O'Farlan's novel," Sally said. "He thought I needed something to read while I was stuck in a chair."

"Oh." He sounded mollified, and Sally relaxed. She wasn't trying to save Prender's pride, but she didn't want him antagonistic to O'Farlan. Robert O'Farlan hadn't seemed to care about that: she was to read it first, he insisted. And after that, Mrs. Peel. And then Atherton Jones could look at it, if he wanted to.

"I've read most of it, of course," Prender was saying. "In fact, I told him he must finish it. Then he seemed to get stuck — wrote nothing for months. But I hope he didn't finish it *too* quickly, in these last weeks. What's the end like?"

"Well, of course I haven't your experience in reading manuscripts," Sally admitted. "If you like it, you'll advise him about a publisher?"

"Of course. Hazleton, Hazel and Birch might be the firm to handle it. I'll judge that once I read the last chapters." He looked at Sally, but she didn't praise them. This book was, after all, Prender's discovery. He had liked the beginning. It wouldn't do if someone else liked the end before he did.

"Would you like to read it now?" Sally asked casually.

"Not at the moment. I'm going upstairs to have a tub. I've found manuscripts hard to deal with in a bath. I'll borrow a book from the library instead." He looked again at the mirror as he left them. His fine spirits were quite restored.

"Hope he doesn't take my pet copy of Dinesen into the bathtub with him," Sally said.

Mrs. Peel, who had been rearranging the remaining mariposa lilies and admiring the pure outline of their cupped white petals, tapped the manuscript. "What about it?" she asked. "It *is* good?"

Sally nodded. "It's a real novel. Plenty of scope and understanding and perspective. He may have got that by waiting so long to write about his idea. And we all thought that slightly comic, didn't we? A novel about the First World War. . . . We keep forgetting that Tolstoy wrote about a war fifty-two years after it was all over."

"And ten years after he had seen any fighting, himself," Mrs. Peel reminded her. "Oh dear! Do you think Prender will write a foreword saying this novel is another *War and Peace?*"

"No doubt," Sally said gloomily. "Ah, well. . . . How was your morning ride?"

"Majestic. I felt like a lady-in-waiting accompanying the Emperor reviewing his troops. But it is a strain, finding trails without gates."

"Why do you ask him to go with you? Sorry for his abandoned state? Your soft heart will undo the lesson he was learning, darling. Reforms are often ruined by the too kind people in this world."

Mrs. Peel smiled disbelievingly. "He talks a great deal. But say what you will, he *can* talk. We had the men of taste in the eighteenth century, all the way from Branch Creek to Two Fork Gap."

"Talking the mountains down, perhaps? Could be. Eighteenth century, age of reason, dislike of scenery as barbarous institution."

"But, Sally, Prender *is* interesting when he gets started."

"When I want a lecture on literature, I'll enroll at Columbia," Sally said. Then her eyes fell on the bills and Mr. Quick's letter, and she frowned suddenly.

"Did the bandage slip?" Mrs. Peel asked sympathetically.

"I've just been forced to remember why I called you into this room," Sally said. She handed the letter to Mrs. Peel.

"Do I *have* to read it now? I did want a bath before Prender used all the hot water."

"I think you'd better."

Mrs. Peel looked at Sally's face and read the letter.

Sally said, "I'm fairly stupid at understanding money matters. You're the expert. Now, is that letter as bad as I think it is?"

"It's so long since I was an expert in money matters," Mrs. Peel said unhappily. She read the letter once more.

"Translate it into English, will you?" Sally asked. "I get baffled when I deal with Mr. Quick's vocabulary."

Mrs. Peel smiled in spite of herself. "Well, cutting out all the notwithstandings and inasmuches, it seems to say that what he warned you about in New York is now more or less true."

"Go on, darling. This is so cozy, isn't it? Just you and I, sitting in our country house, finding out how poor we really are. But how? How, so suddenly? This house was a bargain . . . Why, the furniture alone would cost almost as much as the entire price we — I mean, you — paid. And there *was* money enough, wasn't there?"

"Yes. In a way. But I've been dipping into capital, and forgetting how much capital I had already spent. As Mr. Quick points out, I never got any financial return on any of my *literary* investments. So, what with everything, we've got about six thousand dollars left."

"Some people would say that's a lot of money." Sally cheered up. It seemed quite a lot to her. Enough for Margaret. Sally's cook books, although scarcely gold mines, had always brought in a small steady sum each year to keep her independent in all her own expenses. "Why, that isn't so bad!" she said.

"It is about one hundred and twenty dollars a year, if I leave it as capital. If I spend it, then there will be nothing at all in a year or two." At the present rate of expenditure, she thought, they'd use it up in four months.

There was silence for a very long moment.

"How ever did this sneak up on us?" Sally said. "Six thousand, I mean . . . after all that money you made!"

Mrs. Peel looked extremely guilty. "It should be nearer twenty-five thousand," she said. "That's my fault. I thought — well, seeing it was getting low — that I'd — well, that I'd help it along a little. *You* know — the stock market."

"And you . . . ?"

"And I lost, this time. Either the stock market has changed since 1926, or my luck has gone."

"You lost?" Sally began to laugh.

Mrs. Peel was startled. Then she had to smile. Then she laughed too.

"Fat lot we have to laugh about," Sally said, and went into peals of laughter again.

"Karl and Earl would say it served me right," Mrs. Peel gasped in a sane moment. But this only set them off again.

Sally pointed to her bandaged ribs. "It hurts, it hurts. Oh, stop me, Margaret! Don't let me laugh any more."

"We'll live here, through all the winter snows, and no more traveling ever, and no more cities," Mrs. Peel said, trying to regain her seriousness. Her words helped her, when she really thought about them.

"And we'll rustle Jim's cattle, and eat potatoes, nice white fluffy potatoes," Sally said and burst into another fit of laughter.

Then, at last, quite exhausted, they looked at each other.

"I'll start writing more cook books — lots of them," Sally said. But she knew her income from them wouldn't go very far between two people, so she spoke without much conviction.

"But you can't write them unless you travel. You always wrote that kind of cook book. You just can't invent recipes, and give them foreign places and names to make them palatable. You'll poison your public."

"Not much future in that," Sally agreed. "Six thousand could last you three or four years, here. If you lived *very* quietly. It's possible to live here in the winters if you like being snowed-up, and learn to flop around on snowshoes. Or we could close the house, and get a job somewhere. We'll find something, don't worry. We aren't complete idiots."

"Only in certain directions, and that's all over too. No more travel, no more people. That's one consolation: I'd feel very guilty if I had spent all that money on ourselves. But we didn't. We could have lived in a fashionable part of Paris, or on the Riviera; we could have moved around according to the social season. But we didn't. And we may have collected people in our day, but there never was a title or a millionaire among them. *That's* something we did not do."

"It was fun while it lasted," Sally said. "Look, would you see if this bandage has slipped? That's it. Thanks. Now, you run upstairs and have your bath, and change before lunch."

Mrs. Peel began to walk slowly towards the door. "I suppose we had better cancel that order with Milton Jerks for a new car?"

"The one we've rented from him will have to do. It may be slightly battered, but it isn't temperamental."

"And we can't have anyone to take Drene's place, either. We'll all have to make our own beds and dust around."

"Prender will leave," Sally said delightedly. "Unless Carla feels she has to volunteer to do it for him. Did you know she polishes his boots when she cleans her own?"

"What?"

"We ought to have guessed he never shone those boots, himself."

"One thing I can say for Dewey — he just let his shoes crack up." Mrs. Peel was still shaking her head when she reached the door. But there, she paused again as she had done every few steps across the room. "Sally, you don't think Jim Brent could afford to buy this house back from us?"

"Not this year. Or next. In a few years, perhaps. If he can still get two cents profit on each pound of steer he sells." Or if a grass fire didn't ruin him, or a year of drought.

"That's what I thought. Besides, somehow, I don't really want to give up this house."

"I'm glad of that," Sally said simply and tried to smile to Margaret as she left the room.

The worst of laughter was that, afterwards, it could leave you so depressed. Sally looked out at the mountains. She wondered what sort of job she would find. In America, you could take any job at all providing it was honest. No need to apologize for it, or try to disguise it. And no one would pity you. *You've a job, haven't you? All right, let's see what you can make of it.* That was the attitude. I'll get a job, Sally thought. But Margaret? Margaret is older. Then, if necessary, I'll get a job that will keep two of us.

Mrs. Peel, in dressing gown and slippers, burst into the room.

"Sally, stop worrying! I've decided what to do. It's quite simple. I'll write another novel. I must be a very weak character, don't you think? I've really got to have the wolf not only howling at the door, but scratching the panel out, before I'll work. Don't look so upset, Sally. Why, it might even be fun to write this book! How does an historical novel about Idaho sound to you? After all, it wasn't just discovered by skiers and potato-growers, was it?"

"What name will you use this time? Margaret Peel or Elizabeth Whiffleton?" Sally was trying to smile, to sound encouraging, but her depression only increased.

"I don't know." Mrs. Peel's excitement died away. Then she remembered the bath which was still running, upstairs, and she dashed from the room. She called back, "Depends on who gets control of the novel. But *I'll* put up a good fight this time."

"What fight?" Prender Atherton Jones asked as he came out of his bedroom. He had been thinking, longingly, of a well-cooked luncheon digesting in his well-exercised, pleasantly bathed and freshly dressed body. "Margaret, I've discovered the most amusing book. But can you tell me what on earth this inscription means?"

But Mrs. Peel, not even stopping to look at the book in his hand, only said, "My bath! The library ceiling!" and rushed on frantically.

Fortunately, she found there was still a couple of inches to go before the bath water would pour down into the library. The water was half-cold, for Prender had enjoyed a very good bath indeed. She felt in such a Stoic mood, however, that she scarcely said, "I knew it," and she stepped in for almost a minute.

CHAPTER XIX

Harmony and Discord

Prender Atherton Jones went on his way downstairs. He would show Sally his discovery in literature. It was a kind of period piece, true to the romantic escape of the 1920's: the era when green hats and sheiks and Constantinople sleeping-cars all vied with Huxley and Mencken and e.e.cummings. Not to mention Prohibition, Mayfair parties, raccoon coats, exiled Czarists, and Dada.

He looked at the book with a smile. *The Lady in White Gloves,* by Elizabeth Whiffleton. He must have read it before — probably had only glanced into it: it had been one of those best-sellers — for he remembered he had included it with some other popular novels in a witty review he had written at the time. But now, it had the most peculiar fascination for him; it awakened a nostalgia, as if he were looking at a collection of old photographs, fantastic perhaps, horrible in some ways, and yet reminders of an age when life had been young and gay and very brave-new-world. Even if the twenties had roared more with the hysterical rush of an express train than with the majestic dignity of a lion, they had had their charms in retrospect. They had been almost peace, compared to which the thirties had been a mounting nightmare. And the nineteen-forties — a fitful slumber of exhaustion, tormented by memories of delirium?

Ah, he thought, that's good, that's very good. He halted at the foot of the stairs to take out his little notebook and record it.

He found Sally in the sun porch, but Grubbock and Koffing were with her — Grubbock sitting in a rocking chair, inappropriate but comfortable; Koffing standing at the long wall of window, looking at the mountains with a frown on his face. They were in the middle of an argument about horses.

206

Atherton Jones cleared his throat. Sally looked around.

"Earl and Karl are invited to go with the cowboys on a round-up. And we were discussing —" she explained. Atherton Jones interrupted her with an amused exclamation.

"You *don't* have to go, do you?" he asked the men.

"We'd like to," Earl Grubbock said with a grin. "Why don't you come along? Plenty of scenery. We are sleeping out in the mountains for a couple of nights."

Prender Atherton Jones smiled pityingly.

They went on with the discussion, forgetting Prender entirely. Something to do with Karl's horse and Jim Brent's advice that Karl should stick to his own horse until this trip was over. "I can see his point that you are better off with a horse you know on a trip like this," Sally was saying. And Earl Grubbock was agreeing with her. "What's all the rush, Karl?" he wanted to know. "This trip tomorrow will be difficult enough, perhaps, without worrying about a strange horse." Yes, said Sally, or having a horse worry about a strange rider.

Horses, Atherton Jones thought angrily as he turned on his heel and left the room, they made everyone equally stupid. Horses, dogs and babies should be banned from all conversation.

He went into the library, and made himself a Tom Collins. (Margaret had listened to his humorous comments on the evils of Prohibition, and had set up a tray for emergency thirsts.) He was still bridling over his reception by Sally and the others. Ah well, he thought grimly, he had become accustomed to the selfish egotism of youth in these last weeks. It was true that you had to live with people to find what they really were. The little things about them, which amused you when you only met them once a month or so, became absolutely intolerable when you were in constant contact with them. Margaret Peel was the only person here who was at all sympathetic. It was a pity her mind was so slow and her reactions so simple. Still, as Koffing had pointed out, she was the product of her environment: her life had been an easy and comfortable one, no worries, no work. As for her little experiences in occupied France, they probably existed mostly in her imagination. (Sally hadn't even mentioned them.) What would seem normal to most men would seem highly exciting to a nonadventurous woman. Margaret Peel wasn't the Mata Hari type. The truth was she needed someone to look after her.

He sat down in the most comfortable chair to wait, partly for luncheon, partly for Margaret Peel. If you had discovered an amusing book and amusing phrases to describe it, then it was a pity to let them go unused. Margaret Peel was the perfect audience.

He stretched his long legs, admired them, looked around the pleasant room; and in that moment of well-being, he felt the charm of the whole house. It wouldn't be a bad life to have a place like this — nearer New York, of course, where one would have an equally comfortable apartment. As a *pied-à-terre,* naturally. For there was Paris. Margaret had had a flat in Paris, and a villa in Italy. Did she still own them?

It was in moments like these that he regretted his return to bachelor life, although he had welcomed its freedom on the death of his second wife. A man needed a woman to take care of the bothersome details of existence. Perhaps it was that discovery which had almost driven him into a third marriage: Mimi would have been the perfect ornament for his home. But she would have been demanding and self-centered. He saw that clearly now. As a man got wiser, what he wanted was comfort and peace of mind so that he could live as a civilized being and have the leisure to write his books. It was all very well to have fame as a talker, as an encourager of the arts, but words had a way of vanishing if they weren't enclosed between the covers of a book. Mimi would have indeed been a grave mistake. He complimented himself on the perspicacity and solid good sense which had kept him free of her.

Then, thinking of Mimi, he somehow thought of Dewey Schmetterling. And he opened *The Lady in White Gloves* to read the puzzling inscription again. It was definitely in Dewey's writing. The book must have belonged to Dewey, and he had left it in the library by mistake and Mrs. Gunn's niece had just jammed it into any shelf. (Prender had found it tucked inappropriately among a row of Dickens novels.)

Dewey had written on the flyleaf: "To the modest author, from one of her unconscious public — a token of his esteem." Prender, the expert on Dewey's prose style, diagnosed a play on the word "unconscious." And there was a peculiar twist to the phrase "a token of his esteem," for the novel was a battered old copy, coming apart in several places, with the name of a very small town library stamped across the pages at ruthless intervals. Dewey must have intended to give it to the authoress, and then, in the excitement of his unexpected departure, had left it behind. Elizabeth Whiffleton . . . Prender searched his memory. No, he didn't know her. In fact, no one ever seemed to have known Elizabeth Whiffleton. Except Dewey. Trust Dewey to find out. . . .

This new idea took away much of the charm of the book. Dewey had discovered it first. Prender Atherton Jones frowned, hesitated, and then went over to the bookcase where he had found the novel. He had lost interest. Dewey would no doubt write to ask for the book (he would treasure it highly), once he was beyond his present stage of forgetting everything for the sake of two little golden pigtails and tight pearl-gray frontier pants. Ah, Dewey . . . He smiled. He must start writing his letters this afternoon.

When Atherton Jones had left the sun porch, Earl Grubbock interrupted his argument with Karl Koffing to say to Sally, "Whose idea was it, by the way, that Atherton Jones should move into our cabin?"

Sally was startled. "Not ours," she said hastily. "You mean he tried to get you both to move out, as soon as Dewey left?"

"It was implied that you'd like it that way. However, we had a few doubts about that. So we stayed where we were."

Sally shook her head in amazement as she marveled over Prender.

Grubbock looked at Karl Koffing. "See?" his eyes seemed to say. Then he spoke to Sally again. "Dewey Schmetterling wasn't a particular friend of yours, was he?"

"Not very." She smiled at her understatement.

"And Esther Park isn't here because you happen to know her family?"

"No." This time, Sally was angry.

"Now I'm beginning to get things straight." He looked at Karl again.

"You must have a poor opinion of Margaret and me, Karl," Sally said. She tried to make a joke of it, but she was hurt.

"Well, why do you have people you don't like?" Karl Koffing asked accusingly.

"We didn't have Dewey. He came, and he stayed. What can you do? I mean, if you are a woman?"

That obviously didn't seem any answer to Karl. He shrugged his shoulders and turned to look out of the window again.

Grubbock smiled. "I see. A man could tell Dewey Schmetterling to get the hell out. A woman — well, what does a woman do?"

"Worries. Gets cross," Sally said. She laughed. "And Karl, if you have any ideas how we can ask Miss Park to leave, without hurting her feelings, we'd be very grateful to you."

"I don't think my ideas interest you much," he said, facing her. "You never see my viewpoint about anything — not even in this matter of Jim Brent and his precious horses."

"I do see your point of view, Karl. Only I see the other points of view, too. And I choose whatever I think is best and that becomes *my* point of view. Of course, I may be wrong often enough. None of us is perfect."

Earl Grubbock's eyes were amused. "But didn't you know that Karl's ideal State is going to make everything and everyone perfect?"

"That's a tall order," Sally said.

Karl looked at Grubbock angrily. Then he turned on Sally. "It's easy to laugh if you prefer injustice and intolerance."

"Hey!" Grubbock said. "Wait a minute! What makes you think you have cornered the market in justice and tolerance?"

Sally said gently, "You know, Karl, there are people who may think quite differently from you but who want these things too."

"But do they work for them, fight for them? They talk. They are shams."

"You aren't being exactly fair to your country's history," Sally said.

"Look at it!" he said bitterly. "Republicans and Democrats have been shaping this country for almost two hundred years, and what have we got?"

Sally glanced at Grubbock. She said with a touch of irony, "We haven't done too badly, compared with most other countries." Then her voice became serious, "And I'm not talking about one small group in our population. I'm talking about the average man."

"So you don't think changes are necessary? It's all just perfect for you?" he asked mockingly.

"No," she said, trying to keep her temper. "I'd admit what was good in our country, and go on with reforms from there."

"You're afraid of change," he told her. "You want to patch up an old system to keep it from falling to pieces."

"And what new system do you suggest?"

"In —" He stopped. You had to be careful nowadays not to say "in Soviet Russia." Two years ago, you could have used it as a powerful argument. Four years ago, everyone — except for a few crypto-fascists — would have applauded. But now, they'd look at you, call you a Communist.

"In fact, there isn't a new system," Sally said quietly. "Even Communism has been tested for thirty years. And I'm sure you couldn't possibly suggest that the system that suited Russia, thirty years ago, would suit America in 1948? Or even what suits Russia today would suit us?"

"And what do you know about Russia today, except what you read in the capitalist press?" he asked. That started him off.

Ah, me! thought Sally, and I brought this on myself. The same old arguments, the same old phrases and political clichés, the sweeping generalizations, the half-truths presented as whole truths. Even the use of words in a foreign way, such as "lackey." (When, in America, had a lackey served dinner or opened the door or driven your car?) Karl was convinced and sincere about what he said; so convinced, that she watched him and wondered if he had followed these arguments to their logical conclusion.

She felt cold. She shivered in the warm room.

Grubbock had sensed something of her emotions. He rose suddenly. "Look, Karl," he said abruptly, "leave implementing your ideology, and get this question about your horse straightened out. We leave early tomorrow on this trip. Are you going to take Brent's advice, or aren't you?" He glanced at his watch as if to excuse himself. "It is almost lunchtime, and there's your mail to be collected."

"If Brent's afraid for his property, *I* wouldn't want to worry him. The greatest sin of the twentieth century is an attack on property. That's unforgivable. Human beings can be underpaid, starved, overworked. But don't let anyone destroy property. You can get arrested for that."

"That's a good exit line," Grubbock said, trying to make a joke of the fact that Karl was already halfway to the door.

"No one would arrest you for breaking a horse's leg, Karl," Sally said quietly. "So stop hamming. The worst that might happen would be that you'd have to shoot the horse. Wouldn't that worry you?"

She looked after him unhappily. She said to Grubbock, "But what else could I say, there? If I told him he'd probably break his own neck or smash his thigh — which could happen very easily on the kind of horse he wants to ride — he wouldn't have listened. He's proud of being brave."

Grubbock shrugged his shoulders. But he admitted to himself that he had been noticing that, too, in these last weeks.

"He'd be fine," Sally said, "if he stopped straightening other people out, and attended to himself for a change. But he's probably gone away thinking the same thing about me."

Grubbock had to laugh. Karl would be doing that, all right.

"Well, that was a wasted hour," Koffing said, as he and Grubbock reached the cabin. "We might have got some work done. Instead, we listened to a frustrated woman's ideas on a world where the possibility of any change terrifies her."

"If she were frustrated," Grubbock said quietly, "it's possible she'd welcome any change. Hell, where's the whisky? I feel thirsty after all that." He searched for the rye. The bottle was empty.

Karl said, "Forgotten last night's party? Carla and Mimi; and Esther Park arriving uninvited?"

"Now *that* was a wasted hour or two. All Mimi wanted was to talk. . . . Hell, what has Brent got that we haven't?"

"Thirty, or was it fifty, thousand acres."

"Look, Karl, they may have helped to start her off on him. But Mimi's far beyond that stage now. I was sorry for her last night. She's trying to hide it, she thinks. But she's serious, all right."

"With *that* stock character? He's too busy counting his steers to notice anything else. He'll probably realize she was here a year from next Christmas."

"How do you know so much about him?" Grubbock asked evenly. His own guess had been that Jim Brent was handling a difficult situation in his own quiet way.

"He doesn't take much knowing. What makes you so curious?" The two men eyed each other, outwardly still friendly. Karl's brown eyes were smiling. Earl's face, with its broad cheekbones and snub features, looked as placid as ever. But there had been a slight edge to these two last questions.

"Just wondered how you get people straight so easily," Earl said in his easy, lazy way. "Must make novel writing a cinch for you."

Koffing said nothing. His eyes weren't smiling now.

"It's time we were getting down to some real work," Earl went on. "When we get back from this trip, I'm going to start a routine. Less talk; fewer parties."

"Better get Norah to leave, then," Karl suggested. "In this last week, you drop everything the minute you see her." His voice was bitter.

"Sure," Grubbock said ironically. "Let's blame it on everyone except ourselves. And what's making you so goddamned bad-tempered today? I saw O'Farlan's manuscript lying on Sally's table, too."

There was a short silence. Then they both smiled. The quarrel which had been edging nearer for days wasn't going to come off.

"At least, you've started writing," Karl said.

"What's stopping you?"

"I don't know," Karl said worriedly. "I've got stuck with my damned characters."

"Well, if they bore you, throw them out. Get yourself some new ones."

213

Karl's annoyance returned. "I'm not bored by them. I'm writing what I am writing, and no woman is going to change my ideas."

"I haven't changed mine," Earl said, equally sharply. "I haven't changed a damned bit. Except —"

"Except?" Karl asked derisively.

"All right then. Except to concentrate more on human beings and less on type-casting. Perhaps that's all you need, too. Then you'd be so damned interested that nothing would stop you from writing."

"Nothing's going to stop me once I leave this place. Once I'm back in New York —"

"There will be speeches to make and political meetings to attend. That will keep you tied up until November. Then after that — well, there's the next election to work for, isn't there?"

The novel should have been finished this month, Karl thought. That had been the idea — to come here and finish it. Then back to New York, with a clear mind and all his energy now turned to the last six weeks of the election campaign. That had been the idea. Instead, this place had defeated him. Defeated? Not that. Then what had it done?

"I can't work here," he said. "It's narcotic. It's —" He didn't finish the sentence.

"Frankly, I'd say you were getting into a state of mind where you can't work anywhere."

"And what's my state of mind?" Karl was suddenly angrier than Earl had ever seen him.

"You're too damned sure about everything. Anyone outside your group is either a menace or a moron."

"Sounds as if you were trying to say I'm a dyed-in-the-wool Republican."

That's right, Grubbock thought bitterly, joke about it, twist the point of the argument and make me feel a fool. "Look," he said, and his voice was angry now, "do you want the truth or don't you? Scared of it?"

Koffing sat quite still, saying nothing, forcing himself under control. His face became expressionless, he relaxed the muscles in his hands. He had a feeling of triumph, and then he controlled that sudden emotion too. He looked at Grubbock blankly. "Go ahead," he said. "This will be good for a laugh, anyway."

"Yeah. And it may be on you. You keep talking about 'the people,' but you've forgotten what the word means. You used to think about people in terms of human beings — that's how you started worrying about politics to begin with. That's how most of us start worrying about politics and shifting left. And that's all right, as long as you keep thinking about people as human beings. But you didn't. Somewhere along that road you've been traveling, you lost sight of human beings."

Grubbock paused and waited, but Koffing only outstared him. "You don't believe me?" Grubbock's anger increased. "I'm telling you that you only think of people as stereotypes. So how the hell are you going to be a novelist? Better stick to writing political speeches, all black and white. Or finish this novel and use it as a political tract. But for Christ's sake, don't keep bellyaching that you can't write a real novel. You could have; but you killed it. And if you want to blame anything or anyone, blame yourself. It's all your own choice."

Karl had everything under control. He could even produce a smile on his lips. It was, he thought, good training. "Interesting," he said.

Grubbock stared at him. "Okay, okay," he said at last. "I give up." He turned on his heel and left the cabin.

Karl Koffing drew a deep breath. Then he slowly lit a cigarette. He glanced over his shoulder at the door, but it was still closed. Let Grubbock sulk this one out, he thought. When Grubbock cools off, he will begin to feel a fool. That's the time to argue with him.

Koffing rose from his chair and walked over to the window. He stared at the mass of trees encircling the cabin's glade.

It's this damned place, he told himself. I'll leave. As soon as this trip into the mountains is over, I can pack up and get out. Grubbock will be normal once he is back in New York again. And I'll get my novel finished. It's this damned place.

215

CHAPTER XX

Roundup

A PALE golden light spread slowly over the fields and hills, bringing the land to life again. Half an hour ago, it had been a smooth surface of dimmed shapes and black shadows: a picture painted in muted shades on a flat, smooth canvas. But now its furrows and sinews gradually stood out in bold relief. The mountains were no longer a wall of stone, but separate peaks, advancing, receding, rising, falling, each with its own subtle coloring of rock that changed from gray-blue to blue-gray, from white-yellow to white-red, from black crag to red canyon. They were veined and traced by the jagged spines and sharp precipices which slashed through the forests that ringed their lower slopes. Even the trees were different at this hour. The firs were each outlined clearly by the early sun's slanting rays; their dark mass had become an army of fretted shapes advancing down into the valley in close formation. There, the round cottonwood trees and the thin birches seemed to have been cut out of bright green and silvered cardboard, given invisible feet so that they could be arranged around the neat silhouettes of houses and barns. Above, the scattered white clouds, edged with gold and pink, trailed out from the horizon.

That, Earl Grubbock thought, is the final master stroke, carelessly beautiful. I might make a habit of getting up with the dawn and become a painter or a poet. I might. Or I might just see it once in a while, when I have to, and gape and be speechless until I think of some clever remark to show what an opinion man has of himself.

He turned away from the view, back to the problem of fastening his rolled blankets onto the cantle of his saddle. The sharp air made his fingers clumsy. "Cold," he said to Karl Koffing who was working on a slip knot.

"Damn cold." Koffing looked up at the mountains again, looked at the clouds. "I've a theory," he said, tugging at the leather string which had slipped its knot entirely, so that his blanket roll sagged sideways. "Once, most people lived in the country or near enough the country. Once, people went to bed early because they hadn't electric light to keep them sitting up. So once, people got up early and called it normal. And this is what they saw." He nodded to the sky and the sun rising in all its glory. "Hence Tiepolo. All you need up there, at this moment, is a couple of cupids and a few saints and you'd have a Tiepolo picture, full of curves and lights and blue and gold."

Grubbock looked with some surprise at Koffing. But he contented himself with a nod. He didn't feel like talking, somehow. None of the others were. They were working quietly, as if the deep peace of the sky had slipped down from the mountains and the hills, had flowed over and around them.

Koffing stood back to survey the effect of his re-tied saddle string. "Not too bad," he said, as he surveyed his workmanship. "A bit to one side, but it'll look worse before it's unpacked." He lit a cigarette and watched Chuck and Jackson helping Bert and Robb with the pack horse. Ned and Jim Brent were saddling up.

Grubbock, watching them too, noticed that if their movements seemed leisurely, they were efficient enough. They worked precisely, neatly, as men who knew their jobs. It was an expert bit of packing that Bert and Robb were doing, making sure of careful balance in bulk and weight.

"We're late," Karl said, glancing at his watch. But he spoke easily, stating a simple fact, without any touch of criticism except the amused shake of his head. Grubbock thought, Karl's in a good mood: yesterday is forgotten. That was all right with Grubbock. This trip was going to work out well, after all.

Jim Brent came over to them. "All set?" He seemed scarcely to glance at the rolls tied on to their saddles. "Might be a good idea to take a slicker along."

"Just another thing to carry," Koffing said. "The weather looks good to me."

"At the moment," Jim agreed.

Grubbock looked at him. One thing he had discovered out West: you had to listen to what wasn't said, just as much as you listened to words that were spoken. "I'll run down to the cabin and get our raincoats," Grubbock said. He was annoyed with himself; he thought he had remembered everything.

"That'll hold things up," Koffing told him, glancing at his watch again. He was thinking, six o'clock they said, and six o'clock it is; they can't say that we kept them late. "I don't need a raincoat," he added and studied the sky.

"A slicker comes in mighty useful," Jim Brent suggested. "It makes a good ground-sheet, you'll find. We're late in any case. That damned pack horse. They're just naturally mean, it seems." He looked again at the ill-tied bundle on the back of Koffing's saddle. He said nothing about that; but his keen eyes narrowed for a moment and he tilted his head just slightly to one side, as if he were avoiding the smoke that came drifting up from the cigarette in the corner of his mouth.

"Okay," Grubbock said, and moved off down the path towards the cabin. He knew when to take a hint. That was the way advice was given, out here. When you were among the Romans, you might as well listen to them, for they knew what to do. Karl would have to repack that roll; and adding a slicker to it was one way of getting it properly packed this time. Brent would see to that. What Karl needed was some basic training. Then Grubbock thought, that's a hell of an idea for a pacifist to have! But before he could argue that one out, he saw Mimi. He was surprised enough to stop dead in his tracks.

"Hello there!" Mimi said brightly as she passed him. She was walking quickly, determinedly.

"Going to kiss the boys good-by?" Grubbock called over his shoulder. Then he wished he hadn't. Brent had heard him. Brent was looking down the path towards Mimi. And for a moment Mimi hesitated, and the smile was less confident.

"Well, well," Grubbock said to himself, and continued his way to the cabin.

Brent and Koffing were silent as they watched Mimi approach the corral. Her hat, crisply shaped, was set jauntily above the smooth red hair. Her flannel blouse fitted her excellently. (But — as Koffing admitted — it had something to fit. Carla's shirt always seemed too big, Esther Park's a couple of sizes too small.) It opened low, as if a button had been forgotten, and a silk scarf around her neck was folded into the deep neckline. A heavy leather belt was pulled tight almost at hipline, and her blue jeans fitted as neatly and smoothly as any cowboy's. Over one shoulder, she had draped a fringed buckskin jacket.

"Dressed for action," Koffing said. "I have to hand it to Mimi: wherever she is, she looks the part. She's even adopted a new walk."

"These boots aren't ballet slippers," Jim Brent said. He was watching Mimi with a mixture of annoyance and amusement.

Koffing looked at him curiously. All the men Karl knew in New York were willing to bankrupt themselves for a week in order to take Mimi out for an evening. (That was the rottenness of the capitalist system for you.) And there wasn't one man at Rest and Be Thankful who hadn't hoped she'd spend a good deal of her time with him. Dewey Schmetterling had known that, of course; that was the reason he had ditched Mimi before she got around to ditching him, just to be different, just to show the other men he could do it and they couldn't. But here was Brent, eyeing Mimi with no more interest than if she were a new colt. It was the same way Brent and the cow hands looked at these mountains: they looked at them and all they'd say would be "Fine day," or "Seems like it's going to rain."

Mimi Bassinbrook's confidence almost failed her completely as she reached Jim Brent. It was a new and frightening feeling. She changed what she was going to say. Her face changed too: her eyes became hesitant and the smile on her lips was shy. "Hello there!" she said. That was all.

"Hello, Mimi," Koffing said. "You should make a habit of early rising. Brings the color to your cheeks."

She said to Jim Brent, "I always meant to see the sun rise, just once in my life. This seemed as good a morning as any."

"You're a couple of hours late for that," Koffing said sharply. He turned away and walked over to the group around the pack horse.

"Did you have to do that?" Jim Brent asked her. Mimi's eyes opened wide. But he was smiling now, and she relaxed.

"I'm always doing something wrong, it seems," she said with an answering smile. "Although not many others notice it as much as you do, Jim. What's wrong this time?"

"Nothing's wrong. But when a man pays you a compliment you could thank him with a smile. Or do you get too many compliments?"

"Is that why you don't pay me any? Frankly, I didn't notice Koffing. Oh, just blame it on my bad manners. Or on the sunrise." She looked at the hills. And suddenly, she was serious. She stood motionless, completely natural. She wasn't even aware that Jim Brent was watching her.

Earl Grubbock, hurrying back with the slickers over his arm, passed them as he ducked under the hitching-rail to reach his horse. He glanced at Brent's face. Well, he thought in amazement, what did Mimi do to ring the bell this time?

"We'd better get started," Jim Brent said, looking around at Grubbock re-rolling his pack. Koffing was busy on his, too.

"Jim," Mimi began. Then she knew by the smile on his face that he knew her question.

He shook his head. "The answer is no, Mimi. Sorry."

"Don't girls ever go?"

"Sometimes. If they know the rules and can ride well enough. It's a tougher job than you think."

"I can ride as well as Karl does."

He nodded. You can also distract more, he thought.

"I'd like to have gone." She looked at the mountains. "I'll never ride into them, now," she said sadly.

He found himself saying awkwardly, "Well, we'll see about getting you up there before you go back to New York."

She smiled with delight. "That's a promise."

"Sure." And how the hell had he got himself into this? "We'll try and make it," he added.

Something of the happiness in Mimi's face was gone. "We'll try and make it," she agreed, keeping her voice as easy as his. Then she forced a smile and said, "See you in three days. Don't get lost. There's the rodeo on Saturday, you know." And there was to be a dance afterwards.

"We'll be back in good time," he said. "Ned won't let us forget that." He touched his hat and walked towards his horse.

All right, she thought. All right, Mr. Brent. Damn you. She leaned her elbows on the hitching-rail and found the other men more interesting to look at. "I wanted to see the sunrise," she told herself. "So I'm seeing it." But there was a flush on her cheeks and a sharp brightness in her eyes, and the smile on her lips was too set.

"Don't forget to come back for the dance at Sweetwater on Saturday," Mimi called over to Grubbock and Koffing, and gave them a smile all for themselves.

"Technique," Grubbock said in an undertone as he finished strapping Koffing's roll to the cantle. He glanced over at Brent who had heard Mimi's words. "That's what they call technique, brother." But it wasn't as effective as what she had used five minutes ago. He wished that he had arrived a few seconds earlier with the slickers to see how that was done.

The men were mounted. Bert was leading the pack horse. He waited until the others, short-reining their horses, had wheeled around to leave the corral.

"Save a dance for me, too," Ned called across to Mimi.

Grubbock leaned down from his horse to say to her softly, "Cheer up, honey. We'll all be back to dance with you. Even Karl." But he looked at Brent as he turned his horse professionally and rode over to the others.

I hope he falls and breaks his neck, she thought bitterly. Grubbock knew. Karl did, too. How many of the others? She couldn't tell. All she knew was that they liked her, each in his own way. But she felt none of the glow that always accompanied that feeling.

She smiled to them all in turn as they waved to her, giving Jim Brent no more, no less. But as she watched him ride alongside Bert, following Karl and Earl, with Ned and Robb in the lead, all her anger disappeared. She watched them take the trail to the mountains, the dust now rising in a small cloud under the horses' hoofs.

"Always was a pretty sight," Chuck said as he came up with Jackson. They leaned their forearms on the hitching-rail, too. "Yes, a mighty pretty sight in the morning sun."

"Better from horse," Jackson said gloomily.

Chuck nodded, and spat in sympathy.

Mimi looked at Jackson in surprise. "Did you want to go, too?"

At that moment, Ned and Robb spurred their horses into a violent burst of speed and gave a high, ear-splitting whoop that echoed across the valley. Ned was standing in his stirrups. He waved his hat. "Strike for the hills, the dam is broke!" he yelled, and set his horse for the high ground.

"That's Ned," Chuck said. "Always playing up to a pretty face." He grinned as he added, "They won't keep up that pace for long. Seems to me they're all playing up a bit, this morning."

Mimi felt better, somehow. She watched Bert and the pack horse disappear over the hill. "Where do they go?" she asked, staring at the range of mountains.

"It's like this," Chuck said. He pushed back his hat on his head and took his clasp knife slowly out of his pocket. He opened it methodically. Then he dropped on one knee, and drew a line in the loose dirt with the point of the sharp blade "That's the mountains." He made a small square to the east of them: "We're here." He traced a weaving line: "That's Branch Creek, running down to join Crazy Creek in the valley. They're following the trail over that hill to the draw, and that brings them to Branch Creek." As he spoke in his slow, quiet way, he traced each point as he named it. "Up above Branch Creek, there's Two Fork Gap. There, they take the West Thumb, and cross it, about three miles up, at Lazy Way. They climb then, keeping Flashing Smile on their right. Climb for two thousand feet, maybe, up Black Rock mountain. That gets them to Muledeer Pass. They start going down a ways, I reckon about five hundred feet. Boulder Trail, they call it. Then the ground levels out, and that's the plateau they're on. That's where they start working. Park land, and forests, and mountains all around. And not one human being to spoil the view between you and the next eighty miles."

He rose stiffly, wiped off the blade on his blue jeans, and closed the knife with a snap. "There's a good pot of coffee on the stove," he said, looking away from the mountains, pulling his hat back into place over his eyes.

They walked over in silence to Cowpoke's Corner. Just three of us who wanted to go, Mimi thought. "Is it so beautiful up there?" she asked.

Chuck poured out the thick black coffee into three thick mugs, then carefully chose the one without any cracks or chips to give to her.

She thought, at first, that he hadn't heard her question. Then at last he said, "Sure is."

There was another silence. "Sure is," Chuck repeated. "Prettier than the prettiest woman I ever saw."

"Was that why you never got married, Chuck? No woman ever came up to the standards the mountains set?" She was half-joking, but a new idea had taken hold of her mind. She looked through the open door at the mountains. A new kind of competitor, she thought. Well, I'll take you on.

"Was married twice. Buried both of them," Chuck said and rolled a cigarette. "Got two sons and five grandchildren," he added proudly.

"Why —" Mimi looked at him in amazement. "I never thought you had been married, somehow."

"Guess most men try it once. Bert had a wife over in Laramie, mighty nice woman. He buried her last spring. Ned's been often as near married as don't matter. Jim's wife — well," he was too busy licking the cigarette paper to finish that sentence.

"Jim?" Then to save her confusion, she turned to Jackson. "And how many wives have you had, Jackson?" she asked quickly. He had been listening intently to Chuck, smiling when Chuck smiled, as if

223

there was a sense of humor which men alone shared. Now Jackson's broad face grew broader as his grin widened.

"No wives," he said triumphantly.

"Guess he traveled around too fast," Chuck suggested and struck a match on his thigh. "Got away before they catched him, every time." This sent Jackson into a roar of laughter. "But," Chuck went on, a smile coming into his eyes suddenly, "he'll have to step kind of lively when he's over to Sweetwater for a visit. Wouldn't surprise me none if Wyoming don't get her brand on him."

"You seem to know how to keep him amused," Mimi said to Chuck, smiling as she listened to Jackson's deep laugh. Then she remembered the look on Jackson's face as he had stood beside her at the corral and watched the others ride away. "Jackson," she asked gently, "why didn't you go with the boys, today?"

Jackson's dark eyes, under the heavy black eyebrows, said nothing at all.

"Was it because of us — the guests?"

Chuck said tactfully, "He has his reasons." And that, his voice said, is enough. Don't go bothering a man with questions and then complain of a truthful answer.

"Do you like it here, then?" Mimi persisted.

"Sure," Jackson answered.

"Why?" That was a question which she had been asking herself, too, during these last three weeks. Her answer wasn't altogether Jim Brent: there was something about this place. . . . Perhaps if you loved New York's skyscrapers you loved mountains. Prender Atherton Jones didn't like mountains, but he didn't like skyscrapers, either.

But Jackson's answer was something she had never expected. He looked at her as if deciding whether to speak frankly. Afterwards, she was flattered that he had decided to tell her. He said, "In Paris, Rome, London, New York, I am servant. I open door for you. I pour coffee for you, give you cup on tray. Here, I sit and drink coffee with you."

She looked at Chuck. "I see," she said. "And I agree with you. It makes life easier, somehow." She tried to imagine a ranch where the cowboys were treated as servants, where men didn't know their own value or recognize the dignity of others. It was impossible to imagine. It just couldn't be. "It's more pleasant for everyone," she said. She wondered how she could now bring the conversation safely back to Jim Brent, but she had chopped it off and there was no joining it together again. And as she looked at Chuck, she knew he wouldn't talk about Jim and Jim's wife. That, too, was what Jackson liked — the way these people measured their distance between people: they knew how far to come, how far not to go, and they expected the same from you. There was, behind their frankness, a line of respect drawn between friendliness and privacy.

She rose. "Thanks for the coffee, Chuck. Hope I wasn't a nuisance coming up to the corral so early." She tried to sound diffident, but she had already begun to worry about it. She should never have come to the corral, this morning. She knew that now.

"Mighty nice thing to see a smiling face when you set out for the hills," Chuck said.

And that was typical too, she thought as she walked slowly towards Rest and Be Thankful. There were a lot of answers Chuck could have given, and he had chosen the kindest. He knew why she was depressed and he wasn't going to add to her unhappiness.

He knew. Did everyone know? And she thought she had kept it secret. So that she wouldn't look a fool if she didn't win.

She halted, standing in the bright sunshine, frowning away her unexpected tears as she looked at the silent house sheltering behind the tall cottonwood trees. What had happened to her, anyway? Something begun in fun, in a desire for conquest — something that had turned savagely earnest, bitterly real. Yes, people said, you know when it's love, you know: there's no mistaking the real thing. She had thought they lied. She had thought she had been in love, often. There were some men she had wanted to see; she had been happy when they admired her, sought her out, made love to her. For two months, or three — and, once, for almost five — she would persuade herself that this was what people must mean when they talked about love. This was all there was to it. . . . And men, after a while, were all very much the same. They were the same, of a sameness that only was made different by the difference in their

225

looks, by the color of eyes and hair or the set of a chin or a tone of voice. And then . . . barely three weeks ago . . . Jim Brent hadn't sought her out, he hadn't made love to her, he hadn't given her attention or presents or even an admiring look. Well, perhaps he had given her an admiring look, but only as he'd give *any* pretty girl an admiring look. Yet, when he walked towards her, or stood watching her as she talked, or looked at her with that half-smile in his eyes; when he rode beside her, or rode away from her as he had done this morning — well, she knew now. She couldn't explain it. She just knew. And she couldn't do anything about it. People had been right, and she had been wrong: there's no mistaking the real thing.

She began to walk slowly towards Crazy Creek, avoiding the path through the yard where Mrs. Gunn would see her and welcome her in for a cup of coffee. Mrs. Gunn was too quick to notice. . . .

Mimi reached the creek, by way of the field at the side of the garden, and followed its twisting bank. Her feet were soaked with the heavy dew clinging to each blade of thick green grass. It was cold in the hard black shadows of the trees. She was so unhappy that she was afraid. I'm in love, she thought, and I didn't want it this way. I wanted it the simple, easy, happy way. Instead, I don't know even if he likes me. Yes, I do. . . . he does like me. A little? Much? More than I think? He doesn't dislike me. . . . Then why doesn't he fall in love with me? Why did this happen to me? This way? I'm in love for the first time in my life, and I've never been so unhappy. Never, never. I've never been so confused and bewildered and afraid. I hate love. I hate it, hate it, hate it. "I *hate* it!" she said aloud.

"That sounds a bad way to begin a morning." It was Robert O'Farlan's voice. She looked round angrily. Her eyes searched the garden, the trees. Then she saw him. He was standing on the rough stones in the creek's bed, where its waters had gradually receded with summer. The chokecherry bushes had hidden him, but he must have been there ever since she had left the field and reached the garden.

"Better come down here," he said. "These stones are dryer than the grass. You might as well have waded up the creek as through that dew."

She glanced down at her sodden boots. "Oh," she said, "it doesn't matter." But she scrambled down the short bank, through the chokecherry bushes laden with their rich clusters of bright red berries, and he gave her a hand and steadied her.

"Well, what do you see down here?" she asked, in control of herself once more. She looked round, smiled up at him, and shrugged her shoulders. "Do you make a habit of this?"

"It's one way to spend the hour before breakfast," he said. "I seem to waken at six whether I want to or not." The sunlight broke through the leaves overhead, dappling the water and the stones. The wily trout was hiding in the shadows of a pool. He had meant to point out these things to Mimi, but now he didn't want to. The robins had flown, anyway, as she came down the bank. There was only a bold magpie left, staring at them curiously, angrily.

"*You* shouldn't be looking worried," Mimi said. "Now that you've got your book finished, you've got what you wanted."

He seemed startled, tried to smile and failed. "Have I?" he asked. "Mimi, you look cold and peaked. We'll go up to Ma Gunn's kitchen and get a cup of coffee."

"I feel more like a walk," she said. "Will you come with me? I need someone to talk to."

"What's wrong?"

She glanced at him quickly. He was studying her face. It was a habit he had when he thought she wasn't looking. It had amused her secretly. But now it didn't. Here was another man who could fall in love with her if she planned it that way. Now, it only reminded her of a man who couldn't, or wouldn't. . . .

"Me," she said bitterly. "I'm all wrong. Have you ever felt all wrong?"

"Constantly. Haven't you?"

She was surprised, both by his answer and by his question. She had never felt all wrong before, never.

"You should be happy," she said. "You've written a book. And you've a job. Which is more than Earl Grubbock has."

"That's his own choice. He doesn't want a steady job. He says he likes to be free to change," O'Farlan reminded her.

"Well, you've a job that *you* like. Karl hasn't."

"No one is forcing him to write advertising copy. And his boss can't be as bad as Koffing says he is, not if Koffing got a month's vacation in order to finish his book."

"I suppose so." Mimi had been grateful enough to the publishing firm she worked for, when they agreed to an extra week's vacation without pay so that she might come here. Carla was lucky in having her funny little bookstore, down in the Village, close for the hot weeks of August. And Bob O'Farlan, being a schoolteacher, had the summer to himself entirely. He didn't know how lucky he was. "Well, if that doesn't cheer you up, you've got a wife and children. That's what most men want, isn't it? A steady job, a wife, and children."

"Yes," he said, his voice flat and noncommittal.

Mimi looked at him. He liked teaching, she knew.

They climbed along the dry edge of the creek until they came to the bridge. There, they scrambled up the bank to the road. They walked in the direction of Snaggletooth.

"Bob," she said unexpectedly, "why didn't your wife come out here?" She had never thought that important before; this morning, somehow, it was.

"Jenny?" He was startled once more. "Oh, she couldn't. She's got the children."

But they were quite old: fifteen or something. Mimi said, "That may have been an excuse. Perhaps she thought she'd be too alone; after all, when you work you don't think of very much else. Do you always write this way?"

"When I get the time to write." He was half-angry, now.

"I know it's difficult. I've a job, too, you know, to eat up my days."

"And very few free evenings, I'd imagine," he said coldly.

"You think I'll never write anything?" She looked at him in surprise. She had a way of asking questions, her eyes wide, her lips ready to smile as if she hoped the answer would be a kind one. It was hard to disappoint her, he found. His anger left him.

228

He smiled. "No one is going to write the book for you, Mimi. Why worry about it, anyway? You may as well enjoy your life and keep happy. That may be more important than writing a book."

"But I *want* to write."

He didn't answer.

"I know what you are thinking," she said. "I've no self-discipline. Well, I can have it if I want to. How do you think I keep my figure like this, anyway? And I have experienced life, and I have imagination, and I have — why, what are you thinking? I wasn't trying to boast. Is there anything wrong in listing your assets to cheer yourself up a bit?"

He shook his head. Experienced life, she had said. She had always got what she wanted. That wasn't the kind of experience she needed, not if she wanted to write. But he couldn't tell her that.

"This is one of my favorite views," he said, as they climbed the hilly road. He stopped to look at the mountains, rising in uneven rows beyond the green valley. "I think I see the boys," he said suddenly, and pointed. "Up there! On the shoulder of that second hill above Branch Creek."

Mimi didn't look. "Let's go back," she said. "I'm cold."

They said nothing as they walked quickly down the road, but at the bridge she spoke again. "What do *you* mean by self-discipline? Worries and troubles? Well, I've had them. Or disappointments? I've had them too."

"But never very real ones, never very deep ones. You've been luckier than most, Mimi."

"You sound as if you envied me," she said in surprise. "I thought you — well, I just thought, that's all."

"That I was middle-aged, and thoroughly satisfied, and set in my ways? That I never wanted to turn the clock back twenty years and begin again?"

"But if you wanted that, you could."

"Only if others wanted it, too — all the others who are part of my life as I am a part of theirs. But I am not a free agent. No man is."

"You mean that to keep these others happy, you'd be willing to be unhappy?"

"*Not* willing," he admitted. "But it's got to be done. That's all."

Mimi thought suddenly, we are talking about his family, about his wife. She tried to choose her next words carefully, to keep everything as impersonal as possible. "Won't they feel your unwillingness? Won't that make them as unhappy as you will be? So what good is your sacrifice?"

He said sharply, "I've been thinking that out for months." But not exactly in that way, he reminded himself.

"I'm sorry. I wanted to get you to cheer me up. And all I've done is stir up your troubles."

"Don't worry. I've got accustomed to them in the last ten years." He disliked himself for that remark the moment it was made. And perhaps I helped to earn my disappointments, he thought. It was a new idea. He didn't like it. But it stuck with him.

"I think we both need coffee," Mimi said, leading the way into the house. They went through the hall towards the kitchen. Carla was already there, for they could hear her voice as they approached its door. ". . . . haunted by her. A man can easily get rid of a woman." Mrs. Gunn said, "Can he?" in that dry way of hers, and Carla said, "At least, you'd . . ."

But Mimi had moved away from the kitchen door. She looked down at her boots. "I suppose I'd better change them first," she said.

"A good idea," O'Farlan said quickly.

She looked back when she was nearly at the top of the staircase. He was still standing in the hall, watching her.

She went into her room and sat down on the edge of her unmade bed. Everyone knew. O'Farlan and Mrs. Gunn and Carla, Chuck and Koffing and Grubbock. Once she would have been scornful. Let them talk, she would have said and she'd have laughed. But now, she covered her face with her hands and pressed her cold fingers against the cheeks that were suddenly on fire. Some men might be flattered or amused to have a pretty girl so much interested in them that others could notice. But he wouldn't be either flattered or amused. He'd be as mad as hell. If I don't win him, she realized suddenly, it won't be anything or anyone else that beat me — it won't be the mountains or any other woman. It will be just Mimi Bassinbrook, as I've made her.

Carla Brightjoy had tidied her room, made her bed, and found she was still half an hour early for breakfast. So she went downstairs into the kitchen, as she often did in the mornings, to get an early cup of coffee and help with the orange juice. Now that Drene had gone, Mrs. Gunn needed some extra help.

She needed it especially this morning. Norah, who looked as if she had been crying, was avoiding the kitchen. And Mrs. Gunn, as she mixed the dough for sweet rolls, looked as if she had been making someone cry.

"Come in, come in," she said, when she turned round to see Carla hesitating at the door. "Help yourself to coffee. I won't bite your head off."

Carla drank the cup of coffee without saying anything.

"You're very silent this morning," Mrs. Gunn said, looking up suddenly from her work. She smiled. "I'm not angry with anyone. I'm just worried."

Carla abandoned her silence gladly. "Norah?" she asked.

"Earl Grubbock," Mrs. Gunn corrected her. "Caught him standing out in the yard, this morning, with slickers over his arm, throwing pebbles up at Norah's window to get her out of bed. She was out of it, too, standing at the window, waving to him."

"That seems harmless enough."

"But where's it going to lead to? He will be leaving in little over a week. She'll never see him again."

"Yes, we'll all be leaving," Carla said gloomily. She looked round the friendly kitchen and thought of her bare little room in Greenwich Village. Once, she had thought it romantic. "I suppose it was my own fault that I was lonely in New York," she said. "I used to see plenty of people each day; but if I talked to a customer at all, it was always about some book. That's why I chose the job, of course: I thought books would be the right kind of work for me to do. And I thought if I stayed at home each night and read and wrote, then

231

I'd be a writer. Then I wondered why I got rejection slips. Saying 'Promising. Regrets.' And some just said 'Regrets.' That's as far as I got."

"I guess you were too scared of people."

"I see that now. Funny how you don't see things at the time."

"Well, you aren't scared any more," Mrs. Gunn said.

"Not so much." Carla put down the empty coffee cup, and started halving the oranges. "I've changed a little, haven't I? Am I beginning to do you credit?"

"Me?"

"Yes, you. I keep my glasses for reading and writing. I wear my shirt tucked into my jeans. I've stopped braiding my hair and putting ribbons on it. I've cut it short, and everyone likes it."

"Don't see what I had to do with it," Mrs. Gunn protested. But she was pleased. She added a little twist of decoration to each roll as she shaped it with her firm, light hand.

"Oh, it was just a feeling I got from you. You send out little waves of approval and disapproval, you know," Carla said with a laugh.

"I wish Earl Grubbock felt them."

"Why don't you like him, Mrs. Gunn?"

"I do. Only, I just don't want him being casual with Norah, the way he treated his girls in Europe."

"How do you know if he had any girls in Europe?"

"I can read, can't I? All soldiers had girls, and treated them as if they were a glass of beer or a steak dinner. And if men treated girls that way, abroad — and I can't find any book that tells me different — then that's the way they'll treat them anywhere. And I don't think that's good enough for *any* girl, wherever she lives. A nice girl deserves better than that, doesn't she?"

"But perhaps Earl isn't that kind of man."

"I don't get the feeling he's looking for a wife. He's here for a good time, and a pretty girl is part of it."

"But Norah's awfully sensible, Mrs. Gunn."

"*That's* a new word for staying out until one o'clock every morning." Mrs. Gunn bustled around the kitchen, banged the oven

232

door, slammed the skillet on the stove, as if energy would dissipate her anger. It helped. "As I see it," she said more calmly, "there are several men who wouldn't object to falling in love with Norah, and marrying her, and keeping her happy for the rest of her life. What's wrong with that?"

"Nothing." It made Carla unhappy even to think of it, though.

"So what right have other men to come and enjoy themselves for a few weeks, and make a girl fall in love with them, and then leave her?"

"They don't think of it that way."

"Then it's about time they did. Let them enjoy themselves with girls that follow the same game and know their rules. That's all I'm asking. Is that unfair?"

"But I don't think life was ever fair to women. Or else we'd all be beautiful. Like Drene or Mimi Bassinbrook." Carla thought for a little, and then she added with painful honesty, "You know, if I were a man I suppose I'd be stupid enough to fall for Mimi. She's the most attractive girl." Except Drene, of course, but she hadn't better praise Drene to Mrs. Gunn.

Mrs. Gunn said nothing.

Carla, knowing she was making a mistake, still couldn't resist making it. She had been too fascinated and bewildered by Mimi Bassinbrook, ever since she came here. "Do you think Jim Brent's more in love with her than he admits? It seems strange that he lets himself be haunted by her. A man can easily get rid of a woman."

"Can he?" Mrs. Gunn asked dryly. She was seemingly concentrating on cutting the slab of bacon into neat slices.

"At least, you'd think so," Carla said quickly, appeasingly. "I suppose it must be difficult, too. The trouble is, some girls have so many easy conquests that they think every man could be theirs for the taking."

"Maybe," Mrs. Gunn said.

There was silence. Carla flushed a little. She measured the orange juice with exaggerated care into the nine glasses before her.

"Come in, Mr. O'Farlan," Mrs. Gunn was saying. "Coffee's over there. Help yourself."

233

CHAPTER XXI

Mrs. Peel Changes Her Mind

I T WAS a very peaceful evening, Mrs. Peel thought. She glanced round the living room, and tried to imagine Earl and Karl in the mountains. By this time, they would have made camp for the night: they'd be stretched near their fire, wrapped in warm blankets, looking at the stars. A most poetical experience, if you could judge by all the accounts you had read of sleeping out on mountainsides.

But it was certainly peaceful here. Robert O'Farlan had no one to argue with tonight. He was pretending to be reading a magazine, and not managing it very well. Perhaps he was unsettled by the presence of Prender Atherton Jones, who was reading the last pages of Robert's manuscript with a critical frown. Mimi was sitting as near the fire as possible, with an extra cardigan draped round her shoulders. She was shivering a little, and beginning to sneeze, and she said nothing at all. Carla and Esther were over by the window seat; Esther was talking enthusiastically, Carla was looking a little surprised. Sally was studying the Help Wanted columns in a newspaper, trying to look cheerful, forcing herself to be amused.

Suddenly, Robert O'Farlan rose. "I've got a letter to write," he said, and left the room.

Mimi looked after him. She wondered if it could be a letter to his wife. Then she told herself she was becoming slightly soft in the head with sentimental imaginings. Bob's problems were his own, weren't they? She had enough to think about, in her own life. Only — She got up slowly from her chair. "I think I'm catching a cold," she admitted at last. "I'm going to bed."

"I think that's very wise," Mrs. Peel said. "Take some aspirin."

234

Sally looked up from the newspaper. "I'll get that for you, and a hot-water bottle."

"I can manage," Mimi said sharply. Then she softened her voice and said, "Thanks all the same." She left at once.

Sally and Mrs. Peel exchanged glances. Sally folded the newspaper — not one suitable job unless you could add figures, do shorthand, sew furs, or manicure nails. She left, too, and went into the library to find something for Mimi to read in bed.

Peaceful evening, Mrs. Peel reminded herself with a touch of bitterness. Sally was unhappy and worried. She had been hiding it for days, and her method of hiding it was to be as kind as possible to Mimi. To make up, perhaps, for the unkind thoughts she must have about Mimi. Mrs. Peel, who hadn't allowed herself to be worried about Mimi before, was suddenly depressed. That might be the result of repressing her worries over money matters. But it had seemed wise not to think about approaching bankruptcy until August was over, and the guests had gone away. For the guests would then feel something was wrong, and that would spoil everything for them. Yet worries were never repressible; they just bobbed up in another disguise.

Mimi . . . If Sally were taking this Mimi-Jim Brent affair to heart, then that was really something to worry about. In all those years, Sally had put up a careful guard against men: she was never going to let herself be hurt so violently, so cruelly again. And here, she had relaxed that guard, let it slip just enough. But surely she couldn't be as unhappy as she had been in Paris in 1932. She was older now. She had been barely twenty-one then. Surely that made a difference! I couldn't bear it, Mrs. Peel thought, if I had those weeks in 1932 to go through, all over again. Money worries seemed nothing at this moment: it was one thing to lose your money, but quite another to lose your happiness. No money in the world was going to put that right. Not with someone who felt as deeply as Sally did. How much did she like Jim Brent, anyway? She tried to hide her strongest emotions. That was another bitter lesson she had learned in Paris in those early days. I just couldn't bear it if she got smashed down again, Mrs. Peel thought angrily.

235

Carla, followed by Esther Park, came over to the fireside. Mrs. Peel, putting aside her worries, felt there was an appeal for help in Carla's eyes.

Esther was bubbling over with an idea. "It will be wonderful," she said. "You know, Mrs. Peel, my sister is traveling in Europe next winter. I'm *much* too busy to go with her, and she was worried about leaving me all alone in New York. But she needn't worry any more. Carla is coming to share my apartment in town."

Carla said, "I don't think —"

"It will be perfect," Esther said. "We can talk and write. Just perfect."

"Isn't your apartment uptown? That may be too far away from Carla's job," Mrs. Peel suggested and caught a glance of thanks from Carla.

"Well," Esther said, frowning as she considered that, "perhaps Carla will find a job in a bookstore farther uptown. I know a man who has lots of bookstores. He'll —"

"Why not let Carla arrange her own life?"

"But I was." Esther Park sounded hurt. "Wasn't I, Carla?"

Carla took a deep breath, looked at Mrs. Peel, and then said, "I like my job. And I don't want to change my apartment." But why couldn't I have said that before? she wondered. It was easy enough, after all.

"But you said you didn't like your room," Esther challenged her. "You said —"

"Perhaps Carla didn't mean what she said exactly in the way you interpreted it."

"I was only making conversation," Carla said with a new assurance. "If I don't like my room, that doesn't mean I want to move into an apartment I didn't choose."

Esther Park's eyebrows went up. "I was only trying to help," she said indignantly. She gave Mrs. Peel a bitter look.

She left them and went over to Atherton Jones.

Carla gave Mrs. Peel a smile of thanks. "I think this might be a good time to slip away and finish some work. It's going well, really well."

"I'm glad of that. And I think this might be a very good time."

Mrs. Peel looked over her shoulder to study Atherton Jones, registering alarm, as Esther Park drew up a chair beside him.

"Esther, I am reading," he said in a warning tone. "I am sorry. But I must finish this." He picked up another sheet and gave it all his attention. He didn't answer her next question.

Esther came slowly back to the fire. "Where's Carla gone?"

"She had some work to do."

"It's so dull tonight," Esther said. "Where's Robert O'Farlan?"

"Writing a letter."

"Perhaps he's in the library," Esther said hopefully, and moved towards the door.

"He's very busy. I shouldn't disturb him."

Esther Park studied Mrs. Peel. "You really are very cross tonight," she said. "What have I done?"

Mrs. Peel could only shake her head.

"You don't understand," Esther went on, "but I've *got* to talk to Robert. About something very important. Do you know what he has done?"

Mrs. Peel sighed. What now? Earl Grubbock had made advances to her. Karl Koffing had to be told quite sharply that *she* wasn't that kind of girl; Jackson had forgotten his place; Bert had to be reprimanded; Ned kept looking at her in the most peculiar way. What had poor Robert O'Farlan done?

"Of course," Esther said nobly, "he may not have known what he was doing. But" — she glanced around at Atherton Jones to make sure of a double audience — "he has stolen one of my ideas. And put it in his novel. In the second-last chapter. I told him all about a story I was planning, and he's used it."

Atherton Jones, suddenly sitting very erect, looked over at Esther Park. "And *when* did you see his manuscript? It was never given to you to read."

The anger in his voice startled both women. At last, Mrs. Peel thought thankfully, at last . . .

"I just saw it," Esther Park protested.

"Then you must have read it either in his room or in mine. Who invited you in?"

"He's used my idea."

237

"Nonsense. What idea?"

"About the man who was a failure because his wife underestimated him and then — "

"He told me about that idea more than a year ago. Before you ever met him."

"But I *did* have that idea." She looked pleadingly at them to believe her.

"When you had a look at his manuscript?" Prender Atherton Jones asked cuttingly. Then he picked up the page he had been reading, and concentrated on that.

Mrs. Peel closed her eyes and feigned sleep. It was the weakest evasion she had ever offered, but it worked. When she opened them again, Esther Park had gone. Prender Atherton Jones was standing there instead.

"You're safe now," he said with a smile. Then he became thoughtful, as he placed O'Farlan's manuscript on the mantelpiece. "Something has got to be done about that woman."

"I've been waiting for three whole weeks to hear you say that. Prender, you were wonderful with her. I wish Sally had heard you."

"That kind of thing has to be scotched at once," he said. "It is absolutely intolerable."

Mrs. Peel was thankful that at last he had found something intolerable.

"Something has got to be done," he repeated firmly.

"I agree. And please do it soon, Prender. Yes, you! You know her. I think you might tell her to leave before Karl and Earl get back here."

"It's a most difficult, a most delicate situation." He was less decided now. His anger was leaving him.

Mrs. Peel looked at Prender, thinking that for almost three minutes he had been the Prender she had once known. But now he was retreating into the man whose established position and future plans made him wary of any decisive issue.

He smoothed his hair several times, then looked at the manuscript on the mantelpiece. He laid his hand on it. "Well," he said, "that's that, at least."

238

"Then you like O'Farlan's book?"

He inclined his head. "Yes. On the whole. I have some reservations about the end, though."

"What's wrong with it? It seemed the natural development to me."

"I'm always doubtful of happy endings."

"You mean that the hero ought to have lost his life? He had lost almost everything else he valued. Why, he is like millions of people who keep on going, in spite of everything. That's the whole point about the book, the indestructibility of man's spirit. You'd rather have O'Farlan fake some kind of accident or illness and make his hero die?"

"Well, he's certainly made sure of the book's popularity."

Mrs. Peel stared at him. "Robert wasn't trying for any such thing. He was writing this story as he saw it. If it's a success, good and well."

"A success!" Prender said scornfully. Then he quietened his voice, and even smiled half-sadly. "You've changed your ideas about literature, it seems to me. In the old days in Paris, you used to search for writers who were original and difficult, who had no chance of any popular success whatsoever."

"I still admire originality," she said. "And as for difficulty — well, perhaps I am less of a snob than I used to be. Once, I did think that anything difficult to understand was necessarily important. I got a little thrill — like all snobs — from feeling I was one of the initiated. Yes, I admit it: I paid little attention to the general reading public."

"And now you find them the epitome of all good taste?" He tried to hide his annoyance, but his voice was sarcastic. She might seem to be criticizing herself, yet he felt the quiet voice was criticizing him too.

"No," she said evenly. "I think all taste has to be encouraged and developed. But how can critics like you help it to develop, if you are contemptuous of it? Or don't you *want* it developed?"

"That's a fantastic charge, Margaret." He shrugged his shoulders. Women, he seemed to say, women. . . .

"Well, so far, you've been no help at all! You've shut people out of your literary world, kept it only for the chosen few. You are just as much to blame for any bad taste there is as — as — "

He smiled as he watched her trying to find words; he didn't expect her to finish that sentence.

"As those cynical men who cater to twelve-year-old minds," she said.

He was angry now. He forced himself to be tolerant, and very patient. "I suppose you would say that the critics are to save the people from the snob and the cynic?"

"Why not?" She was in earnest.

"And how many good critics are there in America?" he exploded. She began to count them with infuriating precision.

"Newspaper, magazine hacks," he interrupted her, "all working on a deadline."

That aroused her enough to say, "There you go again, Prender! I suppose if those critics wrote sensitive little pieces for precious little magazines, then you'd think *that* was enough to make them good critics? Really, Prender — don't be like poor Karl Koffing, with everything so neatly black and white."

Sally had entered the room. She said, with a smile, "I always think literary arguments are so invigorating, don't you? Well, Mimi's taken care of. Her tiny hands got frozen this morning, it seems. If her temperature gets any worse, I suppose we ought to send for Dr. Clark. But I think she'll be all right." She settled in a chair near the fire, and then looked up at Prender. "Have a seat, Prender," she said. "You terrify me, looming there like the Empire State Building above me. And what's your new magazine going to be like?" She was trying to change the subject, and she amazed herself. For this was the first time she had ever seen Margaret stand up against Prender. He wasn't enjoying it. He couldn't even talk about his magazine. He didn't even look at Sally.

"What do you mean? I am like Karl Koffing? And aren't *you* a little given to adopting the all black, all white standard? I haven't heard you praise Marie and Charles ever since they took over your printing press in Paris."

"I've never questioned their literary ability," Mrs. Peel said indignantly. "I've only condemned their moral standards in politics. It is their duplicity and treachery that I'm against. Shouldn't I be?"

Sally said, "Prender, what's your new magazine going to be like?"

He answered her this time, although he still didn't look at her. "Margaret will find it precious, I'm sure," he said bitterly. "But I believe it will be important. Not in the materialistic sense, of course. And so I am quite resigned to the fact that it will get little support from the public, despite Margaret's violent belief in their natural good taste."

"But I never said good taste is natural. Taste is something that can be helped, or discouraged." Mrs. Peel looked at him angrily. He could argue so meanly, she thought. "I said — "

"I'm afraid you won't approve of my first editorial," he went on, regaining some of his good humor as he watched her. "I am going to arraign public taste. I am writing a blistering indictment of materialism in America."

"Only in America?" Sally asked. She smiled as he gave her his attention for the first time tonight. "Why, Prender, you've lived long enough in Europe to know the facts of life. There's materialism everywhere. In Europe, they've had longer practice in disguising it, that's all."

"Now, Sally, I can't at all — "

"Take lecturers, for example," Sally said, giving Prender some of his own treatment as she interrupted him skillfully. The word "lecturers" caught his attention. "Few European writers will come to America," she went on smoothly, "unless they are paid a top price to lecture. How many would come, do you think, just to see a new world? And you wonder that such people always see America through gold spectacles?"

Prender Atherton Jones was silent. He was thinking, with some bitterness, of the fees which most Europeans insisted on getting before they ever set foot on a ship to cross the Atlantic.

"Yes," Mrs. Peel said, "we see only as far as we can see, as far as our own limitations let us see. We all have our own horizons."

Prender Atherton Jones was thinking he would have been wiser to have negotiated his lecture fees while he was still in Europe. Only,

241

in 1939, one hadn't had much time to think out such matters. A pity, though . . . Then, Sally's amused voice made him listen.

"Your practising materialist, who firmly believes he has a soul above it all, steps off the ship on his return from America, and what has he to say? Nothing about the music he has heard here, the concerts, the symphony orchestras; nothing about our artists and art collections; nothing about the warmth and generosity and friendliness he has found in people. Oh, no! He holds forth about American materialism. Those who listen to him seem only too eager to agree: it is so pleasant to feel superior to those awful Americans!"

"That's much too broad a charge," Prender said, "I agree about some of those lecturers we've had over here, but — "

"Let me give you the proof of it," Sally said. "People, anywhere, don't like a government that leaves them with less than they had. And I am not talking about freedom, or any other spiritual blessing. I am talking about money, jobs, food, clothes, and all the other material blessings that make life comfortable for us. Take them away from us, and then listen to our complaints!"

Prender stared at her.

"So," she finished equably, "you'd have to live with as few demands as a Yogi, or a Wandering Scholar, if you really wanted to avoid being a materialist." And she looked at him.

"Why Prender," Mrs. Peel said delightedly, "there's a *real* crusade for you to have in your new magazine!"

"What?"

"A crusade against hypocrisy. That would cover so much ground — the arts, politics, religion. And it would be *so* international, too. Down with rationalization! Make the world fit for honest men to live in!"

Prender Atherton Jones looked at her thoughtfully. He hadn't taken a chair, but had remained standing with one elbow resting on the mantelpiece and his feet firmly on the stone hearth. This added yet another inch to his Olympian height.

"Now, Margaret," he said reprovingly, "I am editing a little magazine, not an encyclopedia." And there was no need for her to be so damned facetious, either. He kicked the last log until it broke into two charred ends and fell in a shower of sparks. "You have changed, you know. In the old days, you were quite different."

"So were the old days," Sally said, and rose to find some more logs. They were stacked outside in the kitchen yard, which was something Prender knew as well as she did.

But Prender went on with his own thoughts. Only ten minutes ago, he had placed the manuscript on the mantelpiece and thought, now this might be the time to talk to Margaret. Instead of a pleasant discussion on the state of unmarried loneliness, the need for intelligent companionship, there had been an argument which had got completely out of hand. And there would be no more opportunity to talk to Margaret tonight. Sally would bring in some more logs soon. There was no peace, no privacy at all.

He was so obviously disturbed, even worried, that Mrs. Peel tried to cheer him up. As Sally returned with two small logs (she had to be careful about her cracked ribs, even if they were mending nicely), Mrs. Peel said, "Prender, here's one thing that will really amuse you. About the old days. Did you ever know I was in love with you? Of course, most of the women were. I was absolutely crushed when you married two of my friends, one after the other, and never even looked at me in between."

He pretended to join in her laughter, as he would have done a few years ago. He was looking at her coldly, even as he smiled at such amusing nonsense. For she would never have told him this, in front of Sally, if she still had the remotest feeling for him. She would certainly never have made a joke about it. Thank God, he hadn't proposed ten minutes ago. Thank God! For his proposal would certainly have appealed to Margaret's peculiar sense of humor. There was nothing so infuriating as proposing to a woman and seeing her try to disguise her laughter. Ah well, he thought, Margaret is certainly not in the state of mind to finance my magazine, that's obvious. It was fortunate that he had not been exactly rude, even if he had been firm, towards Esther Park.

Sally could only stare at Margaret.

"I must say you hid it remarkably well," Prender said. "Now, if I had known!" He smiled jokingly.

"Of course I hid it," Mrs. Peel said. "I was so scared of you. You were the oracle, and I was just a very minor acolyte. Besides, a widow with money wasn't the kind of thing that attracted you. Remember how you used to hate money? The source of all hideous good, you called it. But I guess I never attracted you, anyway, for even when I was poor you never noticed me very much. Instead, you married a poetess who wrote free verse which never earned a penny."

And after that, Sally thought, a woman playwright who had two artistic flops and three money successes. Getting the best of both worlds, that was . . . a sort of halfway house. She looked bitterly at Atherton Jones. So that was why Margaret was so crushed and humiliated when he wrote scathingly about *The Lady in White Gloves*. That was why Margaret had insisted on remaining the anonymous Elizabeth Whiffleton, had never written another book.

"And I never even guessed," Sally said slowly.

"Well," Atherton Jones said, "those were the old days. Gone altogether?" He asked the question with a humorous smile which would have made Margaret Peel breathless even ten years ago.

"Quite gone," she said, and laughed gaily.

He must go and talk to O'Farlan about the book, Prender said.

Mrs. Gunn brought some more logs into the living room, shaking her head over Norah's forgetfulness: she was getting as bad as Drene, these days.

Mrs. Peel thanked her. "Now do sit down and tell us what's happening. We depend on you for news, you know. How's the new set of twins over at the Double Bee Emm Ranch? And will Bill Jonson's leg be all right to let him enter for the rodeo?"

Mrs. Gunn sat down. But she came straight to her own problem. "I think Norah ought to leave, Mrs. Peel. She's got to get back home to Three Springs, anyway, to pack her books and clothes for college. She may as well leave now as a week later."

"But —"

"I'm not interfering," Mrs. Gunn said stoutly, having heard Mrs. Peel's opinion on Norah and Earl Grubbock only that morning.

244

"I'm just preventing. She's in a worse state this week than she was last week, and worse that week than she was the week before. Give her one more week here, and she'll be going back to school all upset. That's the trouble with girls. They take love so seriously."

"So do some men, I think," Mrs. Peel said.

Sally said nothing.

"Well, I've no way of judging that," Mrs. Gunn replied. "I don't notice Earl Grubbock going off his food or forgetting to do his work."

"I'm sorry," Sally said. "We seem to have added to your troubles this summer."

"You've had plenty, yourself. Tell me, Miss Bly, when you used to have house parties in those foreign places, did you have worries like this?" She shook her head as she looked at them, thinking that some people never learned.

"We seemed to be all more casual about things, somehow," Sally said.

"How?"

Mrs. Peel tried to answer this time. "Well, some of our guests did fall in love; and were unhappy; and got drunk; and misbehaved with the pretty girls in town; and once — " She remembered that what she was about to say would certainly horrify Mrs. Gunn, for it even horrified herself, now, in retrospect. "Well," she finished lamely, "people did behave very badly at times, I suppose. But the rest of us just seemed to pretend we didn't notice."

"And what," Mrs. Gunn wanted to know, "happened in the end to the girls in the town? But maybe that wasn't important?"

Sally was no longer smiling. She looked at Mrs. Peel. "I think you've got something there," Mrs. Peel said. "I suppose no action is completed until all the consequences can be counted, too."

Mrs. Gunn stared at the fire. "I don't want to be unfair. But if he's as much in love with her as she thinks he is, then he'll up and follow her to Three Springs. That's better than her following him to New York, pretending it's a job she is after."

"How will you get Norah to leave?" Mrs. Peel asked.

"I'm hoping you'll tell her you are cutting down on help."

245

"Oh!" Mrs. Peel said.

"Well, I'm glad that's settled," Mrs. Gunn said, rising to her feet and looking more cheerful. "Now, I've got to go back to the kitchen. Chuck and Jackson are coming down to pay me a visit tonight."

"I wonder how the others are getting along," Sally said, thinking of Jim Brent.

"Oh, they're up there, somewheres," Mrs. Gunn said with a smile, sweeping her arm in a general westward direction beyond the fireplace. "It'll be cold. I told Mr. Grubbock and Mr. Koffing to take plenty of clothes with them."

"So did I," Sally said. They looked at each other and began to laugh.

"Well, if they didn't, they'll learn. That's why they went along on this trip, you know."

"Was *this* the plan?" Mrs. Peel asked with sudden interest.

Mrs. Gunn looked puzzled.

"You told me that Jim and the boys would take care of Karl and Earl. Remember I got worried?"

"Jim thought the trip might be the best answer to all their arguments," Mrs. Gunn said. "Kind of wore him down having to explain so much. But I guess," she added cheerfully, "if I visited New York I'd be just as stupid about its ways."

"I do hope nothing out of the ordinary will happen to them," Mrs. Peel said, remembering the cowboys' strong, if silent and unexpected, sense of humor.

"Nothing out of the ordinary," Mrs. Gunn assured her. "That's why Jim didn't want Mr. Koffing to be riding a difficult horse — that would have added to his troubles. He and Mr. Grubbock will just have a short trip into the mountains and see all about an eight-hour day, up there, for themselves."

Mrs. Peel, brooding over an afterthought, went towards the kitchen to get some more reassuring information from Mrs. Gunn, but Chuck and Jackson were already there and enjoying themselves too much to be disturbed. As Mrs. Peel hesitated for a moment in the pantry, Chuck's voice halted her completely. He was talking in his slow, deliberate way.

" . . . And they'll be figuring the lay of the land, just so's they'll make a fair count of them twenty-four acres that's coming my way when they get it all parceled out. I'm kind of worried about them twenty-four acres. Are they standing up, or laying down, or just kind of leaning tilt-wise?"

At that point, Mrs. Peel shed all guilt over eavesdropping, and stood listening with a spreading smile on her face.

"What if they tell me that's my share, and it turns out to be a canyon wall? Could be. We've canyons to spare. Some fellow is going to be caught with one. What'd my one and a fifth steer do then? Perhaps they've got that taken care of, though, along with all them other improvements. Always did need a new breed of steer in Wyoming that could hang on with its horns. Guess I can manage to round up one cow without too much trouble, but that fifth of a steer — that's another thing that is bothering me. Haven't slept a night ever since I hear of it, trying to figure out a way. Could be me and four other fellows just leave it intact, let it graze in turn on our parcels of land. Could be we'd be saving us a heap of trouble if we just killed it and stopped counting, and had it for meat in the winter. Sure hope I don't get the neck end. Now, there's another problem. If five fellows divide up a steer, the one whose luck with the dice is running low is going to be left hanging on to a tail. And . . ."

But Mrs. Peel had left. The sound of laughter from the kitchen had been too infectious. Even Norah was laughing. And Jackson had the most amazing *basso profundo*.

She went into the library to get herself a book.

She walked slowly along the bookshelves. Dickens. That's how she felt, tonight, she thought. Perhaps *Our Mutual Friend,* with Mr. Boffin being mesmerized by the decline and fall off the Rooshan Empire.

Then she stood very still, staring at the shelf. "What on earth — " she said aloud. She picked out the tattered, torn, and all forlorn copy of Elizabeth Whiffleton's *The Lady in White Gloves*.

* * *

In the living room, Esther Park had returned to talk about her family's place on Shenquetucket Island to Sally. Rescue me, Sally seemed to be saying as she turned to look at Mrs. Peel.

"Sally, I'd like to see you. Will you come into the sitting room?"

Sally rose at once and followed her. She closed the sitting room door and locked it. "Thank you, Margaret. I'll do the same for you, someday. She began by saying she had a cold just as bad as Mimi's. But when I offered to take her temperature, she switched to a long account of her family. My trouble is that I never look at the *Social Register,* so I wasn't impressed. Poor Esther, what *will* she try next?"

"Sally, look at this!" She held out a book. "Dewey knows."

"Dewey Schmetterling knows what?" Sally took the book. Her eyes widened. "Oh!" she said, and then read the inscription. "Dewey's last word. We might have guessed."

Mrs. Peel didn't seem so upset. She said, "I'm glad. I've begun to feel guilty about Elizabeth Whiffleton. I've treated her shabbily. In fact, I nearly told Prender about her this evening when I was admitting I had once been a bit of an intellectual snob. You didn't hear that? I wish you had. I've been wanting to say something like that to Prender ever since I went to some of his dreary parties in New York, last winter. Heavens, they *were* dreary. . . . Not one decent, heartwarming laugh all evening. Just people taking themselves much too seriously, or taking others too seriously. I begin to think that we'd all be saner if we'd argue the way Chuck does. Theories have got to be good to win over that kind of hard-riding logic."

"Darling — " Sally said, wondering if Margaret were slightly hysterical.

"You know, Sally, this is all really very funny. I've been thinking for some weeks about identifying poor Elizabeth Whiffleton. I've been making up my mind to write my agent, and to tell her to go ahead and release the truth. Meanwhile, Dewey is enjoying himself, imagining how upset I'll be when I know that he has found out. He thinks I'll be crushed, that he can always hold Elizabeth Whiffleton over me as a kind of threat. And he feels very superior because he knows the truth, and no one else does."

248

"Yes, Dewey would enjoy all that. He could have a lot of fun out of it, in his own little way." Sally imagined how he'd steer the conversation when he'd meet Margaret at parties; the clever innuendoes, the knowing smile, the constant threat of revelation. He would take care to meet Margaret again, of course. Or else, to avoid him she would find herself living in the middle of the Arizona desert.

"But if there is one thing that gives me real pleasure, it is to disappoint Mr. Dewey Schmetterling. So here's my decision in the form of a telegram. I was coming to it, anyway. Dewey just hastened it, that's all."

Then she looked down at the sheet of paper which lay on her writing table. "How's this?" she asked. "ELIZABETH WHIFFLETON NO LONGER ANONYMOUS. DEWEY SCHMETTERLING MADE AN HONEST WOMAN OUT OF HER. WRITING. LOVE, KISSES, AND REMORSE, MARGARET. Sally, would you be an angel and cope with the telephone exchange in Sweetwater for me? Get Miss Snodgrass to send this telegram to my agent."

"I'm so glad, Margaret," Sally said. "You *do* mean this?"

"When I make up my mind, I make up my mind. As you ought to know by this time, darling."

Sally picked up the telegram.

"It will be a relief to poor Elizabeth," Mrs. Peel said. "She may even find she enjoys writing, now."

"How's the historical novel about Idaho coming along?"

"Not very well. Elizabeth seems rather against it, somehow."

Sally laughed and kissed her friend suddenly.

"Demonstrative tonight, aren't we?" But Mrs. Peel smiled happily.

"I'm just *so* glad," Sally said, and she hurried into the hall towards the telephone.

By the time she returned to the sitting room, she found Mrs. Peel almost at the end of the first chapter of *The Lady in White Gloves*.

"You know," Mrs. Peel said, looking up with surprise, "it isn't as bad as I thought. It's just terribly nineteen-twentyish, that's all. It has a certain cadaverous charm, like looking at a one-time beauty of the ball. And however did Elizabeth Whiffleton think of all these things! Telegram off safely?"

249

"Miss Snodgrass is fully in charge. By the way, her nephew won the local 4-H prize in steer raising. Complete treatment, as far as I could gather. He brought it up and lifted it too. He's going to be in the first float on Saturday."

"4-H?" Mrs. Peel asked, leaving the lady in white gloves walking through the dining car of the Simplon Express.

"Head, Heart, Hands and Health."

"No hearth or home? But perhaps that's for the older ones. And floating — floating where?"

"In the parade through Sweetwater before the rodeo on Saturday, darling. Trucks all disguised into tableaux with crepe paper and branches and things."

"Ah," Mrs. Peel said understandingly. "Like Nice."

"Exactly. Only no emphasis on *l'amour*. All very hearty and healthy."

Mrs. Peel nodded. "How Prender will hate it," she said with pleasure. She picked up the battered copy of *The Lady in White Gloves* once more. "Now, darling, if you don't mind, I'd like to finish this book."

CHAPTER XXII

Return from the Mountains

THREE DAYS passed. Four. It was the fifth day, already late in the afternoon, and Earl Grubbock and Karl Koffing were still in the mountains.

Rest and Be Thankful was alarmed. Only Mrs. Gunn seemed to take the delay as something quite normal, but the more she kept calm and unruffled the more the others were convinced that something must have happened. Chuck and Jackson were just as baffling as Mrs. Gunn.

"Sure," Chuck said to Carla, who had been worrying him with questions, "they've had a bit of a skirmish with hostiles. Or maybe they've gone hunting bear. Bringing home one apiece so you can take them back to New York, along with them elk horns you've been collecting."

Carla then had to spend a heated half-hour trying to convince her shadow, Esther Park, that Chuck was joking, so all must be well. Esther said, "He wasn't. He didn't smile one bit." And she went back to Chuck and pestered him with predictions of possible gloom until he said, "Sure. That's it. They got lost. Wouldn't be surprised if they reached Yellowstone by Christmas." Jackson had to laugh, that time, so Esther Park knew she was meant to laugh too.

"Still," she said with her usual perseverance, "people could get lost."

"Sure." Chuck was being serious now, if you cared to watch his eyes. "If a man don't know them mountains, he's just kind of asking for trouble getting mixed up with them. There were a young fellow, over at the Bar Ex Gee last summer, he made a pack-trip by himself

251

up over Muledeer. Didn't want no guide along. Just himself and nature. Well, reckon he got that all right. Took us the best part of a week to find him. Weren't a ranch or a forest station round here, for near a hundred miles, what weren't out looking for him. Cost us a heap of sleep and good working time. Him and nature."

"Was he alive?"

"He weren't dead." He'd been kind of lucky, that fellow.

Esther saw Prender Atherton Jones in the distance, and so she abandoned Chuck and Jackson who didn't seem too crushed by such neglect. Prender had gone into the saddle barn, which was strange; but stranger still, when she searched there he wasn't to be found. He must have taken the side door out. So he couldn't have seen her waving to him, after all.

She went back to the house. Robert O'Farlan was busy, he said. And Carla was at work, too. After ten minutes with each of them, she found Mrs. Peel in her sitting room. But she was writing and didn't even look up. Sally was in the library, and she said, "Hello! Glad you're free, Esther. I've a job of work for you to do." Esther said she'd love to, but she had to see Mrs. Gunn first about something important. So Mrs. Gunn, returning to the kitchen from a visit to the chicken house, found Esther Park sitting in the rocking chair.

"I think it is all very silly," Esther Park said.

"What's silly?" Mrs. Gunn had to recount the eggs she had brought with her.

"All this fuss everyone is making over Karl and Earl."

Mrs. Gunn looked at her in surprise. She thought of all the horrible ideas that Miss Park had produced at the luncheon table today, worrying everyone with her questions. "Who's making a fuss?" she asked.

"Why, everyone. Just like the silly fuss they make over Mimi."

Mrs. Gunn selected the eggs she was going to use for dinner, and walked into the pantry to store the others carefully away in the big refrigerator. Miss Bly was there, signaling with a finger to her lip. "Thought you'd need some help," she whispered. "I've found the cure: give her some work to do."

Mrs. Gunn stared.

"Work," repeated Sally, "that's all."

Mrs. Gunn went back to the kitchen, hoping it was now empty. But it wasn't. Miss Park was rocking gently in the chair, her eyes fixed on an invisible object on the wall in front of her.

If only she keeps quiet, Mrs. Gunn thought, that won't be so bad. It's not that she's ugly — I've seen worse. It's her expression. It's a good lesson to all of us that we've got to look after the thoughts we think, or just look what happens. Now, that's a cruel thing to say, Isabella Gunn! But it is funny, though, the harder Miss Park tries to make people like her, the less they do. But then, she ought to make *herself* more likable. She has money and a famous family and all that, and they don't seem to matter one bit to anyone else. Not that they should. It would be a poor lookout for the world if people were judged by money or family.

"Do you think Mimi Bassinbrook's going to have pneumonia?" Esther Park asked suddenly.

Mrs. Gunn gave her a sharp look. "No," she said shortly.

"Imagine!" Esther Park said scornfully. "Imagine the doctor being brought all the way from Sweetwater for only a cold."

"Dr. Clark has cured her pretty quick, hasn't he?" Mrs. Gunn stared angrily at the woman rocking so placidly in her armchair. Pensomething-or-other, he had given Miss Bassinbrook. She'd be all right for the dance on Saturday. More was the pity, perhaps.

"I've had pneumonia," Esther Park said. "My doctor warned me to be very careful in future. That's why I was so worried a few days ago when I had that terrible cold. Of course, *I* didn't want to bother anyone."

But you tried hard, Mrs. Gunn thought grimly. Then she said, "Why, here are five pounds of peas to be shelled for dinner! And I just needed someone to help me."

"I'd love to," Esther Park said slowly. She looked at the mountain of green peas on the table, at Mrs. Gunn placing an enormous bowl invitingly beside them. She arose. "But I did promise Mimi I'd go upstairs and see her before dinner. I tell you what, I'll go and cheer Mimi up, then I'll come back and help you."

"Fine. I'll need some help with peeling the potatoes, too."

253

Perhaps, Mrs. Gunn thought hopefully as she looked at the chair rocking peacefully and still more peacefully by itself until it at last came to rest, perhaps she won't even stay once Norah is away and there will be work to do. And Miss Bly, she thought admiringly, Miss Bly is no fool.

She couldn't have paid Sally higher praise.

Before dinner, Mrs. Peel made a habit of taking two carrots up to the corral. Sally came along with her this evening. Both of them looked towards the hills, but there was still no sign of any riders. They did not notice that Chuck and Jackson were sitting outside the saddle barn, waiting and watching too.

Chuck was squatting in his favorite position, his left leg kneeling with the weight of his body balanced on its heel, his right elbow resting on the bended right knee. He shook his head at the carrots in Mrs. Peel's hand. "Look at that, will you?" he seemed to say.

Jackson grinned, partly in agreement, partly in anticipation. It wasn't, by any wrangler's standards, the way to treat a horse, but Jackson had seen Mrs. Peel at work on many an evening.

"Next thing they'll be tying blue ribbons on its tail," Chuck said as he watched Mrs. Peel and Miss Bly walk over to the fence. His voice was low, for sound carried easily across the stillness of the evening. Nice women, but kind of crazy, he had long since decided.

Mrs. Peel's voice, unaware of its audience, was clear and confident. "Here, Boy!" she called. "Golden Boy!"

The horses, grazing quietly in the west pasture, went on grazing quietly. Except the palomino, who lifted his head and looked around in an inquiring manner.

"Is that call for me? Put it through, will you?" Sally said and began to laugh.

"Be quiet, Sally. He'll hear you."

Sally looked at the horse, a golden statue with its head turned towards them. She looked at the other horses, their heads stretched down to the grass. Perhaps, she thought, I will have to learn to paint: I just can't go on like this, wishing I could paint. "Look at the design they make, Margaret! And their colors against that gold·

254

green grass!" White, sorrel — one a darker chestnut than the other, rich bay brown, black, cream buckskin . . . "This is what I like best: to see them together, to watch them free. It must have been magnificent when there was a remuda of hundreds."

"A what?"

"A cavy. At least, I think that's it. Oh, a herd, if you prefer that."

"Boy!" Mrs. Peel called again. "See, he's coming! I don't even have to wave the carrots now."

The golden palomino left the others. He walked slowly, pausing now and again to stretch his long graceful neck towards a tuft of tempting grass.

"He takes his time," Mrs. Peel explained, "to show us that he has an independence above carrots. He is being polite, making up his mind to receive visitors with an elegant air. He's like one of those horses in a baroque painting, isn't he? When he shies, you know, he tosses his mane, dilates his nostrils, and widens his eyes. All he needs is Louis XIV on his back, pointing a finger upwards and onwards through a froth of lace round his cuff. He's completely baroque. In fact, it's so funny to watch him that I forget even to be frightened when he shies. It really isn't so unpleasant as I used to think it was — it's rather like chassez-ing sideways on a dance floor. Perfectly safe if you don't come loose from your partner."

"I'm sure he's a first cousin to a Hollywood blonde with a shoulder-bob. Why not rename him Glamour Boy?"

"And he would throw me, just to teach me how to behave. Don't laugh, Sally. He has his own ways of thinking, and they get him along all right. How would *you* like to spend the winters out in these hills? If self-preservation doesn't involve some form of thinking, then — Boy, here Boy!"

The palomino quickened his pace suddenly, and swerved at a trot towards the fence.

Jackson looked at Chuck. "Well?" he asked with a broad grin.

"Well," Chuck said, and pushed his hat back off his forehead. "She'll be learning the bastard to count next. Then he'll be laying down for his country and rising for the Star-Spangled Banner.

What's this, anyways? A goddamned ranch or a jigging circus?"
But he was smiling. "And what's baroak?"

Jackson shook his head.

"That's what she said, wasn't it? Baroak . . ." How do they get round to talking that way? he wondered. Sure must tire them out. Guess some folks use their voices as others use their eyes. Baroak. It had a good sound to it. Come in handy when he was having a little talk with his own pony. You goddamned sonofabitchn baroak pony, you. That would get it listening. She was right, too: horses had their own ways of figuring out people.

"Mighty nice woman, that," he said to Jackson, whose dark serious eyes suddenly smiled with real pleasure. "Don't you worry, Jack. When you tell her you're staying here and not driving to California or any other such place, she'll understand." He went back to watching Mrs. Peel, who had now clambered through the fence and was walking a few paces beside the palomino with her hand on its neck. Then she gave it a few brisk claps, and it broke away to return to the horses on the hillside. Some people, Chuck had heard, had their own way of explaining a friendship like that: sure, they said, a childless woman, a lonely man, is always losing their hearts to a dog or a horse. But they only proved one thing for sure: they hadn't ever had a dog or a horse that liked them enough to let them know what they were missing.

Sally turned round, ready to walk back to the house. "Hello!" she called, as she suddenly saw Jackson and Chuck. She walked across the dusty corral towards them. "Come down and enjoy Ma Gunn's cooking, won't you? The boys won't be here for supper tonight, I'm afraid."

"I'm not so sure about that," Chuck said, looking beyond her to the hills.

"What? Have you seen them?" Sally turned round quickly and looked once more. "Margaret," she called, "Chuck's seen them!"

Chuck, who had been watching the small cloud of dust for almost half an hour when he hadn't been studying Mrs. Peel, nodded. He pointed. "Heading for the south pasture. Can't move them steers too quick. Lose weight if you look at them, almost."

"Where are they?" Sally asked, her eyes still on the hills.

"I can't see them either," Mrs. Peel said as she joined the little group.

Chuck explained patiently, using a cloud in the sky, a red-walled canyon, a hill with sawtoothed rocks and a green-edged creek to mark the exact spot. "Give them about an hour, maybe," he said, timing their arrival at the south pasture. "Well, I think I'll go peel a lot of potatoes." He touched his hat and moved away, and Jackson went with him.

"Jackson," Mrs. Peel said to Sally, as they walked quickly towards the house to warn Mrs. Gunn about dinner, "is no longer Jackson. The other day, he passed by when I was talking to someone, and I saw him out of the corner of my eye. I thought, 'Well, we've a new cowboy.' And then I looked properly, and it was Jackson."

"They call him Jack."

"Jack. Formerly Jackson. Formerly Tisza Szénchenyi." Mrs. Peel smiled. "He's traveled a long way," she said softly.

"So have we, I think," Sally said and linked her arm through Margaret's.

"Will you do something for me?" Mrs. Peel asked unexpectedly. "Will you stop being foolish? The next evening you want to go riding, will you go riding? Instead of refusing and finding some old excuse?"

Sally was silent. Then she said at last, "Mimi is young and she's very pretty. If I were a man — "

"I wish women would stop making men seem more stupid than they are. I know all about Mimi. I saw her that very first night. She came up to the corral, all ready to go riding by herself, just as you and Jim were setting out. Naturally you asked her to go along. Naturally you found yourself riding alone, while she edged in beside Jim Brent on the narrow trails. And she repeated all these little stratagems every evening after that, didn't she? Until you began to say you were too busy to go, that you had a headache, or that you couldn't ride because of your accident. Just any old excuse, Sally Bly. And you were a fool. You didn't help Jim very much, did you?"

"Perhaps he didn't want that kind of help. Besides, why should I bother, anyway? It's none of my business." Sally's voice was on the defensive now. "Why should it be?"

"Because," Mrs. Peel's voice said gently, "I'm a complete idiot about horses, and your horse is putting on weight."

Sally had to smile. "You're a sweet liar," she said, "but I'll listen to you. I'll start exercising him again."

"In the evenings?" Mrs. Peel insisted.

Sally hesitated. "If I am asked," she said at last, and the smile disappeared from her eyes.

The pack horse came first, running free, streaming ahead of the others, its head pointed unerringly to the ranch. Bert followed it at a fast canter. Behind him, keeping up with him, was Karl Koffing. And then, five minutes later, the group of four men, taking it more easily, riding close together.

They hadn't spoken much for the last hour. And that, Earl Grubbock decided as he tried to ease his blistered thighs by standing up in the stirrups, was a damned good idea. He saw the waiting crowd at the corral, and he groaned. At this stage, all a man wanted to do was to get off his horse thankfully, look back at the mountains, and say to himself, "Well, I made it." No questions, no fuss. Just a bath with real hot water. Food and drink. And bed. A real honest-to-God bed with a mattress and springs underneath and four blankets over you. And sleep. Real, deep-down sleep in a dark sheltered room with every noise held away from you. No waking up with a start when a coyote howled in your ear, or a wind moaned through the trees, or a porcupine rustled the dry twigs near you as it wandered around looking for some leather to eat. No waking up when the temperature dropped another ten degrees, and you were so damned frozen already that you couldn't even pull the blanket more tightly round your chin. No more sudden flurries of snow or icy hail to beat round your ears or make the horses restless. You'd lie there, wondering what the hell made them restless this time — they always had some reason; you'd found that out — wondering if you had tethered your horse securely enough, or would you have to walk five, six or seven miles to find him tomorrow morning? So there you'd be lying on the hard, hard earth, trying to fall into an uneasy sleep, trying to forget that the horses might break loose at any minute. And if they did — well, you lay there trying not to think about that, trying to forget you were miles from the nearest lonely ranch, with nothing but mountains and trees and creeks and parkland between you and it. That made you think of your boots — and you suddenly remembered that if you hadn't hung them high enough, they'd now be making a blue-plate special for a porcupine. So you got out of your blanket and sleeping-bag, and made sure of your boots. Then you had to wind yourself up like a cocoon, again; doing it quietly so as not to waken the others. And you looked at the humped, still figures on the earth around you, and wondered how they could sleep and you couldn't. And as soon as you started getting mad about that, then you slept no more, just lay there counting the drafts.

Grubbock eased himself on his saddle. He looked pityingly at Koffing ahead of him, keeping up his lead. Boy, I bet that hurts, he thought.

Jackson opened the gate and let the pack horse run into the corral. Bert let out a cheery war whoop. The others waved.

"Well, they look all right," Mrs. Peel said with relief. "Just a little more grimy and unwashed than usual."

"Karl has a bandaged wrist," Esther Park announced.

Karl Koffing was sitting on his horse, resting his elbow on the saddle horn. He was looking at the sunset. Nature was giving them a welcome home as spectacular as her early-morning farewell. Nature had won out all around, whether she was setting out to charm or to dominate. One snowstorm, one thunder-and-lightning display, one hail attack with each icy stone as big as a giant-sized pea, one wind and dust storm, opalescent dawns with clouds beneath you, flaming sunsets with beaten-brass skies above you. Not to mention, Karl thought, mountains of twelve thousand feet that stretched for a hundred miles as rhythmically as if they were just the ordinary waves in an ordinary ocean. And forests that never ended, big enough to swallow up a city's millions and have them wandering around, lost and alone, without touch of each other.

"Karl, did you get hurt?" Esther Park was asking.

He shook his head. He was still looking at the range of mountains. Once he had thought them imposing; now he knew that they were only the outer wall to a giant fortress.

"Then why are you wearing a bandage?" Esther asked.

God, Karl thought, I'll have to dismount. Bert was already on his feet, unsaddling, unbridling, getting the pack horse unloaded. I'll have to get this damned saddle off, too, Karl thought. But the problem is to get myself off, first. The last canter had done it. He'd have been wiser to come trotting along leisurely into the corral like Grubbock. But now, as he looked across at Earl, it seemed that he was also resting for a moment before he tried swinging a leg up and over. This was one night Koffing and Grubbock could have done without an audience. They were all there, except Mimi and Atherton Jones.

Fortunately, the audience was now too busy asking questions of Bert and Ned to notice Karl Koffing's silence. The damnedest piece of foolishness was this raw patch of flesh, where the inside seam of his jeans had ground the skin away. He walked stiffly, trying not to limp or hobble, as he uncinched the saddle and carried it to the corral rail. Earl Grubbock, he was relieved to see, was moving just as slowly and carefully.

"How did you get on?" Mrs. Peel was asking Jim Brent.

"Fine." He had worked quickly, and was now turning his horse loose into the pasture. He walked over to the group.

"Run into any trouble?" Robert O'Farlan asked, and everyone waited eagerly for the answer.

"No more than usual. Lost some time trying to find some strays."

"How was the weather up there?" Carla asked. "We had a very cold wind and some rain, two days ago."

"Just what you'd expect," Jim Brent answered her.

And the damned thing was, Koffing thought, Brent really meant it.

"Was it wonderful, Earl?" Carla asked suddenly.

"Ask me in three days' time, and I'll give you a fair answer," Grubbock said with a smile.

260

"Didn't you enjoy it?" Mrs. Peel wanted to know. She looked at him, and then at Karl, anxiously.

"Sure. By November, we'll be talking about it with tears in our eyes. Won't we, Karl?"

Karl nodded. It was easy for Grubbock to admit it had been a tough five days. Grubbock had been in the Army. No one was going to think he couldn't take it.

Sally said, "Mrs. Gunn's cooking a special dinner for you. So what about a bath, first of all? You'll have time. We've got the water piping hot."

"Fine," Karl said. And then, he thought, it wasn't so fine. For Bert and Ned were walking over to their bunkhouse for a quick wash in cold water, and Robb was about to follow them.

"Hell, I don't need a hot bath," Karl said suddenly.

"The hell you don't," Grubbock said and gripped his arm to lead him away. "And I want to see that wrist of yours too, and get a good tight bandage on it."

Mrs. Peel looked inquiringly at Jim Brent. "It's nothing too serious," he assured her. "He was lucky. Now, I'll get cleaned up, too." He looked at Sally as he passed her. "Hello, stranger," he said, "good to see you around the corral again. Do you never go riding any more?"

"If I'm asked," Sally said, her cheeks coloring, her eyes looking very blue and startled.

"Getting formal, aren't we?" he teased her. "Looks as if I'll have to start keeping an engagement diary. See you later."

Now what did that mean? Mrs. Peel wondered. Was it good, was it bad, or was it just . . . ? She glanced at Sally, who had a way of understanding what was meant when it wasn't said. It must be good, for Sally was smiling as she gave Jim Brent a casual nod.

Carla and Esther and O'Farlan turned to walk back to the house. "It must have been wonderful," Carla said, looking at the hills lying golden in the sunset. O'Farlan said yes, he envied Koffing and Grubbock: one summer, some years ago, he had gone mountain climbing and he had enough to think about for months afterwards.

"I've climbed mountains, too," Esther Park said eagerly. And she went on talking as they left the corral.

Mrs. Peel looked after her pityingly. Whatever poor Esther did, and she seemingly had done a lot of things, she would never have anything to think about except herself.

Robb was wasting time. He hadn't left the corral with the other cowboys. Now he came over to Mrs. Peel and Sally as they turned to go down to the house. He has something to say to us, Mrs. Peel thought as she halted. But she had learned how to wait. So had Sally.

"Yes," Robb said at last, as if in answer to a question, "it's mighty pretty up there."

"Almost as pretty as Montana?" Sally asked. She looked at the thin, strong-featured face, at the healthy skin that was tight-drawn over the high cheekbones and firm jaw. There was a gentleness round his mouth that might seem weakness unless you also noticed the steady, far-seeing blue eyes. Now, as they smiled back at her, she remembered that she had never heard him say an unjust or petty thing about any other human being. There was no malice, no cynicism in his heart, no hatred of others' virtues or strength which might be greater than his own. He had seen life at its grimmest reality—for war was the hardest schoolmaster, and Robb had chosen one of its toughest assignments: a parachutist, trained in demolition, who jumped ahead of the air-borne troops—and it hadn't beaten him down. He doesn't know it, Sally thought, but he has a warmth in him that kindles warmth, in what he writes and in those who read.

"Almost," Robb was saying in his slow, quiet voice, making two unhurried words out of one. Then the thoughtful eyes turned to Mrs. Peel. "That book you lent me, Mrs. Peel—" he stopped, half-frowning.

"You liked it?" Mrs. Peel asked anxiously. "That's the poem about the Argentine gaucho," she explained quickly to Sally.

"Sure did," Robb said. "Kept me thinking all the way up the trail and back. He knew what he was writing about, all right. Seems to me"—and he looked, now, up towards the hills—"a poem could be written about that too. Not the way Hernández wrote. The way one of us might write it. Just about a five-day trip into the mountains, going up, being there, bringing the steers back. Just all that."

"Yes," Mrs. Peel said quietly. "A poem about that would be something I'd like to read."

"Is that right?" His frank eyes turned to study her face, as if looking for the truth. "It would be a long poem," he said, "as long as a novel almost. But different as it went along. There's one way of writing to get the rhythm of setting out and then climbing the trail, when everyone's hoping it will be a good journey. Then coming out on top of the plateau, and the world's before you. And then the day's work; that would be different again. And then the nights, and talk, and a bit of remembering, and thoughts about all those others who've sat, just as you are doing now, around a dying fire in the wilderness. And then sleep, when you don't sleep but just lie thinking. That's a mighty queer thing: you're lying in the middle of nature and what you think about is men; you even start planning, seeing things more clearly, right and wrong is easy to understand. And you know it is easier to understand than men make it. All they have to do is to feel the way you're feeling — for you're one of them, and they're a part of you — as you lie out there, listening to the mountains and the night sky. There wouldn't be so much trouble then. You not only feel it, you begin to know it. Then dawn comes up, and you see nothing but pink clouds below you, and the world is blotted out. You're a man, you belong to them down there below these clouds, and yet you aren't a man. You've no fears or troubles or hates left in you. You look at these clouds, and they are not the way you see them from the earth. They are a floor of gold and pink and purple and blue, of colors you don't even know the names of. For a bit, you stand and stare. You begin thinking about the way the Greeks made their gods live, high in the mountains, and that makes sense. You even feel you could leap right forward into these clouds, you could fall ten thousand feet and not get hurt. And that's the thought that makes you know you're a man, again; gods don't have to think about getting hurt."

He smiled, then. He paused, and when neither of the women

spoke, he said awkwardly, "That's as far as I've got it thought out. The last bit of the poem will be the journey back to earth, I guess. And you're getting mixed up with men again, and you can't plan for them any more, and everything is less clear, and the truths become colorless like the way the clouds are turning as you look up at them now. And you look back at the mountains, too, and all you can say is that it's mighty pretty up there."

Chuck's shout broke through the evening silence. "Hey, Robb! Come and get it!"

Robb grinned. He touched his hat. They watched him walk away, his lean body slouching a little, moving deliberately, with the leather chaps round the thin blue-jeaned legs still encumbering his stiff stride.

Chuck was yelling, unaware of his audience, "It's pork chops, tonight, split and blast you, not a pot of stew that don't mind waiting." He talked for two more sentences about Robb, without failing in his descriptive vocabulary.

Mrs. Peel, who could never stop flinching when she heard a swear word — the only remaining relic of her Calvinist upbringing, she thought — now listened in calm wonder. It was strange how they could use an oath so that it was really only the normal way to address a friend. It was, in its rhythm and imagination, a kind of poetry, too. But how had she imagined that she heard the word "baroque"?

"I was wrong to suggest that he should go East this winter," Sally said as they walked towards the house. "New York or Chicago would be no good for Robb. Not at the moment. Not until he gets that poem all out of his heart, just as it is, without other influences spoiling its simplicity."

"He's got to live on something. He's got to earn money, somehow. If he stays in the West, he'll probably go with Ned to Arizona to work on a ranch there for the winter."

"Yes. If only he could stay here! He'd get plenty of time to work here, in the winter."

"The ranch is half-closed. Old Chuck and Bert have priority on jobs here over him."

"What about Rest and Be Thankful?" Sally asked thoughtfully.

"He earns his own way," Mrs. Peel told her. "Sally, I'd spend every last penny I had on keeping the house open this winter, but do you see him living here as our guest?"

Sally shook her head.

"If we could give him a job, not a faked one, a real one . . ." Mrs. Peel hesitated, trying to think of such a job. "We've got to try and arrange that, Sally. Somehow. He should stay here, within sight and touch of these mountains."

"Arrange it without arranging it. Take an interest without seeming to take interest. Margaret, you're facing a riddle more elaborate than Cocteau's Sphinx."

Mrs. Peel's delicate eyebrows were set in a determined frown.

"It was the highest compliment ever paid us," Sally said, "when he talked to us, like that."

Mrs. Peel nodded, still frowning, but she said nothing.

"And to think I once thought *I* could write poetry," Sally went on. "All I worried about was the lisp of a consonant or the echo of vowel sounds, or how free in meter or rhyme I could be. Like the young bard of Japan, whose verses never would scan . . ."

Mrs. Peel smiled at that. She even finished the limerick. "Because I try to get as many words into the last line as I possibly can."

They were laughing as they entered the house. And then Mrs. Peel, remembering Karl and Earl, became serious. "I'm going to look for some Band-Aid," she announced.

CHAPTER XXIII

The Bear and Mr. Jerks
Share an Evening

Eᴀʀʟ ɢʀᴜʙʙᴏᴄᴋ and Karl Koffing had thought that, after one of Mrs. Gunn's biggest and best dinners, they might slip away from the living room with a nonchalant air and set a straight course for their beds. But it was pleasant to be given the two most comfortable armchairs in front of a roaring fire, and have all the others — even Prender Atherton Jones — gather around with questions. Mimi had threatened to come downstairs if she was going to miss all the fun, and had only stopped climbing out of bed when she had been promised that Earl and Karl would pay her a visit before they went back to the cottage.

"If we can get up these stairs," Grubbock admitted frankly. He had already been put through that test when he borrowed one of the bathrooms in the house. (Koffing had reached the bath in the cabin, first.) "You never know how many muscles you've been born with, until you start climbing stairs."

Koffing was still not admitting anything. In any case, there was more reason for him to be silent: his arm hurt badly, in spite of the neat bandages which Ned had wrapped round the swollen wrist and forearm. Ned, when he had come over here after supper to look at Karl's arm, had said he didn't like the look of it too much and that Karl might be wise to see Dr. Clark in Sweetwater tomorrow. Sally suggested that it might be even wiser to drive into Sweetwater with Jackson tonight. Karl refused this idea so vehemently that Mrs. Peel then remembered the quantity of iodine, zinc ointment, sticking plaster, talcum powder, *and* Band-Aid which Grubbock had collected from her in a very offhand way. She wondered how she could suggest that Ned ought to be invited back to do a little more extensive bandaging. After all, there was such a thing as blood poisoning. And when Earl Grubbock made a joke about barbed wire being the one thing he couldn't argue with, and pulled up his sleeve to show an iodined gash in his forearm so that Esther Park would stop suggesting that Karl was halfway to tetanus, Mrs. Peel rose unobtrusively and went into the hall.

Miss Snodgrass at the Sweetwater telephone exchange said why of course she'd find out if Dr. Clark was too busy tonight; glad to, no trouble at all.

And after a conversation with Mrs. Clark, mostly about the two Clark children who were going to be on one of the 4-H floats on Saturday, Miss Snodgrass could report back that Dr. Clark was attending a meeting of the Sweetwater Improvement Committee this evening at the Purple Rim Bar. Did Mrs. Peel want to be put through to him there?

"Just a minute, Miss Snodgrass. Let me think this out," Mrs. Peel said, discovering she hated to disturb Dr. Clark enjoying one free evening.

"Sure," Miss Snodgrass said helpfully. "I'll wait. Choose your words." Mrs. Peel stared thoughtfully at the receiver in her hand for a full minute while she listened to the clack of Miss Snodgrass's knitting needles.

"I've decided just to ask his advice," she said at last. And after a three-minute wait, Dr. Clark's calm voice was produced out of a background of cheerful noise.

"It's nothing serious," Mrs. Peel began, "but they won't listen to anything except professional advice, I know." She began to explain. "You see, it isn't very much. But what does worry me is the fact that he's a writer. If something is wrong with a bone or ligament, then he may not be able to write or type for weeks. *That's* what is serious. I should insist that he come and see you tomorrow, shouldn't I?"

Even with the door of the Purple Rim's telephone booth firmly shut, it was difficult to hear Dr. Clark's voice. He was, she found after two wrong guesses, interested in open wounds.

"Just small ones," she said reassuringly. "And Ned got all the gravel out of them, I'm positive. The arm is swollen, but that's because it is badly bruised. And the other writer has a two-inch tear, barbed wire, but not very deep. What's that? Sorry. Tetanus shots? Well, one of them was in the Army and I'm sure he must be *full* of shots . . . I don't know at all about the other one . . . No, he wasn't in the Army or anything . . . Then I'll send them both in to see you tomorrow. Even if I have to drug their breakfast coffee and bring them stretched out in the ranch truck. No, there's no need for you to come over tonight, absolutely not. No. See you tomorrow. I just needed your authority, that was all. Good night and thank you."

And that, Mrs. Peel thought, was exactly what I wanted to know. Sweetwater tomorrow, and no protests from any heroic young men.

She returned as quietly to the living room as she had left it. They were discussing cowboy clothes. Earl Grubbock was saying they were certainly practical. Karl Koffing agreed.

"There's nothing comic about cowboy dress, once you've found that out," Grubbock insisted, watching the smile on Atherton Jones's face. "There's a meaning for everything. Take these chaps they wear buckled round their legs, for instance. Wish I had been wearing chaps when we went through that brush: thorns as long as your little finger. My legs began to feel like pincushions. Or take these high heels we've all been laughing about." He looked pointedly at Atherton Jones's flat-heeled riding boots. "If you're hanging onto a steer's head while he's pushing you along, you've got to be able to brake his force with your heels stuck out in front of you."

"I can't imagine the circumstances arising," Atherton Jones said, "when I should ever be hanging on to a steer's head, or a cow's tail."

Everyone, except Earl and Karl, thought this was funny.

"I am prepared for the most florid effects at the rodeo on Saturday," Prender Atherton Jones went on. "Oscar Wilde would no doubt have approved of the colorful clothes we'll find there. He thought the Californian miners were the best-dressed men he had seen in America: they combined the practical with the ornamental in the right proportions."

268

"I'll give you one word of advice," Grubbock said. "I wouldn't tell the cowboys about Oscar Wilde's possible approval. I've got a feeling that that wouldn't appeal to them, somehow."

"Probably never heard of Oscar Wilde, to begin with," Atherton Jones said. "And if there is one thing I dislike it is adding footnotes to a joke." He looked at Grubbock reprovingly. A word of advice, indeed. . . .

"I hope your arm is better by Saturday, Karl," Mrs. Peel said trying to change the conversation and bring it around to Dr. Clark's advice. She only half-succeeded.

"How did it happen, anyway?" Robert O'Farlan asked, pointing to Karl's arm.

"Did you fall off your horse?" Esther Park asked. "That *must* have been funny."

"It wasn't so funny," Earl said, frowning at Esther Park, then breaking into a grin to belie his words. "At least, no one thought it was funny except me. And I didn't think it was funny until Karl had got up on his feet again. Say, Bert was quick at catching your horse, wasn't he?"

Karl, feeling the pain in his hand and arm, didn't share Earl's amusement. He had the impulse to say he was going to bed, and leave them all to laugh over his accident. That's what they wanted to do, anyway.

Mrs. Peel was watching his face closely. She said, "Karl, why don't you go to bed and rest your arm? Tomorrow, we can —"

"Go ahead and tell them," Karl said to Earl Grubbock, and he settled back firmly in his chair. "It's nothing," he said equally firmly to Mrs. Peel.

Grubbock hesitated for a moment. "Well," he said, "last night we were coming back to camp. When I say 'camp,' I mean we had found a place as sheltered as possible, which wasn't much, near some water. And when you come riding into camp after a day's work, you've got to make it. You attend to your horse, unpack your roll, gather wood, build a fire, and cook your food. Then, after you've eaten, you've to get all the damned litter buried and burned, and the greasy pans washed in ice-cold water. And after all that — if there

269

isn't something else to be done — you can sit down and relax by the fire, and you have half an hour to get warm before you hit the sack because you're up at the crack of dawn to start everything all over again in reverse. It's strange, you know—"

"Cut out all the sidetracking," Karl Koffing said. "Go ahead and tell them. What's wrong, Earl? Sparing my feelings?" He smiled mockingly. Earl hadn't spared them much, during these last five days. And now, Earl was the one who was talking about discomforts. He hadn't stopped talking all evening.

But O'Farlan, who had been a soldier too, recognized the symptoms. Every post-mortem on any mission, successfully completed, carried its own privileges of grousing. "Must have reminded you of the Army, in some ways," he said to Grubbock. "Except that you weren't being shot over."

Karl Koffing rose. "I'm hitting the sack," he said. "Goodnight." He walked out of the room.

"What's wrong, now?" O'Farlan asked irritably.

"His arm is more painful than we think," Mrs. Peel said.

"Well," Sally said, "he's learned a new phrase, at least." But she looked after Karl worriedly, too.

"How did he fall?" Prender Atherton Jones wanted to know. "Was he bucked off?"

Earl Grubbock didn't answer. He knew what was wrong with Koffing. It wasn't the arm, though that probably hurt like hell and Karl wouldn't admit it. It was O'Farlan's way of talking about the war. Karl had some kind of guilt about that, and what it was you couldn't find out. But frankly, it was getting a bit tiresome. Especially for five days on end, when Karl was so damned intent on proving he was braver, quicker, tougher than any of the rest of them. No one questioned the fact that Koffing had guts. Except himself, seemingly.

"Was anyone to blame?" Mrs. Peel asked. That had been worrying her.

Grubbock shook his head. "No," he said, "it was all his own darned fault. Yesterday evening, Karl and Bert and I were riding back together. We had been out looking for strays. We'd found none.

We were taking a short cut to camp, following a fairly narrow trail that would lead us through a small canyon. At the moment, we were on the open hillside with Karl riding some distance ahead of us. On our right, there was a sheer wall of rock rising straight up from the edge of the trail. On our left, the ground dropped away in a steep slope of grass, sprinkled with boulders and young pine trees. Karl was just reaching the entrance to the canyon. We could see it, narrow and deep, with giant teeth of rock lining its sides, and blue spruce and pine trees trying to climb up between its crags. Then, suddenly, Karl's horse stopped dead in its tracks."

"And Karl fell off," Esther Park said quickly.

Grubbock looked at her. Everyone silenced her nervous laugh with a combined glare. Even Atherton Jones, caught up in the picture of three men on this mountain trail, stared at her angrily.

Grubbock said, "The horse stopped dead on its tracks, and it refused to move. That was what I noticed most — the horse. I could feel something dangerous, I could feel it right from that horse. Bert said, 'Hey, there!' quite quietly, almost to himself. We both reined up automatically. Karl urged his horse on. It wouldn't move. He kicked it. It started turning round. He turned it back and pulled its head to face the canyon."

"Quite right," Atherton Jones said. "Horses have got to be mastered."

"But it wouldn't go into that canyon. It turned off the trail, down the slope of the hillside. Karl yanked it back onto the trail. It turned, it twisted. He pulled it round to face the canyon. And this time it went rigid. He really gave it the heel then, and he lashed it. That was when the Wild West show started. After the third buck, Karl was thrown, rolling down the hillside until he ended up against one of those doll-sized fir trees. The horse turned and bolted.

"Now, this all happened so quickly — a matter of seconds — that I was still puzzling out the rigid horse when Bert passed me. He went right into a canter and then into a lope, cutting down the hillside at a sharp angle to turn off Karl's horse. I didn't see how he caught it — that must have been spectacular on the sloping hillside with its scattered boulders and pint-sized trees. I was too busy trying to reach Karl. I dismounted, but I kept a pretty tight grip on my horse's reins, for he was beginning to act up a bit too. And in those wide open spaces, a horse is the best friend your feet ever had. But just as I was scrambling down the hill, leading my horse — I wouldn't have ridden down there if you had paid me — I saw Karl rise. That's when I began to think it was funny. He had rolled down there like a snowball. He was lucky, though. When he was thrown, he landed clear; one foot might easily have been caught in the stirrup and then he would have been dragged. And when he landed, he didn't fall on rock; and he could put out an arm to break his fall. Then even the way he didn't roll far was lucky: he was stopped by one of those trees instead of landing up against a boulder."

"And what then?" Robert O'Farlan asked. "Did you go through the canyon with Bert leading?"

Grubbock shook his head. "We joined Bert far down the hillside, reached the creek in the valley, and followed its trail to the camp where we were meeting the others."

Prender Atherton Jones said, "You mean to say that Bert, a professional cowboy, let a horse get away with that?" He looked around in amazement, shaking his head disapprovingly. Such slackness was not tolerated in Central Park, he seemed to say.

"Bert said he could take a telling. We could beat our horses all we wanted but they still wouldn't go down that canyon. There was just one thing that made a horse behave the way Karl's did: the smell of bear."

"Well, I'm glad you didn't beat the horses and force them into the canyon," Mrs. Peel said. "What pleasure is there in mastering anyone, anyway, if you have to lash him and beat him?"

"That wasn't the end of the story, though," Earl Grubbock said, watching Atherton Jones with a smile. "There we were, Karl and I, both cursing his horse for having added a good five miles to our journey to the camp. We even thought Bert was a bit of a dope. Then we found the others at the camp. Ned and Robb had been looking for strays round the other end of the canyon. They had ridden up a high trail, where they could get a good view of it. There wasn't a stray in the canyon. But they did see a bear, a quarter of a mile away, right down near the beginning of the spruce forest."

"Good God!" said Atherton Jones. "How far is the canyon from here?"

"Far enough. Still, a lone bear can cover a lot of territory. Every now and again, it seems, a bear comes straying through these mountains. 'Traveled a fur piece,' as Bert said."

"Appropriate remark," Prender Atherton Jones said. "I suppose this specimen got disgruntled with Yellowstone Park? The tourists can't be so entertaining this summer." He looked round with an encouraging smile.

"And what did Karl say then?" Sally asked.

"Nothing very much," Grubbock looked at the scuffed toe of his boot. Shut up, he told himself: you've done a lot of criticizing in these last few days, and no doubt Karl found just as much in you to criticize. A trip into the mountains was certainly one way of getting to know a man.

"Anyway," Earl Grubbock said suddenly, "Karl has plenty of courage." That was one thing Karl had plenty of. Damfool courage, sometimes, but courage.

"But you were all afraid of an old bear," Esther Park said.

He studied her face. "Ned, Robb and Bert wanted to go after it and rope it. Jim said what the hell, it was doing no harm. When it started causing trouble, they could go on a hunting trip."

"But what would you do *if* you met a bear?" Carla asked, wide-eyed and troubled.

"I asked Bert. Seemingly you walk, don't run, to the nearest exit."

"But how do your legs obey you?"

"Bert said he had often wondered about that."

"But bears are *sweet*," Esther Park said. "Why, I've fed them in Yellowstone! They come right up to your car, and — "

"I think we may take it from Bert that a stray bear isn't one that likes tourists," Grubbock said. "Or do we know more than Bert does?"

This was such a new line for Grubbock that Mrs. Peel stared. Then she smiled. "Earl's right," she said. "There's a hospital in

Yellowstone Park that's kept to sew up tourists after they've fed the bears. I believe that over sixty people, last year, had themselves scalped and de-armed and otherwise torn about. And these are the nice, safe bears, Esther, not the bad-tempered strays."

"Do you mean to say that we taxpayers," Atherton Jones began, "have to keep up that hospital and pay for — " But at that moment Mrs. Gunn entered to say that Milton Jerks had just driven up from Sweetwater in his new car, and Dr. Clark was with him. They were talking to Jim, now, out in the yard.

As Mrs. Peel started to explain about the doctor's unexpected visit, Mrs. Gunn passed over a note to Sally. It was addressed to her in Jim's handwriting. She opened it and read it.

The note was written with extreme correctness, following the usual pattern of a formal invitation. "Mr. James Brent requests the pleasure of Miss Sarah Bly's company at the corral of Flying Tail Ranch on the evening of Friday, the twenty-seventh of August, at seven o'clock." Down in one corner was "R.S.V.P." while up in another was "Western Saddle."

Idiot, thought Sally happily, complete idiot. *Hello stranger, do you never go riding any more? . . . When I'm asked. . . . Getting formal, aren't we?* We were, she thought, but I'm not going to be a fool any longer. That is all past tense, Sally Bly.

"Well, who is it this time?" Dr. Clark said when he entered the living room, followed by Mr. Milton Jerks carrying newspapers safely tucked under his arm.

Mrs. Peel apologized for the trouble she had given them.

"No trouble at all," Milton Jerks said, replying for both of them. Dr. Clark was too busy talking to Earl Grubbock, anyway. "No trouble at all. We were at the meeting — Sweetwater Improvement Committee — when this call came through. And Doc, after sitting down and thinking about it, said he was coming out here after all. That broke up the poker game, anyways, so I figured I'd just come along and give Doc a lift in my car. It's a whole lot quicker than his old rattletrap. Eh, Doc? About time you were getting a new one."

"When prices come down, Milt," Dr. Clark said amiably. "Well, Mrs. Peel, it is just as we thought. Booster shot needed here. And your other writer needs the whole works. I'll give him an antitoxin test first, just to make sure. Brought everything along with me. Come on, Grubbock, we'll get over to the cabin." Grubbock followed him out of the room with only an eyebrow raised by way of objection.

"What on earth was he talking about?" Prender Atherton Jones asked.

"Tetanus injections. Wherever you've got horses, you've got tetanus," Milton Jerks said with the wise air of a man raised on a ranch. Mrs. Gunn sniffed quite openly. That salesman from St. Louis, she thought.

Everyone turned to look at the round, red face of Mr. Jerks, beaming with good will and pleasure, but his elaborate costume made them speechless. He bowed to Mrs. Peel. "Brought you the papers, ma'am," he said, and presented them with a flourish. "Guessed you wouldn't get them until the mail carrier came tomorrow. Why keep good news? That's what I say. It's a real pleasure and honor to meet you, Mrs. Peel."

That reminded Sally that she hadn't introduced Mr. Jerks to anyone, although they must have seen many signs of him around Sweetwater.

"This is Mr. Milton Jerks," she said, "who runs the Fill-Up Gas Station, the airfield, the Western Supply — "

"*With* the hitching-rail at the door," Mr. Milton Jerks emended. "Sorry we don't see you all using it more this summer, but the doods from Double Tee Emm and Fennimore's, not to mention the Lazy Runaround, all find it kind of handy. Yes sir, it's become a mighty popular place, the old Western Supply. The best silver jewelry, rugs, bead-work and hand-painted cushions you'll find anywhere in the state of Wyoming. Or Colorado or Montana, for that matter."

"What's wrong with Arizona, Idaho, New Mexico?" asked Carla, and then giggled.

"Sure, them too," Milt Jerks said generously. "Got all the best

Indian work you ever saw. I'm a blood-brother of three tribes, the Iropshaws, the Squeehawks, and the Flatfeet. Yes, sir." He looked at Sally expectantly. "Sorry, ma'am. I interrupted you."

"But I've now forgotten all the other things you do, Mr. Jerks."

"There's the Rocky Mountain Regal Palace Cinema," he prompted her.

"Oh, yes . . . And the Wigwam Laundry Service."

"The one with the tepee, outside?" Carla asked. "Is it a *real* one, Mr. Jerks?"

"Straight from the Squeehawks. Chief Bird-in-Hand gave it to me himself. He bought his new 1948 super-coupe model from me. And I got it for him before his cousin, Chief Two-in-the-Bush, managed to get his 1948 super-coupe from the dealer over in Three Springs."

"I take it that meant a lot to Chief Bird-in-Hand?" O'Farlan asked. "Then he could add another coup to his stick?" He grinned around delightedly. He hadn't made a silly joke like that for years. A wonderful feeling. Also, he was proud of the Indian knowledge he had been collecting from Mrs. Peel's library ever since he had arrived. The others, startled at first, began to laugh.

As well they might, Milt Jerks thought. "He added the coupe to his garage," he explained patiently. "He's got three cars now. His squaw drives one, and the kids have the third to rattle around in."

"And how many cars has Two-in-the-Bush?" Mrs. Peel asked.

"The same. They've always got to have the same. That's how they got their names. Been rivals ever since they were strapped to their mothers' backs."

"Oh . . ." Mrs. Peel was horribly conscious of the strained look on her guests'. faces. So she smiled and said quickly, "Do tell us about the Indians. Do you know many of them, Mr. Jerks?"

"Sure. And just call me Milt. Everyone does. Eh, Ma Gunn?"

"What about a nice cup of coffee?" Mrs. Gunn asked pointedly, preparing to leave the room and hoping to take Milt Jerks with her. And don't "Ma" me, she thought angrily. And "Milt, that Jerk," is what Cheesit Bridger and Chuck call you. Dr. Clark says you're all right, just need a bit of getting accustomed to. He even says that Sweetwater needed someone like you, and if all the things you started here were taken away from us, we'd miss them. But Cheesit says he doesn't trust anyone who can make money as fast as you can, it just isn't natural. Still, you're generous too. . . . Mrs. Gunn left the room then, for she wanted to fix something for the doctor to eat; but she was still puzzling over the problem of Milt Jerks, much as she had done for the last fifteen years ever since he stepped off the train at Three Springs.

"Well," Mrs. Peel said, as Mrs. Gunn went and Milt Jerks didn't budge, "do sit down. And if you don't like coffee, what can we offer you? We've beer, and some Scotch I think, and . . ."

"Teetotaler from the day born," Milt Jerks said, waving his refusal as he took a chair. "Smoking likewise. I'm a Holy Roller."

"A holy what?" Mrs. Peel asked faintly. Then, ever the polite hostess, "Ah, yes . . . I'm a Presbyterian, myself. I didn't know you had a Holy Rolling Church in Sweetwater." I was only doing my best, she thought unhappily, watching Carla suddenly leave the room mumbling something about hay fever and handkerchief. The others looked as if they needed a good excuse too. Mrs. Peel frowned at them slightly, and listened with rapt attention to Milt Jerks.

"We don't," Milt Jerks was saying gloomily. "That's one thing I can't persuade them to have. I'm the only Holy Roller in the place."

"How lonely for you," Mrs. Peel said sympathetically. "I mean, all by yourself."

O'Farlan spilled the entire contents of the cigarette box with which he had been playing nervously, and went down on his knees to gather them together.

Mrs. Peel, conscious that his head was bent, that the others were laughing quite beyond all reason, could only shrug her shoulders and try to give a calm smile to Mr. Jerks. He was shaking his head over the uproar which had burst on the room so suddenly. They hadn't much to laugh at, he thought, as he watched the thin, gray-haired fellow crawl around on all fours. They were all nuts. Writers of course.

The girl with hay fever came hurrying back and joined in the laughter. Just nuts, Milt Jerks thought. Only Mrs. Peel was not laughing very much, trying to show the rest of them how sane people behave.

Then Earl Grubbock returned from the cabin. He stood bewildered. He had never seen Prender Atherton Jones enjoying himself so wholeheartedly.

"Hello, Earl," Esther Park said, suddenly serious. "You're just in time. But I think it's awful of us," she added virtuously, "I really do!"

That silenced everyone, and they looked at her in dismay, waiting for her next words.

"So do I," Sally said quickly, breathlessly. "We should all have helped Robert."

"Yes, indeed," Prender Atherton Jones said and frowned so heavily that Esther's mouth, open to speak, just stayed open.

"Must be quite a handful," Milt Jerks said mildly, and at that moment Mrs. Peel forgave him his extraordinary clothes which out-Westerned all Easterners.

"What is?" Atherton Jones asked, hoping that the evening's entertainment was not yet over.

"You all," Milt Jerks said bluntly. "But I guess you folks are grateful to Mrs. Peel, here, for the trouble she's taken to make you all as comfortable as she could. I've talked with her over the phone, often enough, so I know what I'm saying."

"Really — " Mrs. Peel began, her cheeks coloring violently.

"And we were all talking about you, tonight, Mrs. Peel. Sweetwater is buzzing. It isn't every day we find a famous writer living among us, and it's not every famous writer that comes and doesn't let folks know about it." For a moment he thought regretfully of the higher prices he might have charged if he had only known about Mrs. Peel. Then he became conscious that there was complete silence in the room. He rose to the occasion, literally and figuratively. He pointed to the folded newspapers which Mrs. Peel still held unopened in her lap. "Don't you want to read what the papers are saying about you? I brought you my *Sweetwater Sentinel* as well as your *New York Times*."

278

"What on earth is this man talking about?" Prender Atherton Jones asked, and looked with suspicion at the self-avowed teetotaler.

Sally said, "Merely that Margaret wrote a novel once. It was published in 1925, translated into fourteen languages, made into a movie which ran for years. In addition to all that, it inspired a musical comedy called *Inside Utopia*. Its title was *The Lady in White Gloves,* by Elizabeth Whiffleton. Margaret is Elizabeth Whiffleton."

"That's the name," Milt Jerks said cheerfully. "It was on the tip of my tongue. Elizabeth Whippleton. Miss Whippleton, I'd like to — "

"May I see these newspapers, Margaret?" Atherton Jones asked.

Sally took them and unfolded them. "As we can't all see them at once, I think someone ought to read them aloud. Margaret has always been much too modest about her work, so I'd better do the reading. In fact, I seem to be the only person here who is calm enough. Now, let me see. . . . With due thanks to Mr. Jerks, we'll begin with his *Sweetwater Sentinel.*"

Milt Jerks nodded his approval. "Page one," he told her.

"Here it is. . . . 'FAMOUS AUTHORESS CHOOSES UPSHOT COUNTY FOR RESIDENCE.' " Sally paused to let the headline sink in, and then she read on: " 'News has just reached us that the world-renowned authoress, Elizabeth Whiffleton, who wrote the *Lady in Gloves,* sensation of the 1920's in America and Europe, is none other than Mrs. Margaret Hunterbriar Tharkington Peel who purchased her present residence, Rest and Be Thankful, from James Brent of Flying Tail Ranch early this summer. Mrs. Peel, who is of a retiring disposition, has been living quietly at her beautiful home. She is well-known to the residents of Sweetwater, however, who have remarked on the charm of her delightful conversations over the telephone with them. Our reporter, who tried to reach Mrs. Peel on the telephone this afternoon, but without any success unfortunately, hopes to be able to interview her before our next issue appears next week.

" 'Meanwhile, we know that everyone joins us in wishing Mrs. Peel a long and happy life in her new home. It is situated in one of the most beautiful parts of the State, and is rich in historical associations besides, for which Upshot County is justly famous. It was over the old Stoneyway Trail, which passes through Stoneyway Valley where Rest and Be Thankful is located, that Portugee Phillips brought to Fort Laramie the tragic news from Fort Phil Kearney of the Fetterman Massacre in his famous ride, which broke all records for speed and endurance, in the hard winter of 1866. Some historians claim that Portugee Phillips took the Bozeman Trail, and that may be true to a certain extent, but there is proof that he took the cutoff at Coolwater Creek, which brought him over the Stoneyway Trail for a distance of at least six miles in his record ride to Fort Laramie, there to give warning of the Sioux uprising. Mrs. Isabella Lang of 15 Cottonwood Street, Sweetwater, recalls the fact that her father, John MacIvar, was a small boy when he saw the snow-covered horseman gallop past his father's cabin on the Stoneyway Trail, early in the afternoon of 24th December, 1866. "There was a dark gray sky and the snow was falling," John MacIvar said. Portugee Phillips shouted to John MacIvar to tell his father to gather in all the livestock, and shutter the cabin and keep the guns mounted, and he (Portugee Phillips) would bring help from Laramie. John MacIvar, a resident of Sweetwater until his untimely death at the age of 89 last year, was fond of recounting this story. Mr. MacIvar was a guide along with our Joshua (Cheesit) Bridger, no relation of Jim Bridger, in the 1876 expedition to Yellowstone Park under Gibbon's command.

" 'Sweetwater and Three Springs, indeed the whole of Upshot County, are proud to welcome you, Mrs. Peel!' "

There was a small, subdued silence.

The shock, Sally thought thankfully, had been too great. She poured herself a glass of water.

Milt Jerks, who had been watching Mrs. Peel's face with admiration and sympathy, registered the fact (for the next issue of the *Sentinel*) that Mrs. Peel seemed overcome with emotion.

"Now," Sally said, "for the *New York Times*."

"Page twenty-two," Milt Jerks said.

Sally cleared her throat. " 'Elizabeth Whiffleton, author of *The*

Lady in White Gloves, is now revealed as Mrs. Jonathan Peel. The novel created much interest in 1925, when it was issued here by Hitchpfeffer and McMullins. The book was also published in Austria, Denmark, England, France, Germany, Hungary, Italy, Norway, Russia, Sweden and various other countries. Mrs. Jonathan Peel, who was connected with the Calvados Press in Paris before the war, resided in France until 1942. She is now in the United States.'"

There was a long, intense silence.

Robert O'Farlan came over to Mrs. Peel and took her hand. "How wonderful!" Carla said, and ran to take Mrs. Peel's other hand.

Sally stood back and let the others rush forward, offering their congratulations, talking with a sudden outburst of energy and excitement.

"How fantastic!" Prender Atherton Jones said before he could stop himself. "But what on earth made you keep it a secret, Margaret?"

Mrs. Peel only smiled as she looked at him.

"Why don't we celebrate?" Carla cried gaily. "Let's go up and rout out the boys and get them to come over. We'll have a dance. Go on, Earl, tell them all to come. And Ned must bring his guitar."

"Good idea," Grubbock said, "but I guess tonight's the wrong night for it." He sat down stiffly on a chair near Mrs. Peel. "Dr. Clark will be over here soon," he said quietly. "Everything's all right. But Karl will have to take things easy for a day or two. Dr. Clark said he was glad you called him, though." Then he dropped his voice still more. "What's this I hear about Norah? Is she leaving?"

"Tomorrow, I think." Mrs. Peel watched his face carefully. "After all, it is only a few days earlier than she had planned. Partings can't be postponed, can they? People come and people go. Don't they?"

"Yes," Earl Grubbock said gloomily, "I suppose they do." He sat staring at the fire.

"But Earl," Carla called over, "the evening's quite young. It's only a little after nine o'clock. Well if you won't go — Robert, you go and get the boys. Isn't it a good idea, Mrs. Peel?"

"If they feel like it," Mrs. Peel said doubtfully.

Carla laughed as if it were all decided, and began kicking the rugs back from the polished floor. "Come on, Prender," she said, "I'm going to teach you some real dancing. The Varsoviana, or the Marsoviana, or whatever it's called. You know . . . 'Put your little foot there.' Bert showed me how. It's fun. Why" — she stared at the doorway — "here's Mimi come down to join us!"

Mimi came into the room. She looked as decorative as ever in her man-tailored, feminine-chosen negligee. "I heard the most extraordinary sounds," she said, "and no one came upstairs to tell me why." She looked at the disheveled room and the smiling faces. "What's it all about?"

As Carla, hindered by Esther, told the story all over again, the men from the ranch began to arrive. Jim Brent was there, too.

Mrs. Peel looked at Mimi doubtfully. "Do you think it's wise coming downstairs?" she asked.

"My temperature's normal," Mimi said. "I'm getting better every minute. I'll be at the rodeo *and* the dance on Saturday." She smiled at Jim Brent, settled in the chair nearest the fire, and draped the long wide skirt of her robe around her legs. Most of the men seemed impressed. Mrs. Peel glanced quickly at Sally, but Sally was somehow looking remarkably untroubled. In fact, Sally wasn't even avoiding Jim Brent now. She was talking to him. So Mrs. Peel relaxed and listened to Mimi's congratulations about her book with real pleasure.

Everyone was there, now, except Karl Koffing. Even old Chuck had come to listen to the music and the laughter.

His quick eyes watched tolerantly. The young folks didn't know much about the old dances, but what they didn't know in steps they made up in noise. Now when I were a young fellow, he thought, I could keep neat time, never miss a beat. And the girls, with their long wide skirts swinging out above their trim ankles, was as light as a floating feather. But young fellows was different nowadays.

282

Couldn't keep their legs moving — all them darned sit-and-take-it-easy gadgets like automobiles. Young Grubbock, for instance, was a fine healthy-looking young fellow, but he wasn't dancing. Just sitting there with a cloud of gloom on his face. Yet once, after a couple of weeks on the trail, we'd be coming back to dance until sunup. A celebration was what we'd been planning, all the way back down the trail, and a celebration we had. Why, even Ned and Robb and Bert, by the time it got round to one or two o'clock in the morning, would be saying they had to sack in and get a couple of hours' sleep. Young Koffing were already in bed, and now Grubbock looked as if he were leaving.

Then the sharp old eyes noticed that Norah had just gone from the room, and Mrs. Gunn was too busy pairing off with Dr. Clark in the Virginia reel to see it. But Mrs. Peel, swinging as neatly as a girl of eighteen on Jackson's arm, had noticed it all too. She smiled happily, and Chuck nodded. His hands began to clap the rhythm, just to help them all along.

CHAPTER XXIV

Alarms and Excursions

O N THE DAY before the rodeo in Sweetwater, for which great plans were being made at both Flying Tail Ranch and Rest and Be Thankful, Esther Park began her adventure.

It puzzled the others at first. That was before they started being alarmed. But as they had been puzzled by Esther Park when they had first met her, and then had stopped thinking about her (except as something to be avoided if possible, like drafts or bad cooking), her disappearance didn't trouble them until the evening came and she was about to miss a second meal. That, as Mimi said, was really very odd.

At luncheon, they had only noticed that for the first time in four weeks there was no Esther to keep inserting herself. There was a feeling of relief, mixed with mild speculation about where she had gone for her picnic (for Mrs. Gunn had reported that Miss Park had taken some food from the pantry that morning, when she was leaving after an early breakfast); and luncheon was an amiable meal.

"By the way," Mrs. Peel said suddenly, after the lemon meringue pie had melted away and Prender Atherton Jones had enjoyed his Bel Paese too, "I had a letter this morning that might interest all of you. It was from Drene."

Everyone stopped talking.

"She's well, and very happy. They have been staying in Colorado Springs, and they are now going to Hollywood. I gathered Dewey may work there — Firmament Films seem interested in him. And Drene's learning French; because, after Hollywood, they are going to the Riviera."

284

"Do let us see the letter," Prender urged, forgetting noble attitudes in his amazement and curiosity.

"Oh," Mrs. Peel said lightly, "that's all there was to see." She didn't produce the letter. It was written in violet ink on the palest of pink paper with a purple monogram. Its sentences were kept short, and simple, and free from the hazards of punctuation. Dewey, or whoever was teaching her, was very wise. He would have to attend to her spelling, though. But that was always difficult: most women preferred simplified spelling.

"And Dewey Schmetterling married Drene Travers!" Mimi was incredulous.

"Definitely," Mrs. Peel said, remembering the end of the letter. *Say hello to all the gang for me. I am well. Hopping you are too, Truly yours, Mrs. Dewey Schmetterling. (Diana Travers Schmetterling.)*

"I wonder if Dewey knew she had written you," Prender Atherton Jones said.

Mrs. Peel, still remembering the end of the letter, only smiled.

"Dewey is really very clever," Sally said. "Colorado Springs, Hollywood, the Riviera."

"Just made to order for his problem," Robert O'Farlan agreed. "Then after a year or two, he won't have any problem left."

"Just a very spectacular production," Karl Koffing said.

"I don't suppose he will ever finish his book, now. That's the end of his literary career." Prender Atherton Jones spoke regretfully even if he felt somewhat relieved.

"I don't know," Sally said. "Once he has collected his money from Hollywood, he'll no doubt write a satire about it. Then later on, he can write a novel about the Riviera — it is even a richer field for satire than Hollywood."

"But he will have to keep moving all the time," Carla said. "I mean, people aren't going to speak to him once he tears them apart in a book."

"Dewey doesn't listen to people, anyway," Sally said. "He just likes to see them perform. And he hates to stay in one place."

"How long has he actually lived in America?" Koffing asked.

"He went to live with an aunt in Paris when he was a child. I don't think he ever set foot in America again until the war started. But Prender can tell you much more about him: he's the authority on Dewey."

"I've known him a considerable time," Prender Atherton Jones admitted. "We'd keep meeting. London, Paris, Rome."

"Oh," Carla said and sighed. "I've always wanted to travel. How wonderful to be able to say London, Paris, Rome, just like that."

"You can have all those other places," Mimi said, "I'll take Paris."

"The grass is always greener . . ." Sally said with a smile. "The girls I met in Rome used to talk about New York. And I've rarely met a London girl whose eyes didn't shine when she thought of a holiday in Paris or Rome."

"What about the girls in Paris?" Earl Grubbock asked, breaking his gloomy silence. "Where do they want to go?"

Mrs. Peel smiled as she punctured Sally's theory. "Paris," she said.

They all laughed, and went back to discussing Dewey.

Their laughter would have sounded bitter in the ears of Esther Park. For, at that moment, she was imagining them round the dining table, tortured with anxiety.

They would be talking worriedly. They couldn't eat much. And they'd all feel guilty. Look at the fuss they had made about Drene, and Sally, and Mimi, and Karl. You'd have thought that Earl and Karl were heroes when they got back from that trip into the mountains. Well, they could start worrying now about her. Yes, they'd be talking about her, arranging to send out search parties.

She hoped it wouldn't take long before they found her. She was bored. She had been here for hours. She was hungry. She had eaten the doughnuts and sweet rolls which she had taken from the pantry, this morning, when Mrs. Gunn had been too busy in the kitchen to notice. She had also finished the two bars of chocolate, brought with her in the pocket of her buckskin jacket. All she had to do was to wait.

It was so silent, silent and strange. Almost as if she *were* lost. But she wasn't. She was well hidden from the ranch, though. For when she left the trail, she had followed a path through a little wood; and then she had climbed round a small hill, crossed a shallow stream and entered this high glade through another little wood. It was quite simple, she reassured herself. She had ridden miles and miles on the trail, but the distance from the trail to the glade was short, short and twisted and safe. Then she looked around her, and noticed there were several little woods to be seen from the high glade where she sat. And although she was positive she knew the hill which she had skirted, she could count three small hills all folding into each other from the direction she had traveled.

"Well," she said aloud, "there was a canyon opposite me when I came out of the first wood. There was a canyon with yellow cliffs." But even when she rose to her feet, she could only see the topmost cliffs of that canyon; or *was* it that canyon, for the rocks were now white in the blazing sunshine? And there were other little canyons and cliffs, all hunching their rocky spines, one behind the other, until your eyes were dazzled with their sharpness and brightness. She looked away, at the green restful forest climbing up the mountainside on her left; then she looked again at the stretching teeth of rock rising from the hilly fields in front of her. But they were more muddled than ever, and it seemed, even in that moment, they had changed their shape. As if someone had swung the whole countryside around on an axis, like a globe, and what you saw this morning you didn't see now, and what you hadn't seen then, you noticed now.

Suddenly, she wanted to cry out. She was trembling.

"But you aren't lost," she said. "When you want to go back, all you do is get on your horse and then he'll take you to the ranch. Just leave it to him."

She looked around to reassure herself, and her long-suffering horse looked at her patiently and mournfully. She had tied the end of the reins to the branch of a fir tree, so that he wouldn't wander. He was standing there, trying every now and again to lower his head to the grass at his feet. But she had chosen too high a branch. As she looked round, he stopped straining at the reins and resigned himself to waiting. He closed his eyes.

That was a good idea, Esther thought, and she searched for a place where she could sleep, too, in the heat of the day. She left the boulder, against which she had rested when she had eaten her eleven o'clock picnic, and went over to another tree where she would have pleasant shade. The glade sloped down, in front of her, towards a little stream; behind, there was a thin wood straggling along the crest of a small hill. On her left, were the forest and the mountain. On her right, there lay the wood through which she had entered the glade, and the path which could lead her over the stream towards the trail. It could, but it wasn't going to. She was safe here, no one could see her. She had thought the glade was a pretty place when she had first entered it, but she was beginning to hate it. She glared around it, now, before she sat under the large solitary pine tree where the grass looked comfortable. The horse was restive again; the flies were bothering him, but she was just far enough away so that they wouldn't bother her. She stretched out in the shade of the tree, stared up at the blue sky showing through the bristling fingers of pine, listened to the silly stream chattering away to itself as it wound in and out among the sloping fields and hills, and she hated everything.

I was so nice to everyone, she thought, I really was. They are not worth bothering about, and the women are worse than the men. Jealous, mean. And the meanest is Margaret Peel. She's to blame. But she's afraid of me. Because I know. And no one else knows. Sally Bly wouldn't even listen when I tried to tell her. No one knows but me. I saw her gathering up the empty bottles from behind the couch when she thought no one was there. And she keeps her sitting-room door locked all the time. And when she talks to me, she says "Yes?" and smiles, but her eyes wander. A secret drinker, and no one knows. No one but me. That's why she hates me. And she's jealous, too. She separated Sally from me when we could have been friends, she took Carla away from me when we were making plans for next winter; she takes the side of the men. None of them can do anything wrong, they are all angels as far

288

as she is concerned, so that they will smile to her and talk to her. She went riding with Prender, and she's been talking to him a lot. About me. What lies does she tell? He believed her at first, and I could feel him being turned against me. But he's too clever for her after all. Last night, he talked to me in the old way, so he knows what she is. Almost . . . I'll tell him everything about Margaret Peel when we leave. To think what I've had to suffer this month, for his sake. He must know that. He must know everything.

Elizabeth Whiffleton . . . I don't believe it. She never wrote a book in her life. She hasn't the brains. She got someone to write it for her and paid him to keep silent. And perhaps he died last week. Then she was free to speak and claim the book was hers. Would anyone keep silent for all these years about a book she had really written?

On the day the others leave, I'll pack my trunks and leave too. With dignity. I may even forgive her. I can't help being like that. I'll forgive her. But I'll never forget the way she begged me to come here — telephoned and wrote — and then did everything to make me unhappy. Even this very last touch — this plan to send Norah away, leaving us with all the work to do — that was done to humiliate me. But she can't drive me away. I'll go when I please.

Esther Park watched a lazy white cloud float lightly over the cobalt sky. But she neither saw its delicacy nor felt its mysery. The soft air, warm with the perfume of pine forests, of sagebushes on the hills, touched her cheek lightly and passed unnoticed. She was thinking with increasing bitterness of Margaret Peel, who had tried to take away her revolver and leave her helpless. "But she didn't!" Esther said triumphantly, putting her hand quickly to her side where the spectacle-case was neatly held by her belt. "She didn't," Esther repeated, smiled happily, felt assured of everything, and drowsed into sleep.

"It's almost three o'clock," Mrs. Peel said. "I'm going up to the corral to see if Esther has returned."

"I'll come with you," Sally said.

The others watched them walk away from the group of lazy, contented people gathered on the lawn at the creek's edge.

"Do they like her?" Karl Koffing asked in wonder.

"What do you think?" Earl Grubbock asked. He was in a bad temper: Norah was leaving at four o'clock, and Mrs. Gunn was guarding the stairway to Norah's room. After two attempts to see Norah, he had come back to the garden.

"Well, why bother about Park? She's well able to take care of herself."

"She takes better care of herself than anyone I've ever met," Carla said angrily. "It's just like her to ride back slowly, so that we'll start worrying."

"Who's going to start worrying?" Mimi asked. "She said some pretty nasty things about all of us behind our backs. She even tried to drop the idea into Mrs. Gunn's mind that Sally didn't approve of Western cooking and was sorry she hadn't hired a cook in New York."

"I bet Ma Gunn dropped that idea right back where it came from," Earl Grubbock said.

"She did."

"What makes Esther Park like this, anyway?" Carla asked. "Oh, no, Karl. Don't give me that economic environment stuff: the fault lies somewhere within Esther. She's twisted. She isn't crazy. She's twisted."

"What's the difference?" Robert O'Farlan asked.

"She's all her own fault. She would be perfectly all right if she'd be content with herself as she is, and do the best she could with that."

Mimi giggled. "Isn't that asking an awful lot of her?"

Everyone laughed except Prender Atherton Jones. He looked up from his book with some surprise. He had been listening in spite of himself, and he didn't particularly like the conversation. He said, benevolently but reprovingly, "And since when did Carla start analyzing people?"

Carla blushed. But she answered him, her voice trembling slightly at first until she got it under control. "I may be wrong, but I think

Esther is ambitious, and she has nothing to be ambitious on. She wants to be the center of interest always. I'm sure she started being literary just to be different from all the people who live beside her. I mean, they must have money and fine houses and clothes and all that; but she wanted to become something they couldn't be. So she came to New York to write. But she can't write. And she has no ideas of her own: when she gives an opinion, she is only quoting a review or a critical essay on some well-known author. That didn't cut much ice with us, did it? So she started throwing her family, and money, and the house with two gardeners at us. Because none of us own such things. And we were just as bored with her as her rich acquaintances must be when she starts throwing literature at them. That's what I mean when I say she is all her own fault. Why, we'd *all* like to be the center of attention."

"Not bad," Earl Grubbock said, "not bad at all, Carla." Then he looked at his watch, wondered if Norah had finished packing, decided to wait for another ten minutes. There was no use aggravating Mrs. Gunn.

Carla smiled with pleasure at her artistic triumph.

"That's Esther," Mimi agreed. "But I'd add a middle stage between the great literary mind and the wealthy landowner. She wanted to be the irresistible woman. Didn't you notice the trouble she tried to start? I expect you all heard what I was supposed to think about you; I certainly heard all of your opinions about me."

"What?" several voices asked in a broken chorus. And the men (who had been thinking that if you wanted a woman analyzed, then all you had to do was to let another woman take on the job and to hell with all these psychiatrists at twenty-five dollars an hour) looked at each other.

Prender Atherton Jones closed his book and laid it aside. "What do you mean? If a woman thinks she is irresistible then why should she start making trouble between people?"

"Because," Mimi said, "if you think you are irresistible, you try very hard to prove it." She looked a little embarrassed for a moment. Then, "That's true enough for all women, I guess," she said frankly. The men, watching her, knowing what she meant, thought she had never been more charming. She gave them all a warm smile to add to their admiration.

"And one way of proving it," Carla explained, "is to separate people. If you can't attract, then you distract. Isn't that what you meant, Mimi?"

"Yes," Mimi said slowly, looking down at her slender hands.

"Not that I know much about it, not being an irresistible woman," Carla said quickly, trying to hide Mimi's confusion. "And I'm not the wealthy kind, either. Guess I'll just have to concentrate on writing stories, and hope for the best." She laughed as the others laughed.

"I liked the story you've just written," Atherton Jones said. "Of course, it needs a little polishing, a little editing. But it promises very well, I think."

"Thank you," Carla said. She thought, how strange that I now feel so unmoved by his praise. Yesterday, Mrs. Peel had said, "It's good, Carla. I love it. Don't let anyone change one comma!" And Carla had hugged her with delight. She looked at Atherton Jones to see if he had noticed her coolness. But he was thinking over some problem of his own. I know what is wrong with him, Carla thought. He keeps shutting people out. He lets them in when he pleases, and he closes the door when he pleases. I don't believe he cares about any of us at all, certainly not as human beings. Then why does he bother with us? There was a new problem for her to solve.

O'Farlan, watching the smile on her face, asked, "And what's pleasing you now?" Once, he thought in amazement, I called her a timid and worried little marmoset.

"People," Carla answered, "people are so interesting."

It was four o'clock.

Grubbock was saying good-by to Norah. With a million other people, he thought angrily.

"What's your address? Will Three Springs find you?" he asked at the last minute.

"Until Labor Day. After that, I'm in Laramie." Norah looked at him, and then didn't look at him.

"Maybe I'll be seeing you. I might hitch a ride home and drop in to see you at Three Springs."

"That would be fine," Norah said, but the voice wasn't Norah's.

Hell, he thought, she's just another girl. He looked at the others, avoided Karl's amused eye, and looked again at Norah. But the car was already slowly moving out of the yard. Jackson and Norah and O'Farlan were all crowded together in the front seat. O'Farlan had asked for a lift into Sweetwater: he wanted to buy some presents to take home. Why didn't I fake some excuse to get a lift? Grubbock thought suddenly. But it was too late, now. The car disappeared between the cottonwood trees.

"Think I'll do some work," Grubbock said. He began walking towards the cabin.

"It's four o'clock. I'm getting really worried about Esther," Mrs. Peel was saying.

Earl Grubbock went on walking to the cabin. I've got worries enough, he was thinking, without adding that woman to them.

Mrs. Peel and Sally went up to the corral again. They could see nothing on the hillsides, except horses and steers. The ranch, itself, was deserted. The only person left in it was Chuck. They found him in his kitchen.

Robb and Ned were busy in the alfalfa field today. Fine crop this year, with all that rain in June, and the warm weather in August.

Bert was looking over the three-year-old colts which he was going to start breaking in on Sunday. Or Monday. As soon as he recovered, anyway, from the rodeo on Saturday. Bulldogging could shake a man up.

Jim was out having a look at the steers in the south pasture with a couple of dealers, who had arrived by plane at Sweetwater that morning. They wanted to look over the steers before they made any contract for them, although the steers wouldn't be shipped east until as late in September as possible. Jim had bought them a little late, this year, so they needed all the weeks they could get to put some beef on their bones. After the dealers had seen them, they'd argue a bit in Jim's cabin, and drink his whisky, and try to beat him down to less than two cents profit a pound, no doubt.

"Then I'll get Prender," Mrs. Peel said to Sally. Karl's arm kept him from riding. Earl was in a fiendish temper, and he was still limping badly. Robert O'Farlan had gone into Sweetwater. "Prender will just *have* to go, along with Carla and me. No, Sally, you aren't fit to ride very far, yet. Nor is Mimi."

Chuck looked at them both. He put aside the potatoes he had been peeling, stuck the knife into the table, and said, "Guess I'll catch me a horse and take a little ride."

They watched him saddle up, and mount with an agility that Mrs. Peel envied.

"I'll ride up the trail a piece," he said. "She went thisaway. Saw her leave this morning." Like a drooping daisy, he thought; hanging on, she had been, with both hands. At a slow walk, too. "She ain't the kind to be throwed," he said consolingly, and he rode off.

"I wish I had been a pretty young girl in 1880," Mrs. Peel said. "Or was it '70? Chuck says he's tried to forget his age so often that it just doesn't come remembered any more."

"You'd have taken him, language and all?" Sally teased her.

"Chuck would be a very comforting kind of man to have around your life," Mrs. Peel said. "Language and all."

Sally picked up a potato, pulled the small-bladed knife out of the table, and sat down beside a pail of water. "How do I look as a frontier woman?" she asked, beginning to work. "Now, you go and drag Prender away from his precious book and tell him what to do." But what? Sally thought of the miles of hills and mountains. "She'll turn up," she said comfortingly. "Don't get worried, darling. The Esther Parks in this world always turn up."

Prender Atherton Jones said, "Margaret, what *can* we do? It's all very well to say 'Ride out and find her,' but *where* do we start searching? And aren't we probably worrying a little needlessly? She can't have gone so very far. She doesn't enjoy riding at all, you know. She's no doubt persuading herself that she is communing with nature. My dear, don't look so horrified . . . that's one of her phrases. Don't blame me for it."

"I wasn't," Mrs. Peel said bitterly.

He laid aside *Verve* regretfully. "Very well," he said, not unkindly, "let me come and worry with you, if that will bring her home more quickly. But I am a little bewildered. You blamed Esther when she didn't want to be alone, and now that she has the good sense to leave us in peace for one day, you blame her again."

"If she isn't here by dinnertime —"

"She'll be here by that time. It begins to get quite dark by eight o'clock, nowadays." No one with any sense would stay out in the hills, then. And Esther had quite a strong sense of self-preservation.

"*That* is what worries me," Mrs. Peel said.

By six o'clock, everyone had returned except Esther Park.

Chuck had come back, having ridden five miles out by the Timber Trail. "Saw nothing," he reported to Sally, who was just finishing seasoning the stew which she had cooked for the boys' supper. Ned, Robb and Bert were gathered round her admiringly as they listened to Chuck's news. "I hollered a bit," Chuck went on, "but I heard nothing. I rode up that trail quite a piece. Stopped off at Laughing Creek where the Seven Sisters begin."

"Oh, the seven small canyons . . ." Sally said, following him by memory.

"I hollered some more there. And I listened a bit. Saw nor heard nothing of Miss Park."

"We'll eat," Bert said, "then we'll take our turn."

"But tomorrow's a big day for all of you," Sally said. "Oh, I do hope she comes riding in, before we have to — In any case, this is our worry, not yours."

The men said nothing.

"Talking of tomorrow," Chuck said, dishing the stew without more waste of time, "there's one thing I did see. Saw some Injuns coming over the Far Hill. Squeehawks by the look of them."

Bert groaned. "Now, we'll have to get all the horses corraled. It's too near sundown for the Squeehawks to travel to Sweetwater.

They'll camp here for the night. Wait till you see!" He waved a fork in Robb's face. "Come on, let's eat. There's a helluva — pardon, Miss Bly — there's a lot to get done tonight."

Sally decided it was time to leave and let them start eating. At the door of the cookhouse, she met Jim and Jackson.

"What's this about Miss Park?" Jim asked quietly.

"Just all that," Sally said. "And I mustn't keep you, Jim. Seemingly there's a helluva lot to get done tonight." She tried to smile. If the men hadn't been watching her, she might have burst into tears. It was the concern in all their faces and the worry in Jim's voice that had touched her. She gave them a wave and hurried down the house.

"See you at the corral," Jim called after her. He stood there, watching her.

"Nice woman that," Bert said, looking at the excellent stew in front of him. "Hope she's as good a cook as she is pretty. Come and get it, Jim. Don't look to me as if we'll be poisoned, after all."

"But *what* are we to do?" Prender Atherton Jones asked at the end of the quickly served, quickly eaten dinner.

"Find her," Sally said. "Look, Prender, the cowboys are all going out to search for her. Are we going to let them do our work for us?"

Everyone looked angrily at Prender Atherton Jones. They were now all having the first pangs of conscience about the casual way they had talked of Esther Park all day.

"Sally, you shouldn't ride far," Mrs. Peel said. "And I don't think Mimi should be out in the night air, either. And as for Karl — why, it's madness for him to ride with that arm."

"Don't worry," Karl said, "I'm not falling off a horse again."

"But in the darkness, you could strike your arm against a branch of a tree." Mrs. Peel began thinking of blood poisoning and all kinds of complications.

"We'll see," Sally said appeasingly, and exchanged looks with Mimi and Karl. "Now, let's get *warm* clothes. See you at the corral in two minutes."

They all arrived at the corral in less than four minutes, which proved that everyone, even Prender Atherton Jones, had begun really to worry.

"At least, the weather is good," Carla said miserably, and looked over the fields, clear and golden in the rays of the evening sun.

"There's Ned and Robb, and there's Bert!" Earl Grubbock said, as he pointed to three horsemen spreading up towards the canyons. "They began early."

"They certainly did," Karl Koffing said, looking with surprise at all the horses — except those that were saddled and hitched to the rail — now clustered together inside the corral. "What's the idea?"

"Thought they looked kind of cozy in here," Chuck answered. He was leaning on the hitching-rail, and he exchanged that peculiar smile-that-wasn't-a-smile with Jim. Jim Brent was mounted, waiting for all the guests to gather.

Then Karl noticed that his horse wasn't among those saddled. Neither was Mimi's. Nor Sally's.

"Look, Jim," he began angrily, but Jim Brent just shook his head.

"None of you are fit to ride," Jim Brent said quietly.

"But Jim," Mimi said indignantly, "I — "

"Will you all stop talking and get moving?" the quiet voice went on. "Karl, we need a man at the corral, just to keep Chuck company. Sally, you can stay there, too. Mimi, you get back to the house and help Ma Gunn get everything ready for our return."

No one contradicted him this time.

"Now," Jim said, "Jones will ride with Carla as far as Ironstone Ridge, and no further. Mrs. Peel with O'Farlan as far as Blue Hill, no further. Earl, you'll keep within shouting distance of Jackson and me. We're fanning out in the direction of the Seven Sisters. Got that, all of you? Now, point out to me where you're going. Jones?"

Atherton Jones, scarcely recognizing himself by that name, pointed obediently. He looked again, incredulous. "Good God!" he said in alarm. Everyone turned to look.

Carla and Mimi screamed.

The others stared.

"Indians!" Mrs. Peel said faintly.

Over the hill came the Indians, riding in a tight group, wheeling in a circle, making for the high field that stood behind the ranch.

"On their way to the rodeo," Sally explained quickly. "They are staying here for the night. Isn't that right, Jim?"

"They usually do," he said. He grinned. "It's all right. They aren't hostiles. Never killed a white man except in self-defense."

"Well, I'm glad of that," Atherton Jones said so thankfully that he raised a smile all around the group. They were mounting, now.

"And wigwams!" Carla said, suddenly noticing the white-winged, cross-poled tepees that were being erected in a small line under the shelter of the hill. Further east, on the road from Snaggletooth, several cars were parked along the grass edge, and a straggling group of shawled women and small children were climbing up towards the camp.

"I think it might be a good idea to keep your mind on your horse, Carla," Jim said.

"Of all nights for Esther to choose to get lost in!" Carla said, and then felt ashamed of herself. She paid attention to her horse.

"Got your holts?" Chuck asked, as he watched them sitting on horseback.

"And one last thing," Jim said. "If you find her with any blood around, don't, for God's sake, try to get her on a horse. One of you stay and let the other ride back for help." He turned his horse and rode off, with Jackson and Earl following him. The others chose their appointed directions.

"Jesus Christ," Karl said under his breath. "I bet that stiffened all of them."

Chuck said nothing, just looked at the horses.

"It stiffened me," Sally said.

"Blood," Mimi said. "You know, I hadn't even thought of that. And the things we said today! We've all disliked her, you know. Even Prender."

"Oh, shut up, Mimi," Karl said. "Hell's bells, what a mess . . ."

"Shut up yourself, Karl," Mimi said.

He looked at the horses in the corral, then at the Indians on the hill. "Any connection?" he asked Chuck suddenly. I'm damned, Karl thought, if I'll keep guard around the corral. Didn't Jim Brent realize the Indians would notice the carefully corraled horses? Fine way to treat friends.

"Sure," Chuck admitted frankly. "And we couldn't pay them a bigger compliment. The Squeehawks say they can beat the Crows any day when it comes to being horse fanciers."

"Well, I'm not staying here to insult any Indian," Karl said.

Chuck looked at him, pulled his hat further down over his eyes. "Leaving your post, son?" he asked quietly, almost casually.

"That's right," Mimi said quickly. "You go and help Mrs. Gunn, and I'll stay here in your place."

"Argue it out with Jim," Sally said. "But you better wait until he gets back before you go making your change in his plans."

Karl said nothing. But he stayed. He'd argue it out with Brent.

Mimi was watching Jim in the distance. He was riding towards the Indians who had traveled over the hill. Indians, she thought, Indians coming over the hill. I've never seen anything, imagined anything like this. It's a matter-of-fact thing to Chuck here, to Jim, to all the boys. But I've never known anything like this. "And we'll probably never be able to see them," she said gloomily, thinking of Esther Park and a night of worry and trouble. Trust Esther to choose today. . . .

"You'll be hearing Injuns plenty," Chuck said as if he had been reading her thoughts. "After they set up their tepees and the women start cooking, and they eat, and they do a bit of talking, they'll be singing and dancing half the night. They're kind of slow to get started on it, but once they get going they keep it up. You'll be hearing them plenty. But first, we'll find Miss Park."

"Yes, Chuck," Mimi said. And for penance, she turned away from the blue-rimmed mountains and the golden hillside and the white-pinioned tepees, and she marched down towards Mrs. Gunn and a stack of dirty dishes, and fires to be lit, and sandwiches to be made.

"And what do we do?" Karl asked. "Just stand here counting the blasted horses every five minutes?"

"There's worse things to look at nor a horse," Chuck said amiably. Then, as Karl and Sally both stood silently beside him, he began to tell of the winter when he lived with the Squeehawks on their reservation which lay eighty-odd miles away to the south. They were good ranchers. Not like the Iropshaws who rented out their land to others and spent too much on joy-water, when they could get it, and then never had a penny for their families. Now, take the Squeehawks. . . .

Karl listened, not altogether pleased with what he heard. Neither the prosperity of the Squeehawks nor the laziness of the Iropshaws fitted into his picture of Indians. Soon, he stopped listening and just looked at the horses.

CHAPTER XXV

The Waiting Maiden

E STHER PARK awoke from a deep untroubled sleep. She felt good. The air was still warm, and she lay under the tree and looked up at the sky. Then she noticed it was less brilliant and the sun was farther away. It was after five o'clock by her watch. She rose, stretching herself stiffly. The horse was still switching his long tail restlessly, tossing his head as much as the tight reins would let him. I'm thirsty, I'm thirsty and hungry, Esther Park thought. She walked down towards the little stream. It had a silly name, she remembered, but that was all she could remember about it. The water was shallow, flowing clearly over the small rounded pebbles; it tasted cold, cold as if the snows were just melting.

As she knelt at the edge of its bank, she heard a shout. It was Chuck's voice. They had begun searching for her. About time, too, she thought angrily. Why, they should have found her hours ago. And she would have now been sitting in the living room at Rest and Be Thankful with everyone gathered around her. "We were so worried, Esther," they were saying. "How did it happen? Tell us." And she would begin to speak, describing how she had ridden far into the mountains. Coming back, the horse took fright — perhaps he smelled a bear — and she was thrown. Stunned. The horse came back to her, and stood beside her. She couldn't rise. She lay there. She must have fainted. She didn't remember much after that until she heard a faint shout in the distance, and she revived in time to cry out weakly in answer — just when they might have gone on and never found her.

She heard Chuck's voice again, calling repeatedly. He was farther down the stream, hidden by the small wood. Well, she wouldn't answer him. He was the one who made fun of her. No human being ever caught distemper, she had found out. Let him search, she thought. Then she wanted to laugh. "I could have called but I didn't," she said aloud. "I didn't." Let them all search!

Then after she was sure Chuck had gone, she walked up the sloping ground towards the tree where she had slept. She glanced at the horse to see if he were safe. He whinnied. She must remember to untie him before the search party found her. She wished she had something to eat, something better to drink than water. It was cruel of them to keep her waiting like this. But they were all thoughtless and selfish, all of them. She sat down on the grass, her elbows resting on her knees, and she stared moodily ahead of her. She stared over the tops of the scattered pines and birches that grew down the slope of the stream's little valley, at the thick wood beyond the stream, at the canyons beyond the wood. The sun's rays were less bright now. The forests round the mountains were somber and silent, the crags became a darker, colder gray as they fell into deepening shadows. She sat, quite motionless, staring at the miles of land in front of her, seeing nothing. If they don't come by six o'clock, she thought, I'll get on my horse and let him take me home. I'll come slowly into the ranch, and they'll see how near to complete exhaustion I am. And they'll have to admit that I've courage. "How wonderful of you, Esther," Carla would say, "to be able to ride home by yourself after what you went through. Did you see the bear?"

The two Indian boys, racing their horses ahead of the others as they crossed Far Hill and reached Flying Tail territory, saw Chuck in the distance near Laughing Creek. They reined in abruptly and sat watching him. But whether it was with interest or amusement no one could have told.

"Old-timer," the smaller boy said, looking at Chuck's hat. He tilted his own battered felt hat still more in the style of the younger cowboys.

His cousin nodded.

They kept motionless, sheltered by three stray trees and a clump

302

of boulders. They watched Chuck turn round and ride away, back towards the ranch.

"Why was he calling?" the younger one asked.

His cousin sat listening, slouching on his horse, his body resting. His long legs dangled against the dark streaks of sweat on his horse's flanks. Then, without a word, he kicked his horse and pointed its head towards Laughing Creek. The other boy followed him, racing his horse, too, up the sloping ground to the sparse pine trees that grew on the miniature hill above the creek.

As they rode, anyone behind them would have thought they were cowboys, for they wore blue jeans and tightly fitted shirts and high-heeled boots and battered old felt hats on their heads. The hats were shaped correctly, and they were proud of them. (Their fathers and grandfathers wore their broad-brimmed hats straight on their heads, with the high crowns undented and a feather stuck in the bands. That was old-fashioned, like the long thin plaits of hair that fell below the high-crowned hats.) But as they dismounted near the crest of the small hill, and looked around to see how far behind were the rest of their families, they were no longer cowboys. For they had slipped off the bare backs of their horses with a quickness and supple grace that didn't belong to a paleface.

"That was a horse," the older boy said. He nodded. He had heard a faint whinny, brought to him on the wind which came in his direction, just after the old-timer had ridden away. He had been sure it was a horse. And now he heard a restless horse no more than thirty paces away, just beyond the trees over the small ridge.

"But why search for a horse by shouting?" the smaller boy asked.

They looked at each other, each seeing a reflection of his own face. The thick black hair fell over the broad smooth brow in straight heavy locks. The eyes slanted, wide apart above the broad cheekbones. The flat cheeks and the heavy broad nose added to the width of the face above the mouth. But below the lips, the whole face suddenly narrowed and sharpened into a pointed chin, long-jawed. The skin was brown. The fine eyes were almost black. The older boy suffered, like most boys of sixteen, from a skin eruption. The younger cousin had inherited his family's perpetual cold.

At this moment, they were serious, sensing a mystery and excitement. But if anyone had thought this normal, he would have been as mistaken as he was in guessing that two young cowboys were riding in front of him. They had been joking, laughing, yelling, giggling, for the last fifteen miles. They had been scouts for Custer — the ones he hadn't listened to; then a Squeehawk raiding party against a Sioux village; then cavalry charging the Germans whom their uncle, Bob Big-Foot-in-the-Shoe, had beaten. And just before they had seen Chuck, they had been the two bravest leaders of the Light Brigade, which they had learned about in Sixth Grade English last year. Now, at this moment, they were just Cedric Slow-to-Move and Harold Running-Nose, curious, alert, eager to solve the problem about which their instinct had warned them.

Cedric, because he was six months older and half an inch taller than Harold, led the way. They tethered their horses securely and crept forward silently to the crest of the hill, taking shelter behind a clump of trees. In the open ground that sloped away in front of them, a woman sat under a solitary pine. That was nothing remarkable. The Indians had always called this little hidden slope with the magnificent view the Waiting Maiden, just as the canyons ahead were called the Seven Sisters. It was appropriate that a woman should sit here and look into space. Cedric's great-grandfather told a story that lasted three nights about just such a woman in this very place.

"Aw, nuts," whispered Harold in his best Sixth Grade English.

"*She* didn't neigh," Cedric whispered back, his keen eyes searching the rest of the glade and finding the horse. He smiled.

"She could, I bet," Harold said, looking at her closely. Then he saw the horse, and he smiled too. It was standing very still, its head high: it had sensed them. The horse has more brains than she has, he thought. He looked at Cedric, but Cedric was standing as still as the horse.

"I'll give my bear's roar," Harold whispered, and he began to laugh silently. He slid onto the grass, holding his ribs, and rolled around as he enjoyed his joke. He could see it all — the bear that roared, the woman in flight, the horse that wouldn't move because it knew what was a bear and what wasn't. Then Harold stopped laughing, exhausted and happy, and lay watching Cedric with interest. Cedric had another idea. Horses always gave Cedric ideas.

"I bet my two-bladed knife to your new belt buckle that she would never know," Cedric said softly. He was talking in Squeehawk now, dropping into the old language as he dropped into the old challenge.

Harold measured the distance from the group of trees to the single pine where the horse was tethered. He fingered the new silver buckle which his father, John Running-Nose, had given him only last week for killing his first bison in this year's Big Hunt. Then he nodded his agreement. The distance was too great.

His critical eyes watched Cedric Slow-to-Move, who, after handing over the boots which he didn't like but wanted to wear, had begun a side approach under cover of the fringe of trees until he halted at the group of pines nearest the horse. Then he rose to his feet, stood there, letting the horse see him, smell him. He had reached it now, coming to the horse face-on, slowly, calmly. He stroked its nose and talked softly into its ear as his right hand slipped up to the knotted reins. Harold Running-Nose had to smile, even if he did lose his silver buckle, even if he did get a beating from his mother that would take the skin off his back.

The evening silence increased. The breeze had dropped. Nothing stirred. Even the horse was quiet. It's lonely here, Esther Park thought. I'll loosen the horse from the tree. Shall I begin riding back to the ranch? Or shall I wait some more? They must be coming soon to find me. She rose, and turned towards the horse. But the horse was not there.

She ran up to the tree. The horse was not there.

"Where, oh where?" she cried.

Had it smelled a bear, broken loose, gone galloping off?

"But I would have heard it," she said. And there had been nothing to hear.

Then, because she had been thinking of bears for the last ten minutes, thinking how bravely she had lain still when she had fallen from her horse and the bear hadn't come any nearer, and the startled horse had run away and then, later, had come back to stay beside her, she now became terrified. She was alone. She was helpless. She had no horse. The ranch was miles away. She was alone and the forest up on the mountains was thick and menacing. She stood uncertainly. Then she gave a cry and began to run awkwardly in her heavy, high-heeled boots.

She didn't run very far, for the wood near the stream had darkened in the lengthening shadow of the mountain. The path she had followed this morning was no longer clear. The wood was black and silent and filled with threats. She took ten paces into it. Then she knew she had lost the path. She stumbled back over a fallen tree and scattered twigs. She reached the glade again. The path was near here. But there seemed so many paths, so many openings through the trees that started closing around you once you stepped into them. On the other side of the stream there were deeper woods. Behind her was the mountain and its grim forest. A rabbit skeltered across the glade. She screamed. Then she called wildly. "Chuck, Chuck," she called. She called the others, too. But there was no one to hear. Then she screamed once more, and wept, and fell on the ground.

When the Indian camp had been made in the field overlooking Flying Tail Ranch, John Running-Nose examined the horse which his son and his nephew had brought so quietly and carefully to join the others. And like the other horses, it was hobbled to keep it from wandering.

"That's a good one," he said to his son. "Where did you find it?"

Harold said, "We found it near the Waiting Maiden."

"A wild horse with a saddle growing on its back? They breed rich horses here."

The group of old men in their high-crowned hats, and young men in low-crowned hats, burst into laughter. The shawled squaws, cooking pemmican into a broth over oilstoves, giggled and put up a polite hand to cover their remaining teeth. The young girls, in tight blue jeans and tailored shirts, with their pretty dark hair hanging loose to their shoulders in glamour-bob style, looked up and smiled. They wore lipstick. And they didn't have to hide their teeth, for they had grown up in orange-juice days. Then they went back to their tasks of helping the squaws, or of looking after the swarm of children that fell over each other, laughed, cried, giggled, sniffed, and fell over each other.

John Running-Nose was still waiting for an answer.

"At some distance off," Harold said slowly, "there was a woman. She liked to sit and watch the mountains." His father insisted on honesty between blood relations.

"He speaks the truth," Cedric Slow-to-Move said, eyeing his father who had the same standards as John Running-Nose.

Then John Running-Nose said to his son, "And where is your new buckle of the best silver?"

Harold looked at Pretty Smile, his mother. "I lost it," he said, and followed Pretty Smile into the family tepee which held thirty on good nights, thirty-six at a crush.

"No sign?" Sally asked.

"Nothing," Prender Atherton Jones said. He helped Mrs. Peel dismount. "It is almost dark now." It is useless, his tone of voice said.

"Bert and Ned came back for lanterns. They've gone out again. Robb is still searching through Yellowrock Canyon."

Carla and O'Farlan stood silently beside Sally. Grubbock had just ridden back, too. He said quietly, "A human being is too small a thing to get lost in that rock pile."

"What now?" Koffing asked.

Jackson said, "Lanterns, like Bert and Ned."

Sally suggested, "Let's wait until Jim finishes talking to the Indians."

"They saw no one on their way here to the ranch," Grubbock said. "Jim went and asked them specially, just before we rode out."

"Well, they've been talking to him long enough since he came in." Sally looked across at the barn, whose lighted doorway showed three Indians in full, resplendent dress. In the elaborate costumes, they looked both majestic and terrifying. "Why have they put on their special clothes?" she asked.

Chuck said, "They are paying us a visit. I guess they came to give

307

us an invitation to watch them dance. Sort of dress rehearsal for tomorrow when they perform at the rodeo. They're friends of Jim. Guess they kind of expected him to entertain them as usual. They made him a blood brother ten years ago. Strong-Wind-in-the-Mountain they call him."

"What's the name they gave you?" Sally asked. Any talk was better than just staring at the dark hills and forests, thinking how vast they were.

"Now that's a mighty strange thing." Chuck said. "They give a name that fits. Or they give a name that's opposite, so everyone knows it fits extra well. Like the wife of John Running-Nose. His name fits, but hers is Pretty Smile, and she's had about three teeth in her head since she was sixteen and had her first son. That's the opposite kind of name. See?" It's good to keep talking, he thought as he watched the strained faces around him. "Now, when it came to giving me a name, you'd be surprised what they thought up."

"What?" Sally asked.

"They call me Long-in-the-Tongue. That's a heck of a name." And I don't go spreading it around, either. Only, he thought, tonight's different. "There's Jim coming back now," he reported suddenly.

Everyone turned to watch Jim, as if they could judge the news he brought by the way he walked. Behind him, the three Indians were stalking back towards their camp in the growing darkness.

"What on earth had they to say?" Prender Atherton Jones asked angrily. "They've wasted more than ten minutes."

"You can't hurry that kind of talk," Jim said. "But I did find out something. Two of their boys saw a woman. Just after five o'clock. Up on that small park called the Waiting Maiden."

"But I was there," Chuck burst out. "Or a couple of hundred yards at most from it. I hollered good and loud. There weren't no woman on that hillside."

"Cedric Slow-to-Move and Harold Running-Nose say they saw her."

"They're good boys," Chuck admitted. "Truthful. Except when it comes to horses, like all Squeehawks. Say, Jim, they didn't see any horse, did they?"

308

"That wasn't mentioned. I got the feeling that the horse delayed our conversation a bit."

"So them boys lifted it, saddle and all?" Chuck's lips tightened. He looked as if he were trying hard to keep some well-chosen words from exploding.

"How *can* they behave like that?" Atherton Jones said, staring angrily at the receding figures of the Indians. Only two minutes ago he had been reflecting on the nobility of the Indian in all his array, making the white man (Jim, in this case) look insignificant. "A human life is at stake," he went on, "and they hedge because of a horse which they don't want to give up. I presume they *have* stolen it?"

"Take it easy," Jim said sharply. "They're good guys. They're worried about this darned horse business, and they took a chance of losing it back to us when they came over here to tell us about Miss Park."

"This is too involved for us to understand, Jim," Mrs. Peel said appeasingly.

He gave her a smile. "I'm taking Jackson, and we are riding out with Bird-in-Hand, Two-in-the-Bush, Running-Nose and Slow-to-Move. We'll signal to Bert and Ned and Robb and get them off their trail. And I've an invitation for all of you to visit the Indian camp as their guests. Don't ask me how they knew you were here. But they knew. And they knew about Mrs. Peel. They are sorry that their tribe doesn't go in for initiating women, but they've got an honorary name chosen for her. Flowing Ink." He lifted one of the lanterns that Jackson had lighted, and swung himself easily onto his horse. He paused only to look down at Atherton Jones and say, "Sure, the Indians have their little ways. And we have ours. Guess some of them don't look too good either, sometimes."

Never, Sally thought, had she seen Prender so properly silenced. Strong-Wind-in-the-Mountains had done it.

"We'll all go back to the house and get everything ready," Mrs. Peel said. "And I'll ask the Indians to be *our* guests; then Mimi won't catch pneumonia out in the night air. Perhaps they'll dance on the lawn."

"We'll see how Esther is, first," Sally reminded her. And she wondered, as she thought of the mass of children playing over the hillside, whether an Indian camp might not be a better place for the party than a lawn and a house with many doors. Tonight was sufficiently complicated. This, Sally decided, is one time I'm going to say no to Margaret. Mimi could go wrapped up in blankets, which would be appropriate enough.

"Oh, of course," Mrs. Peel said. "I'm afraid Flowing Ink went right to my head. But I don't think Esther is hurt, do you? Jim seemed relieved, didn't he?"

They all began talking. The sense of disaster was beginning to dissipate, and relief over Esther and excitement over the Indians took its place. "It's wonderful!" Carla said about everything. And they all began to move towards the house.

"Coming?" Earl Grubbock asked Koffing.

"I'm still on duty." Karl glanced at the horses. "Looks as if my job is just starting. Why didn't you go out again with Jim and Jackson?"

"Couldn't sit a horse any more," Earl admitted frankly. "Guess this is something like sun-tanning: a second burn on top of the first one raises pure hell." He looked at Chuck and tried a Western joke by way of general apology. "Got enough rawhide on my tail to make a brand new saddle." And once, he thought, I used to pity the Infantry. He set out determinedly towards the cabin.

Under cover of the darkness, Chuck smiled openly. He had liked the way young Grubbock could keep his face straight. "See you later," he called after him.

Karl was watching the lanterns moving swiftly out by the Timber Trail towards the Seven Sisters. "I wonder why she didn't hear you," he said. That stopped Chuck's enjoyment of the joke. He went back to brooding over Esther Park. And why hadn't she heard him? It was the kind of failure he didn't like. He was going to think this one out.

The men, guided by the two subdued boys, rode out to find Esther Park. They rode quickly up the dark trail, but when they reached

Laughing Creek and crossed over into the black wood, their pace slackened. This path was treacherous by night.

Jim Brent called out to reassure her. There was no answer. He called again, as they came out of the wood and reached the glade.

"Isn't here," Hubert Slow-to-Move said, and looked at his son Cedric.

"She was here," Cedric said, and his cousin Harold nodded.

They searched the ground by the light of the lanterns. The Indians pointed out where she had sat — there were scraps of silver paper and the crumpled wrappers of chocolate bars on the ground beside a rock. There, the Indians said as they came to a tree, she had lain down for a long time. Perhaps had slept. They said nothing of the obvious traces of a horse which Jim's quick eye had noticed, too, by another lonely pine tree. He said nothing, either.

They all gathered together and talked. Daylight would be better. "It has to be tonight," Jim said.

They gathered together again, and they talked some more. Then, with the lanterns held high, they began to search the ground very carefully.

"This way," Chief Two-in-the-Bush said at last. It was difficult to judge at night, but he was sure she had taken this way.

"This way," Chief Bird-in-Hand said almost simultaneously. He spoke with equal conviction. Then, in silence, they led the way over the crest of the sloping hill that sheltered the glade, through the scattered pine trees out into rough open ground covered with boulders. The others followed, bringing the horses.

It was then that Esther Park wakened. First, she heard the night wind sighing through the fir trees. And then she saw the darkness above her, around her, blacker and deeper than it had been before she had fallen asleep. She sat slowly up on the rock where she lay. She had climbed there before the darkness fell, climbed to get away from the ground and the animals that haunted the ground. She felt tired and ill, hungry and sore. She had wept and shouted so long, before she had fallen into a deep sleep that was almost unconsciousness, that she had no strength left in her throat. But I must shout when they come, she told herself. They will see me easily on this rock. They must come. . . . She lifted her eyes and stared wearily into the blackness that surrounded her. The tears were running down her cheeks once more. Then her body stiffened. Lights. Lights wandering down there on the hillside below the rock. Horses, there were horses, and there were men. She tried to call, and she couldn't.

She tried to call again, but now she saw the two men with the lanterns. She saw the dark, frowning faces, the painted brows, the long thin plaits of hair, the tall feathers rising sharply from the narrow headbands. Indians. Indians pointing towards her, running towards her. She moaned in terror, she didn't hear Jim Brent's voice calling to her. She only heard the high-pitched shout of an Indian. She screamed and rose. She turned to run, forgetting the high rock onto which she had climbed; and she fell, still screaming, down into the darkness.

CHAPTER XXVI
Jim Brent Takes Charge

M<small>RS. PEEL</small>, wrapped in a heavy wool dressing gown, came into the kitchen to get warm. She placed the kettle on the electric stove in the pantry, and then sat down in Mrs. Gunn's rocking chair. It was four o'clock in the morning. The house had fallen into sleep at last. Mrs. Peel was supposed to be in bed, too, but after she had made the coffee and drunk it, she didn't go back upstairs. She threw some kindling into the wood stove in the kitchen, and drew the rocking chair to face the flames. The fire caught, and held. If it hadn't, she thought, I might have burst into tears. That was how she admitted she was near the breaking point. Then she found she was crying a little, anyway.

She was still sitting there, watching the flames when Jim Brent came in.

"I saw the light and thought I might be in time for a cup of coffee," he said. And he had hoped it would be Sally who was in the kitchen. But he hid his disappointment. After a quick glance at Mrs. Peel's face, he went on talking while he searched for some dishes and bread and butter and the frying pan. "Breakfast is what we need," he said, and began cooking the eggs. "Well, the Squeehawks have gone. Robb, Chuck and I saw them off. Rode as far as Flashing Smile with them."

Mrs. Peel rose to help. She was quite calm now, and all traces of tears had been quietly wiped away, but she was white-faced and haggard. "Then you never got to bed?" she asked.

"We talked a bit after the dancing and singing was all over, and the women and children were packed off to sleep. Then before dawn, they all began getting ready to move. They'll reach Sweetwater in

313

time to set up their camp near the Iropshaw and Flatfeet Indians—you'll see quite a collection of tepees at the side of the rodeo field—and they'll rest a bit, and then they'll get ready to ride in the parade. The young girls won't be wearing blue jeans and cowboy shirts. They'll be riding sidesaddle in white buckskin dresses. Pity the women couldn't dress for you last night—too busy, I guess, setting up the tepees and cooking and keeping the children out of harm. But wait until you see them today: shawls of every color, buckskin leggings and moccasins, all beaded and embroidered with porcupine quills. They dye them every color in the rainbow, you know."

"I don't think I'll see the parade or the rodeo," she said. "I don't feel like it, somehow."

He pretended to be studying the slices of toast which Mrs. Peel had managed to burn.

"Just wait until you've had breakfast," he advised her, "and had a short sleep, and got dressed, and driven down to Sweetwater. When you feel the sunshine and see all the laughing faces around you, you'll enjoy yourself too."

Mrs. Peel shook her head, perhaps over her efforts at toast making.

"Stop thinking about Esther Park," he said. "She's alive, isn't she? And no thanks to her. The—" He controlled his language. "The silliest piece of stupidity . . . She could have followed Laughing Creek right downhill to where it joins Crazy Creek, and she would have been on the road. Then all she had to do was to keep the mountains on her left hand, and she would have been here by midday."

"But she wouldn't know *where* to keep the mountains," Mrs. Peel said, remembering her own experiences on a trail.

"She had the mountains on her right, when she rode out. Obviously, you keep them on your left when you ride in."

Mrs. Peel smiled faintly. "You make it sound easy, Jim."

"It is. Good heavens, she was no distance at all from the ranch—five or six miles at the most." It was easy, if you really wanted to find your way back. He looked at Mrs. Peel. I won't tell her that unless I've got to, he thought.

"How long will it take a broken thigh to mend?" she asked.

314

"That depends on the person with the broken thigh."

"And she may have other injuries. Dr. Clark said he would call us around six o'clock and give a full report."

"Well, she's in good hands. Three Springs Hospital is up-to-date. And it has had a lot of experience in broken thighs and smashed legs." He set the plates of ham and eggs on the table. "Come and eat. And we'll stop talking about her until we've been fed."

Mrs. Peel obeyed him, thinking how pleasant it was to have some-one to take charge and give orders and make up her mind for her when she was so dazed that all she would have done would have been to sit hunched over a fire and wait for Dr. Clark's telephone call and try to get everything sorted out in her own mind and decided and — oh, she couldn't even take care of her sentences any more, things were just running away from her.

After breakfast, which she ate with an appetite that surprised her, they sat with their elbows on the kitchen table, talking over their fourth cup of coffee and a cigarette. She was warm enough now to throw off the wool dressing gown which had covered her tweed suit and sweater, and somehow, everything began to look less difficult to solve.

"Thank you, Jim," she said, "for taking charge last night."

"Someone had to, I guess." The younger men didn't feel they ought to take charge, and Atherton Jones had just dithered around stroking his hair and saying "Good Heavens, this is terrible, terrible!" It had been easy enough to take charge, Jim thought. All he had done was to get Dr. Clark to bring up the ambulance and get Esther Park out of the house.

"She didn't want to go to the hospital. She wanted to stay here. That's worried me, Jim. Could we have nursed her here?"

"And kept you tied to her room for months? No. Besides, she was Jones's friend, wasn't she?"

"It was puzzling the way she didn't want to go to the hospital. No one knew her there, she kept saying."

"I wired for her sister to come and take charge," Jim said.

"I think I'll go down to Three Springs and stay until the sister arrives."

Jim Brent looked at her thoughtfully. "It seems to me," he said slowly, "that there are nurses and doctors in a hospital. And her sister, if she likes to catch the first plane from New York to Denver, could be in Three Springs by this evening."

"Perhaps she won't, though."

"Look, you are not going down to Three Springs. You are just about ready to be ill, yourself. If anyone should hang around Three Springs until the sister arrives, it should be Atherton Jones. He knows the family. Let him deal with this. He started it all, in the first place. I told him as much, last night."

"You told him?"

"Well, he was making quite a speech about someone having to go down to Three Springs — what would the sister think, and all that stuff. I said, sure, what would the sister think if she found the family friend was still having a holiday some thirty-five miles away from the hospital."

"Oh, Jim!"

"And before he got his second wind, I told him Jackson would drive him into Three Springs this morning before the parade started through Sweetwater."

"What did Prender say?"

"Oh, he fluffed a bit. But he's leaving here at nine o'clock."

Mrs. Peel said, "Well, it looks as if I'm too late to decide anything." She smiled. "And I'm glad, too. Every time I try to make things simple, I always end up complicated."

"It was rough justice, perhaps," Jim admitted. "But sometimes that's the most honest kind of justice. And I shouldn't worry too much about Esther Park, either. She asked for this."

"Now, Jim," Mrs. Peel said, "that's not like you to say that. People do get lost, and frightened. And seeing the Indians in the dark . . ." Mrs. Peel shook her head sadly.

"Look, where does she get her ideas about people? This is 1948."

"But you've been brought up among Indians, Jim. You know them. We don't. Look how we all got so excited last night, once Esther was safely away in the ambulance and we could have our party with the Indians. It was the most fantastic and exciting experience for all of us. I know they were drinking coffee and talking with me ten minutes before, and we had all laughed together. But once they started dancing, I was scared. I just stood, unable to speak, or even to move. And so were the others. Even Grubbock and Koffing were impressed."

Before the drums started to beat, Earl and Karl had been discussing a lot of things that caught their fancy. The Indians' long, tight red woolen underwear, for instance, which now took the place of the red paint which once had covered their bodies. Was it, Earl wanted to know, the happiest solution for the problem of skin that had become accustomed to warm clothing? Karl said the white man had given the Indians all his worst faults — colds, drink, and modesty. He thought it was comic, too, that Cowboys and Indians had become a historic game, for now there were only Indian cowboys. Earl Grubbock wondered if Pocahontas would have seemed as romantic to John Smith if she had worn lipstick and blue jeans and a permanent wave? But both Karl and Earl stopped joking when the drums began. Then a silence fell. And the men began to dance, moving in a circle around the central pole where, once, an enormous fire would have blazed. Their intent, painted faces, their elaborately dressed bodies were lighted by the flares that hissed and spluttered on the grass. Their feet stamped the rhythms of the discordant drums. The women and children watched and listened, quiet, motionless. And behind them all stood the tall white tepees with the dried scalps hanging from them, like ghosts in the shadows under a cold, hard sky.

"Yes," Mrs. Peel said, remembering, "we all stood silent then. Even if there *was* red woolen underwear beneath the shoulder capes and breechclouts and beads and feathers, that didn't matter. For there was something else — strong and deep. Something terrifying, as all old primitive ideas can be terrifying. Perhaps because they are so real. Don't you see, Jim?"

"Yes." He looked at her again, and this time he decided to tell her. "But what I had in mind, mostly, was this. Esther Park didn't have to be on that rock in the darkness. She asked for all that happened to her. Look, Mrs. Peel, she must have heard Chuck. The Indian

317

boys described exactly how she was sitting, and where she was sitting, when they reached her just ten minutes after Chuck was calling. They heard Chuck, remember. Now, when you questioned her, she told you she was too weak and exhausted to call back. But she could still have pulled the trigger of that gun of hers. Sally and I had a look at it. It hadn't been fired." He took the gun out of his pocket, and placed it on the table. "Why didn't you tell me she was wandering around all month with this gadget at her belt? We'd have stopped that mighty quick, I can tell you."

"Well, no one took me very seriously about that, and I didn't want to bother you. Besides, she never used it, did she?"

"And if she had? Don't you kind of think that trouble is best taken care of before it starts?"

"Yes, I see that now." But the others had seemed to think that any interference was an attack on Esther Park's personal freedom: she liked having a gun, and that was her own business. No more dangerous, Prender had said, than owning a car that tempted you to drive at eighty miles an hour. None of them had approved of the gun, of course, but none of them had wanted to interfere, either. "It's a wonder she didn't shoot the Indians," Mrs. Peel said thankfully.

"She tried to, when she was lying on the ground screaming her head off. The Indians stopped to let me reach her first. I saw her struggling to pull something out of that purse on her belt. Lucky the lamp shone on it. I kicked it out of her hand, and hit her over the head to keep her quiet. Couldn't have got her back to the ranch if I hadn't."

"That's why she kept saying the Indians scalped her! I had the most frightful time explaining they couldn't have, because her hair was still on her head. But she said they had. She felt the blow of the tomahawk."

Jim shook his head. "If that woman weren't such a tragedy, she'd be a comedy. Didn't she realize that if you carry a gun and are lost, then you fire the gun to attract attention? Or didn't she think that we'd notice this?" He pulled out the torn wrappers of the chocolate bars which he had found in the glade. "Two half-pound slabs. Who takes that with them for a morning ride, anyway? Wonder she wasn't as sick as a dog," he added in disgust. "And another thing, did she think you can tie a horse to a tree for hours and it won't leave any traces?"

"Then she planned it all," Mrs. Peel said, suddenly angry.

"And she got more than she bargained for."

"Does anyone else know about this?" Mrs. Peel thought of what the others would say.

"Best keep it quiet," Jim said. "She's away. That's the main thing."

Mrs. Peel agreed. "If the Indian boys hadn't admitted seeing her, why we'd have been searching all night!" And other accidents could have happened on the dark trails. And the rodeo would have been ruined for everyone. And Ned — with his entry money paid. And Bert, too, who hoped to win something at bulldogging. For the cowboys would have searched all night through and all day, if necessary. "Jim," she asked suddenly, "what about the horse? Did you ask for it?"

He smiled. "Not this time. But I got the saddle and bridle back. I let Slow-to-Move and Running-Nose learn that I knew the horse had wandered. I said that you were worried about the saddle and bridle, because they were your favorites."

"I was worried?"

"Well, I said Flowing Ink was worried. I also said you would give the horse as a present to the boy who was clever enough to find it and bring back the harness. The saddle was sitting on the hitching-rail by three o'clock this morning."

"Flowing Ink will pay for the horse, certainly," Mrs. Peel said with a smile. "But Jim, aren't you angry about it all?"

"I don't see what good that can do, now. There had to be a slight balancing of accounts, and the horse did it. You see, the Indians took some trouble finding Esther Park last night — that interfered with all their own arrangements. And John Running-Nose lost a silver buckle through some bet that his son made, I heard. And Hubert Slow-to-Move lost a valuable tailfeather in the pine woods. Belonged to his great-grandfather. So I knew then the horse was gone for good, no matter what I said."

"What if a horse had been stolen from the corral, and there had been no trouble about Esther?" Mrs. Peel asked. It was all, as she had said earlier this evening, very involved. And yet logical, too.

"I'd have made a good try at getting it back. It's a matter of who's to laugh last. The Indians like a joke. Keeps them happy for years. If you see an Indian laughing at something that doesn't seem funny to you, he's remembering how a joke once began just with the same kind of situation he sees round him now. And he's thinking that the joke could be repeated again. It might not be, but it could, and he's enjoying it in any case."

"And once I thought Indians were a grave and gloomy people," Mrs. Peel said, remembering the laughter and talk and noise and bustle of the Indian camp last night.

"That's when they are among strangers," Jim said. "But yesterday, they were your hosts. Well, now, we'd both better get a couple of hours' sleep." He left, without wasting any more time on unnecessary good-bys.

Mrs. Peel watched him for a moment. There's another comforting kind of man to have around your life, she thought. Then she had no more time to think of Jim or of Sally, for the telephone bell rang sharply in the hall. It was Dr. Clark with reassuring news. There were no further complications. Just a nice straightforward fracture which would keep Esther out of mischief for a few months. There was nothing to worry about, everything was well under control. And he had found just the right nurse, too. He didn't say that the rest of the hospital staff called her the Holy Terror. Instead, he ended with a cheery, "See you at the rodeo!"

Mrs. Peel climbed the stairs happily to her bedroom. She lowered the shades and drew the curtains to keep the sun out. And within five minutes she was deeply, wonderfully asleep.

CHAPTER XXVII

Sweetwater Stampede

M RS. PEEL, Sally and Earl Grubbock arrived in Sweetwater well before the parade was due to start. They drove in with Jackson and Prender Atherton Jones, who was all packed and prepared for Three Springs. This was Mrs. Peel's first journey down to Sweetwater — her arrival at Rest and Be Thankful by the Snaggletooth road had been almost enough to cure her of travel — so that she found herself excited and curious as they approached the little town.

It lay at the beginning of a plain stretching eastwards, rippling in waves of small hills, spreading into infinite distance. The plain was a dust-colored green, covered with sagebrush and buffalo grass. Some ten miles away (although, if the map hadn't insisted on ten, Mrs. Peel would have said two) a small puff of white smoke traced the path of a train on the single-track railroad, winding its way towards three neat circles of blue water. That would be Three Springs, proud possessor of a railroad station. Distances within distance were peculiar, Mrs. Peel thought. These strange islands of stone called "buttes," for instance, which rose sharply and unexpectedly out of the distant plains: bare mountains with their peaks cut off, flatly, evenly, their steep sides clearly balanced and outlined. They looked as if they had been built by a forgotten race of giants who liked their tables pyramid-style. She couldn't believe that the nearest butte was over seventy miles away, and the farthest one was a hundred and ten miles distant. But Sally said it was true enough, and had given her the map to prove it.

As they drove down the twisting road into Sweetwater and entered the cluster of doll's houses and treetops, which suddenly became real houses and shaded gardens, they began to forget the lonely miles of plain which stretched out so hungrily towards the town. Sweetwater had obviously no fears that it could be swallowed up. The log cabins were substantial, and there to stay. The white-painted houses had their plots of well-tended grass and bright flowers. And Main Street, looking very different from the buffalo trail that had wandered over the giant plain only seventy years ago, was a smiling host. Banners and flags were strung overhead across the street; every store was decorated; and the biggest sign of all, stretching from an upper window in the two-storied Courthouse to the roof of the Teton Bar opposite, bade them WELCOME, STRANGER, TO THE SWEETWATER STAMPEDE!

It was there that Prender Atherton Jones began to flinch. But the others, most annoyingly, were too busy enjoying themselves as Jackson drove the car slowly along the bustling street, avoiding the darting children, the arriving cars and the tethered horses. Sally knew everyone, it seemed, and everyone knew Sally.

Mrs. Dan Givings stood at the doorway of her Western General Emporium and gave them the first wave. Next, there was Milt Jerks with his new white beaver felt. He was standing outside the B Q Bar discussing the day's events with a group of men. This was, as Sally pointed out, an astute middle-point between the Wigwam Laundry, the Fill-Up Gas Station ("We Check Your Water, We Measure Your Oil, We Do All We Oughter, And Save You Toil"), the Rocky Mountain Regal Palace Cinema (*Roaring Gulch* and *Two-Gun Hennessey,* grand double feature, air-conditioned), and the Western Supply with the hitching-rail, well hitched this morning, at its doors. "I suppose the airfield will just have to take care of itself, today," Sally said. She waved back to the dazzling Jerks hat, once she had recovered from the electric-blue satin tie and the embroidered shirt with its silver buttons.

Outside the Purple Rim, Cheesit Bridger and his friends were grouped in more normal attire, having contented themselves with a fresh cotton shirt and a good shave. Their best hats looked remarkably like their usual hats, except that they were twelve years or so younger. They weren't the kind of hats that waved at ten o'clock in the morning, but the way they were pulled down a little more over the friendly eyes made Sally and Mrs. Peel feel welcomed, not just for this day but for any other day too.

There ended the first block, and Ed Yonker, the Undersheriff, doing traffic-duty for the day, waved them on against the lights. He gave them a broad smile, called "Hello, Miss Bly! Going to enter for the bronc riding?" and went back to his own conversation with three friends who were grouped around him. In the second block in Main Street, Bill's Drugstore said WE WELCOME YOU! And Mrs. Bill, of the Zenith Beauty Shop upstairs, had a commendable placard saying Us TOO! The Methodist Church welcomed all and everyone. VIC Matteotti, Boots Soled and Bought, had an outsize American flag. Cas Morawski, of the Elk Café, had two flags. The Evangelical Lutheran welcomed one and all. The office of the *Sweetwater Sentinel* had its welcome (WELCOME!) framed in the flags of the United Nations. This idea had almost caused the staff, who had worked all night in the best newspaper tradition, to have nervous prostration deciding which flag was upside down and which wasn't even if it looked as if it were.

Young Bill, son of Bill of Bill's Drugstore (and of Mrs. Bill) was doing his job of traffic-directing towards the third block in grand style. He had been a traffic M.P. at Remagen Bridge, and his short efficient gestures were so unmistakably clear and commanding, even to the most frenzied farmer's wife in a car packed with swarming children, that his admiring audience on the sidewalk all said it was no wonder Bradley got across the Rhine so damned quick. Young Bill was doing such good business that J. Huff Top Quality Groceries must have wondered why he had spent so much time on a window display. Still, for those who cared to turn round, it was a sight worth seeing: an artistic Empire State Building, worked out in cans of Sheridan Export from one of J. Huff's postal card collection. Next door, a large banner in red letters told you PETE KENNEDY's MEN'S WEAR BIDS YOU WELCOME! The window of Mat Billings, Meat Market, was quite filled by the head of a buffalo with a formidable frown and a curly forelock. Henry Adelbert, Apothecary, had a stuffed rattlesnake fighting it out with a ruffled eagle (suspended by wires) which also helped, trust Henry, to emphasize his window display on antidote for snakebites. Bartlett's Billiards had washed its windows. The Bank was closing its doors. And Joe's Barbershop, overflowing with last-minute customers who wanted a haircut to set off their best hats, had produced a genuine wooden Indian which two Iropshaws and a Flatfeet were studying with interest.

"Or *do* you say a Flatfeet?" Mrs. Peel wondered aloud as the car stopped at a clear space on the sidewalk.

Prender Atherton Jones, about to deliver his farewell, touching lightly (but surely) on the self-sacrifice he had volunteered to make, looked at Mrs. Peel in bewilderment.

"One Flatfoot, surely," she said, convinced she was making everything clear. "Oh Prender, do look at these pioneer children on horseback, and that frontier girl riding sidesaddle. Why, the costumes are authentic 1870. . . . And look, there's a covered wagon, and two Indian guides, and a crowd of trappers! They must all be starting to gather for the parade. Do stay, Prender. You'll still have plenty of time to reach Three Springs for luncheon at the Inn. Unless you care to join us at Bill's Drugstore or the Elk Café?"

Sally saw him flinch this time. "Everything is going to be so crowded," she said gaily, "that we'll probably eat at a hot-dog stand in the rodeo grounds. Won't you stay, Prender?"

Prender could not bear the word "hot dog," far less eat the object. He flinched for all to see. He looked at the growing crowds now beginning to jam the sidewalks, at the cars bringing people from all over Upshot County and beyond. Then he looked back at the interested faces of Margaret Peel and Sally Bly, so delighted with what was happening around them that they scarcely noticed him now. Earl Grubbock, standing on the running board of the car to get a better view of the faces that passed him, was equally neglectful.

"Look!" Mrs. Peel cried again, for a group of men on magnificent horses with elaborately worked saddles and silver-decorated bridles were riding past towards the starting point of the parade. The horses almost outshone the men, and that was something Mrs. Peel had thought impossible. She looked round her, watching the pretty girls in gay Western clothes or bright cotton dresses, watching the sun-tanned men in their handsome shirts and best boots and newest hats, watching the excited children with well-polished cheeks and healthy bodies, watching the quiet content of the old people, watching the laughing faces and the eyes that looked at her so candidly. "Why, Prender," she said, suddenly noticing him again, "you aren't looking at anything."

"Not my line," Prender said, gazing intently at the giant banner swaying lightly in a touch of breeze. WELCOME, STRANGER, TO THE SWEETWATER STAMPEDE!

"There are the Indians!" Mrs. Peel cried.

"And there are Bert and Ned and Jim on horseback," Sally said. "Flying Tail Ranch is looking very grand today. Where have they been keeping all these clothes?" But there was a smile of pride on her face, the same smile that was on all the faces around her as they identified their friends and neighbors.

"Are these Iropshaws?" Mrs. Peel was asking. "Flatfeet have circles of tailfeathers. And there are our Indians! There's Hubert Slow-to-Move. And he knew us! Prender, did you see that? He straightened an eyebrow. And look at his daughters, today — white buckskin, beads, pink silk scarves and shawls. Why, I never saw so much Shocking Pink outside of Schiaparelli's showrooms."

"Hello, Miss Bly," said the Sheriff, on horseback. "And this is Mrs. Peel? Glad to see you, Mrs. Peel. Well, we're kind of trying to clear the cars off the street now. Got to get the parade started."

"The car's just leaving," Sally said.

"No hurry. Just thought I'd drop the word." He saluted and rode off.

"That's much the nicest parking ticket we've ever been given," Mrs. Peel told Jackson, who only looked at her pleadingly. If I don't get this car to Three Springs and back soon, I'll miss all the fun here, he seemed to say. He had worn his new black hat, too, and his equally new silver belt.

"Good-by, Prender," Mrs. Peel said quickly, and startled him, although he had been trying to leave for the last five minutes.

"Good-by." He didn't make his speech. He didn't feel he was

making any sacrifice at the moment. He wouldn't have stayed here unless he had been tied down with chains.

"Good-by," Sally said, as Jackson ground the car into first gear warningly.

Grubbock jumped off the running board in time, and yelled a belated good-by after the departing car. He watched it negotiate the last difficult stretch of Main Street, and smiled as it was chased down the Three Springs road by a chorus of cowboy yells. That's Ned and Bert, he thought. "By the way," he asked, "did I hear anyone say thank you?"

"Prender never actually does, you know," Mrs. Peel said.

"It's not his line either?"

Sally said, "If this had been the annual festival in a little town in Mexico, or the South of France, he would have stood for hours and applauded. He would have talked about it for months afterwards. Authentic folk art. The Color of the Soil." Blast him, she thought; he'd almost spoiled her day.

"Temper, temper," Earl Grubbock said, watching her face, but he gave a sympathetic smile. "Does he have to stiffen quite so artistically when a hot dog is mentioned?"

"Prender's trouble is that he has never been really hungry in all his life," Mrs. Peel said unexpectedly. "If he had stayed in Paris as we did, for part of the war, he would have had wild dreams about all the food he had ever refused. But that was naughty of you, Sally. You know how he feels about sausages."

"I only brought up the humble hot dog to correspond to something like tamales. He wouldn't have refused them at a Mexican fiesta. And he missed the whole point, why you and I are so happy. . . . Doesn't he know the joy of seeing ordinary hard-working people looking so prosperous and proud of their lives? Doesn't that tell him anything?"

But Earl Grubbock, his eyes once more searching the sidewalk, wasn't listening.

"Perhaps she is on the other side of the street," Sally suggested.

He smiled, then. "I've been trying to watch both sides," he confessed, "but—" His voice changed. It became very matter-of-fact.

326

"There she is," he said, and he stared angrily at three handsome young men who were escorting Norah through the crowd. He didn't move towards them, didn't even let them see him. He just stood there, watching Norah.

At that moment, a dazzling white hat struggled in Mrs. Peel's direction. "Hello, Miss Whikkleton, how are *you?* I've been trying to reach you for twenty minutes. Want you to meet some of the folks. Make you feel right at home. Big day today, for this little old cow town. Sure is." Milt Jerks looked round with pride on his adopted realm.

"Mr. Jerks," Sally said, trying not to look at the blue embroidery on the white satin shirt, "who are these boys over there, standing in front of the wooden Indian?"

"You mean the Brebner boys?"

"Brebner?" Sally smiled at Earl. "Then they must be Norah's brothers." Or cousins . . . In Wyoming, people had so many cousins.

"Sure. One's studying to be a doctor somewheres in Michigan. And one's managing the Bee Ex Bar Ranch down in Montana—a big outfit, they tell me. And the youngest, he's still at school, going to be a lawyer, I hear. Come all the way for the Sweetwater Stampede. Yes sir, none of these young fellows miss it if they can help it."

You would have thought Milt Jerks had lived here all his life, Sally thought, and she found his enthusiasm touching. Then she noticed that Chuck and his friend Cheesit Bridger had moved up to this part of Main Street, too. They had made no attempt to come forward, but had propped their backs comfortably against the rattlesnake window, and were keeping a seemingly casual eye on everything.

"Now, Miss Whittleton," Milt Jerks was saying, grabbing hold of passing arms, "let me present my old friends John Jackson of the Tee Bar You and Judd James of the Double Ex Gee. Hey, Mrs. Christie, want you to meet my friend Miss Elizabeth Whifferton. Mrs. Christie's the wife of our banker, Bob Christie. And here's Miss Snodgrass of the telephone exchange, and Mrs. Bill Buell of the Zenith Beauty Shop. All the stores closing now? Getting ready to begin, eh? Half an hour late, Sweetwater time, eh?"

As Milt Jerks made himself master of ceremonies, Sally was watching Earl Grubbock. "It looks as if Margaret and I are going to be well taken care of," she suggested. "And I notice that Mimi and Carla and Robert and Karl are standing across the street, so everyone is safely here. We'll meet you at the rodeo."

"Fine," Earl Grubbock said, gave her a half-embarrassed smile, and left as quickly as possible. Sally wondered if people in love were always so obvious to other people, sometimes even more obvious than they were to themselves. She kept wondering about that, and she was suddenly as embarrassed as Earl Grubbock had been. Fortunately, Milt Jerks was still introducing people. He managed a slight variation on Whiffleton at every try. Once, towards the end, Sally was sure she heard "Whittington."

Chuck and Cheesit Bridger looked as if they wondered whether things were getting out of hand, whether any action had to be taken. But the group that Milt Jerks had created swallowed him up, and Mrs. Christie and Mrs. Bill and Judd James and Miss Snodgrass formed a quiet phalanx around Margaret Peel as if they had been reading her mind. Chuck and Cheesit Bridger gave Sally a nod and went on their way.

The last children were allowed through the waiting crowd (the smallest ones were passed overhead) to find a good view and a seat at the edge of the sidewalk. A silence fell, and all heads were turned to look along Main Street in the direction of a sudden blast of music.

"That's the school band," Mrs. Christie explained. "There's my Tommy, see, with the trumpet!" She pointed to a ten-year-old blowing manfully. She forgot all the agonies she had endured, this last month of practising, and she clapped as delightedly as all the other mothers were clapping for their musicians.

"That's my niece with the flute," Miss Snodgrass said, waving to a fair-haired girl no more than eight. "And there's Young Bill's boy with the drum. My! How he's grown since last year. He's almost as big as it is now." And she turned to congratulate his proud grandmother on Little Bill, who might not be keeping very good step but certainly could keep up the right bangs.

Bands, Mrs. Peel thought, always make me cry, especially if they play "My country, 'tis of thee" just a touch off key, and march so determinedly out of step. She looked quickly away, blinking in the bright sunlight, towards the rest of the parade.

The prettiest girl in the whole of Upshot County came first, riding the noblest horse. "Her dad runs a small ranch just out of Sweetwater a piece," Miss Snodgrass explained. "Getting married next month. Look, there's her boy. He's riding with the men from the ranches, just behind her. My! Isn't she pretty in her Western clothes? Milt Jerks wanted her to wear white satin, but we soon put a stop to that."

The crowd cheered the groups in turn — the men from the ranches; the men who had come from Montana and Colorado and Idaho to take part in the rodeo; the cowgirls; the old-timers, still able to sit a horse even if they were reaching ninety. Cheesit Bridger was in this group, but Chuck wasn't old enough to qualify seemingly. As she looked at them, Sally thought that if they had vied with each other, when young, in being quick on the draw, in loving fast women and beautiful horses, in holding ten gallons of raw liquor, in shooting bears and bison and any Indian that didn't seem to appreciate the white man's westward march, they now had a rivalry between each other to see who'd last longest. Old-timers didn't die, they only faded away.

Then the children came riding along, all the way from the kindergarten on Shetland ponies to the bareback riders in the Eighth Grade. One very small boy almost fell off his nervous pony, but a businessman of the town (identifiable, although he wore cowboy clothes, by his more expansive waistline) wheeled his horse to dash to the rescue and raised a cheer. "Nearly fell off yourself, Bob," a man's voice called. "Turned so darned quick, you just about left your horse standing." Bob, trying not to look too proud, rode back to his place at the side of the parade. He wiped his brow and said he'd given his old saddle a right good coating of glue that morning, so they all could stop worrying.

The cheers, the offered advice, the friendly laughter over the inevitable predicaments, drew the spectators and riders together until

329

they became one. Everyone was in the parade, Sally thought. The watchers laughed and suffered with those who rode, as floats stopped floating and had to be pushed. Or there was the horse that started bucking with one of the local policemen, who just managed to keep his seat but lost his hat, while the crowd roared with delight and cheered the horse on. Or the pioneer woman, driving a jerky, who started to travel in circles until two substantial townsmen on suitably substantial horses got her headed in the right direction. Yes, everyone was in the parade: those who stood on the sidewalks and cheered, or watched with critical silence, or admired with quick comments, were all riding down the center of Main Street, too.

After the highly decorated floats, with their tableaux of frontier days, had reminded everyone that life was not always a matter of a steady job, a cinema on Main Street, or Main Street itself, there came the newest tractors and reaping machines with waving arms and reaching teeth magically lowered to pass under the street's banners. They were applauded, too; and then, as if to apologize for this sudden interest in the machine, the horses that followed were given double cheers. Here were the bright sorrels, the creamy buckskins with their dark manes and tails, the golden palominos, and the Appaloosas. "What on earth is that?" Mrs. Peel said aloud, staring at an Appaloosa. But everyone around her, although more accustomed to the idea of a horse that reminded you of silver leopards and zebras and still didn't let you solve the problem, agreed with her bewilderment. "It's just," Miss Snodgrass said, shaking her head, "an Appaloosie."

"They love it. They know they're beautiful," Mrs. Peel said, referring mostly to her favorite palominos, although she included buckskins and sorrels too. "They're like Ziegfeld Girls coming down a runway. Or am I a little mixed?"

"A little," Sally said. "But they've certainly been glorified. Everyone within miles of Sweetwater must have stayed up all night polishing his horses. If you ask me, the horse's best friend is man."

Just then, a deep silence fell on the crowd. The Indians were coming, riding in the full array of their tribe. Then the cheers burst out, as rich and full as they had been for anything else that day.

330

"They love it, too," Sally said quietly. "And so would I, if I were one of them. It is something to have been an enemy and to have become a friend." And she watched the rest of the parade in thoughtful silence.

At its end, Mrs. Peel shook her violently by the arm and pointed. "Do you see what I see?" she asked. It was the last group, cow hands and wranglers and ranchers, bringing the parade — symbolically enough — to a workaday close. And there, riding between Jim Brent and Chuck, his face beaming with pleasure, his borrowed horse well under control, his black hat pulled over his black eyebrows, his silver belt gleaming round his staunch waistline, was Jackson.

CHAPTER XXVIII

Jim and Sally

M IMI was rather subdued by the time the rodeo had ended. It could very well be hunger, Mrs. Peel thought; or it could be five hours of sitting on a hard wooden bench; or it could be five hours of watching quick movement in bright sunlight, of your blood pressure rising when a triumph was won, of your heart sinking when a man lay on the ground unable to rise and the ambulance drove slowly into the rodeo field. For Mrs. Peel was suffering from all these things. She was as emotionally purged as if she had been attending a Greek tragedy.

"Home for me," she said to Sally. "But you stay for the dance."

Sally shook her head. She was watching the judges' stand. Jim Brent was leaving it now. "No," she said, "of course I shan't." She tried to sound as if she weren't disappointed. She even smiled. But there was disappointment in her eyes.

"I'll take Mrs. Peel home," Robert O'Farlan said. "I'm a rotten dancer, anyway."

"But Sweetwater is something to see tonight," Sally said. "It will be wide open. It's said to be the next wildest Western town to Jackson Hole, once the night begins."

"What fun!" Carla said. "Why, Jackson Hole is the wildest place after Butte, isn't it? And Butte's the wildest town in all the West. So that gives Sweetwater third place!" That made her think of Ned. "Too bad," she said, becoming serious again, "about Ned, I mean. And he missed it by so little, only a quarter of a second."

"Well, he got second place," Mimi said. "That's always something, I suppose."

"But he has made better time before. Why, I've seen him rope a calf in fourteen seconds. Today, he took fifteen and a half."

"That's the unpleasant thing about losing," Mimi said. "You know you could have done better, somehow — if you had only known what to do." She was watching Jim Brent riding slowly over the rodeo field towards them. But you haven't lost yet, she told herself: he's been nicer to you in these last two days than he's ever been. She glanced at Sally. Yes, she's attractive, very attractive: there's something about the way she looks at you, the way she smiles; her skin is good, and she has that soft blonde coloring that some men seem to like; her figure's all right, too. Wonder if I'll look as well as that when I'm her age? Or was she joking about her age? But whatever her age is, I'm younger. And I'm not unattractive, either. And one sure way of losing is to tell yourself that you've lost. She looked around at the grandstand, now slowly emptying, and chased away the doubts that had been forming all this afternoon in her mind. After all, she thought, Jim Brent doesn't have to live here always. . . .

Karl stood up and stretched himself. "The crowd's clearing," he said. "We could start leaving, ourselves." He looked at the rows of benches, littered with pop-bottles and spilled peanuts and popcorn. "There is going to be a lot of sick kids in Upshot County, tonight. Or are they toughened from the cradle onwards? Come on, Mimi, let's get going." He looked after Earl Grubbock and Norah, who had slipped away quietly by themselves even as he was talking.

But Mimi waited. "I'm still recovering from the wild horse race," she told him. "Karl, you should have entered for that."

"On which side?" Robert O'Farlan asked with a grin.

Mrs. Peel thought how extraordinarily sympathetic Mimi had become. After steer riding, calf roping, saddle bronc riding, calf roping, ladies' horse race, Indian relay race, bareback bronc riding, calf roping, kids' pony race, bulldogging, calf roping, pony express race, sheep catching contest, calf roping, half-mile race, cow-cutting contest, the wild horse race had *her* roped and blindfolded. "I know just how those wild horses felt," she murmured. "Especially the ones

333

that ran the wrong way when they were saddled and mounted, and the blindfold was removed."

"Some are still running," Robert O'Farlan said, trying to see into the far distance. "What do their riders do, eventually? Make their way back on foot from the mountains?"

"Yellowstone by Christmas," Carla said and laughed. She had adopted Chuck's catch phrase, and found it constantly useful. Then, as Jim Brent came riding up at last to them (he had stopped to talk with five different sets of wranglers and their wives, Mimi noticed) Carla said, "Jim, it was wonderful!" Both Mimi and Sally let her do the talking, about Ned, about Bert (who had done well although he had won nothing), about the Indian cowboys who had ridden Brahma bulls as if they had been buffalos.

"Glad you enjoyed it," Jim managed to say at last.

Mrs. Peel said, "To be frank, we are sitting here recovering. At least, I am; and the others feel guilty about leaving me. But I'm feeling guilty, too, because I want to go home and Sally insists she is taking me there."

"Well," Mimi said, suddenly quite recovered, "let's all go into Sweetwater and have dinner. And then those who are staying for the dance, stay. What's the dance like, Jim?"

"Just a little shindig," he said with a grin.

"Jim Brent, you are the most annoying man," Mimi declared with a warm smile.

"You'll see for yourself. I guess you'll have a good time. Just don't get lost, that's all."

Robert O'Farlan said, "We'll see the girls safely back to Rest and Be Thankful."

"Aren't you going to the dance, Jim?" Mimi asked.

"No. I'll drive Sally and Mrs. Peel back to the ranch, if they don't mind being in a car with a horse trailer behind it. The rest of you can borrow Mrs. Peel's car for the ride home. It will be more comfortable than the truck you arrived in." Then he looked at Sally. "See you at the car."

She nodded. "Yes, Jim," she said, trying to keep the happiness

334

out of her voice. Her eyes smiled, too. He touched his hat, shortened the reins, turned his horse round neatly, and rode off.

"He's so — so definite," Carla said. "And how beautifully he rides."

Karl was watching the horseman. "Yes," he said.

"They all do," Mimi said, and rose abruptly to her feet. She seemed more interested in three Indian women, surrounded by their children, who were moving with slow, silent footsteps from their seats. Like all squaws, they were short, broad, massive under the bright enveloping shawls that hid their dresses. Their skirts were short, ending just below the knees. And their legs were encased, stiffly, thickly, in tight white buckskin leggings; their feet were neat and small, gloved like a dancer's. Their straight black hair was braided. Their rich black eyes were slanting. This season's crop of babies was carried in their arms. They grasped the babies with one arm crooked round the small waists, holding them vertical, keeping them face-out. Their other children, the girls in white buckskin tunics embroidered with beads and dyed porcupine quills, the boys in small cowboy suits, followed them like a straggling convoy, with faces that — laughing or crying — were stickied over with candy, lime pop, and sniffles.

Then a voice from the judges' stand halted everyone as it came over the loudspeaker, blurred at first and then clear. The same voice had announced various pieces of advice at intervals through the long afternoon, whether it was to tell them all to stand up and put their weight on their feet for a change, or to encourage a rider — "That boy had bad luck. Give him a hand, folks." Now, the pleasant deep-voiced drawl stopped the moving crowd. The heads all turned, not to the loudspeaker overhead, but to the invisible man in the distant box. "You'll be right glad to hear that the boy who's in hospital is doing all right. Doc Clark has just sent word to us here that Russ Murray is okay. He'll be up and around in a few weeks. And Jep Jonson, who had a little bit of trouble with his Brahma bull, has got no worse than a couple of ribs and an arm broken. He's right here with me now. Says he's a refugee from an ambulance. Well, that's all. You can go out and enjoy yourselves, now. Thought you'd kind of feel better if you heard."

And the thousand and more who had stopped to listen in silence, began talking, began moving out more quickly. The sound of their voices proved they did feel kind of better. And Robert O'Farlan, watching their faces, was sure that they'd enjoy themselves better too.

He looked back at the judges' box. "You know," he said quietly, "I liked that. Sort of a climax to the whole show, somehow. Can't explain it exactly, but —" He shook his head and followed the others, with a very silent Mimi close beside him.

In Main Street, all the shops were open again, and the drugstore and cafeteria and the Elk Café were filled to overflowing. The Purple Rim and the Foot Rail were ablaze with lights and bursting with noise. The Teton Bar had its new neon sign — a cow with green hoofs and a long, dry tongue hanging out — in flashing display. The sidewalks were crowded with discussion groups exchanging news or analyzing the rodeo. Horses were tethered to the hitching-rails, and the little colored lights around the banners and signs had all been turned on. Hundreds of parked cars not only crowded the side roads, but even edged out the horses on Main Street.

Jim drove carefully, watching out for children and dogs. Sally sat beside him, and Mrs. Peel was comfortably fitted into the back seat between a coil of rope, a new lamp shade, chaps, half a sack of flour, half a dozen cartons of cigarettes, a new ledger, beer, three detective stories, a heap of magazines, and a set of records. Bachelor shopping, Mrs. Peel thought. She picked up one of the books and found it interesting enough to start reading.

Jim braked suddenly, and swore under his breath at a daring wrangler who didn't believe in traffic lights. "Sorry," he said. "Nearly had him. But this is the only way out of town for us."

Sally, recovering herself from the jolt, looked round. Mrs. Peel had saved the lamp shade, and everything else was so tightly packed that it hadn't been damaged. Then Sally looked at the trailer behind the car. But the horse was all right, too. In fact, Ginger seemed rather

336

to be enjoying his triumphal progress through Main Street, jolts and stops and starts and all. He had even stuck his head out, at the side of the windshield on the trailer, to get a better view.

"He likes the big city," Jim said. "He and the children in the cars."

Then Sally noticed that all the parked cars were filled with people, farm hands, small homesteaders from lonely cabins, all with their wives and children. They sat in silence, just looking, and the children's eyes were round and wondering. As Jim slowed the car again to avoid a stream of jaywalkers, she looked into the back of one of the parked cars. The three little fair-haired boys didn't notice her at first. When they did, she gave them a smile. They drew back tense, ready for flight. Then the oldest boy gave a small shy smile, and bent quickly down to hide his temerity. When she looked back again, they had forgotten about her. All they saw was the town.

"A lot of people must have lonely lives," she said. "Yet they look happy people." They were healthy, neatly dressed, and their faces, quiet and watchful, were friendly faces.

"I guess they're thinking it's a nice place to visit but they wouldn't like to live here," Jim said with a grin.

Sally looked at him. "Do you know New York?" she asked in surprise. Then she wished she hadn't asked. His face had tightened.

"Sure," he said at last. "That was where I met my wife."

"Was it?"

"You knew I was married?"

"Mimi told me," Sally's even voice said. There were so many gaps in our lives, in his and in mine, she thought, that we don't know about. Once I didn't think they mattered. But they do. They belong to the past and the past is over, and yet their shadow falls coldly over the present. She pretended to look behind the car at the trailer. Now that they had climbed the hill out of Sweetwater, they were starting to twist and turn up to Stoneyway Valley. Margaret, she noted, was asleep or pretending to be asleep.

"He's all right," Jim said, looking at the trailer too for a moment, and then concentrating on the road. "He's traveled to California with me in that contraption. He seems to enjoy it."

"You get around," Sally said. Shadows, she was thinking, were never so cold and terrifying once she knew what caused them; but would she ever know, or would he? We come so near to explaining them, and then we don't; and we can't ignore them either. What was part of our past is still part of us now.

"Used to."

"You sound settled, now," she said, trying to keep her voice as casual as his.

"I am." He was wondering when Mimi had told Sally about his wife. Probably only in these last few days. And that explained something that had worried him; it seemed, recently, as if Sally were further away from him. Instead of getting to know her better, he had got to know her less. He had thought that was perhaps the way she had wanted it. Perhaps. A wife hadn't seemed to make much difference to Mimi. But to Sally? That proved something about Sally, and he liked what it proved.

The silence embarrassed Sally. "Robb," she said suddenly — "Robb wasn't at the parade or at the rodeo."

"He stayed in charge of the ranch. Said he had some work to do. I'll take over when we get back, and he can get into Sweetwater for the dance."

"Oh." So that was why Jim hadn't waited for the dance. You hope too much, she told herself, that's why you always get disappointed. She said, "Then come over and have dinner with us, if you'll trust my cooking. Mrs. Gunn is staying overnight with her friends in Sweetwater. You know, I think she is beginning to approve of Earl Grubbock. At least, there were plenty of other pretty girls around, today, and he didn't bother about them at all. I'm glad, for Margaret and I were aiding and abetting him, you know."

"Can't he make up his own mind?"

"He is beginning to, I think. I suppose he suddenly realized he was never going to meet Norah again unless he did make up his mind. As long as she was at Rest and Be Thankful — well, it was a nice luxury not to make up his mind, wasn't it?"

Jim looked at her sharply. "I suppose so," he said. "You sound as if you believed that Earl and Norah will never meet anyone else they'd — well, fall in love with."

"But they *are* in love. Have you seen them when they are anywhere near each other? It would be a waste, wouldn't it, to throw it all away because they didn't realize in time how much they . . . ?" She stopped, pretending to laugh at her romanticism, but she averted her head and looked out at the hills and studied the evening sky. This conversation about love, about someone else in love — yet not someone else, either — this conversation, this was so unlike Jim. He was waiting for her, now, to go on. As if he wanted to hear what she believed. But she couldn't go on. "Is that rain over that mountain?" she asked.

He burst out laughing.

"What's funny about that, Jim?"

"Everything."

She smiled, too. She felt her cheeks were on fire. "This is getting to be a difficult conversation," she said, keeping a joke in her voice.

"I never was good at — " He didn't finish the sentence except in his own mind. At making polite conversation when there's something else to be decided. "By the way, Mimi hasn't got all the details quite straight. I haven't been married for a number of years."

Then as Sally said nothing, he went on, "We separated before we each ruined the other's life. I met her in New York, just after I had gone there from Chicago. I was going to be an illustrator, I thought. She was on the stage. She had to be in New York. She didn't want to leave it. I liked New York, too. But after a bit, I found I wasn't any good as an illustrator. I suppose when I set out for Chicago to learn to be an artist, I was having a kind of revolt against being a rancher. I had three years in Chicago, and then I went to New York with a job there. And I had nearly two years in New York before I got wise to myself. I wanted to come back here. My revolt was over. Ranching was a job I could do well. This was where I was happy, where I was needed. I wasn't much needed in New York. I wasn't going to stay there, and be a kind of hanger-on. So I came back to Wyoming. At the end of the second year."

"She wouldn't come?"

"No."

"Not even to see it?"

"She took one look at the map and screamed." He was smiling. "Didn't seem so funny to me at the time, though."

"Is she famous, now?"

His voice became cold and emotionless. "She had one or two parts — just enough to keep her convinced she was good. She married an agent. And she was just getting into star parts when — well, they were driving out for a week end in Pennsylvania and they had a bad smash. She was killed."

Sally said nothing more. She suddenly realized she knew more about Jim and his wife than anyone else did. He had really been in love, had gone on hoping that she would come out here after all. Until she married the other man. And he had killed her.

"That was just before the war started," Jim said. And after that, he thought, he hadn't had so much time to think about himself and what might have been and what hadn't. When you got caught up in a war, personal pride and admissions of defeat in your private life didn't seem so damned important.

He brought the car carefully over the bridge and stopped it before the house.

Mrs. Peel opened her eyes. "Rest and Be Thankful," she said gratefully.

"You'll be able to do that once your guests clear out," Jim said with a smile. "They've given you a busy month." Too damned busy, he thought as he looked at Sally.

"Except that Sally is talking of leaving."

"What?" For once, the tightly controlled face was completely caught off guard.

"To take a job in Chicago as a publisher's reader," Mrs. Peel said.

"Margaret," Sally said quickly, "you know we agreed not to talk about — "

"Jim isn't just one of the others. He's our friend. He may as well know, now."

"I'm going to start dinner," Sally said. "I'm hungry. And Robb will be waiting for you, Jim. See you later." She walked quickly into the house.

340

Mrs. Peel still sat in the car.

"You've been a long time together, haven't you?" Jim asked unexpectedly.

"Yes. Ever since 1932. I was alone, she was alone. It seemed a good idea to travel together. Of course, I had known Sally for two years before that, ever since she arrived in Paris. She was going to write poetry. And she was very much in love with a man and he seemed to be in love with her."

Jim turned to look at her. There was a question in his eyes.

"He was a writer — one of our little group. She had followed him from America to Paris. He had asked her. Her family and all her friends in Boston were absolutely against him. You know, I've often thought that was the reason why she stayed in Europe for so long. She waited, although she never admitted it, until most people who had known him had forgotten about her. When she left here, you see, they all thought he was going to marry her."

"Where is he now?"

"In Italy, I hear. Quite a famous dramatist nowadays. He's had two wives and a brood of children. Memories didn't worry him at all, seemingly." Mrs. Peel disentangled herself from the back of the car. "I like your choice in lamp shades, Jim. And may I borrow this novel? I began it before I fell asleep."

And did you fall asleep? he wondered. Then he gave her a smile, and she looked less nervous. "Sure," he said. "And what time is supper?"

"Give us an hour. Or will that be too late?"

"Fine. I've some things to see to." Principally a lot of ideas to be rearranged, a lot of thinking to be done. That had always been his failing — his unwillingness to face a situation that really affected him deeply. Like the two years of his life wasted in New York, when one year, or six months, should have been enough to tell him. Yet he could act quickly enough — sometimes too damned thoughtlessly — in other matters. It was only in things that he wanted to hide, deep down reasons, that he postponed the problems. Pride, he told himself, was always your trouble; and it's a bad one.

He gave Mrs. Peel a wave of his hand and drove towards the

ranch, sounding the horn with three short blasts so that Robb would be ready to leave.

Sally cooked dinner, borrowing from Mrs. Gunn's well-prepared larder, while Margaret attended to making the dining room as attractive as possible with flowers and candles and a roaring log fire. Then, with all the clutter of cooking cleared away, Sally dashed upstairs to dress. She had exactly eight minutes. As she threw off her blue linen suit, and slipped into a white wool dress with a long sweeping skirt ("so suitable for dining at home in the winter evenings," the New York catalogue had said — which made it just about right for six thousand feet high in Wyoming at the end of August) she wondered along with forty million other women just how anyone ever had the time to lie down for an hour with cream on her face, and pads over her eyes, and relax before dinner. She folded a green silk scarf into the neckline of her dress, clasped a gold bracelet on its tight, narrow cuff, and slipped her feet into her gold slippers. Why not? She hadn't been so happy as this for a long time. She hadn't been as happy as this since she was eighteen; perhaps she hadn't been as happy then as she was now. The difference between feeling happy at eighteen and feeling happy at thirty-seven was that you appreciated it when you were thirty-seven. She looked in the mirror on her dressing table and laughed. Then, to see if the hem on her dress looked right, she climbed up on a chair.

"Sally!" Mrs. Peel said in amazement, looking into the room to see if she were ready. Why, Mrs. Peel thought, Sally is getting prettier and prettier: some women are lucky, that way; while others, as lovely as Mimi when they were young, either fade or coarsen. "You could have used the long mirror in Prender's room, or have you forgotten he has gone?"

Sally had.

"Well, I'll serve dinner," Mrs. Peel said philosophically. "That dress was made for nothing more arduous than tossing a salad."

"I'll put my trust in one of Mrs. Gunn's enormous aprons," Sally said. "Now let's go downstairs. Do I look all right?"

342

"Very much all right. You know, it must be an awful gamble to be a man and marry a young girl for her looks. You'll never know what you'll get by the time she's forty." Sally wasn't really listening, though, so she wasn't as baffled by Margaret's way of speaking only half her thoughts as she might have been. Sally had heard Jim come into the house. She hurried Mrs. Peel by the arm towards the staircase.

Jim was waiting in the hall. He turned to look up at her as she came downstairs. He smiled, and there was a mixture of admiration and pleasure in his eyes. Then he noticed her dress and the gold slippers. She is halfway to Chicago, he thought, and the happiness left his eyes. And Sally felt it. What had gone wrong? Everything had been right. When he waited for her at the foot of the stairs, everything had been all right. Then suddenly, without warning, it had gone wrong. She could have wept.

After dinner, they went into the sitting room where Mrs. Peel had arranged another cheerful fire. She left them, there, with some pretext that sounded almost reasonable. It didn't matter anyway, Sally thought. Everything was so wrong since that moment in the hall when Jim looked at her and then stopped looking at her, that Margaret's subterfuge didn't embarrass her in the least.

It was all so matter of fact, to sit here and make conversation and be a polite hostess. She wasn't happy any more. She was back to normal. And angry, angry with herself. It's my fate, she thought, to be romantic and silly, and then to be angry. Angry and ashamed. Women have too many false hopes, too many bitter disappointments. If men could only see into our hearts, how pitying and amused they'd be. For women, right from the day they went to their first party, always hoped too much: how many dances, seemingly successful, had been grim failures covered over with a smile; how many invitations accepted became invitations regretted; how many plans and dreams had become stupidities; how much pretence that all was well, when it wasn't? We are too personal, she thought, in the way we interpret a look, a tone of voice, a smile. How lucky to be a man and never pay attention to the little things; how fortunate to take people as they are, and not to suffer from taking them as you would like them to be. How terrible it is to be a woman, to feel the difference between the dream and the reality, and yet to keep on dreaming in spite of reality.

She was looking at the flames leaping gaily around the neat pine logs. She was talking about Robb. "We didn't tell anyone about his poem," she was saying, as if she had no other thoughts. "Ideas like Robb's are best left alone, not talked over, until they come alive on paper. Our guests might have killed his idea with their enthusiasm and interest. And the cowboys might have killed it with good-natured amusement. Prender Atherton Jones, of course, was quite useless to approach; he only likes folk epic when it belongs to certain languages, certain centuries. But we have a problem, Jim. Robb ought to stay here this winter, when there isn't much outside work to take up his time. But how can we help him without seeming to help? He's so independent."

She lifted her head and looked at Jim. Why didn't he answer? He was sitting opposite her, watching her, silent.

"What's wrong?" she asked quickly. "Do you think Margaret and I are being just — just silly? But you know there's a real poet in Robb. Don't you, Jim?" Why didn't he speak? He wasn't the kind of man to laugh at poetry. When she had gone riding out with him, in those far-off pleasant evenings before Mimi ever arrived on the scene, he had a way of describing a mountain or a trail or a fragment of history so simply, so vividly, that she had been amazed and delighted.

"Yes," he said at last.

"Then you are on our side," she said. "But there is something puzzling you. Don't you see why we want to help Robb?"

"It's you that's puzzling me. I thought I knew you. And then, tonight, I suddenly realized I don't. Why are you going to Chicago?"

"What brought that up?" she asked, startled.

He looked at the elegant dress and slippers. "You're halfway there, now."

"I — why, Jim — I — " She looked down at her dress. I was

344

only trying to look my prettiest, she thought. But she couldn't say that.

"Why Chicago?" he insisted. "Or New York, or Paris? You can't forget the cities?"

She stared at him; and then, out of relief and of the happiness that came surging back into her heart — women, she tried to tell herself, women keep making the same mistakes over and over again — out of relief and renewed happiness she said, "Does that matter?"

"Yes." He rose, leaned an arm on the mantelpiece, and looked down at her.

"There's a job in Chicago," she said.

"But why? Are you bored here, or what?"

"Money," she said.

"You've money enough," he said, suddenly angry. He hadn't been able to keep the bitterness of his disappointment out of his voice.

"But we haven't," she said protestingly.

"You haven't?" He was amazed. And then it seemed to her he was pleased, still puzzled, but pleased.

"It has a way of disappearing," she said, trying to make a joke out of it. "I've been looking for a job for the last two weeks. There's one in Chicago that I could take. The money from that, along with the little income I have from my cook books, would be enough to keep both Margaret and me. She could live here for most of the year, and do her writing — yes, she's started writing again, didn't you know? — and I could come to Wyoming for my summer vacation. You see, Jim, I owe a lot to Margaret — not just those years we've traveled together, but — well, other things. . . . She, well, without being dramatic about it, it's simply this: she saved me at one time. She saved my life. That was how our friendship really began."

Sally hesitated. I must tell him, she thought. I must clear up all the shadows now. "I was in love. No, I didn't *think* I was in love. I was in love. And he seemed to be in love with me. Just nine days before the wedding — he — Well, he left Paris with my best friend, and that was that. I was sort of intense, I suppose, about things in those days. I had given him so much of myself that there didn't seem anything left. . . . That was when I decided to kill myself. I was trying to get up enough courage—it takes a lot of courage, Jim—when Margaret arrived to see me. Just accidentally, about nothing important." She paused, as if she were remembering. "And so I got over that bad patch in my life; and I went on living. People said I took it very well." She laughed. Then she said, half-surprised, "That's the first time I've laughed at it, though." And the first time I've ever talked about it, either, she thought. "I'm glad, I'm glad I told you," she added, and there was relief in her voice. And then, without warning, her eyes filled with tears, and her head drooped, and her lips trembled.

He stepped forward, and reached for her hands, and pulled her slowly to her feet, pulled her towards him until she stood against him. "I'm glad, too," he said gently, and he kissed her.

At midnight, Mrs. Peel gave up all hope and went to bed. "From now on," she told herself, "you are going to have a lot of evenings by yourself. You may as well start getting used to them, Margaret Peel." She adjusted the pillows comfortably behind her back, tucked the blankets tightly round her waist, and buttoned up her warm bedjacket. Sally, when she came in to say good night, would be disappointed if she were asleep. Sally would want to tell her the news that was no news. Margaret Peel opened the detective story, which she hoped would keep her awake. She read for an hour. In spite of two sudden deaths and a third to come at any moment, her eyes began to close.

Sally came in as the book was slipping to the floor.

"Hello," Margaret Peel said, opening her eyes. "Had a nice walk?"

"Wonderful." Sally's eyes were as bright as the stars in the sky out-side. "Jim and I went up towards Snaggletooth."

"Where he first met us. . . . And *how* he shouted, remember?" She looked at Sally's golden slippers, now dust-covered and streaked with grass. "I suppose they were expendable. And your dress, Sally! What a pity . . . I rather liked that one."

"Margaret, guess what's happened?"

"I couldn't possibly."

346

Sally laughed. "Oh, you knew after all!" she said.

"And did you accept?" Mrs. Peel tried not to smile, but it was difficult. "Well, darling," she said appeasingly, "I'm really very happy that you both came to your senses. How on earth did that happen? I nearly threw hysterics at dinner, tonight."

"Something to do with Chicago and the big cities, something to do with living in Wyoming, something to do with the fact that I'm not rich, something to do with me bursting into tears like a fool. I don't know. It was just all sort of mixed up."

"It usually is," Mrs. Peel said. "And you don't make it any clearer. Was he actually worried about asking you to live here? Why, if his job were in Alaska, or Pittsburgh, or Rio de Janeiro, it would have been all the same to you. When are you getting married? Christmas weddings are charming."

Sally laughed. "We're getting married in four weeks."

Mrs. Peel said, "Well!" Then regaining her breath, she added, "Why wait even four weeks?"

"By that time, all the cattle will have been driven down to the railway. That's a busy time for everyone on the ranch, you know. Now, what's so funny about that?"

"Nothing." Mrs. Peel managed to control her laughter. "If your Jim heard you, he wouldn't be worried about making you a rancher's wife. Now, I've teased you enough. I'm very, very happy. Go to bed, darling. You can tell me in the morning how wonderful he is, and how handsome, and how wonderful. He is, you know. You're a lucky girl. Good night, Sally."

Sally put out the light. "Margaret," she said thoughtfully, "about tomorrow — do you think I ought to wait until Mimi leaves before I spread the news?"

"Look," Mrs. Peel said angrily, sitting up in bed, "do you think for one moment that she would have spared your feelings? Besides, do you think for one moment that Jim is going to keep this news from the boys? And he never gave a serious thought to Mimi, so don't go embarrassing him. He only admired her as all men admire a pretty face. There would be something rather odd about us all if we didn't."

347

"But Mimi is young." Sally's voice was expressionless.

"So are a hundred girls in Upshot County, all as pretty as she is. You saw them today. Sally Bly, are you forcing me to tell you how pretty and attractive you are? You are one of the prettiest women I have ever met in any county. If that's all you needed to reassure you, I could have told you it two months ago." She lay down, drawing the blankets closely around her frozen shoulders.

Sally said, "Good night, Margaret," and closed the door quietly.

Women, Mrs. Peel thought, what strange creatures we are, always worrying and wondering and hoping and being afraid. And men? They were just as much a set of contradictions in their own way. It was a miracle that the human race had done as well for itself as it had, in the fifty thousand-odd years it had complicated this world. No doubt, at this moment, Jim was pouring a third drink and pacing around his room, wondering what he had done to deserve Sally. And Sally would be brushing her pretty hair, and looking at her charming face in the mirror, and forgetting all about the warmth and sincerity that lay within, and wondering what she had done to deserve Jim. That being the case, and Mrs. Peel decided it would be, then this was going to be a very happy marriage. Tomorrow, Jim would be round here first thing to see Sally, to make sure that everything was all right, that tonight hadn't been a dream. That was the pattern, Mrs. Peel thought sleepily, and it was the best pattern in all the world. "Sentimentalist," she chided herself, and smiled, and fell asleep.

CHAPTER XXIX
Memento from the West

I⊤ was the last day, a day made perfect with the very best Wyoming weather.

Everyone seemed so unwilling to pack, that Mrs. Peel was almost moved to ask them to stay a week longer if they could arrange it. But Sally said, "Now, be careful!" And Mrs. Peel, remembering her genius for complicating life — not only her own life, which was hers to complicate if she chose, but also the lives of others who didn't want them complicated at all — was careful.

The ordeal of packing had been left to the afternoon, when lunch was over and they felt unhurried. But after one of Mrs. Gunn's most inspired meals, they felt so completely unhurried that they drifted out of their rooms into the garden, leaving opened bags and suitcases to yawn hungrily on littered beds. Somehow, they found themselves grouped around Mrs. Peel and Sally in their favorite place near the creek. The men lay on the grass, but Carla and Mimi, conscious of their city clothes, sat more decorously on chairs.

"I've got the labels written," Carla said. "And it won't take me so long to pack once I do begin. I know where everything goes. I hope."

Mrs. Peel said, "I didn't know how tanned you all were until you put on your city clothes."

Mimi looked around at them all. "We look disgustingly healthy," she announced. "And in two days we'll be back in New York. Humidity and all. You know, I've forgotten how it is to melt in New York heat."

"So have I," Carla said. "And I bet we are bewildered by all

349

the traffic, at first, and we'll leave our purses and gloves all over the place, and the men will be hobbling around on their flat heels."

"Then, after a few days, you'll look round and say 'New York!' And there will be affection and amazement in your voice," Mrs. Peel reminded them.

"I'm already beginning to say it," Mimi admitted. "I loved being here, of course, but — "

"I know," Mrs. Peel said with a smile. Sally looked at her quickly. You don't have to say that, Margaret, she thought: Jim and I are not going to chase you away from here. Or was Margaret getting restless? Perhaps the sight of all the city clothes and opened suit-cases was having an unsettling effect.

"I don't know," Grubbock said unexpectedly. He sat up and moved his shoulders irritably under the restricting jacket of his suit. His clothes were much looser on him, especially round the waist and hips, and that had pleased him. But they were damned uncomfortable all the same. "A city is a hard place to take when you haven't got much money. You begin to think that money is more important than it is. Either your standards get twisted, or your own mind gets twisted." He glanced for a moment at Karl Koffing.

"Cheer up, Karl," Mimi said. "You'll soon be back where you can get your own newspaper on the day it is published. What a re-lief that will be for you!"

Robert O'Farlan smiled in spite of himself. He had been de-pressed all day. But he took himself away from his own worries to look at Karl. The others were laughing good-naturedly, and Karl had the sense and the control to say nothing. They were laughing good-naturedly — for they had liked Karl — and yet with a touch of uneasiness as if they were now worried by him. As well they might be, O'Farlan thought. Karl had made them all politically conscious — conscious of Karl's politics. And the more the others had a close look at them, the less they liked them.

Koffing, keeping a smile on his face, decided he would go and finish his packing. But not yet; in a couple of minutes. He out-stared O'Farlan. To leave now would be to look like retreating. But how had they all changed as they had? O'Farlan had never liked him from the first. But Mimi, Carla, Grubbock? Who was to blame? He looked at Sally and Mrs. Peel. Well, they didn't manage to bribe me, he thought. I'm as free and independent as when I came here. I've kept that, even if I got no work done. A wasted month. Nothing gained from it. But they didn't bribe me with kindness, as they hoped to. They didn't change me and won't. I'm stronger than any of them. A thousand of us are stronger than a million of them. They don't know how strong yet. This time, his smile was genuine.

"That," Mimi said, "was a long silence. What were you thinking, Karl?"

"That it was a pity Sally and Jim didn't have their wedding when we were here. I've always wanted to see a real old-fashioned feudal wedding with all the trimmings. I suppose people will be riding in for miles around?"

Sally colored, and tried not to look at Mimi. Carla and Mrs. Peel both began talking at once.

But Mimi looked at Karl, quite self-contained and even smiling. Then she looked up at the sky and studied the shapes of the white clouds. I don't need Sally's pity, she thought. I was in love, and I am in love, but I don't need pity. Someday I'll even congratulate myself on my escape. I would never have made a rancher's wife. For on Saturday, I sat for five hours at a rodeo and watched the people around me. I would have had to change me, inside and outside and every which way, to be like them, to be happy with the things that made them happy. And when I had finished with that change? I wouldn't be Mimi. I'm young, and I've a lot of life to live and a lot of places to see. That's my choice. Bob O'Farlan would say it was my character that had made that choice. Bob's no fool. The more you know him, the more there is worth knowing.

She closed her eyes. How lucky for me, she told herself, that Jim didn't fall in love with me. How lucky for him that he didn't give me the chance to accept him. Ah, well . . .

She was almost persuaded. Give me another two months with New York to help me, Mimi thought, and I'll be quite persuaded. I hope.

351

She opened her eyes to see Mrs. Peel was watching her. "Carla is coming to share my two-room apartment, this fall," Mimi said quickly. "Tell them, Carla!"

"Why, Mimi, I've just been talking about that. Weren't you listening?"

"I was straightening out some accounts in my mind," Mimi said with a smile. "I'm depending on you next winter, Carla, to keep me out of the red."

"I'm not awfully good at accounts," Carla said.

"Well, you'll be good for me anyway. Whenever I start accepting too many invitations, you'll point sternly to the typewriter. Oh yes, I'm going to write a novel. In fact, I've got the first chapter all mapped out. And what's more important, I know what comes after that too. I'm using one of Chuck's stories, frankly. About Crazy Woman Creek."

"That's a true story," Sally said. "And a powerful one." But could Mimi manage it?

"Oh, I know it isn't an original story. But if most of the big writers in the world were humble enough to borrow most of their stories, who am I to be proud?" Mimi said. Then she noticed that Bob O'Farlan was watching her, waiting for her to go on. And somehow she did. "It's the story of a white woman who had the courage to go against tradition and marry a half-Indian. She went to live with his tribe. But courage wasn't enough. Those for whom she gave up everything murdered her happiness. No one could help her then. She wandered near the Creek where her husband had been killed before her eyes, and would let no one come near her, not even the Indians who became sorry for her."

"You could hardly blame her for that," Grubbock said. "They had murdered her husband. Or perhaps executed is the better word. It was his own fault. Greed and treachery. But say, you've added something to the character of the woman. I used to think that it was just the shock of seeing her husband killed that drove her crazy. What do you know? We've got a writer in Mimi, after all!"

"After all!" Mimi said indignantly. "Well, Mr. Grubbock, that story is copyright now. Listening?"

352

"It's all yours," Earl said. "Besides, there are plenty of stories in this part of the world for us all to pick up and use. I'm sorry I didn't get around more. It wouldn't be a bad idea, not a bad idea at all, to stay in the West for a few months. Get a job here, somewhere. Newspaper work, perhaps. It's got its attractions."

"Yes," Sally said, with a smile for her own private enthusiasm. She wondered if Earl would be most attracted in the direction of Three Springs and then Laramie.

"For instance," he went on, "I'm interested in that story about the newspaper editor who fought on the side of the homesteaders and small ranchers around Buffalo. Back in 1892, as Chuck would say. About the time of the Texas Invasion, anyway. He took a beating, at first. Lost everything, it seemed. Except he got the people behind him in the end. Sort of encouraging to see ordinary people decide what is right, by themselves, and then go out and win with all the odds against them. Nice touch that, somehow." He pulled a handful of grass and studied it. "Say, Karl, you wanted to go north to see that place near Buffalo called Ten Sleep, where the Mexicans work in the beet fields. I'd like to see Buffalo. Why don't we travel up there together?"

"That's an idea," Karl said, interested.

"You'd enjoy it," Mrs. Peel said. "I hear Ten Sleep is as pretty as its name. And you could study conditions among the Basque sheepherders near Buffalo, too. Did you know they've a *jai alai* court, right in the middle of Wyoming?"

Karl looked at her. Then he said, "I'm due back in New York. I've got a job to worry about."

Earl threw down the crumpled blades of grass. For someone who hated the lousy capitalist system, Karl stuck to pulling in the do-re-mi. "Sure," Earl said evenly, "you've more important work to do than go studying conditions where they are pleasant to study. What's the point in that?"

"I envy you, Earl," Robert O'Farlan said. "That's what I'd like to do for a bit — wander around the country."

"You are going to have a pretty good time in New York signing contracts. You can wander around, there, celebrating."

Robert O'Farlan half-smiled. It worried him slightly that they all assumed his novel was going to be accepted. All that had happened, so far, was that Mrs. Peel's agent had sent an enthusiastic letter about his manuscript; and this morning, she had sent an enthusiastic telegram about the reactions of a publisher's reader. But there was at least one more publisher's reader to please, not to mention the publishers, before the book reached a contract stage.

"How happy your wife must be," Mrs. Peel said, trying to cheer him up. He had been so silent all day. Not the way you expected a practically accepted author to behave. Perhaps he had worked so long over the book that people's approval had bewildered him. Didn't he know how good the novel was? "Have you wired her about latest developments?" she asked with a sympathetic smile.

He shook his head. "Not yet. After all, there's nothing definite . . ." Would Jenny be pleased? In the way he wanted her to be pleased? If it isn't too late, he thought. For all the letters he had written recently had been answered, but not answered in the way he had hoped. If it took two people to build a hidden, smoldering quarrel, it took two of them to put these fires out and rekindle a purer, better flame. God knows, he thought, remembering their first years together, God knows I'm willing to try. But I can't do it alone. Well, he thought unhappily, I'll go on trying. But how long? Until he knew definitely it was no good? But how did you ever know definitely, so that you would have no remorse later?

"You're our great success," Carla said. "Will you come to our parties so that Mimi and I can show you off? And we'd like to meet your wife, wouldn't we, Mimi?"

"Yes." Mimi met Bob's eyes. (She was the only one who called him Bob. He never seemed to object.) Two unhappy people, she thought. Two much-envied people, by those who didn't know. Two very unhappy people, you and I. I am unhappy out of my own weakness; you are unhappy because of your strength. For you are strong, Bob. You're like Jim Brent in that: you've argued out right and wrong. She said, "You're our very own literary lion, Bob. But we'll have to teach you how to roar. You are much too modest, you know. You don't realize your own value. Why, when you arrived here, how

354

many of us could ever have guessed you had a major work practically finished?" She smiled wholeheartedly.

"The only time he roars is when Karl waves a red flag," Carla said, and went into a fit of giggling.

"Carla, scallions to you!" Mimi said in mock horror.

"Oh, that's nothing," Carla said airily. "Just you wait until next year. I'm going back to New York to write a play. About people like us, falling over one another emotionally. And for its title, I might borrow Dewey Schmetterling's phrase. Six Authors in Search of a Character. Or is that too close to Pirandello? Still, it would be appropriate . . ." She looked at Mrs. Peel. "You are the sixth, although you've graduated ahead of us. And to tell the truth, you'll be my favorite author." Then she rose, looking at her watch, and ran quickly to the house.

"And that," Mimi said, rising from her chair, "leaves the rest of us with no exit lines worth saying. Coming, Bob? You've got to help Carla get these blasted elk horns into her suitcase. I absolutely refuse to travel with them naked. Can you imagine the apartment in New York, all in French Provincial and Grand Rapids Modern, with antlers around the wall? Carla says they'll be wonderful for drying stockings on. I begin to wonder what I've let myself in for!" As she walked away with Robert O'Farlan, she was talking enough nonsense to keep him smiling.

I hope, Mrs. Peel thought as she looked after them, that Jenny O'Farlan is a wise woman. For her own sake. So far, judging from Robert's face each time he read one of her letters, she wasn't very wise. Whatever she wrote was not what he wanted to read, what he had hoped to read. It was almost too painful to see him lift the letter so eagerly from the hall table, go upstairs to read it, and then come down later with his eyes cold and his voice too controlled. Why did she do it? Or did she think it was enough to be a clever housewife and a devoted mother? Didn't she ever wonder why a man had married her?

"Look," Earl Grubbock said suddenly, "I'm not going back to New York. Not yet. While I'm out here, I may as well explore a bit. New York will still be there when I decide to see it again." He rose

355

to his feet. He gave Sally a grin. "You don't look too surprised," he said.

"Perhaps I felt a surprise coming," Sally said. "You are an independent kind of man, and with that kind anything can happen."

Karl looked at him. Independent, he thought, and he could have laughed. "I suppose you are traveling as far as Three Springs in the car with the rest of us?" Karl asked. "Or are you too independent for that?"

"No. I guess Three Springs is a good place to decide where next," Earl said, and looked at Karl as if he dared him to say it.

Karl didn't. He was the last of the guests to leave the garden. He had meant to be the first. And then he had waited. For Grubbock? That forlorn hope, he thought bitterly. A fascist. A potential traitor.

Mrs. Peel watched him leave.

Something of her thoughts must have appeared on her face, for Sally said, "He will be happy once he is back in his own group again. This place baffled him. But first, he is going to have a depressing journey back to New York. Two thousand miles of farmland and villages and small towns, where people live as happily as they live in Sweetwater. And the more prosperity he sees, the more depressed he will be. He will comfort himself with the hope that it won't last."

They were both silent for a long minute.

"There is something evil," Sally said, "in a mind that wishes ill-fortune on others who have done him no harm. I think it is all the more evil for disguising itself as idealism."

"He was talking about the election yesterday. He predicted there would be a fascist upswing in America. Everyone in Wyoming proves it, seemingly."

"Remind me to tell Chuck about upswing. That's another for his repertoire."

"Oh, Chuck's got it! And he's adopted 'exploited,' as well. You exploited upswung sonofabitchn old pony you. A few other words are there too, if only I could remember them. I'm sure I heard baroque among them. Now where did he get that? I'm sure it was baroque, and not a peculiar Anglo-Saxon word that Vassar didn't teach me in my Beowulf class."

356

But that problem wasn't solved, for Sally suddenly said, "There's Jim." And she forgot everything else.

Mrs. Peel left them together as quickly as she could. She entered the house. It was beginning to look lonely even now. The living room was deserted. The dining table was shrunken into its smallest size. The library looked too neat.

I ought to go away, Mrs. Peel thought; I ought to go away until Sally and Jim aren't too occupied being married. I ought to go away for many months. Long enough, anyway, to let them know they don't have to invite me over to their cabin for dinner because they are sorry for me being alone. Long enough to establish the habit of only treating me as a neighbor, and not as a third member of the family. But that, Mrs. Peel decided, is up to me. I've got to be the one who does it.

She went into her sitting room. Her correspondence for these last few days had been left unanswered. She picked up the letter from her agent, which had brought the good news about Robert O'Farlan. There was a long paragraph for her, too. At first, she had read it and laughed. Now, she read it.

Hollywood . . . It would be interesting to see. But to work there? She glanced at the letter again. "All the publicity about Elizabeth Whiffleton has stimulated new interest in *The Lady in White Gloves*. Firmament Films have some idea about a remake, as they hold all the rights which you sold them in 1926. That means you won't get any money, I'm afraid. But after I had spent three hours on the phone with them today, they agree you should at least be the consultant on historical background. They offer five hundred a week for six weeks (that being their limit for historical details, seemingly) and it isn't bad as a price now that everyone on the Coast is down to their last two swimming pools. Much worse, I think, is the fact that you'll be working with Dewey Schmetterling who — for a mere two thousand a week — is going to show you just how you should have written the story in the first place. I hear he has a very beautiful but expensive wife, so there isn't much hope he will refuse Firmament's offer. It must have taken some of the joy out of his contract when he realized that he helped to start this new interest in

The Lady in W.G. If he hadn't tried to get his claws into you, he might have been working on a story of his own, with all the screen credits for writing given to Schmetterling. Let me know before Tuesday if you find this idea amusing in its own way. It might be fun."

My agent has a sense of humor, Mrs. Peel decided. Historical background . . . Am I as old as all that? Then she laughed, thinking of Dewey working on the script of *The Lady in White Gloves*. He was going to sweat blood for his two thousand dollars a week.

But not Hollywood with Dewey, she thought suddenly: that would be too much. What else, though?

She went over to her writing table, opened its drawer, and picked up the manuscript which she had begun. It was a play. Not a historical novel after all; a play. Really, Elizabeth Whiffleton pulled the most peculiar jokes on her. Well, she had the first act completely written, and the other two were mapped out. She had written it so easily that she was a little bit frightened. Or perhaps the explanation was that she never had found conversation difficult; in fact, all her life she had loved talk much too much. And in a play, she could talk to her heart's content. And meet such funny people . . . Yes, writing plays would certainly keep her from being lonely. But would it keep her alive, too? "Elizabeth," she said suddenly, "are you going to be good this time, or aren't you?"

Then she laid the manuscript back in the drawer. "Well, I'm backing you anyway, Elizabeth," she said. And she tore up the letter. It was a strange feeling, tearing up five hundred dollars a week, even if it were only for six weeks. But grand gestures were always pleasant, for the moment at least. She went into the hall, dictated a telegram to Miss Snodgrass for her agent in New York, and then had a pleasant conversation about The Wedding. Seemingly, in Milt Jerks's phrase, Sweetwater was buzzing.

Carla said, "I've tried and tried. They just won't go in, anywhere. And Mimi says I can't possibly travel with them." She looked at the elk horns despairingly. She had collected them so carefully, bringing in only the very best specimens from the hillsides, where she had

358

found them lying bleached by sun and rain. There were four sets of antlers, standing over three feet high, branching and pointed with twists and flourishes.

"Mimi is right," Sally said. "I can't imagine you climbing into an upper berth ornamented with these."

Mimi said, "Nor could you even hold them in your lap for the journey to Sweetwater. Milt Jerks is waiting outside with his newest station wagon. You daren't risk scratching one of his beloved red leather seats, far less putting one of my eyes out, or maiming Bob for life. You'll just have to leave them."

Jackson, who was standing beside Mrs. Gunn and Mrs. Peel, ready to help with last emergencies, said, "Leave them. I'll find big box. I'll send."

"Jackson, you're an angel!" Carla cried. "How wonderful! I did want a memento of the West, you know."

"Fine," Mimi said philosophically, wondering how antlers would look on terra-cotta walls under a black ceiling. "We can always start a vogue for hoopla. We'll teach our guests to throw their hats on the points, like the way Bert and Ned do it. No drink until a hat is caught and held. Why, that *will* save lots of money. Now, what about that train we have to catch?"

"You all look wonderful," Mrs. Peel said as she escorted them towards the station wagon.

"Mimi made me throw away my hat," Carla said. "She lent me this beret. All right?"

"Very much so," Sally said.

Carla halted, suddenly remembering. "I wonder if we'll see Prender Atherton Jones in Three Springs?" She didn't sound overjoyed.

"He left yesterday," Sally reassured her.

"What about Esther?"

"Big sister chartered a plane and hired a nurse to take Esther back to civilization and Shenquetucket Island."

Mrs. Peel said, "And Esther seems almost herself, again. She plans to sue everyone in Upshot County."

Carla shook her head.

359

"Cheer up, Carla," Sally said. "You won't see Esther in New York for a long time."

"When are you coming to New York?"

Sally smiled and shook her head. But Mrs. Peel said, "I'll be there. I've got some work to finish."

"Let us know when you are coming," Mimi said.

"Don't forget that," Robert O'Farlan added.

"And I'm coming back here whenever you ask me again," Carla warned them.

"It was an interesting month," Karl Koffing said.

"I'll send you postal cards and keep you amused meanwhile," Earl Grubbock suggested, with a broad grin on his face.

As farewells were being repeated, Jim Brent came round the corner of the house. He had, Mimi thought, timed it beautifully. He said good-by briefly to each of them, giving each a warm smile and a friendly handshake. Then they climbed into the station wagon, while Milt Jerks looked at his watch and shook his head. Jim Brent stood beside Sally, while Mrs. Peel and Mrs. Gunn tried not to be sentimental (they both were easily saddened when the word good-by was said, especially when those who said good-by looked as if they didn't want to say it), and Jackson waved a fourteen-point antler.

Carla twisted round to watch Sally and Jim. "They look just exactly right together," she said with difficulty. (She shared Mrs. Peel's and Mrs. Gunn's weakness.) "I know they'll be terribly terribly happy." She sighed, wiped her eyes, and turned away as the trees closed in and the house was blotted out except for a lazy spiral of smoke. She wondered what it would be like to be Sally, standing there beside Jim Brent. Better than having money like Esther Park, or even fame like Mrs. Peel. Then she looked at Mimi's face, and she fell silent.

The others were silent, too. They looked out of the windows to see the last of the mountains. Milt Jerks did the talking. They were late, but this new car was a good one, plenty of power to it. And people didn't have to worry about the train because it didn't pay much attention to timetables: you could rely on it being later than you were. They listened politely, for they knew it was a mark of honor that he himself had come to drive them to Three Springs. There wasn't anything he wouldn't do to oblige Miss Whirrelton, he told them for the third time.

"Well, I'll be — " Earl said suddenly, interrupting Milt Jerks. He pointed, and then took off his hat to cheer. Over the brow of a hill came Ned and Robb and Bert, riding at full speed, racing the car.

"We'll see about that," Milt Jerks said with a grin, and stepped on the accelerator.

"Good-by," Carla called, although they couldn't possibly hear her. She waved wildly, as all the others were waving.

Then the car twisted out of sight, leaving Ned and Bert and Robb grouped together on the hillside. They were waving, too, sweeping their hats in wide circles above their heads, while Ned's piercing cowboy yell echoed across the valley.

CHAPTER XXX

The Waiting House

"So SHE wants a memento of the West," Chuck said reflectively. He looked at the antlers, he looked at Jackson, and then he looked at the rest of the cowpokes who had gathered around.

"Memento," Jackson repeated. "That's what Carla said."

"She meant a souvenir, something to remember us by," Robb explained.

"Sure wouldn't want to disappoint her." Chuck studied the large box which Jackson had unearthed in the storeroom and dragged up to the corral. He eyed the antlers again. "I think they'll look kind of lonely in there. Better make it a real good memento."

The others nodded.

Bert looked around the corral for inspiration.

Ned looked too, picked up a worn horseshoe, and flung it neatly into the box.

Robb found part of an ancient bridle and added that.

Ned discovered two large nails, bent and rusted. "Real genuine antiques," he said.

Jackson found an old saddle blanket, with more holes than pattern left.

Chuck added two empty cans of Sheridan Export and a can of baked beans.

Robb produced a cracked stirrup and a piece of frayed rope.

Bert returned from his voyage of exploration with six inches of horse's tail, tied with a piece of string and decorated with a stalk of Indian paintbrush.

Chuck next arrived, with some corral sweepings on a shovel. "Just to give the right aroma," he said as he emptied it into the box.

"Atmosphere," Bert said. "That was one of Mimi's favorite words. Used to think it meant something you breathed. Seems that words mean a lot of different things in different places." Darling, for instance. Angel, for another.

Chuck thought over atmosphere. Weren't no useful kind of word. Memento. Well, memento might do. You goddamned sonofabitchn old memento, you. That was a good word, come in right useful. It had a real sound to it.

"She's as full as she'll go," Jackson said. "Okay?"

"Close her up," Chuck said.

They roped the box thoroughly. And they solemnly nailed on a large label, while Ned searched in his little diary for Mimi's address.

"Hey, Jim, will you step over here for a minute?" Bert called, as Jim and Sally came up to the corral for their evening ride. "It's Carla's memento," he explained while Jackson found a pen.

Then they all grouped around Jim as he printed the address. "It needs just a touch more," he said, and he decorated the label with a bowlegged man, a laughing horse, and a contemplative cow.

No, Mrs. Peel had said after dinner, she really didn't feel like riding tonight. And so Sally and Jim, trying not to look too relieved, had set out by themselves.

Mrs. Peel sat in front of the fire, rearranging her life. There was, she had discovered, a considerable amount to be rearranged. But perhaps it was good for one to have a general overhaul in plans every now and again. Then, through the quiet hall came the sound of laughter from the kitchen. She recognized Jackson's deep voice. Jackson . . . How was he going to fit in to all these new plans? She rose and went towards the kitchen. He was talking about some memento which he had brought down to the house, all ready for delivery to New York.

"Jackson," Mrs. Peel said, "I'm so glad to be able to see you. We've a few things to talk about. What about your vacation? And after that?" How can I start telling him I can't afford to pay him any more, she wondered miserably.

"Well . . ." Jackson said. And then he stood, turning his hat in his hand as if his thoughts were moving in a similar circle and he hardly knew where to cut through the chain to find the first one. He looked at Mrs. Gunn for help.

"No, you do it," she said.

Mrs. Peel stared at Jackson's face. "Why, Jackson, do you want to stay here? Always?"

He nodded.

"But won't you find it lonely?"

He smiled, shaking his head. "Not lonely here. Enough people. Enough time. Real friends."

"And to think I've been worried about you all these weeks! I've been avoiding you, I didn't want to hear that you were leaving. For we couldn't have done without you, Jackson."

"That's the one thing that's worrying Jackson right now," Mrs. Gunn said. "If he stays here, how are you going to set out traveling for California?"

"I'm not going there. Oh yes, I know we were traveling there when I insisted on taking the wrong road. Remember, Jackson? But I've changed my ideas, just like Jackson. I'll wait here for the wedding, and then I'm going back to New York and finish some work."

"We'll miss you," Mrs. Gunn said.

Mrs. Peel looked at her quickly. "But I'll be back here in the spring." Then she half-smiled. "I'll certainly come back every summer for a visit," she said. Then she looked at Jackson, again. "Can Jim give you a job?" she asked anxiously.

"We'll be taking on some new hands next spring," Mrs. Gunn said. "We'll be needing them. And in the winter, well, we need a good handyman around the place. Chuck thinks he will retire for the bad months, this year. He's got a nice little cabin outside of Sweetwater, and he'll take it easy there for the real cold weather. Ned's going to Arizona for the winter. And Bert thinks he'll get himself a job there, too, as corral boss on a dude ranch. Guess he figures dudes are easy, after this month. So Jim has asked Robb to stay on here and help keep things going. And there's room for Jackson, too."

364

"But won't you all be isolated? When the snows come?"

"Once the snowplow clears the road, we can get down into Sweetwater. Jackson's aiming to do that quite a lot, aren't you, Jackson?"

For the first time in her life, Mrs. Peel saw Jackson blush. Then she looked at Mrs. Gunn's laughing face. Jackson, confused but smiling, said he was needed at the corral.

"Funny thing about weddings," Mrs. Gunn said cheerfully, as she looked after Jackson walking quickly towards the ranch, "as soon as one happens, several happen. As if they were catching, like measles."

"Jackson? Married?"

"Oh, it will take him the winter to make up his mind. But I'm thinking he's caught, this time. She's a nice girl. Lives over in Sweetwater. Wish Ned would look at that kind." Mrs. Gunn shook her head dolefully.

"Is Ned in trouble again?"

"Sure. Didn't you see her sitting over by the chutes at the rodeo on Saturday, with Ned perched beside her on the rail? Pretty as anything. A blonde with blue eyes. Wants to be a rodeo star someday. Ned was disappointed your guests were all going away, as she could have come out here to help me."

"Perhaps this one will marry him," Mrs. Peel said. "But, of course, it is just possible that Ned doesn't really want to marry anyone. Isn't it?"

"Could be," Mrs. Gunn agreed. "Anyway, we're back to normal, again." She began arranging the newly made doughnuts on an outsize platter. Tomorrow the boys would be in here for breakfast.

Mrs. Peel went into the garden. She walked there for a little. Then she looked at the house, and she stopped walking to stand hesitatingly before it. In the quiet evening, it loomed dark and lonely.

Yes, I know, Mrs. Peel answered it. You aren't the kind of house that should be left dark and silent. You like people. And you could have people: you could have Jim and his wife and their children and all their friends. I don't amount to much, compared to all

365

that, do I? I'm not very good for you all alone by myself. Of course I could have guests here in the summer. But I've always depended on Sally to cope with a house full of guests. (And what's more, I've got to spend more time on working and less time on people.) From now on, Sally is going to have her own life quite apart from mine. And I must shape my own life, quite apart from hers. But what about you? Jim can't buy you back, not yet. And he won't live here until he can. Solve that problem for me, will you?

She began to pace slowly back and forward, stopping now and again to look at the house. There's one possible way, she thought. . . . If only I can make it sound practical, intelligent and cheerful. You've got to help me, she told the waiting house.

She heard Sally's voice down by the bridge, and then Jim laughed. She waited beside the house. They were taking a long time to come. Mrs. Peel smiled. Well, she could always bury herself in work until the wedding; and then, after that, New York was a safe distance from a newly married couple. She waited patiently until she saw them stroll leisurely on to the lawn. "Sally, Jim!" she called, and surprised them, for they had not seen her in the shadows.

"Hello," Jim said, "what are you doing out here? You'll catch cold, Margaret. The dew's heavy tonight."

"I'm too excited to catch cold," she said smiling. "I've just had the most intelligent idea, and it's so simple I just can't think why it never dawned on me before. Jim, would you buy back this house? I don't want all the money at once, for it would all get used up too quickly I know. What I need is a steady income for the next eight or ten years. So if you would buy the house, and pay me a certain amount every year until you've bought it completely, I'd be so happy. You see, with a steady income for the next few years, I could work as I want to work. I'd be able to write what I want to write."

"But, Margaret," Sally said, "you've never loved a house as much as you've loved this one. Perhaps you'll have a success with this play you are writing, and you won't have to worry about a steady income."

"But I also love traveling," Margaret Peel reminded her. "And

366

I'm beginning to feel the most awful homesickness for New York. Don't laugh. It's perfectly true."

"I don't like the idea of you being alone," Sally said worriedly.

"Why not? It will be a completely new kind of adventure. I'm looking forward to it, frankly."

Sally glanced at Jim. She was a little hurt, a little bewildered. But it was true: Margaret had always liked change. "I had hoped you'd settle here, and perhaps write. You've never given yourself much time to do that." Then she stopped persuading, simply because their long friendship had been built on freedom of choice. For years, their inclinations had coincided. Now they were separating.

Margaret turned to look at the house. "It needs lights. It needs voices. It needs people. Do you see what I mean?"

Sally and Jim could say nothing. The house answered for them.

"Think it over, Jim," Margaret said. "It would suit me financially, you know. And then, I could stop worrying."

"It suits me financially, too," he said frankly. "I couldn't manage to buy it back otherwise. But — "

"Good. We'll talk about it tomorrow, shall we? Now I'm going to take some carrots to the corral, even if it is late. You know, Jim, I think I'll learn to drive a car and borrow your trailer and take Golden Boy with me to New York. How would he look attached to a hitching-rail outside my apartment?" She laughed, gave a wave of her hand, and walked around the dark house to the kitchen garden.

"Do you think she really wants it this way?" Jim asked. He slipped his arm around Sally, his eyes still watching the house. Margaret was right. It needed people. That was one of the reasons why he had let himself sell it, in the first place. "Does she mean it?"

Sally said slowly, "I usually can tell when Margaret doesn't mean something. When she was talking to you, I watched her face and I listened to every inflection in her voice. And I could find nothing, except that she meant it."

His arm tightened around her shoulders.

"Just a minute, Jim," Sally said quickly. She reached up to kiss him swiftly on the cheek, and then she left him, running towards the house. He watched the lights being switched on, one by one, in the hall, in the living room, in the dining room, bringing the house to life again. She must have run upstairs, for the light in the main bedroom suddenly blazed into the night. He smiled, then, as he waited by the cottonwood trees beside the creek.

She came running back to him, and as he caught her, she said, "Look, Jim! That's much better, isn't it?" She was half-laughing, half-serious.

"Yes," he said, but he looked only at her. "Yes," he said again. And he kissed her.

Then holding each other, silent now, they turned to look with one heart towards the house. Behind it, the fields and hills had become formless shadows. The forests were lost in the solid blackness of the mountains. A faint light etched a line along the jagged edges of the peaks. Then that last sign of the invisible sun was gone, and the dark blue sky stretched over a sleeping land. The first stars glowed faintly down on shadows and silence.

Jim looked at Sally. Even she had become a shadow, something that might slip from his grasp, vanish into the darkness. He kissed her with a violence that startled her.

"Never leave me, Sally," he said. "Never."

For a moment, the intensity in his voice frightened her. "Never," she said. She reached up to kiss him, to seal that promise. "Oh, Jim! You do love me . . ."

"I love you," he said.

Afterwards, she might tease him that it had taken him three days to say these words in that way. But not now. Now it was enough to walk, with his arm holding her, across the dark shadows to the welcoming house.